EL CAMINO

Ken Baysinger

KEN BAYSINGER

EL CAMINO

Published by Yorkshire Publishing
3207 South Norwood Ave.
Tulsa, Oklahoma 74137 USA
918.394.2665
www.yorkshirepublishing.com

Book design copyright © 2017 by Ken Baysinger. All rights reserved.
Cover design by Junriel Boquecosa
Interior design by Mary Jean Archival

Published in the United States of America
ISBN: 978-1-947491-98-4

1. Fiction / Mystery & Detective / General
2. Fiction / Mystery & Detective / Private Investigators
13.11.20

CHAPTER 1

SATURDAY, JUNE 11

"**W**hat are the symptoms of rat poison?" Leann Riverton asked me.

"Rat poison doesn't *have* symptoms," I corrected. "It *causes* symptoms."

"Don't be a pain in the ass," Riverton complained. "Just tell me what happens when someone is fed rat poison."

"There are several different kinds of rat poison. The most common rat poisons are anticoagulants, usually containing warfarin—the same stuff that people take to prevent heart attacks and strokes. It reduces the viscosity of the blood. In rats, it causes massive internal bleeding. But if someone is trying to kill a person with warfarin, it would take too large a dose to be done without the victim's knowledge."

"I thought rat poison was made of strychnine or arsenic, stuff like that."

"That was a hundred years ago. Now it's either warfarin or zinc phosphide. Zinc phosphide has a very strong smell. I don't think you could sneak it into a person's food and expect him to eat it. But rats? They don't care how their food smells. They scarf it down, and then the phosphide reacts with their stomach acid to produce phosphine gas. Very bad for the rats."

"Okay, well then, what would cause me to feel sick and nauseous the day after having dinner at my ex-husband's house?"

"Lots of things. But not rat poison. Is there a reason you think your ex-husband might want to poison you?"

"Not that I know of, but we didn't like each other enough to stay married."

"Then why were you having dinner with him?"

"Because it was Thursday," she said impatiently, as if that should have been obvious. "I always go over to his place for dinner on Thursday. And then I noticed that I was getting sick every Friday. Actually, my boss noticed it. He accused me of faking it just to get off work early, but then I barfed on his desk."

"How many times has this happened?"

"I only barfed on his desk once. Then he believed me."

"No, I mean how many times did you feel sick on Friday after having dinner with your husband on Thursday?"

"Oh, I think maybe five or six times. That's what made me start to wonder."

"Leann, if you think your husband is trying to kill you, you should go to the police."

"Oh no, I couldn't do that. If I called the cops on him and it turned out that Roger *wasn't* trying to kill me, then he might decide that he *does* want to kill me."

I couldn't argue with that logic. "Then why don't you just stop going over there and see if you stop getting sick?"

"Because he buys steaks and gives me nice wine. I can't afford that kind of dinner myself."

It didn't seem to me that a guy who is trying to poison his wife would spend money on steaks and nice wines to do it. There had to be a different answer. It was pretty clear that Leann was a creature of habit. She went to dinner on Thursday because it was Thursday. What else did she habitually do that might make her sick?

"When do you start feeling sick?" I asked.

"It starts in the afternoon and lasts until the next morning."

"What do you eat for lunch?"

"I always pack a sandwich. On Friday, I have tuna fish. I'm Catholic, you know."

Okay, why do people say "tuna fish?" If it's tuna, don't you *assume* that it's fish? Nobody ever says "salmon fish" or "chicken bird." It's just another of life's mysteries.

"Didn't the church get over that whole fish-on-Friday thing?" I asked.

"I guess so, but I don't want to take any chances," she said. "I mean, the nuns always told me I'd go to hell if I ever ate a hamburger on Friday."

"I'd like to take a look at your kitchen. Maybe I can find something there.

"Like a clue?"

"Yes, a clue."

An hour later, I stood in her kitchen looking around. If I'd expected to find her living in squalor and poisoning herself on her own filth, I couldn't have been more wrong. Her kitchen was immaculate. The jars and cans were carefully arranged by their contents, stacked in straight rows. I like a neat pantry, but this was borderline spooky.

"I buy my canned goods by the case," she explained. "It's a lot cheaper that way. I go to Salvage Mart where they sell the surplus food that the regular stores don't want."

On the right-hand side of the pantry, on the lower shelf, there was a stack of canned tuna. I picked up a can and looked it over carefully.

"Is this what you make your sandwiches with on Fridays?" I asked.

"Yes. You know, I got a whole case—24 cans—for three dollars. In the regular stores, it's a dollar thirty-nine a can!" she said proudly.

Today's crime was about to be solved. "Do you ever look at the expiration dates on these cans?"

I pointed to the date on the can I was holding. It said July 2006.

"Oh, that doesn't mean anything," she objected. "Once it's in the can, it can't go bad."

"Actually, that's not true," I explained. "Let me take this. The county has a place where I can have it tested—I'll call you with the result—and don't eat any more of that tuna!"

"Really?" She looked disappointed, like she'd really wanted me to prove she was the victim of a crime—although, I guess that selling outdated tuna might be a crime of some kind. It ought to be, if it isn't. Or maybe she was just disappointed at having to throw out her bargain tuna.

CHAPTER 2

For Bill and Sharon Warren, that same Saturday started out on a discouraging note. They arrived early at the boat ramp in West Linn, wanting to get on the river and do some morning skiing before the hoards of wakeboard boats arrived to chop up the water and make real water skiing impossible.

"We'll tie up over there," Bill said, pointing toward the new transient dock off to the left of the two-lane boat ramp. "I'll suit up on the dock before we go out."

The shortie wetsuit Bill tossed into the boat was his concession to the early season cold water. In June, the water temperature in the Willamette River was still below sixty degrees, a bit too chilly for comfort. He removed the tie-down straps and installed the stern plug, while Sharon and their daughter, Stephanie, loaded the ice chest and picnic basket into the boat.

With Sharon at the controls in the boat, Bill backed down the concrete ramp. When the back of the boat was in the water, Sharon pressed the trim button, lowering the engine. With a sputter and a momentary cloud of two-stroke oil smoke, the big Mercury outboard fired up.

She backed carefully off the trailer and then idled over to the transient dock to wait for Bill to park the rig and walk down to the boat. As she stepped from the boat and secured a line to the dock, she noticed the strong smell of gasoline. Immediately, she jumped back into the boat and shut down the engine.

"I think we have a gas leak," Sharon called to Bill as he walked down the ramp to the dock. "I smell gas, so I killed the engine."

Even before he got to the boat, Bill could see the rainbow sheen on the surface of the water. He climbed into the boat and pulled the portable fire extinguisher from its mount. Cautiously, he released the latches on the engine cover, ready to jump back if a flash fire erupted.

When nothing happened, he lifted the cover from the classic Black Max motor and set it aside. Studying the exposed engine, he searched for the source of the fuel spill. The engine was clean and dry. He traced the lines from the fuel pump to the carburetors and still found no signs of leakage. But the fuel slick on the water was unmistakable, and his was the only boat around.

The amount of fuel on the water suggested a major leak, and yet he could not see any clue where it was coming from. Looking over the side, he could see that the fuel slick was starting to stick to his boat, forming an ugly yellowish stain at the waterline. Something definitely wasn't right.

"I think it's coming from over there," Stephanie said, pointing to a spot midway between the boat ramp and the dock where they were tied up. Sure enough, Bill could see the place where the slick originated. Every few seconds, a fresh bubble of fuel would rise to the surface and spread out across the water, drifting slowly downstream on the gentle current. He studied the rising fuel for several seconds before confirming what Stephanie had said.

"We'd better report this," Bill said, pulling his phone from the little backpack he had carried to the boat.

Within ten minutes, a Clackamas County Sheriff patrol car arrived at the boat ramp. The deputy walked down onto the dock where Bill and Sharon were waiting. They had moved their boat around to the inboard side of the dock, out of the fuel slick.

Pointing to the spot where the fuel was rising to the surface, Bill said, "Something under there is really spewing out the gas."

The deputy used his portable radio to call his dispatcher and report what he'd found. "We've got something in the water down here, and it's pouring gasoline into the river. There's a fuel slick that goes as far as I can see. We'll need hazmat, and you better send search and rescue too."

The dispatcher contacted the marine unit. The Clackamas County Sheriff's Office Marine Unit was in charge of the Willamette River, and it would be their responsibility to deal with whatever was happening at the boat ramp.

Bill and Sharon walked their boat back over to the boat ramp. They'd load it up and take it home to wash the fuel stains from the hull. Maybe there'd still be time to go to the Hebb Park boat ramp five miles upstream and do their skiing there.

CHAPTER 3

Deputy Kim Stayton was a 13-year veteran of the department, and was the senior deputy on the Clackamas County Sheriff's Office Marine Unit. She brought the 22-foot Jetcraft patrol boat upriver from its moorage at the top of the Willamette Falls Locks. Onboard with her was a member of the hazmat team and two other marine unit deputies.

Stayton idled up next to the dock that ran down from the boat ramp, separating the two launch lanes. She could plainly see the fuel slick. There was a lot of gas on the water. She directed the patrol car deputy to close the boat ramp. She didn't want any more boats in the water until she figured out what this was all about.

"We need a dive team down at the Willamette Park boat ramp," she said into her radio. "It looks like something's gone to the bottom here. It's leaking a lot of gas," she added.

The dive team arrived an hour later on the department's high-speed search and rescue craft, a rigid hull inflatable powered by a 150-horsepower jet outboard. Two divers spent the next half hour putting on their scuba gear and preparing for the dive.

After less than a minute underwater, they came to the surface and shouted to Kim, "There's a car down here. We'll check for occupants."

With that, the divers again went under. Minutes passed. Kim watched the bubbles, tracking the divers' position as they searched the submerged car. At last, they came to the surface and swam over next to the boats. Their lack of urgency suggested that the car was unoccupied.

"We've got only a couple of feet of visibility, so it's hard to say for sure, but it appears that nobody's down there," the diver reported, confirming what Kim had already guessed. Then the diver added, "But there's more than one car. At least three, maybe more."

The other diver held out an underwater writing slate. On it he'd written the license plate numbers from the cars they'd found. "Looks like the latest one sank right on top of the others," he commented.

"It's a late-model Honda Accord," the first diver told Kim. "The other cars look like they've been down there awhile. They're coated with silt."

"Joy riders?" Kim speculated.

"That'd be my guess," the diver said. "They steal 'em, and then when they're tired of driving 'em around, they bring 'em down here. Drive 'em in just to watch 'em sink."

"Don't kids today know how to toilet paper houses?" Kim asked nobody in particular. "Well, looks like we have a project. I'll call in the reinforcements."

The cars sat in water twenty-five feet deep, about thirty yards off shore, slightly downstream from the boat ramp. By noon, the hazmat team had rigged a containment boom around the site to keep the fuel from drifting downstream. Absorbent pads were floating inside the ring to soak up the gasoline. A Channel 8 news van was in the parking lot, and already the reporter and cameraman were on the dock.

"What will be the long-term environmental damage from this oil spill?" the reporter asked, thrusting a microphone at Deputy Stayton.

Kim rolled her eyes.

"This isn't the Exxon Valdez," she explained impatiently. "It's gasoline, not oil. What got away before we rigged the containment boom will simply evaporate."

The reporter nodded gravely, pretending to understand. "Have you determined the source of the spill?"

"There are several cars down there," Kim answered.

For the next ten minutes, the reporter continued to pester Kim with inane questions until the deputy finally said, "You'll have to excuse me. We have a lot to do here."

The tugboat *Sarah B* arrived, pushing a tall barge-mounted crane. Kim directed them to anchor alongside the containment boom. It took the better part of an hour to set the four anchors and get the barge properly positioned to raise the wrecks. Divers by this time had found the source of the gasoline leak. The Accord was missing its gas cap, as if the car thieves had wanted to maximize the damage they were causing. The divers managed to curtail the leakage by cramming a rag into the filler pipe, but by then, most of the fuel was already gone.

On shore, three flatbed tow trucks stood by. Two technicians from the crime scene investigation unit were on hand to secure what evidence could be obtained from the vehicles. The plate numbers had been run through DMV, confirming that all three cars had been reported stolen. The Honda had disappeared from a parking lot in Portland the previous evening. The other two cars had been stolen several weeks earlier.

As soon as Kim and the hazmat team had the containment booms out of the way, the divers went back into the river. This time they used a hookah rig instead of scuba tanks. The divers' regulators were connected to hoses from a compressor onboard their support boat. The full-face dive masks they wore contained a hard-wired communication system that allowed the divers to talk with the deputies in the boat above.

They directed the crane operator to lower his cable into the water. A pair of wide nylon slings attached to a framework on the end of the cable would be used to lift the cars. The divers positioned the slings under the ends of the Accord and called for the crane operator to take up the slack. The news cameras were rolling when the Honda was lifted to the surface and set down onto the barge. Water poured out when the CSI techs opened the doors.

"Nobody here," they called out.

Breathlessly, the reporter relayed the news to the camera. "The investigative team is reporting that the car is empty, but it's too soon to say for sure whether or not anybody was in the car when it went into the river. While the underwater search continues, we can only hope that this is nothing more than an act of vandalism and not a human tragedy."

Two hours later, all three cars were on the barge and the divers were on the dock, peeling off their dry suits. The crime-scene techs were going over the cars, but there was little hope that they'd find any useful evidence. It was late in the afternoon when the barge was pushed close to shore so the crane could lift the waterlogged cars onto the boat ramp.

With nothing better to do, the search-and-rescue team began conducting a magnetometer search of the area, in case other cars were in the water. They ran a grid pattern back and forth over the water, gradually widening the search area, watching for telltale spikes on the instrument's video display.

"Hey! We have a hit," the deputy operating the magnetometer exclaimed.

They were just beyond the far-western edge of their search pattern, actually upstream from the boat ramps. It was not where they expected to find anything. The only reason they were in that particular spot was to swing the boat around and set up for another pass over the target area.

"Give me another pass," he said to the boat driver. "The profile looks right."

After making two more passes over the area, he got on the radio and told Stayton what he had. "Too big to be anything but a car," he told her. "About twenty feet down."

"Okay," Kim radioed back. "Drop a marker buoy, and I'll have the divers check it out." She'd been there all day, and the last thing she wanted was to find another car. But it was her job. She walked over to the divers, who were packing up their gear.

"I hate to do this to you, but it looks like we have another car down there," she told the divers. They'd been in and out of the water all day, and looked exhausted.

"Can you muster up enough energy to make one more dive? Just to check it out?" she asked.

"You're a real slave driver, Stayton," one of the divers grumbled in mock protest.

"Listen to you," Kim shot back. "Here the generous taxpayers of Clackamas County give you a nice, new, fast boat and all this state-of-the-art dive gear, and they even pay you to go out and play in the water, and all you can do is complain."

"I'm not complaining," he said. "I'm just saying…"

The sun had gone behind the hills, and the area was in shadow by the time the divers got back in the water. They swam over to the marker buoy, signaled each other, and released the air from their buoyancy compensators.

Kim stood on shore watching the bubbles. The divers finally surfaced and swam to the boat ramp. They peeled off their fins and then waded ashore.

"It's a car, all right," the lead diver told her, "and it's been down there a long time. It's completely covered. Must be a foot of mud over it. I think it's a Ranchero, or maybe an El Camino. You know, one of those little pickups that are half-car, half-truck?"

"Well, if it's been down there long enough to collect a foot of silt. Another day won't hurt it. Let's wrap it up for today and come back in the morning."

She radioed in her report and told the dispatcher that they'd have to have someone on-site overnight, and they'd have to keep the boat ramp closed the next day too.

CHAPTER 4

After solving the mystery of Leann Riverton's weekly poisoning, I spent the rest of my Saturday onboard *Annabel Lee*, my own personal sailing ship and lifetime project.

Originally named *Chrisholm*, she was built in 1885 in Lowestoft, England, as a fishing schooner and was used in that capacity on the North Sea for at least fifty years. Inevitably, there came a time when a two-masted sailing vessel could no longer be competitive in the commercial fishing fleet, so in about 1930, she was refitted with auxiliary power. This gave her a reprieve from the scrap yards where most other vessels of her age and design were being torn down for salvage.

The Second World War made fishing the North Sea an unreasonably hazardous occupation, so *Chrisholm* remained dockside until 1946. She was found there by a movie producer who purchased her and had her sailed to San Diego. During the 1950s and 1960s, she was used in the production of many movies and television shows. She had been used as everything from a pirate ship to a luxury yacht in the movies, but by 1970, that genre was dead.

In 1974, she was purchased by a group of investors who renamed her *Southern Cross* and sailed to Cabo San Lucas for a new life running sunset cruises for tourists. That was a good business for thirty years, but a series of poor business decisions coupled with the worldwide economic downturn put the owner in bankruptcy. I ran across the bankruptcy auction online and put in a perfunctory bid of five thousand dollars.

Now the truth is I never expected to win the auction. I had placed the bid on a whim, thinking that it would be cool to own a 110-foot schooner if I could buy it for five grand. I'd never sailed anything bigger than a Sea Snark—a nine-foot sailboat made of plastic foam, but I was dazzled by the notion that I could cruise the world on my own nineteenth century schooner. I was completely dumbfounded when I was notified that I'd won the auction. I paid for it with my Visa card.

I was past due for some R and R, so I booked a flight to Cabo to see what I'd bought. At the Port of Cabo San Lucas, I found the harbor master and asked if he could direct me to the *Southern Cross*. He pointed at the biggest vessel in the harbor. She hadn't looked that big in the photos online.

But she had a nice look to her. She was painted a dark green with black trim, which gave her a dignified, even stately, look. Her bow was absolutely vertical. I later learned that the design feature is properly called a plumb stem. The English originally designed the plumb stem for ramming other ships but soon found that because this design resulted in a lengthening of the waterline, it gave the vessel an advantage in sailing speed and stability. The main thing, as far as I was concerned, was that she looked very classy.

"There she sits," the harbor master said, "and she has about a week left to sit there."

"What do you mean?" I asked.

"The moorage fee is paid up until the end of the month. After that, she has to go."

"Nobody mentioned that when I bought her."

"So you're March Corrigan?"

"Just 'Corrigan,' please," I said for about the half-millionth time in my life. Nobody *ever* calls me March.

"How much is the moorage fee?" I asked.

"Doesn't matter," the harbor master said. "I've already leased the moorage to someone else. You'll have to get your vessel out of here."

Great! I didn't even know if she was seaworthy, and I had not the slightest idea how to sail her. The harbor master led me out to where my ship was tied up and wished me luck. I stepped onboard and entered a whole new world. She seemed to be relatively clean and well cared for. Sure, the paint was chipped and faded, the varnish was peeling in places, but overall, she looked pretty solid.

I went back to my hotel, paid the tab for the room I hadn't slept in, and hauled my luggage down to my yacht. I picked the best stateroom and declared it mine. For the rest of the day, I compiled a list of things I had to do. At the top of the list was to determine if *Southern Cross* was seaworthy.

In the morning I found a licensed marine surveyor who spent all afternoon studying every part of the vessel. His report, delivered to me the next day, was as big as a phone book and listed so many defects that I was sure I'd have to pay someone to take the ship out and sink her. But his summary report said otherwise.

"Basically, she's a sound vessel, remarkably well maintained and in wonderful condition for her age," the surveyor told me.

"Is she fit to sail?" I asked, going straight to the heart of the matter. "Can she make a two-thousand-mile voyage on the Pacific Ocean?"

"In the right hands, she can sail around the world," he said, "but she'll need some work here and there. I've marked the critical things."

With help from the surveyor and the harbor master, I recruited a crew of six to help me sail from Cabo up the West Coast to Oregon. We had an uneventful three week cruise up the coast to Astoria, during which I had ample time to figure out what I was going to do with her. I even figured out what I'd name her. *Annabel Lee*. My plan was to live aboard, refurbish her from stem to stern, and then sail her across the Pacific. Somehow between now and then, I'd learn how to sail.

A longtime friend, Angelo Garibaldi, had a private dock on the Willamette River in West Linn. He owed me for a six-month investigation that I'd done for him the previous year that ultimately led to the conviction and imprisonment of his company bookkeeper for fraud and embezzlement. But he never recovered any of the money that had been taken from him, and so I hadn't been paid for my work. He offered to pay me with a place to tie-up my ship at his dock.

When we arrived at Astoria, I paid off the crewmen and they went back to Cabo. I arranged to have *Southern Cross* towed up the Columbia and Willamette Rivers to Garibaldi's dock in West Linn. With her ten-and-a-half foot draft, that was as far as she could go. In fact, it was pretty touchy getting her that far.

That was three years ago. By the time I tied up my *Annabel Lee* in West Linn, I knew that she was in no condition for me to live aboard. For starters, all of the drains discharged directly overboard. That alone made her legally uninhabitable, but there were many other things as well, ranging from inadequate electrical wiring to the total lack of a heating system.

I needed a pile of money to finance this new project, so I sold the house and banked the two hundred thousand dollars that I netted on the sale. I was sure that I'd be able to do the whole job for half that amount, but it wouldn't hurt to have a buffer.

Kaylin Beatty, my real estate agent, led me to a little cottage a block from where she lived in Canemah, separated from the riverfront only by the Union Pacific Railroad. Total price was sixty nine thousand dollars, three percent down on a 203K loan, which even gave me a few bucks to spend upgrading the kitchen. Cheap living—just what I needed.

I set up my office in the living room and hung my cleverly worded neon sign—*Discreet Investigations*—in the front window. It was a convenient location, and I liked the fact that it was next to the river. It would do nicely until I could get *Annabel Lee* ready for occupancy.

❧

While Deputy Stayton was fishing cars out of the river, I was busy installing the last few pieces of about a mile of conduit for the new wiring. What made the job tedious was my determination to keep all of the wiring concealed to maintain the ship's historical character. Easier said than done!

Back home, I peeled off my stained coveralls, opened a beer, and flopped down into my plush sofa to watch the evening news. I switched on the television just in time to see a reporter poke a microphone into Kim Stayton's face and ask, "What will be the long-term environmental damage from this oil spill?"

I knew Kim well enough to know how much a stupid question like that annoyed her. I was actually impressed by how relatively civil her response was. But I did notice the eye roll. I decided to give her a call.

"Hey, sweetheart, you made the six o'clock news," I said when she answered.

"Oh, did they show the part where I stuffed that ignorant reporter's microphone down his throat?" she asked.

"I guess I missed that part. I tuned-in in the middle of the story. So what *is* the story?"

"I'm still on the scene. We're just wrapping it up for the day. Someone's been stealing cars and rolling them down the boat ramp into the river, and now we have to pull them out."

"How many?"

"We've pulled out three so far. There's one more, but it's been down there a long time—totally buried in silt and mud. We'd have never even found it without the magnetometer. Anyway, we'll try to get it out tomorrow."

"In that case, why not save yourself the drive home and spend the night here?"

"Is there wine involved?"

"Cabernet Sauvignon, Sonoma Valley, 2004," I read from the bottle.

"You're a sweet talker, Corrigan."

CHAPTER 5

SUNDAY JUNE 12

S unday was another beautiful day. The first boaters arrived at the boat ramp before 7:00 a.m. and grumbled when the deputy on-site turned them away.

"Will you let us launch if we share our donuts?" one of the boaters asked.

The deputy groaned. He'd been out there all night, and now he had to deal with donut jokes. "What kind of donuts?" he asked.

"Any kind you want," the boater said.

"Krispy Kremes, but only if they're warm," the deputy said.

"You're asking a lot," the boater answered. "Do you know if Hebb Park is open?"

"As far as I know, it is," the deputy told him. "And that's your best bet because I don't think we'll get this park reopened today. They're going to be pulling more cars out."

The boaters climbed back into their SUV and drove back out to the road. Watching them leave, the deputy silently wished that they really had brought donuts. A couple of warm Krispy Kremes and some hot coffee would have been pretty good right then.

Kim Stayton and the marine patrol unit arrived back on-scene at 8:30 a.m. Search and rescue motored in a few minutes later.

"First thing we need to do is figure out what it's going to take to get that car out of there," Kim told the divers.

"If it's sunk into the mud, we'll have to dig it out before we can lift it."

"I like the way you say 'we.' Are you planning to come down and help?" Sammy Cushman, one of the divers, commented as he climbed into his drysuit.

"No," Kim said, "but I'll provide moral support."

"Moral support, yeah, that'll be a big help," Sammy grumbled. "How much moral support does it take to dig a car out of the mud?"

"Hey, you guys live for this kind of stuff," she reminded him. "If there weren't mutts out there dumping cars into the river, you'd be out of work."

"Yeah, yeah, yeah..." Sammy said, "and I'd be home watching baseball on TV."

The divers finished suiting up, and after checking their equipment, they swam over to the marker buoy. They looked at each other and nodded. Pressing the buttons on their buoyancy compensators, they released air and disappeared under the water. Kim leaned back in her seat on the patrol boat, enjoying the warm sun, watching the divers' bubbles rise to the surface.

Twenty minutes later, the divers came to the surface and swam over to the boat ramp. The first diver tossed a license plate onto the dock and pulled his mask off. The plate was one of the old yellow-and-blue Oregon plates. It was coated with river slime but was otherwise undamaged. It read LPO 476, and the date stickers indicated that it had expired in November 1981.

"We're going to need some equipment to dig that thing out," Cushman told Kim. "We were able to get to the tailgate and pull the plate, but the front is really buried. It's an old Chevy Malibu."

Kim carried the license plate to her boat and called it in. The dispatcher asked the urgency of the request, and Kim said, "Just routine. It's been down there more than thirty years. I don't think the owners are too concerned about getting their car back."

Kim got back with the divers to work out a plan. She needed to get the car fished out as soon as possible so they could reopen the boat ramp. There had been a steady procession of disappointed boaters being turned away all morning. It was one thing for a closed highway to make people late to work, but interfering with their recreation was something on a whole different level. There'd be a stack of complaints on Kim's desk the next day, and the longer she kept the boat ramp closed, the more hostile they'd be.

Sammy Cushman said, "I think we'll have to just leave that car where it is. It'll take a month to dig it out. In fact, about the only way we'll be able to dig that thing out is with an underwater vacuum cleaner of some kind. Something that'll suck up the mud and carry it away from the site. Just digging out the license plate stirred up so much silt we had zero visibility."

"How about one of those things that treasure hunters use to dig out the doubloons from Spanish galleons?" the other diver suggested.

"An air lift. Are there any treasure hunters around here?" Sammy asked.

"No, but maybe we could get our hands on a gold dredge," the other diver answered.

"That might work," Kim said. "People use those things down in Southern Oregon to excavate sediment out of the riverbeds in hopes of finding gold."

"You know any gold miners?" Sammy asked.

"None that I can think of. But I'll bet we could rent a dredge somewhere," Kim mused. She turned to one of the other deputies and said, "Get on the radio and see if somebody can hunt down a gold dredge."

"We'll have to move all of the silt off of the car, and then we'll have to dig underneath it to rig the slings,"

Sammy commented. "That's got to be a couple of tons of mud."

"Make that a big gold dredge," he called after the deputy.

"How long will it take after we get the machine?" Kim asked

"Who knows," Sammy said, "I've never used a dredge. It could take days to dig the thing out."

Kim groaned. She waved the patrol car deputy over. "How about making a food run?" she suggested. "Looks like we're going to be here awhile."

Kim's shoulder radio made a sharp beep, followed by the dispatcher's voice. "We have a hit on that license plate."

"Go ahead," Kim answered.

"That car is a 1978 El Camino, registered to a Randall Mendelson," the dispatcher said. "He's the one who—"

"I know who he is!" Kim interrupted. And then to herself she whispered, "This just gets better and better."

CHAPTER 6

T he Mendelson-Devonshire disappearance was legendary. It was also political dynamite. In 1980, the disappearance of Jessie Devonshire and Randy Mendelson had been Portland's biggest news story. It remained the region's most notorious unsolved case.

It couldn't even be properly called an unsolved crime because it had never been proven that a crime had been committed. All that was known was that fifteen-year-old Jessie Devonshire had vanished without a trace and that Randy Mendelson, a twenty-year-old landscaper, had disappeared at the same time.

The consensus of opinion was that the two cases were connected, but the only direct evidence of that was the fact that Randy Mendelson had done yard work at Devonshire's home. Had Mendelson abducted Jessie? Had they struck up a romance and run off together?

Toward the end of 1980 and into 1981, a pattern of murders developed up and down Interstate 5 from California to Washington, and many people speculated that the Mendelson and Devonshire disappearances might be the work of the serial killer who became known as the I-5 Killer. Even after Randall Woodfield was arrested and convicted as the I-5 Killer, many people remained convinced that Mendelson and Devonshire had been victims of his murder spree.

Everyone had a theory, but facts were in short supply. The one fact that everyone knew was that Jessie Devonshire was the stepdaughter of Wilson Landis Devonshire, top aide to then Portland mayor, former Oregon governor, and current US Senator Alan Blalock. Blalock was the most powerful man in Oregon politics, and in 1980, Devonshire was his protégé, a rising star in the Oregon Democratic Party. In the mid-1980s, Devonshire was appointed by the governor to fill a vacancy on the Oregon Supreme Court and had served there ever since.

The Mendelson-Devonshire case had been the biggest hot potato in Clackamas County law enforcement for at least ten years following the disappearances. At least three careers had ended because detectives had been unable to provide the answers that the politically connected principals in the case demanded. And now Kim Stayton found herself right in the eye of the political hurricane.

On the radio, Kim ordered the dispatcher, "Don't say another word! There will be no further discussion of this over the radio. Understood?"

"Ten-four," the dispatcher said, using the officially obsolete but still broadly used ten-code reply.

"If you have any additional information for me, call me on my personal cell phone," Kim commanded. "And do not share this information with anyone!"

"I understand," the dispatcher confirmed.

Kim clicked-off the radio, picked up her cell phone and touched speed-dial number two.

"Sheriff Kerby," the strong voice answered.

"Sheriff, this is Deputy Stayton on the marine unit. We've been pulling cars out of the river at the West Linn boat ramp, and we have a situation here that you need to know about," Kim began.

"Go ahead."

"Sheriff, one of the cars is a '78 El Camino, and it has just been identified as belonging to Randall Mendelson"

"Jesus Christ!" Kerby muttered. "Who knows about this?"

"Somebody in headquarters ran the plates. Probably just that person and the dispatcher who called me. I told him to say nothing more about it. Then I called you. But if anyone happened to be listening in on a scanner, they could have heard it."

"Okay, you keep a lid on this. I'll get right over there."

Kim folded her phone and clipped it back onto her duty belt. She took a deep breath and looked around. The media vans that had been there the day before had not returned.

Back on the radio, she told the dispatcher, "I need three units over here. No lights or sirens, but I want them here quick." To the patrol officer who was already there, she said, "Park your car in the road. Block anybody from getting down here. Other units are on the way. Have them set up a secure perimeter, and don't let anybody through until Kerby gets here."

The deputy looked bewildered and asked, "What's going on?"

"Never mind—just do it!"

Hurrying back out onto the dock, Kim waved to Sammy. "From this moment, we treat this as a major crime scene, got it? Nobody goes in the water, and nobody touches the car!"

"Jesus, Kim, what is this?"

"It's just the biggest career wrecker in this department's history. That El Camino belongs to Randy Mendelson."

Cushman threw up his hands. "I knew I should have stayed home and watched baseball."

"Listen," Kim said. "Get busy trying to chase down that dredging machine. We're going to need it here today. And for Christ's sake, don't tell anybody what we have here!"

The screech of tires and the slamming of a car door announced the arrival of Sheriff Kerby, barely five minutes after Kim's phone call. Kim filled him in on the events leading up to the discovery of the El Camino, and then she told him what action she had taken. While they talked, the first of the three patrol units arrived.

A barrier of yellow crime scene tape began to form around the park. Two more cars arrived, and more deputies set up portable barricades at both ends of the road leading past the boat ramp. Curious neighbors began appearing along the edges of the park, wondering the reason for such a flurry of activity on a Sunday morning.

And then the media began to show up. The first to arrive was the Channel 12 helicopter, circling overhead, hoping to be the first to tell the world what was happening. Kim could only shake her head in despair. Of course, all of the newsrooms had somebody assigned to monitor the police radio channels. It was inevitable that someone had picked up on Randy Mendelson's name, and now the feeding frenzy was on.

News vans soon surrounded the park, and reporters, cameramen, and technicians climbed over one another trying to get the best vantage point. A pair of crime-scene vans arrived, and crept their way through the crowd to the barricade. Deputies moved a patrol car and let them through and then quickly blocked the opening.

Despite the presence of Sheriff Kerby, Kim was still the officer in charge. "We really need Cal Westfall down here," she suggested to Kerby. "He knows how to talk to these people." She gestured toward the mob of reporters.

Without discussion, the sheriff got on his radio and ordered the dispatcher, "Get Deputy Westfall down here. We need someone to deal with the press."

Westfall had been the public information officer for the Clackamas County Sheriff's Office for the last five years, ever since his predecessor had left law enforcement to narrate "reality" shows on television. On just about any night, you could find Deputy Jim Riddle on the Tru-TV channel providing commentary on videos of police chases, car wrecks, and shoot-outs.

To hold off the media until Westfall arrived, Sheriff Kerby made a quick check of his uniform and then strode toward the shouting reporters. For an elected official, Sheriff Kerby was surprisingly shy in front of the news media. He wasn't very diplomatic, and he knew it. It was best to let the professional spokesman do the talking, but somebody had to say something now, or the reporters would make something up.

Kim walked back to the boat ramp, where a command center of sorts was being constructed. Sammy Cushman spotted her and waved frantically.

"Hey, I think we're in luck," he said. "There's a commercial dive company that has the equipment we need—something called a venturi dredge."

"Great, what do we have to do to get it here?" she asked.

"That's the best thing. It's already here." He gestured out toward the river, where a work barge was moored a quarter mile downstream. "They've been working on an underwater pipeline. The dredging machine is right there, tied up to the barge." He pointed to what appeared to be a pontoon boat loaded-up with machinery and hoses. On the railing of the craft was a sign that said Pacific-Western Diving in blue and green letters.

"What do we need to do to get it over here?" Kim asked urgently.

"I'm already on it. I know the lead diver on that job—Dan Barlow. He lives right down there." Sammy gestured downstream.

"You mean Big Dan? I know that guy."

"Yeah, *everyone* knows Big Dan. I called him, and he gave me his boss's number."

"Good," Kim said. "Get him on the phone and say whatever it takes to get that machine over here!"

"Already done," Sammy answered. "I gave him your name in lieu of a purchase order—told him it was a blank check. Hope that's okay."

"Somehow, I don't think anyone's going to worry about the cost on this one. So what's the plan?"

"A dive company boat is tied up at Big Dan's dock in Canemah. As we speak, Dan is putting his gear onboard, and his equipment operator is on the way. He said they'd be here within the hour. They'll bring the dredge over, and all we'll need to do is tell them where to set up." He paused and then added, "Just one thing."

Kim gave him her best "What now?" look.

"Environmental issues," Sammy explained. "Dan says that this job could send up a mud cloud that'll mess up the river all the way to Portland. He says they could face big fines if they do that."

"Well, tell him to get that rig ready to go, and in the meantime, we'll see what we can do to protect the environment from mud." She couldn't keep a trace of sarcasm out of her voice.

She spotted Cal Westfall heading toward the command center. He approached her, and she quickly briefed him on the situation.

"But listen. Before you go face the jackals, do you know anybody who can advise us on the question of muddying up the river? The dive company thinks we'll have DEQ all over us if we stir up the mud."

"Yeah," Cal said, "they're probably right. But let me make a couple of calls. Sometimes if you talk to them first, they'll look the other way. It's when you ignore them that they get their bureaucratic panties in a wad."

For the next hour, Westfall worked on contacting the right people up and down the chain of command in the Department of Environmental Quality. It was Sunday, so nobody was in the office. The only way he could get home phone numbers was by calling someone who knew someone. It was a tedious process, explaining that they wouldn't be creating an environmental catastrophe.

"It isn't nuclear waste, dioxin or PCBs, we're dealing with here," Westfall patiently told DeAnn Fields, a mid-level manager at DEQ on the other end of the phone line. "It's mud—just plain old river mud, the stuff the riverbed is made of."

Three different people had already told him that they didn't have the authority to approve the excavation. Each time they referred him to a higher level in the DEQ food chain. He was interrupted by the young deputy who was serving as the incident command post's dispatcher.

"I have a call you need to take," the deputy said.

Westfall silently lipped, "Who?"

"It's the governor."

"Excuse me, Ms. Fields," Westfall said into the phone, interrupting her carefully worded passing of the buck, "I have the governor on another line, so I'm going to have to hang up. Is there anything you'd like me to tell him?"

After a long pause, Ms. Fields said, "No, but if you'll call me in the office tomorrow, we'll initiate the paperwork."

Westfall didn't hear her. He'd already disconnected.

"Yes, Governor," he said into the other phone.

The governor didn't beat around the bush. "Are the news reports accurate? Have you found Randy Mendelson's car?"

"Yes, sir. That appears to be the case. All we have so far is a license plate, but it's the right make and model."

"When will you know for sure?"

"Not until we get the car out of the river."

"How long?"

Westfall saw his chance. "That, I can't say. We're going to have to stir up some mud in order to get the car out of the riverbed. I've been talking with DEQ about what kind of permits we need."

He heard the governor sigh. "Listen to me. You do whatever it takes to get that car out of the river, and I mean today! I'll take care of DEQ. You just get on with the job. Understood?"

"Yes, sir. And thank you."

While all of this was taking place on land, Big Dan brought the dive company boat up from Canemah and pulled in next to the boat ramp dock, where Deputies Stayton and Cushman waited. Dan introduced his equipment operator as Idaho Slim.

"So what's the situation here?" Dan inquired.

"We need to excavate an underwater crime scene," Kim told him. "There's a car down there buried in mud. We need to bring it to the surface without disturbing whatever might be inside."

"Yeah, that's what Sammy told me," Dan said. "What about the environmental crap? I don't want my name to show up on some bureaucrat's desk tomorrow morning."

As if on cue, Cal Westfall joined the group on the dock. "I just got off the phone with the governor. He has given his personal guarantee that there'll be no problem with DEQ."

With that settled, Big Dan and Idaho Slim motored downstream to the work barge and returned with the dredging machine. Sammy showed them where to anchor, a few yards downstream from the buoy marking the location of the El Camino. The big barge with the crane was still tied alongside the transient dock, waiting to be called in to lift the car after the excavation.

Kim watched the dive crew set out a four-point anchor system to ensure that Dan's boat and the dredge float couldn't drift out of position.

"Has anybody done anything about getting some food delivered down here?" she asked nobody in particular.

She stood in the command center, trying to stamp out brushfires as they broke out. Spectators in boats had begun to arrive in such numbers that she had to call for help from neighboring Yamhill County's marine unit to cordon off the river. And then, seeing that they would be there into the night, she had called the Oregon Department of Transportation to borrow some of their portable generator and flood light systems.

"Got a load of pizza on the way," a deputy said. "Compliments of Bellagios."

"Phone call for Deputy Stayton," someone shouted.

Kim waved and threaded her way through the chaos to take the call. It was DeAnn Fields's boss at DEQ.

"Go ahead and do what you have to do," the voice on the phone said. And then he asked, "I don't suppose you can do this after dark, can you?"

"It may end up that way, whether we want to or not," Kim explained. "The divers say it doesn't make any difference to them since they won't be able to see anything anyway. There's just no visibility down there."

"It will save us all some headaches if nobody sees the mud you stir up." Then he added, "Boy, someone sure pulled some strings on this."

But that's how things worked. All it took was to drop the name Devonshire, and bureaucrats all over the state came to attention. Nobody—even the governor—wanted it ever said that he'd been the one who stood in the way of this investigation.

As slices of warm pepperoni pizza were passed around, Cal hurriedly put together a press release that gave the media something to put on the evening news. It was mostly background, plus confirmation that the car had been tentatively identified as belonging to Randall Mendelson. No, there was no word on what, if anything was in the car.

"Have human remains been found?" a reporter shouted.

"Nothing has been found. The car is buried in sediment," Cal patiently explained for the third time. "It will take some time to excavate it."

"When will you know?" someone else asked.

"We don't have a timetable. Divers are working on it, but we have to be sure that no evidence is lost in the excavation process."

"What kind of evidence?"

"We won't know that until we find it."

"Are you looking for bodies?"

Kim shook her head in awe at Westfall's ability to field these questions without losing his patience and saying something that would turn the media against the department. She could never have done it.

The two sheriff's department divers and Big Dan entered the water and swam on the surface to the marker buoy above the El Camino. Dan signaled for Idaho Slim to fire up the dredge pump. The divers descended the twenty feet to the muddy lump that covered the car. They worked their way around to the back, where the mud layer seemed to be thinnest.

The deputies each held a high-powered light, while Big Dan ran the dredge. He twisted the lever, opening the valve that controlled the suction, and then pressed the four-inch nozzle against the mud. Like a giant vacuum cleaner, the dredge started slurping up silt. The six-inch discharge hose had been laid out on the riverbed, snaking about fifty feet downstream from the worksite.

After ten minutes, they could see the top edge of the tailgate. In another ten minutes, they had the entire tailgate and rear bumper exposed.

Kim watched as the first traces of silt erupted on the calm surface of the water. Within minutes, a muddy plume started to spread downstream from the dredge outlet hose. After half an hour, the plume had engulfed whole area around the dock and reached half a mile downstream. The complaints would start coming any minute.

The process continued uninterrupted for nearly two hours. When the divers came up for a break, the plume of silt extended all the way to Willamette Falls, a mile downstream. They reported that they had uncovered the entire rear portion of the El Camino and had the roof and windows of the cab uncovered.

"Can you see anything inside the cab?" Deputy Stayton inquired.

"Just mud," Big Dan replied. "All of the glass is intact, but the windows were open a crack—just enough to let silted water get in. It looks like the entire cab is filled with silt."

"Any idea how much longer it'll take to finish the excavation?"

"At least two hours. Probably more by the time we dig out some workroom around the car."

"Can you keep working, or would it be better to wait until morning?"

"I'd rather wait. The thing is we won't be able to lift it in the dark anyway, so there's no hurry to dig it out tonight."

"No, it's only a question of the mud we're sending downstream. Someone is bound to start complaining that we're hurting the salmon or owls or something."

"Well, if you want to keep working, I'm game."

Stayton looked at the two Sheriff's department divers.

"I can handle a little more overtime," one of them said, and the other nodded in agreement.

After a half-hour break, the divers went back into the water. It was after 10:00 p.m. when they came back up and announced that the excavation was finished.

"We have the entire vehicle uncovered, and I sucked out as much mud as I could from around the car," Big Dan told Stayton.

"You think we're ready to lift it?" Stayton asked.

"We're ready to *try*," he explained. "The thing is it's going to be damn heavy. I'd like to get the mud out of the cab, but you'd lose whatever else is in there."

"No, we can't take a chance on losing evidence. We'll try to lift it as is, and if that doesn't work, then we'll talk options." She spoke loudly to everyone on the dock, "Okay, let's wrap it up for the night. Be back here at eight in the morning, ready to get this finished."

CHAPTER 7

worked all that day on *Annabel Lee*, and although every joint in my body ached from the contortions I had to do in the process of installing the conduit, I ended the day with the satisfaction that I was done with that particular phase of the Project. I didn't look at any of this as work. I loved being onboard *Annabel Lee*, and I looked forward to the day when I could live aboard. I just wished I could make it happen sooner.

I'd heard helicopters flying overhead, and at one point, I went up on deck for a beer and looked up toward Willamette Falls, thinking that there must be some kind of protracted rescue operation taking place. Seeing nothing, I finished my beer and went back to what I'd been doing.

Back at my place that evening, I turned on TV and found wall-to-wall news coverage of Kim's car recovery at the West Linn boat ramp. That was when I learned that she'd found Randy Mendelson's El Camino. I didn't need the reporters to tell me what the Mendelson-Devonshire case was all about. Even though I had not even lived in Oregon in 1980, I had the names of Randy Mendelson and Jessie Devonshire permanently burned into my memory by the nationwide media coverage.

There were several things about the 1980 investigation that had raised questions in my mind that remained unresolved. I recalled seeing interviews with the missing girl's mother and her husband. They were played over and over on TV, and to me, both the mother and the stepfather looked like they were lying. I could never understand why the investigators couldn't read their body language or why they had so quickly dismissed the Devonshires as suspects.

It was no secret that Wilson Devonshire was the top aide to Portland Mayor Alan Blalock, arguably the most influential man in Oregon politics—then and now. I'd always speculated to what degree their political power had influenced the investigation.

When there isn't any tangible evidence, the best way to close a case is to pin it on someone who isn't around to defend himself—in this case, Randy Mendelson. But I'd always felt that there was more to it than the gardener abducting or running away with the underage rich girl, which was the media story line.

In the first place, the Devonshires weren't rich. They lived in a nice neighborhood in West Linn, but they were no higher than upper middle class. In the second place, Mendelson was more than just a gardener. He had been a local legend on his high school football and basketball teams until a knee injury ended his future as an athlete.

The Mendelson family was pure working class. Randy's old man worked at the paper mill and brought home enough money to take care of his family, but not enough to pay college tuition. So upon graduation— and lacking the athletic scholarship everyone had expected him to win— Randy did what he'd been doing during every summer since he was ten. He mowed lawns.

But the thing that set him apart from every other teenage kid with a lawn mower was that he *marketed* what he did. And he had great instincts for business. While other kids simply mowed lawns, Randy marketed full-service landscape maintenance. In those days, long before undocumented workers took over the landscaping market, Randy sold affluent people on the concept of paying a monthly fee that covered a whole range of services, including mowing, fertilizing, weeding, trimming, pruning, barking, and watering.

Within two years, he had sold enough of those contracts to hire three other kids to help with the work and to pay for a pair of used pickup trucks to get to and from the job. At the age of nineteen, he was able to pay cash for a year-old El Camino, the car of his dreams—the very car that Kim was digging out of the Willamette River mud.

With Kim on my mind, I decided to take an evening stroll out to the houseboats, a hundred yards up the railroad tracks—mostly just to shake the cramps out of my muscles, but also to get a better vantage point to look upriver for a clue as to whether or not Kim would be stopping by that evening. From the end of the houseboat docks, I could see the portable floodlights at the West Linn boat ramp. The helicopters had gone away when the sun went down, but it was clear that there was still a lot going on up there. I concluded that I probably wouldn't see Kim that night.

Walking back home I passed the travel trailer belonging to a lady I knew as Rosie. I happened to glance in that direction at precisely the moment that Rosie looked out her window. That guaranteed a half-hour conversation. For a semi-elderly, vastly overweight woman, she sure could move fast. She got out the door around, the back of her trailer, and was talking about what a nice evening it was before I could look the other way and pretend to be deaf.

"Yeah, real nice day," I echoed.

"They say another storm's coming in," she said.

"Around here, you can count on that," I answered, setting my mouth on autopilot while my brain searched for a viable getaway plan.

"Storm won't be here for a couple of days, though."

"Yeah, you have to make the most of the nice weather because it never lasts."

"Hey, you want a glass of wine?"

I knew better but said, "Sure, that would be nice." It's way too easy to overdo politeness.

On a picnic table next to the trailer sat a jug of wine and a mismatched selection of plastic tumblers. Rosie snatched up the jug and poured a way too generous quantity of wine-colored liquid into each of two glasses.

"To the weather," she said and took a big gulp.

I glanced at the label on the jug—not that I'm a snob for wine labels. I just like to know what I'm drinking. There was a line drawing of a steam locomotive billowing smoke as it rounded a bend in the railroad tracks. Bold lettering spelled out Night Train Express. No vintage was stated on the label. My best guess was that it was early last week. The wine smelled a bit like the stuff I use to clean engine parts.

"Pretty good wine," Rosie proclaimed. "Not the best, but pretty good and not too expensive."

"Mmmm." Tentatively, I took a sip. Moments before, I'd been mildly concerned about the hygiene of Rosie's glassware—or plastic ware. But I need not have worried about that. I'm pretty sure Rosie's wine has at least the same disinfectant power as iodine. And it tasted about the same too.

"I see Big Dan is working today," Rosie commented.

Relieved to have something to say, I told her, "Yeah, they're pulling an old car out of the river over at the boat ramp." As long as I kept on talking, I couldn't drink the wine, so I told her everything I knew about what was going on, even mentioning that Kim was supervising the job.

"She that cute little deputy I see over at your place all the time? Corrigan, you ought to wrap her up and keep her. She's a gem, she is."

Great. Relationship counseling. And I didn't even have to pay for it.

Rosie finished off her glass and reached for the jug. She made a gesture offering to top off my glass, but I waved her off.

"I'd like to stay around and chat," I told her, "but I have to get back. I'm expecting a phone call." I put down my glass and got up to leave. "Thanks for the wine, Rosie."

As I walked away, Rosie picked up my glass, sniffed the wine, shrugged, and took a big gulp. No sense letting fine wine go to waste.

The ten o'clock news opened with the continuing story of Kim's attempt to recover the car that might finally provide the elusive solution the Mendelson-Devonshire case. The lengthy report summarized the investigation that had followed the 1980 disappearances and then went on to describe Kim's discovery of the sunken El Camino.

Accompanying video showed the three cars that had been lifted out of the river on Saturday, with a reporter speculating on what connection they might have to the case.

The report ended with a recording of Kim's radio conversation with the dispatcher when she first learned the identity of the car's owner. The wide-eyed reporter revealed to the world that "Deputy Kim Stayton, the marine-unit supervisor on the scene, attempted to suppress public knowledge of the vehicle's identity."

In the middle of a sports reporter's attempt at making yet another 0-0 Portland Timbers soccer game sound exciting, I heard the distinctive rumble of Kim's Jetcraft. I killed the TV and walked out onto my porch as she pulled up to my dock and cut the engine.

"You've become a celebrity," I said when she came up the steps.

She groaned. "You've been watching the news. So you know what's been going on."

"I'm not sure that *both* of those things are true," I said, and then recounted what I'd seen on TV.

"They actually played a *recording* of that?" she complained

"Bad deputy," I teased. "They even said that you've been stonewalling them."

"Yeah, it's Watergate all over. Consider the source. That's how my day went. How was yours?"

"I spent most of the day on the Project. Then I shared some fine wine with Rosie. She has a high opinion of you, by the way. Of course, all that could change if she watches the news."

Kim sighed. "If only *that* were the worst of my problems."

"Think you'll find anything in the El Camino?"

"It'll be a big letdown if we don't. I expect to find Mendelson and Devonshire inside. It's the only thing that makes sense. If either of them were alive, something would have turned up. But in thirty-two years, there hasn't been so much as a hint, and that tells me that they're both dead."

"Heard anything from Wilson Devonshire?"

"Not yet, but the political powers are definitely in play. Even the governor got involved, ordering the DEQ to let us pollute the river if that's what it takes to get the car out. But I don't expect Devonshire to say anything until we know what's in the car."

CHAPTER 8

MONDAY, JUNE 13

The northbound Amtrak Cascade rumbled past my place at 7:15 a.m., shaking the floor and rattling the glassware in my kitchen cupboards. I'd never need an alarm clock as long as I lived in Canemah. While I started making coffee, Kim went out to get the morning paper.

"I got your mail too," she said when she came back inside. "Ooh, this must be important. It's addressed to March F. Corrigan."

"Obviously someone who doesn't know me," I said sourly.

Kim paused long enough to conjure up a serious expression. "Corrigan, I have to know. How in hell did you come to be named March? I've never heard of anyone else named March."

Trying my best to sound like Al Pacino, I held up my hand and said forcefully, "I told you to never ask me questions about my business."

"Aw, come on, Corrigan, we've been together for how long—two years, three? Don't you think it's time to tell me?"

I took a deep breath. I always knew it would come to this. After an appropriately long pause, I explained, "In the sixties, my folks were beatniks or hippies—something like that. I'm lucky they didn't name me something like Dweezle or Star Child."

"So how did they come up with a name like March?"

"It was fashionable in their crowd to assign names that related to when you were born."

"But that doesn't make any sense! You were born in *April*," Kim objected.

"Yeah, but I was *due* in March, and fortunately for me, they'd already settled on the name."

Pressing her luck even further, she asked, "I have to know: what does the F stand for?"

"My birthday is April third," I said, wishing for an end to this line of inquiry.

"I don't get it," she said.

I chewed on my lower lip. "My middle name would have been Third, but that would have made my initials M T—pronounced 'empty.' That simply wouldn't do, so they pretended I was born five minutes later, which would have made my birthday the fourth."

Kim gave that some thought. Her face brightened and she said, "I get it: march forth—double meaning. Cute."

"Good. And now you know why I just stick with 'Corrigan.' So let's have breakfast and get on with our day."

"Right. I need to get out of here before some TV cameraman spots my boat parked at your dock," she said.

"I can see it all now: 'Deputy Stayton's love nest discovered.' Front page news."

"That's not funny, Corrigan."

We had a quick breakfast before walking down to the dock. As Kim was preparing to start the engine on her patrol boat, we spotted Big Dan hurrying down the steps.

"Stayton," he called out, "can you spare a minute?"

Kim turned and said, "Sure, what's up?"

"Look, it's your show. I'm just there to run the dredge. But I've done a lot of salvage work over the years, and I'm concerned about this lift." He gestured toward the boat landing upstream. "I think we're going about it the wrong way."

"Why do you say that?"

"It's too much weight."

"It worked fine for the three cars on Saturday."

Big Dan rubbed his forehead and explained, "Yeah, but this one is different. Like I told you yesterday, it looks like the cab is filled with mud. I'm guessing that the interior capacity of the El Camino is something like seventy-five to a hundred cubic feet. That much mud will weigh five or six tons. I think that if you try to lift that much weight using slings under the ends of the car, the way you lifted the other three, you'll overload the El Camino's frame. If the frame fails, the cab will rupture, and whatever's in it will be lost."

"So what do you suggest?" Kim asked.

"You need to run two heavy beams under the car—one right behind the front wheels, and the other just in front of the rear wheels. That'll center the lift under the heaviest part of the load. You'll need cross-members between the two beams to hold them the right distance apart."

"How do we get that framework under the car?"

"We'll have to take the frame down in pieces. We'll push the dredge under the car to open up tunnels that we can pull the heavy beams through. Then we'll bolt the cross-members in, and we'll be ready to lift."

"Where can we get the materials to make this thing?" Kim asked.

"There's a guy at Clackamas Steel who will do the calculations and get you the right size beams. Just tell him what the total load will be—let's see—allow two tons for the El Camino plus six tons for the mud. If each beam can carry a center load of eight tons, that'll give us a 100 percent design margin. Make the beams ten feet long."

"You give your friend a call," Kim told Big Dan. "Tell him I'll have a truck heading his way to pick it up."

"I need one more thing," he said. "Can you have one of your divers go down and measure the distance between the front and rear wheels. We need to know how long to make the cross-members."

"Good point. I'd better get up there and get someone into the water. You have them start rounding up the materials. I'll get the dimensions."

On the radio, she called dispatch and requested a flatbed truck. "I need it at Clackamas Steel at nine-thirty."

Big Dan nodded and headed back toward his place while I untied Kim's dock lines.

Kim called after him, "Have them drill the beams and cross-members and give us the hardware to assemble it all."

CHAPTER 9

It was mid-afternoon when Big Dan came to the surface and reported that he had the lift frame assembled under the El Camino. If everything went right, the car would be on dry land in another hour. The divers went back under and made a final check.

When he was sure that everything was ready, Dan gave the order to start lifting. There were groans of steel against steel as the cables went taut and the beams came up in contact with the El Camino's frame.

"Hold there," Dan ordered. "She's stuck like a suction cup on a mirror. We have to break the vacuum in order to get her loose. I'm coming up."

Swimming up next to the Pacific-Western dive boat, Dan described what he needed. "I want the water hose for the dredge. Screw a gate valve and a three-foot piece of one-inch pipe onto the end, and I'll use that to try to hose out the mud."

After assembling the makeshift nozzle, Idaho Slim fired up the pump. Dan went back carrying his water cannon. He pushed the end of the pipe into the right front fender well and opened the valve.

"Okay," he said over the com system, "keep a nice, steady pull. Not too much, but keep the rigging tight. I'll keep poking around until something comes loose."

The blast of water from the pipe instantly stirred up a cloud of silt, and visibility went to zero. The divers were enveloped in blackness as the silt blocked out all light from the surface.

"Sammy, you hear me?" Dan asked.

"Ten-four."

"Keep a hand on the corner of the car, and tell me if you feel it move."

"No movement yet," Sammy reported.

Dan kept poking the nozzle into the mud all around the front tire and in as far as he could reach under the engine. "Anything yet?"

"Still nothing."

"Okay, stop lifting while I go to the other side," Dan told the crane operator. He felt his way around the car, careful to avoid tangling the hoses with the rigging. He found the left front fender well and started poking the nozzle into the mud around the tire. "Start lifting again," he ordered. "Sammy, you still there?"

"Ten-four."

"Let's give it a go then." Dan opened the valve and was immediately enveloped in a fresh cloud of silt. There was a different noise, and even before Sammy shouted, "It's going up!" Dan knew that the El Camino had moved for the first time since 1980.

He shut off the valve and ordered the crane operator to stop lifting. "Hold on for a few minutes, and let the water clear up some. I want to see what's happening."

The silt plume slowly drifted downstream, and daylight again reached the El Camino. Dan worked his way around the car, carefully looking for any sign that the frame or cab might be failing. When he was certain that everything was okay, he ordered the lift to proceed.

Slowly, the car moved toward the surface, with streamers of silt falling away as it rose. Occasional chunks of mud broke loose and thumped back to the riverbed. Sammy and Dan, on opposite sides of the car, monitored its rise. A cheer rose from everyone on the dock and barge when the roof of the El Camino broke the surface.

Once the car had been set down on the barge, the divers went about the business of reeling in their hoses and putting away their equipment. Meanwhile, the barge was pushed up alongside the dock. A ring of people soon surrounded the El Camino, walking around and inspecting it, trying to see through the muddy glass to determine what was inside. Streams of muddy water trickled out from every part of the vehicle, and chunks of mud piled up on the deck beneath it.

From outside the police lines, TV reporters spoke urgently to their cameras, while other cameramen, with huge telephoto lenses, zoomed in on the barge. Three news helicopters circled overhead, creating a noise that prohibited normal conversation.

The flatbed truck from the Main Street Towing Company backed down the boat ramp to the water's edge. Carefully, the El Camino was lifted from the barge and set down onto the truck. It was left sitting on the lift frame, which was ten feet wide, so pilot cars would be required for the drive to the sheriff's department's vehicle maintenance facility in Oregon City. The procession formed up in the boat-trailer parking area, with West Linn Police Department motorcycles in the lead, blue and red lights flashing.

They led the official pilot car, with its yellow flashing lights and Oversize Load sign on the roof. Next was the flatbed truck, and it was followed by three sheriff's cars. A swarm of vehicles full of media people and other interested citizens joined the parade as it worked its way through the park and up the hill away from the boat ramp. The incessant noise from overhead faded away as the helicopters followed the famous El Camino.

"Okay," Kim shouted to everyone left on scene, "let's all pitch in and get this wrapped up. I want to be out of here before dark."

CHAPTER 10

TUESDAY, JUNE 14

The steel bows that once held huge polyester canopies over the three giant covered wagons at the End of the Oregon Trail Interpretive Center are streaked with rust stains, sad victims of the Great Recession. A couple of blocks beyond the mothballed museum is a long row of nondescript buildings belonging to Clackamas County, among them the sheriff's office vehicle-maintenance facility.

It was here that the El Camino was unloaded from the flatbed and moved into a garage that had been hastily cleared out for this job. Deputies had been stationed at the entrances to prevent anyone from disturbing the car, which continued to drip river water through the night.

At eight Tuesday morning, the homicide and violent crimes unit gathered in the meeting room at the sheriff's office headquarters on Sunnybrook Boulevard in Clackamas. HVCU consisted of seven detectives, two crime-scene investigators, and a forensic artist. This morning's meeting would be led by Sheriff Kerby.

When Kerby walked to the front of the room, everyone found seats, and all conversation ended.

"Is there anybody here who does not understand the importance of what you're going to do today?" he asked rhetorically. "This will be the most important day in your career. I'm the only one in this room who was with the department when this case began. The discovery of Randall Mendelson's vehicle is the first break in this case in thirty-two years. Now it is yours to solve."

Although she wouldn't have any further involvement in the investigation, Kim had been invited to sit in on the meeting. Kerby motioned her to the front of the room and said, "I'm going to let Deputy Stayton describe how the vehicle was found and recovered."

Kim spent the next few minutes describing the events of the weekend, making a special point of emphasizing the steps taken to ensure the preservation of whatever evidence the El Camino might contain. She kept her comments to a minimum, knowing that her presence there was mainly a gesture of courtesy.

Next, Kerby called Detective Larry Jamieson to the front of the room. "Detective Jamieson will be lead detective on this case. He will tell you what has already been done."

"Silverton and Elkton are in charge of the crime scene." Jamieson motioned to the CSI unit criminalists, Carrie Silverton and David Elkton. "They have consulted with an archeology professor at Oregon State University because what we're facing is essentially an archeological dig. As you probably have heard, the vehicle is filled with mud. The plan is to wash the mud through strainers to catch anything that comes out."

When Jamieson finished, Kerby repeated the importance of full cooperation, concluding with, "Okay, now let's go to work."

When the meeting broke up, everyone headed out to their cars for the short drive to the maintenance garage in Oregon City. Only Jamieson, Silverton, and Elkton had official roles in the investigation at this point, but many others found some excuse to be there. It was an event that nobody wanted to miss.

Floodlights, work tables, and tool boxes now surrounded the El Camino that had been Randy Mendelson's pride and joy. The investigators walked around the car, finally deciding that the passenger side door was the best place to start.

"When you're ready," Jamieson said to Elkton.

Elkton and Silverton positioned their freshly constructed strainer on the concrete, directly beneath the El Camino's door. The strainer consisted of a rectangular box made of two-by-six lumber with eighth-inch screen mesh in the bottom. A short piece of two-by-four was placed under each corner to hold the strainer off of the concrete.

"Here it goes," Elkton said as he lifted the door handle. The door didn't budge. "Either it's locked, or the latch is seized up."

That was hardly unexpected. He gave another tug, getting the same result. From his tool box, he produced a twenty-four-inch crowbar. He jammed it into the gap where he guessed the latch was located. While

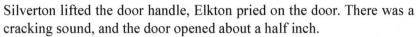

Silverton lifted the door handle, Elkton pried on the door. There was a cracking sound, and the door opened about a half inch.

"That's it," Elkton said with satisfaction. "Here we go."

Slowly, he pulled the door open. The silt inside formed a wall of mud that stayed mostly intact as the door was opened. Little gullies formed as water drizzled down the mud.

"Let's get the door out of the way," Elkton said. He motioned to a couple of CCSO mechanics, and they wheeled an oxyacetylene kit over next to the car. A transmission jack was placed beneath the door, and then the hinges were cut. The door was moved off to the side, where it would later be rinsed off and processed for prints.

As the mechanics finished their work, Silverton moved in with a garden hose. With the nozzle set to a soft spray, she started washing away the mud. Over the decades, it had settled and become compressed into a firm mass that eroded away slowly. The air was electric with anticipation as the mud eroded into the strainer below.

"I have hair here," Silverton announced.

Everyone strained to see. Down at seat level, strands of long blonde hair protruded from the mud. She continued rinsing away the mud.

"There's a skull," she said. The bone was as brown as the mud, but it clearly was a human skull.

"Major trauma to top of the skull. Compression fracture, probably fatal," Elkton observed. He placed the skull in a plastic tub filled with water to prevent the rapid deterioration that might occur if the bone was allowed to dry. In the lab, forensic pathologists would finish cleaning the bones and remove the mud from inside. It would be their job to officially determine cause and manner of death.

Silverton continued spraying the wall of mud that still filled most of the cab, trying to work from the top down. She had taken off only a couple of inches when she found the second skull perched on top of the backrest, leaning against the rear window of the cab.

"Let's open the other door," she suggested.

The driver's door opened without prying, and as they'd done on the other side, the mechanics cut the hinges. As Elkton lifted the skull out of the car, he pointed out a small round hole in the left rear.

"Definitely a bullet hole. Small caliber," he commented.

There was a moment of perfect silence as everybody grasped the meaning of the bullet hole in the second skull. They were dealing with a double homicide. Until that moment, everyone had assumed that the remains would confirm the murder-suicide theory. But the bullet hole was in the wrong place for a suicide.

Jamieson picked up his phone and called Sheriff Kerby. "You need to see what we have here," he said.

Twenty minutes later, Kerby entered the garage. Jamieson showed him what the investigators had found.

"I want everyone's attention," Kerby announced. "What you've seen here is not to be shared with anyone outside this room. You say something to your wife, your neighbor, your mother or your dog, and I'll have your badge. Is that absolutely clear?"

There was a disorganized chorus of acknowledgment from around the room. With that, he turned and walked out of the garage, leaving everyone else standing and looking at one another, wondering why they had wanted to be there.

Elkton took over the job of washing the mud out of the El Camino. What gradually emerged was a scene of horror preserved in mud for over three decades. The remains of the two victims were totally skeletonized, but a good deal of connective tissue remained intact since there had been no scavenging animals to tear the bones apart and scatter them around.

Much of the victim's clothing remained intact as well—testimony to the longevity of man-made fibers. The small bones of the hands were loose and had fallen to the floor before the car had filled with silt, but the major bones were still attached together, looking like bizarre headless Halloween characters in their stained clothing.

The smaller skeleton, presumed to be Jessie Devonshire, lying sideways on the seat, was dressed in what appeared to be a full-length pink satin negligee over a lace-trimmed babydoll with matching panties. The larger skeleton sat upright behind the steering wheel, dressed in an Oregon State University t-shirt, blue jeans, and Red Wing work boots.

"It doesn't look like they were out on a date," Elkton observed.

"Those match the clothes that Mendelson's mom said he was wearing when he left the house that day," Jamieson commented. "I reviewed the investigation summary yesterday. We never had a description of what the girl was wearing. The stepfather said he hadn't seen her leave the house."

"Then why did he say she'd gone out on a date?" Silverton asked.

"Devonshire's statement was that she'd told him earlier in the day that she was going out. He said that she wasn't there when he got home," Jamieson explained. "He logically assumed that she had left for her date."

"She didn't go on a date dressed like that," Silverton argued.

"I agree," Jamieson said. "So what could have made her leave the house dressed in lingerie?"

"Jailbait night at the local massage parlor?" one of the other detectives quipped.

"Maybe Mendelson knocked on the door to ask about pruning a tree, saw the chick in her sexy little nightie, and was overtaken by lust. He drags her out to his car, she fights, he hits her with a landscape brick," another detective speculated.

"Could be," Jamieson mused. "Let's finish with the mud and turn the remains over to the pathologist."

Silverton picked up the hose and went back to spraying. The mud in the floor pans was harder to get out since it had to be sprayed or scooped up over the sill. On the driver's side, she carefully worked around the Red Wing boots, which had not yet been moved.

"I have a gun here," Silverton suddenly announced.

She continued washing until the gun was fully exposed. It was a single-action .22 revolver with a Ruger medallion visible on the walnut grip. Elkton used forceps to lift the weapon out of the car and place it in a pan of distilled water pending further examination. It would take days, perhaps weeks, to analyze all of the evidence and develop a solid theory about what had happened on July 25, 1980.

In the meantime, Jamieson had to come up with something to tell the reporters, who were ready to pounce on anyone who came out. So far, those leaving had managed to escape by saying—truthfully—that they weren't authorized to say anything. It wouldn't be so easy for Jamieson. He picked up his phone and dialed.

"We need to schedule a press conference," he told Sheriff Kerby. "And before anyone says anything, we have to figure out how much we're going to make public. The reporters are just outside the door, and they're going to demand something from me as soon as I go outside."

"Tell them there'll be a press conference at five," Kerby said. "No, make that four, so they'll have time to get it on the five o'clock news. Don't say anything else."

CHAPTER 11

One of the great benefits of being self-employed is that I could work when I wanted to and give myself a day off when I felt like it. Other times, I got a day off simply because I just didn't have anything to do. I went over to *Annabel Lee* and started pulling wires through the conduit. I calculated that it would take over six miles of wire to finish the job. There would be eight AC circuits off a central panel that would be connected to the diesel generator in the engine room.

The DC circuits would be wired to a fuse panel behind a cupboard door in the main salon. Then there would be the communication circuits, computer network, television cable, audio, and navigation circuits. Every wire had to be labeled and numbered according to its function. This was the start of a very long project.

The sheriff's four o'clock press conference was carried live on every television station in Portland. CNN and MSNBC had picked up the story and were carrying the live feed from the Portland stations. Cal Westfall opened with a summary of the events leading up to the day's work on the El Camino.

He was interrupted more than once by reporters impatient to know what they'd found inside, but Cal just put his hand up and waited for them to shut up before continuing his prepared monologue. He had to tell the story his way, starting at the beginning and ending at the end. Having driven the anticipation level as high as it could go without causing some kind of explosion, Cal finally got to why they all were there.

"Today, detectives and investigators from the homicide and violent crimes unit opened the car that was extracted from the Willamette River, which has been positively identified through the vehicle identification number as belonging to Randall Mendelson."

There was a murmur from the audience, and Westfall waited for it to die down.

"Two sets of human remains were found inside the car. Positive identification has not yet been made, but based on what we know right now, we believe that they are the remains of Randall Mendelson and Jessie Devonshire. We believe at this time that at least one of the subjects was the victim of homicide."

The room exploded in questions shouted from every corner. Westfall just stood still, waiting. They finally got the point and fell quiet.

"Over the coming days, the remains will be examined by forensic pathologists, who will attempt to determine the cause and manner of death. Other evidence found in the car will be analyzed in our crime lab and investigators will continue to process the vehicle in search of additional evidence.

"As to what evidence has been found, I will tell you that a weapon was found in the car. A hand gun. We have not yet determined if it will be possible to trace the weapon's ownership or if it played any role in this crime. The weapon will be sent to the state crime lab tomorrow for analysis.

"Those are the basic facts. I will now take your questions."

For twenty minutes, the reporters tried—without success—to get further detail or opinions out of Cal Westfall, who remained absolutely composed and polite throughout the media carnival.

I watched the whole thing on Channel 8 and did a lot of reading between the lines. First, for Westfall to say that "at least" one of the victims had been murdered implied that the old official conclusion of murder-suicide was now uncertain. But if there was the possibility that it had been a double murder, why not say so? The answer was inescapable: because if it was a double murder, the prime suspect was a justice on the state supreme court: Wilson Landis Devonshire.

CHAPTER 12

WEDNESDAY, JUNE 15

Wednesday was a work day. I had two clients on retainer, and I always set aside two days a week to do work for them. I will grant that two days a week is a lot to sacrifice, but these clients were, after all, my bread and butter. As long as they remained in need of my work and kept paying my monthly fee, I would have the freedom to do whatever I wanted for the other five days a week. That didn't seem like such a bad deal.

Xycon is one of those companies that operate well out of the public view. They design and manufacture integrated circuits for highly specialized computer systems, and one of the greatest threats to their operation is employee theft. In the extremely competitive world of computer-processor design, there are people who are not above using corporate espionage to shortcut the hugely expensive engineering process.

Xycon came to me four years ago because they suspected that one of their design engineers was selling proprietary information to a Chinese manufacturer. Upon my successful closure of that investigation, Xycon put me on retainer to monitor certain aspects of their employees' activities for hints of malfeasance.

The thing that has always amazed me about "computer geniuses" is how many of them are so completely stupid in the use of their own computers. Of all people, they are the ones who should know better. They frequently write things on Facebook or Twitter that announce to the world what they are doing, without regard to consequences. I spend eight to ten hours a week reading posts made by Xycon employees.

What I do has prevented at least four major breaches of security, any one of which would have cost Xycon several times more than the total fees they've paid to me. But it is tedious work. Four hits in four years means that nearly everything I read is meaningless in terms of Xycon's security. It takes a lot of coffee to spend hour upon hour reading the mostly innocuous online chatter of about four hundred employees in search of indications that someone might be stealing from Xycon. And that sums up my day—a lot of caffeine and no hits.

Preparing to unwind after my long day of online eavesdropping, I carried a chilled bottle of Chardonnay across the railroad tracks and down to the dock where I keep my ski boat. I poured two glasses of wine and sat down with Kim to watch the only boat out on the river as it labored ponderously through the water, kicking up a huge wake for the would-be wake surfer close behind, who could never quite find equilibrium between the boat and the wave.

"Isn't it kind of dangerous to be that close to the boat?" I asked Kim.

"I sure wouldn't want to be that close to a spinning propeller," she said, "but I've never yet heard of a wake surfer getting the Veg-O-Matic treatment. We *have*, however, had them get sick on the exhaust fumes from the motor."

"Strange what people do for recreation." I watched the surf rider slip out of the sweet spot and sink—for about the tenth time. I hadn't seen him actually stay on the wave for more than a few seconds at a time.

"That would bore me."

"Oh, unlike reading tweets from computer nerds all day," Kim teased.

"That's different. I get paid for it—and rather handsomely, I might add," I said defensively.

"And that takes the boredom out?"

"You have to treat it like a game—a puzzle, where you search for pieces that fit together with other pieces. It's challenging, and that's what keeps me awake. Well, that and a lot of coffee."

"You can have it. I'll stick to what I'm doing."

"Ah, yes. I saw that you were back out on the river today."

"Yeah, my career in major crimes investigation is over—brief but glorious."

"I watched the press conference yesterday. Westfall mentioned evidence of 'at least' one homicide. To me, that implies the possibility that someone else was involved."

"So you picked up on that little faux pas." Kim chuckled. "Kerby was not happy that Cal let that ugly cat out of the bag."

"Kerby doesn't need to worry. Nobody at the *Chronicle* mentioned it."

"Yeah, I don't get that. Why would reporters, who were willing to commit mayhem yesterday in order to learn the grisly details of the contents of the El Camino, now be completely without curiosity as to what the evidence means?"

"Oh, I don't think the reporters missed the meaning of Cal's 'at least' comment. They can't possibly fail to see that if both victims were murdered, Wilson Devonshire would be the prime suspect."

"So why don't they say so?" Kim wondered.

"Because they will do whatever they can to stifle any news that might tarnish the reputations of their anointed leaders. It's no secret that the editorial staff of the *Chronicle* is dominated by liberals—or 'progressives,' as they like to call themselves now. And it's also no secret that the ultra-liberal Wilson Devonshire is among the 'chosen ones' in Oregon politics."

"I didn't know you were such a cynic."

"I don't believe in Santa Claus, the Easter Bunny, or objective journalism. If that makes me a cynic, then I plead guilty," I countered.

"No *Santa Claus*? You really *are* a cynic."

"Okay, so what *did* you find in the El Camino?" I asked, getting back to the original conversation.

"I can repeat only what was said in the press conference. Beyond that, we're sworn to silence."

"But something in that car made Cal Westfall suspect a double homicide," I persisted.

"I can't comment on what Cal Westfall does or doesn't suspect," she evaded. "Nobody is going to draw any conclusions until the lab reports come back."

"When will that be?"

"Don't mention this to anyone, but there'll be a press conference tomorrow for the pathologist's report. We'll also have an inventory on physical evidence. Ballistics and firearm analysis may take longer."

Running low on both Chardonnay and daylight, Kim and I retreated from the dock and made our way back across the tracks and up to the house. I switched on the stereo and put Elvis in charge of the rest of the evening.

CHAPTER 13

THURSDAY, JUNE 16

The mid-afternoon press conference was held in the fourth-floor auditorium at the Sheriff 's Office Sunnybrook Boulevard headquarters and was carried live on Portland's radio and television stations as well as the cable-news networks.

"We want to give you an update on the investigation following the recovery of Randall Mendelson's 1978 Chevrolet El Camino from the Willamette River last Monday," Sheriff Kerby said in opening the press conference. "All resources of this office have been made available to this investigation, and we have been promised the full cooperation of the Oregon State Police crime labs. I will now turn this conference over to Cal Westfall, who will provide full details on the progress of our investigation."

Westfall stepped forward and opened by saying, "I'm going to ask that you hold all questions until after I've completed my update.

"As you know, on Tuesday our crime-scene investigators searched the vehicle recovered from the Willamette River the previous day. During the thirty-two years the car was in the river, silt and mud were carried into the vehicle through partially open windows and completely filled the car's interior with mud. Our investigation started with the careful removal of all that mud.

"Two sets of human remains were recovered from the vehicle, and forensic pathologists have confirmed the identities as Randall Mendelson and Jessie Devonshire. Positive identification was made through dental records and certain personal effects also found in the vehicle.

"The pathologist's report indicates that Jessie Devonshire sustained major blunt-force trauma resulting in multiple fractures of the skull, very likely causing serious injury to the brain. It is believed that this injury was not survivable. There was also a gunshot wound at the back of the skull, and bullet fragments were found inside the skull. This injury would not have been survivable.

"Randall Mendelson sustained a gunshot injury in the parietal area, above and behind the left ear. This injury was not survivable. Bullet fragments were found inside the skull.

"A firearm was recovered from inside the vehicle. It has been tentatively identified as a .22 caliber Ruger New Model Single Six revolver. This weapon is consistent with the composition of the bullet fragments recovered from the victims as well as with the size and nature of the entry wounds. The firearm has been sent to the Oregon State Police ballistics lab for analysis, along with the recovered bullet fragments. That analysis may take several weeks.

"Clothing and other personal effects were found in the vehicle and are being studied in the Sheriff's Office crime lab.

"As to the vehicle itself, it was determined that the transmission was in Drive and the ignition switch was in the On position, suggesting that the vehicle was driven down the boat ramp into the river. The windows on both sides of the vehicle were open about three-fourths of an inch, thus accounting for the accumulation of silt inside the cab.

"Although the investigation is incomplete, the evidence appears to support the long-held belief that Mendelson murdered Devonshire and then took his own life. It is believed that Mendelson may have forcibly abducted Devonshire from her home on July 25, 1980. Evidence indicates that Mendelson delivered a blow to Devonshire's head, either during or following the abduction.

"It is believed that Devonshire may have still shown active vital signs, leading Mendelson to deliver the gunshot wound. He went to the old West Linn boat ramp and drove the vehicle into the river. Rather than die by drowning, Mendelson then put the gun to his own head and fired a fatal shot.

"Please remember that these are preliminary conclusions based on partial evidence. As more is learned from the evidence currently being analyzed, the conclusions may be modified. I will now entertain your questions."

This triggered a feeding frenzy of questions from the reporters. Once again, many of the questions showed a ghoulish interest in the condition of the bodies. Westfall declined to discuss that subject "out of consideration for the families of the victims."

The questioning went on for over half an hour but brought out no new information. I found it interesting that the name of Wilson Devonshire was never mentioned in any context. I felt that the investigators must have some additional information not brought up in the press conference to support their murder-suicide conclusion because based on what they'd said, I would have rejected murder-suicide. But then, if they had additional information to support murder-suicide, why not say so? It made no sense.

Something else about the press conference bothered me. I watched the row of HVCU detectives standing behind Cal Westfall. As he spoke about the evidence supporting the murder-suicide theory, several of the detectives looked very uncomfortable. Larry Jamieson just looked disgusted

.ॐॐ

"Kim, I just don't understand how your detectives could have concluded that the evidence supports murder-suicide," I said over dinner that evening. We were at her place, a modest condominium townhouse on the southern fringe of Oregon City.

"I'm sure they have good reason, but I don't know any more than you do," she said, "and if I did know anything, I couldn't tell you."

"Jamieson looked like he wanted to choke someone when Westfall said it was murder-suicide."

"Like I said—"

"You can't comment on the investigation," I finished for her. "I'll tell you what I think. I think that someone in the investigation has become very lazy or has been pressured to pin the whole thing on Mendelson, no matter what the evidence shows."

Kim repeated, "Like I said…"

CHAPTER 14

MONDAY JUNE 20

The Mendelson-Devonshire case made headlines on Friday, but over the weekend it slipped off the front page, and when I skimmed through the thin Monday morning paper, I found no mention of it at all. Only a week before, it had seemed like the biggest story of the year, and now it was gone.

I was aboard *Annabel Lee*, as I had been all weekend, pulling bundles of wire through conduit. This work was a lot less physically demanding than installing the conduit. But it was tedious. I had to attach a plastic sleeve to each end of every wire, identifying its function, and God help me if I should mis-label one.

My old boom box kept me entertained, either from the case of CDs I kept aboard or from local talk radio. That Monday was the first time I'd heard the icon of Portland talk radio, Lars Larson, comment on the Mendelson case.

"Does it make any sense to you that Randy Mendelson would kill himself twice?" Lars asked. "Either you shoot yourself or you drown yourself. Nobody does both.

"And what about the location of the bullet wound in Randy's skull? It was described as being 'above and behind his left ear.' That isn't where people shoot themselves. They either put the gun to their temples or put it in their mouths. I'm not even sure that it's possible to hold the gun in a position to shoot yourself where they say he did.

"The firearm found in the El Camino is a Ruger New Model Single Six. That's a popular weapon, and I'm very familiar with it. It has a 6 ½ inch barrel, which means that a shooter's hand would be nearly a foot from the muzzle. Go ahead and try to put your hand in that position. You probably can't do it, but even if you can, it isn't comfortable, and it isn't the natural way to hold a gun."

"Lars," the caller named Theodore said in a tone dripping with condescension, "why would the sheriff's office say that Mendelson shot himself if he didn't really do it? What possible reason could they have?"

"Well, I'll tell you what reason they could have," Lars said. "Because if Randy didn't pull the trigger, then somebody else did, and the most likely suspect would be Wilson Landis Devonshire."

"Come on, Lars. You're saying that there is some massive conspiracy involving a supreme court justice and the entire sheriff's office? Do you know how foolish that sounds?" asked Theodore.

"I'm not saying the sheriff's office is involved in a conspiracy," Lars answered. "But you and I both know that a man in Wilson Devonshire's position can exert a huge amount of political pressure on public employees."

"Lars," Theodore insisted, "Devonshire is not even in politics. He's a supreme court justice. He can't put political pressure on anybody!"

"I beg to differ," Lars responded. "Devonshire is where he is because he's part of Alan Blalock's inner circle, and Alan Blalock can put political pressure on anybody in Oregon."

The debate might have gone on longer, but it was the top of the hour, and Lars had to yield to the network news feed. I had to admit to myself that what Lars had said made more sense than what Cal Westfall had said in the press conference.

During the national newscast that followed, my phone started chirping like some kind of mutant mockingbird. Why can't they make a phone that sounds like a phone?

"This is Corrigan," I said.

"Hello, Mr. Corrigan," a woman's voice said, "My name is Lila Mendelson, I'm—"

"Randy Mendelson's mother," I finished for her. "What can I do for you?"

"I want you to prove that Randy didn't kill that girl," Lila said, "and he didn't kill himself, either. Larry Jamieson gave me your name. He's the detective with the sheriff's office who is in charge of the investigation."

That puzzled me. "Why would Detective Jamieson suggest that you call me?"

"He said that you are a good investigator, and that you can do things that he can't."

"What things?"

"I don't know. He just said that you might be able to help me."

"I'll tell you what. Can you meet me at Shari's Restaurant at the Oregon City Shopping Center in half an hour? You know where that is?"

"I can be there. And thank you, Mr. Corrigan!"

An hour later, we sat facing one another in a booth at Shari's. Lila had said that she wasn't hungry, but I talked her into ordering a slice of pie and a glass of iced tea. I ordered a club sandwich and a cup of coffee.

"What they're saying about Randy just isn't true. He wouldn't hurt that girl," Lila said.

"What do you think happened?" I asked.

"I don't know," she said with desperation creeping into her voice. "I just know that it didn't happen the way they're saying. Randy didn't kill himself or anyone else."

"How can you be sure?"

"Because the car was in the river!" Lila cried. "Randy *loved* that car. He saved for two years to buy it. He washed it every day. He would *never* have driven it into the river, no matter what!"

Trying to calm her, I said, "Lila, what can you tell me about the time when Randy and Jessie disappeared?"

"Oh, it was a beautiful summer day," Lila began. "Mount St. Helens blew up that year, and then we had weeks and weeks of rain. I thought it would never stop. But I remember how nice the weather was that day. Randy should have been home for dinner, but when he was late, I just figured it had something to do with his work.

"Then when it started to get dark, I knew that something was wrong. Randy would have called if he was going to be that late. So I called the police, but they told me that Randy was an adult and they wouldn't investigate until he'd been missing for forty-eight hours. They said he'd probably be home by morning.

"But he wasn't. He never came home. And then when I heard on the news that Jessie Devonshire was missing, I called the police again because Randy's work schedule said that he'd been working for someone named Devonshire on Friday.

"Well, that changed their attitude. Before I knew it, my whole living room was full of police and sheriff's officers, all asking questions about

Randy. I didn't know until later that they all thought that Randy had taken the girl away. But that isn't what happened. I just know that isn't," Lila insisted.

"When did the detectives tell you that they thought Randy was a suspect?"

"I don't think they did until they showed up with a search warrant. They went through the whole house. The garage too. They took Randy's business records. That's the only thing they found."

"What did the business records say?"

"Like I told you, Randy's work schedule said he'd be at Devonshire's place after three that Friday afternoon. That's all there was."

"Didn't witnesses say that Randy had been dating Jessie?"

"Randy never dated Jessie. She was only fifteen. I don't think he even knew her," Lila protested.

"But I've always heard—"

"No! The only one who ever said that Jessie went out with Randy was Wilson Devonshire. Nobody else. If you ask me, he's the one who ought to be investigated, not Randy."

"I'm sure he was. It's standard procedure to investigate the people closest to the victim."

"It was no investigation," Lila insisted. "They asked him for a statement, and that was it. He pointed the finger at Randy, and they never looked at old man Devonshire again. And then after the detective died, nobody ever did anything until last week."

"Wait a minute—the detective died?"

"Deputy Gary Turner. He was the lead detective on the case back in 1980. He was killed in a car accident about three months after Randy and Jessie disappeared."

"I hadn't heard that before."

"It was in the news, but none of the reports connected him to Randy. They said that he fell asleep and went off the road. He was found in his car at the bottom of a ravine. It was too bad because Deputy Turner didn't believe that Randy was guilty."

"What makes you say that?"

"He told me. We talked about it a lot. He was looking at old man Devonshire. There was something about the carpet in Devonshire's house. Turner told me that Devonshire had replaced some carpet a few days after the disappearance. He never told me any details, but he said that he was looking into it. And then he died."

That was something else I'd never heard. And it was something that I could investigate. I explained my fees to Lila, doubtful that she could afford to pay for an investigation. But she surprised me.

"I can pay you. Randy had insurance. It was only a five-thousand-dollar policy, but today it's worth over fifty thousand dollars. Now that he's been found, the insurance will pay off," Lila explained.

"Most life insurance policies have an exclusion clause for suicide," I reminded her.

"Yes, of course. But this was a policy that his grandparents bought when he was a baby. The exclusion period was long past. He didn't kill himself, but even if the death certificate says that he did, the policy will pay off."

I wasn't sure that I liked the idea of taking this poor lady's insurance money. She looked like she could use it.

"Please, Mr. Corrigan, this is the only way I can spend that money. I won't take it for myself. It would be like blood money. But if you will help me prove that Randy didn't do what they said, you can have the money.'

"Here's what I'll do, Lila," I finally said. "I'll poke around and see what I can find out. If I don't find anything by the time my bill comes to five thousand dollars, I'll stop wasting your money. The rest of the insurance settlement is interest, and you should take it. It isn't blood money."

"I'll think about that," Lila conceded. "But I know you'll find out that Randy is innocent."

I was convinced that something was there. Larry Jamieson would have never sent Lila to me if he believed that it was a dead end. Perhaps if Lila had been a pest or a hysterical nutcase, Jamieson might have sent her to me just to get her off his back. But she was patient, thoughtful, and intelligent, and for Jamieson to send her to me meant that he believed her. That left me wondering again what Jamieson knew that I didn't.

CHAPTER 15

TUESDAY JUNE 21

I decided that a good starting place would be the "morgue" at the *Chronicle* office, where copies of every edition of the paper dating back into the nineteenth century were stored on microfiche cards. Someday, all of the microfiche files would be copied to computer, but in the meantime, I had no choice but to labor over the dim optical screen.

I was re-familiarizing myself with the case as it developed in the news back in 1980. I didn't learn anything new, but it was good to have the whole story fresh in my mind. The articles confirmed that Gary Turner had been the lead detective on the case. I searched forward into September and October 1980.

The death of Clackamas County Sheriff's Office Deputy Gary Turner was front page news on Tuesday, October 7. He had been found in his private car in a deep ravine below the Clackamas River Highway west of Estacada. Because of the lack of skid marks on the pavement, it was concluded that Turner had fallen asleep at the wheel after dark Sunday evening.

There were no witnesses. The car was spotted by a woman walking her dog on Monday morning. Turner had died of massive head trauma. The article was accompanied by a photo of the car being pulled back up to the roadway. Turner's Buick Regal was wadded into an unrecognizable ball. I found no mention of Turner's involvement in the Mendelson-Devonshire investigation.

Four days later, another article described the deputy's funeral, which featured bagpipes playing "Amazing Grace," in the tradition of all law-enforcement funerals. But again, there was no mention that Turner had been lead detective on the Mendelson-Devonshire case. I wondered how that could possibly be an oversight.

One comment in the article caught my attention. Nobody knew why Turner, who lived in Oregon City, had been heading toward Estacada. The closest thing to an explanation was one deputy's comment that "some of the guys were getting together at the Sahara Club, so maybe Turner was on his way to join them."

Deep inside the same issue, I found an obituary notice for Gary Turner. I made a print of the obituary as well as the article and its accompanying photo of Turner's grieving widow, Leslie Turner. *What had become of her?* I wondered. If there had been anything suspicious about Turner's death, his widow would be the one who would know.

The place to start looking for Mrs. Turner was the county property tax rolls. If she owned property in Clackamas County I could find her—provided she hadn't changed her name. But three hours in the assessor's office produced no results.

Back at my place, I sat down at my computer and looked up Leslie Turner in the White Pages online. I found three people of that name in Oregon, but none was old enough to be the one I was looking for. No surprise there. It was unlikely that Leslie would still be named Turner.

Gary Turner's obituary said that his wife's maiden name had been Leslie Athena. The White Pages yielded just one hit for anyone named Athena in the entire state. Marilyn Athena, age eighty-one, lived on East Fairfield Street in Gladstone. It was a long shot, but she was the right age to be Leslie's mother. There was a phone number, but I opted to visit her in person.

The gray-haired lady who answered the door was rail thin but stood straight and tall. She was about five seven and couldn't have weighed over one hundred pounds. But she was not frail, and her eyes sparkled with life.

"My name is Corrigan," I said, handing my card to Marilyn.

"An investigator," she read. "What does an investigator want with an old lady like me?"

"I'm wondering if you are related to Leslie Athena. Her married name was Turner."

"Well, yes, Leslie is my daughter. Why are you interested in her?"

"She might have information relevant to an investigation that I'm conducting."

With a twinkle in her eyes, Marilyn challenged, "Mr. Corrigan, you didn't really answer my question."

She was pretty sharp. I decided to lay it out. "My investigation involves Leslie's husband, Gary Turner. I'm hoping that Leslie can shed some light on a case he was working on when he died."

"That was a long time ago, Mr. Corrigan. What could possibly be of interest after all these years?"

"Honestly, Mrs. Athena, I'm just looking for whatever I can find. It's a shot in the dark."

"Leslie had a very hard time after Gary died," Marilyn began. "She was devastated. It took years for her to put Gary's death behind her."

"Does she still live in this area?" I asked.

"She lives in Portland, but I don't know if she'll talk to you. She is still pretty touchy on the subject of Gary's death."

"Touchy?"

"At first, she insisted that Gary's death was not an accident. Then she just stopped talking about it—refused to talk to anyone about it."

"Do you think she'd talk to me?"

"Probably not. She wouldn't even go to grief counseling."

"Can you tell me how to get in touch with her?"

"I'm old, but I'm not senile. Of course, I *can* tell you," she chided. "Your question is *will* I tell you."

"Mrs. Athena, you got me. *Will* you tell me?"

"I'll give her your number. If she wants to talk to you, she'll call."

"Fair enough."

CHAPTER 16

"**P**retty warm afternoon," a familiar voice said. I was standing on my porch and had just opened a beer. It was predictable that the sound of a pop-top would get my neighbor's attention.

Bud lived in an old workshop behind the house across the alley from mine. He used to own the house but gave it to his son, Daryl, when he was unable to pay his property taxes. Daryl graciously let Bud live in the old shop.

I'd been inside Bud's shack once. He had thrown up a partition, separating his living quarters from the shop area, which was filled with a lifetime collection of greasy car parts, tools, and junk of undetermined origin. But if forced to make the comparison, I'd say the shop half of the building was cleaner than Bud's half.

Identifiable amid the clutter was a bed, and along one wall was a counter crudely constructed out of scrap lumber. It featured an old, chipped porcelain sink and a Coleman camp stove. A tiny doorless closet in the corner housed an old toilet, with the tank hanging high on the wall. There was nothing resembling a shower, but it's quite possible that Bud never noticed.

"Want a beer?" I offered.

The question was rhetorical. Of course, Bud wanted a beer. I motioned for him to have a seat and went and got another beer from the refrigerator.

"Still working on that ship?" Bud asked.

"Just started pulling wires."

"I could help you with that," Bud offered. "You know, I used to work in electronics."

I knew that Bud had been an electronics technician in the Navy during the Vietnam War, so I guessed that electrical wiring wouldn't be beyond him.

"I appreciate the offer. I'll keep that in mind if the job gets too big for me." I doubted that I could afford the amount of beer it would take to keep Bud adequately fueled-up. At that point, Kim drove up in her sheriff's marine unit SUV.

"Thanks for the beer," Bud said, getting up to leave.

Bud couldn't stay around in the presence of a uniformed deputy.

My plan was to get Deputy Stayton out of uniform as soon as possible, but not for Bud's benefit.

Over our second glass of wine, I broached the subject of the Mendelson-Devonshire investigation.

"Any idea why Larry Jamieson would tell Randy Mendelson's mother to hire a private investigator?" I asked.

She looked surprised. "He did that?"

"According to Mrs. Mendelson, he did."

"And she contacted you?" Kim asked. I nodded, and continued, "What does she want you to do?"

"She wants me to prove that Randy didn't abduct or kill Jessie Devonshire—or himself. But I don't understand why Jamieson would send her to me."

"Not much I can tell you."

"Does that mean you don't know, or does it mean that you're just not talking?"

"Corrigan, I don't think you completely understand how hot this case is. I'm not talking about it because it could cost me my job," she said seriously.

"But I thought the case was closed with the conclusion that it was murder-suicide. Why would it be too hot to talk about?"

"Look, I'll tell you this much, and don't ask me anything else about it. Jamieson was blindsided by the press release, and he doesn't agree with the official findings—which, by the way, are not official. It's open ended, even though the investigation has been suspended. Okay?"

"Okay," I acknowledged. She had just confirmed what I had suspected.

CHAPTER 17

FRIDAY JUNE 24

spent the next couple of days doing work for Xycon and my other bread and butter client, William Gates—not *that* William Gates. Gates is the attorney who made a name for himself by representing Claudia Wendling in her wrongful-death civil suit against Eugene Glenwood, after Glenwood had been acquitted in his criminal trial in the death of Claudia's sister, Harriet Wendling.

Gates won the civil case, giving a small measure of satisfaction to the murder victim's family. They got much greater satisfaction when, a month after his loss in the courtroom, Glenwood was laid flat by a TriMet bus while jaywalking across a four-lane highway.

I'd had little time to devote to Lila's investigation. Nor had Leslie Turner called. So when I picked up my job folder on Friday, it remained very thin. I had the newspaper clippings from the most recent investigation, the microfiche prints relating to Gary Turner's death, and the notes I'd taken when I talked with Lila Mendelson.

I went back to the *Chronicle* archives to follow up on what Lila had said about Gary Turner's discovery that carpeting had been replaced in the Devonshire house shortly after Jessie Devonshire's disappearance. Such a revelation should have completely changed the direction of the investigation, and yet after another six hours in front of the microfiche reader, I still had found no mention of it in the *Chronicle*.

What could that mean? I listed the possibilities on a yellow pad:

1. Lila was mistaken.

2. Turner investigated and determined that the carpet had been replaced, but it had no connection to the case.

3. *Turner established a possible connection between the carpet replacement and the case, but the sheriff's office decided to keep it confidential.*

4. *Turner died before documenting the result of his investigation of the carpet.*

5. *Turner did his investigation of the carpet "off the books," meaning that he didn't put it into the official investigation file.*

Assuming for the moment that number 1 was not true—and I believed it wasn't—that would almost automatically rule out number 2. Turner wouldn't have mentioned the carpet to Lila if the lead hadn't developed some evidence relevant to the case.

Regarding number 3, would the sheriff's office keep such a fact confidential? Often, in the course of an investigation, authorities will keep a material fact confidential as a tool for screening out false witnesses or to avoid alerting potential suspects. But if this was the case, it seemed unlikely that Turner would have confided in Lila Mendelson.

Number 4 had the same problem. If Turner was following protocol, he wouldn't have shared the result of his investigation with Lila Mendelson before putting it into the official investigation file.

So number 5 was the only logical explanation. That begs the question, why was Gary Turner conducting an unauthorized investigation? Perhaps Leslie Turner could shed some light on that question—if she would just call. The only other possibility would be to find someone who'd been inside the original investigation and hope he would talk to me.

I carried home a pile of microfiche prints that included every article I could find about the case from the time of the crime through the following October—a three-month period. I went through every article and wrote down the name of every law enforcement official mentioned.

There was only one official associated with the current investigation who was involved in the 1980 investigation. Clackamas County Sheriff William Kerby had been a uniform deputy in 1980. His name came up in connection with ground searches conducted in the days immediately after Jessie Devonshire was reported missing.

Asking Sheriff Kerby about the case was a monumentally bad idea. We had met several times at CCSO social functions I had attended with Kim. If I were to ask him about Mendelson-Devonshire, it could cost Kim her job. Not to mention the obvious. If the current investigation was being suppressed—and I knew that it was—it was being done at the direction of Sheriff Kerby.

Over the weekend, I spent some time trying to track down the other names on my list of people involved in the 1980 investigation. It wasn't as difficult as tracking down Leslie Turner. All were men, and men rarely change their names. I started with twelve names—eleven after Sheriff Kerby. Of those, I found seven in the obituaries. Three of the remaining four had retired from the Clackamas County Sheriff's Office. I could find no trace of the final person on the list.

On Monday, I went out to talk with former deputies Haines, Buxton, and Odell. Using counterfeit press credentials, I claimed to be writing a feature about the Mendelson-Devonshire case, a "then and now" piece showing how both investigations had reached the same conclusion. I hoped to flatter the former officials with praise of their ability to come up with the right solution, even with the scant evidence they had at the time.

My first stop was at the home of George Haines in Salem. On the phone, I had already established that Haines had left the Clackamas County Sheriff's Office early in 1981 to take a job as a corrections officer at the Oregon State Penitentiary. He retired in 2006.

"Mr. Haines, what was it like working a high-profile case like this back in 1980?" I asked.

"It wasn't any different really. We asked questions, got answers, and followed up leads," he said.

"What was your role in the Mendelson-Devonshire investigation?"

"Wasn't much. I'd have been involved in processing physical evidence, except there wasn't any."

"None at all?" I pressed.

"Oh, we processed some blood spots on the driveway, but they turned out to be not human blood. And we went over some gardening tools that were left in the yard, but didn't find anything. That was it."

"Gardening tools?" That was the first I'd heard about that. "What tools?"

"I don't remember specifically, but you know, pruning tools or clippers. Things like that."

"Mendelson's tools?"

"Never established that for a fact. No prints on them—he probably wore gloves when he worked."

I made a show of flipping through my notes. "There's something in here about carpet," I said, attempting to lead him, but he didn't bite."

"I never tested any carpet."

Haines seemed to be telling me the truth. If Turner had found carpet to be tested, it would have gone to Haines—unless Turner was working off the books, which seemed more and more likely. I thanked Haines and pretended to shoot a photo of him for the fictitious newspaper article.

After the drive back to Portland, my second interview was considerably quicker.

"Deputy Buxton, I'm writing a feature story about the Mendelson-Devonshire investigations," I said, handing him my phony press credentials.

"No," he said.

He tossed my ID back at me and closed the door. That was a very rare thing. Most people like the idea of being able to portray themselves favorably in a newspaper article. At the very least, they show some curiosity about it. Buxton was either stonewalling, or he harbored a grudge toward reporters—as many law-enforcement people do. Either way, I wasn't getting anything out of him.

My third interview was nearly as short. In answer to my opening line, retired deputy Odell squinted and said,

"That old dog is sleeping, and you best just leave it be, son."

As the door was swinging shut, I played my last card.

"What did Gary Turner find?"

The door opened, and Odell glared at me. "He found out how to get dead."

And with that, I found myself staring at the door.

CHAPTER 18

TUESDAY JUNE 28

"Hello?" a woman's voice said nervously.

"My name is Corrigan," I said. "I believe I just missed your call."

"Yes, Mr. Corrigan. My name is Leslie Charleston," she said. "My mother said you wanted to talk to me. Marilyn Athena."

I tried not to sound as excited as I felt. "Yes! I'd like to ask you some questions about your late husband, Gary Turner."

"My mother told me that. She said you are investigating his death."

"That's not exactly correct. I want to ask you some questions about something he was investigating at the time of his death."

There was a long moment of silence.

"It never goes away," Leslie finally said softly. "That investigation cost Gary his life."

"What do you mean?" I asked.

"Isn't it obvious? Gary found something that he wasn't supposed to find, and they killed him."

"Who killed him? Do you know what he found?"

"I can't talk about this. You'll get both of us killed."

The line went dead. I tried calling back, but Leslie wouldn't answer. But I had two things working for me. Number one, Leslie had called me from a land line. Number two, I have a nationwide reverse directory online. Within two minutes, I had the address in northwest Portland where Leslie Charleston had made the call to me.

It was a forty-five-minute drive from my place to hers. She lived in a modestly restored Queen Anne Victorian home in a trendy area just outside of the downtown business district.

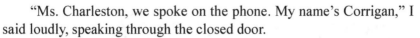

"Ms. Charleston, we spoke on the phone. My name's Corrigan," I said loudly, speaking through the closed door.

"And I told you, I don't want to talk to you," came the voice from inside.

"Are we going to have to carry on this conversation through the door?"

The door opened a crack, security chain in place.

"I figured you wouldn't quit easily after going to the trouble to track me down," a pretty woman with short blonde hair said. "Tell me why I should talk to you."

"You've been following the news?" I asked. "I'm working for the mother of Randy Mendelson. She met Gary Turner during the original investigation in 1980. She believes that Randy was a victim, not a perpetrator, and she thinks that your husband found something to prove it."

With resignation, Leslie said, "You might as well come in. If either of us is being watched, it's already too late."

She unhooked the security chain and held the door open. I stepped inside, and before she closed the door behind me, Leslie took a quick look up and down the block. I assumed she didn't see any black Suburbans.

"Who would be watching us?" I asked.

"I'm not just imagining this," she said. "There really are people who don't want anyone to think that the Mendelson-Devonshire case is anything but a murder-suicide. It was that way in 1980, and it's that way today. My husband was killed because he wouldn't leave it alone. And you saw how quickly the case was put back to bed last week."

"Who do you think did it, if not Mendelson?"

"You're the investigator, Mr. Corrigan. You tell me."

"Logical suspect? Wilson Devonshire."

"Wilson Devonshire," she repeated. "Supreme Court Justice Wilson Landis Devonshire. The politically connected Wilson Devonshire. The Wilson Devonshire whose friends have *owned* Oregon politics for all of my adult life. And you *wonder* who might be watching us?"

"You really think it's that dangerous?"

"Mr. Corrigan, look over there." She pointed to a pair of suitcases standing side by side at the foot of the stairs. "I'm going to be out of town before the evening news comes on. If your body is found floating in the river this afternoon, I won't hear about it because I'll be long gone."

"Leslie, I'm sorry. But I think you're overstating the danger."

"Really?" she snapped. "Really? Tell that to my husband! Tell that to that other detective—Hammond!"

"Wait a minute!" I said, startled. "Hammond? Richard Hammond?" He was the one name on my list of detectives on the case in 1980 for whom I had drawn a blank.

"Yes, Dick Hammond. He died of a heroin overdose two weeks before Gary was killed. They said he was a junkie, but Gary worked with him and had never ever seen any hint of drug use. He was buried without even the benefit of a formal funeral—no recognition, no acknowledgment that he ever existed.

"Gary knew Dick had been murdered. And he knew everything that Dick knew about Devonshire. He figured the only way he could save his own life was to close the case on Devonshire. Officially, he suspended the investigation and locked up all of the investigation files, hoping that would get him off the hook long enough to finish the job.

"And then one night he didn't come home. He was found in a canyon outside Estacada. Fell asleep at the wheel, they said. If I were you, Mr. Corrigan, I'd watch my back!"

"Do you have any idea what evidence Hammond and your husband uncovered?"

"Gary never told me about it. After he was killed, they broke into our house and completely trashed the place."

"You think someone was looking for evidence from your husband's investigation?"

"You'd better hurry up, Mr. Corrigan. You're going to miss your turnip truck."

"Uh…right. So there's no evidence left to substantiate what you've told me."

"I never said that," she corrected, and my pulse rate went up noticeably.

She handed me a key that hung from a round plastic tag. Printed on one side of the tag was "East Side Storage," and below that was handwritten "#56." On the other side was an address: "9969 SE Powell Blvd., Portland, OR."

"That key was hidden inside a hollowed-out bar of soap when they trashed the house. I found it weeks later while taking a bath. I've never been to that storage locker, and I've never seen what's in it. For thirty years, I've paid the rent with untraceable money orders," Leslie explained.

"Ms. Charleston, why are you giving this to me? If there are people out there who would kill to get their hands on the evidence your husband gathered, how do you know that I'm not working for them?"

"Because if you were working for them, I'd already be dead. Now, Mr. Corrigan, you'll have to excuse me. I have a plane to catch."

"Would you like a hand with your bags?" I offered.

"No, thanks. I'm going to take them out the back door while they're watching you go out the front. My car is in the alley."

She closed the door behind me as I stepped outside. I looked up and down the block but still didn't see any surveillance. But then, you wouldn't if they were any good.

Leaving Leslie's place, I drove west on Lovejoy Street, which turned into Cornell Road as it wound up and over the West Hills. Two cars back, there was a gray Ford Taurus. Keeping an eye on the mirror, I turned left onto Skyline Blvd. The fact that the Taurus also turned left didn't mean a thing. It was a pretty popular route.

I drove southeast on Skyline to Burnside, then west on Burnside, which turned into Barnes Road. The Taurus stayed with me. I could see two people in the car but couldn't make out any detail through the tinted glass. From Barnes Road, I got onto Highway 217. This seven-and-a-half-mile highway is the most heavily traveled roadway in Oregon. The Taurus was still behind me when I got to I-5.

Somewhere before I got to the I-205 interchange, the Taurus disappeared, leaving me wondering whether or not they'd really been following me. My best guess is that they were. It seemed highly unlikely that anyone else would choose to drive the circuitous route I'd chosen, and for that driver to be right behind me seemed beyond coincidental.

If indeed someone had been tailing me, they'd made a switch, and some other vehicle would have replaced the Taurus. But over the next fifteen minutes, I was unable to identify any other vehicle following me, despite my speeding up and slowing down and making a loop through the streets of Tualatin. So maybe it had just been a coincidence. Afternoon rush hour on I-205 starts at about three, and I was in the thick of it. Traffic crawled at about fifteen or twenty miles an hour, with frequent stops and starts. It took forty minutes to get to the Powell Blvd. exit.

A few blocks off I-205, I found East Side Storage. I held up the key, and the attendant waved me through the gate. Three rows of cinder-block buildings lay inside the fenced compound. Each row consisted of four buildings. The side walls of the buildings were punctuated with roll-up garage doors. The small walk-in units were located on the ends of the buildings. I stopped in front of unit number 56.

I looked up and down the alleys between the buildings and satisfied myself that nobody was lurking there. Inside unit 56, I found a small wooden table. On it sat two cardboard boxes of the type used to store files. I saw no markings on the boxes to give a clue as to their contents.

I loaded the two boxes into the back of my Yukon, closed up unit 56, and drove back to the gate. I handed the key to the attendant and told him I wouldn't need it anymore. For a case that supposedly had no evidence, it was remarkable that Gary Turner had managed to fill two boxes.

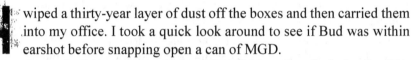

CHAPTER 19

I wiped a thirty-year layer of dust off the boxes and then carried them into my office. I took a quick look around to see if Bud was within earshot before snapping open a can of MGD.

Instead of the neatly organized files I'd hoped to find, the first box contained two loose piles made up of sheets of paper, spiral note pads, file folders, and manila envelopes. In the second box, I hit the mother lode. On one side of the box was a pile similar to those in the first box, but next to it was a stack of three-ring binders, four of them.

The binders were the murder book for the Mendelson-Devonshire investigation. I could see right off that these were not the original murder book, but they were the next-best thing. They were the detective's personal copies of the original documents, which presumably were tucked away somewhere in a CCSO evidence vault.

In the days before desktop computers, the *murder book* was the way that detectives organized the records relating to an investigation. Today, everything but the hard evidence is scanned, indexed, and stored in digital form. With proper cross-referencing of the digital files, detectives can search and retrieve investigation files in seconds, instead of the hours or days it would take to plow through the paper files.

Still, I needed only a quick look at Gary Turner's murder book to see that Wilson Devonshire had been much more a person of interest in the 1980 investigation than had ever been revealed to the public. I decided—for two reasons—that my first task would be to digitize all of the material in the two boxes. The first reason was simply that digitized files are a lot easier and quicker to work with than paper files. The second—and more important—reason was that I didn't want these files in my office. It was simply too dangerous to keep them around.

I settled-in and started going through the first stack of papers. Each time I came to a document of irregular size, I placed it on my copier glass and made a copy on 8½ x 11 plain paper. When I got to the spiral notebooks, I spread them open on the glass and copied every page. Keeping everything in its original order, I inserted the new copies into the stacks of documents in place of the odd sized ones, which I set aside in a different stack.

It was after midnight when I finally finished making copies. The total number of pages to be scanned and saved as PDF files must have been around five or six thousand. While my automatic document feeder fed the pages to my scanner, I warded off drowsiness by reading the murder book.

It was extremely unusual for anyone to drive past my place after midnight. But at 2:30 a.m., I heard the crunch of gravel under the tires of a slow-moving car. No headlight beams swept across my windows as the car turned from Water Street up the alley that separated my place from the neighbor's. The car continued slowly up the alley. I looked out just in time to see it turn onto Highway 99E and disappear. It was not a gray Taurus. It was a black Acura, the kind favored by the local drug dealers and gangstas.

Two hours later, the same thing happened again. Same gangsta car. I guessed there was some possibility that it was just a couple of guys out looking to score some meth, but I was feeling the pressure of too many coincidences in a short period of time. The sooner I could get Gary Turner's files out of my house, the better.

Sometime after sunrise, I made another pot of coffee and fried up some bacon and eggs while the scanner kept churning away on the documents. I didn't see the Acura again, but I did get three hang-up calls. The caller ID said, "Restricted Number." Was it someone checking to see if I was home, not realizing he had called a cell phone? Or was it a simple wrong number? Too many coincidences.

At 3:30 p.m., I put the final load of papers into the document feeder. Ten minutes later, I disconnected the hard drive and locked it in the high-security safe that I had buried in concrete at one corner of my foundation, concealed beneath a bathroom floor tile that could be removed only after moving a clothes hamper that appeared to be permanently attached to the wall. It would require a significant explosion to open that safe without the combination.

Then I carried Gary Turner's file boxes out and put them into the Yukon. I drove to what I believed to be the biggest bank in town, hoping that they would have space in their vault for the documents. The teller leaned over the counter and looked at the two boxes stacked on the hand truck. I lifted the lid off the top box to let her see the contents.

"Sure," the teller said, "we have safe deposit boxes that'll hold the papers—but probably not the file boxes."

"Okay, I'll take one of those."

"Actually, I think it'll take two. Maybe three."

I signed up for two of their largest available safe deposit boxes, and once inside the vault, I transferred all of the papers, notebooks, and binders from the file boxes into the safe deposit boxes. I had to help the teller lift the boxes back into their spaces in the vault. She turned two keys to lock each box in place. I left the bank with two keys in my pocket.

Exhausted, I flopped down on my bed and fell instantly asleep.

CHAPTER 20

WEDNESDAY, JUNE 29

My clock read six twenty-two when I woke up. But what day was it? Tuesday evening? No, that couldn't be. The sun was coming in the back windows. It was morning. Must be Wednesday. It felt like I had a mild case of rigor mortis. I arched my back and stretched—and, in the process, smacked Kim in the head.

"Jesus, Corrigan," she complained, "if you want me to wake up, just shake my shoulder."

"Sorry, babe. I didn't know you were there."

"You were as good as dead when I came in last night," Kim said. "I brought steaks, but you looked so cute I couldn't bear to wake you up. So I ate alone, helped myself to some of your wine—a nice Pinot, thank you very much—and then watched a chick flick on TV."

She was really rubbing it in. I knew how chick flicks and red wine affected Kim. She wanted to be sure I knew that I'd slept through more than just a steak dinner.

"If you're making breakfast, I'll have steak and eggs," I suggested.

"Nice try. Cook your own breakfast." She paused and then asked, "What the hell did you do yesterday, swallow a handful of Quaaludes?"

"No, I worked all night Monday, and when I was finished, I just sort of lapsed into a coma."

"Must have been pretty important to keep you up all night."

"It might turn out that way. In any case, don't ask about it because I can't tell you."

"Or you'd have to kill me," Kim parroted the line from *Top Gun*.

"Yeah, unless someone else decides to do that for me," I mumbled to myself.

"Are you talking or passing gas?"

I shook my head. "It's nothing. How do you want your eggs?"

ﾂﾂﾂ

After Kim was gone, I took a long shower and did a mental review of the events of Monday and Tuesday. Leslie's warnings seemed a lot more real now that I'd read the Devonshire murder book. Then there was the Taurus. And what about the gangstas in the Acura?

If they had returned during the night, they'd have seen Kim's SUV with "Clackamas County Sheriff" emblazoned on the sides in reflective lettering. That would have kept them from stopping. I reminded myself to double-check my security system.

My first task of the day was to go out and buy another external hard drive. I got the original hard drive out of the safe and then set one of my computers to the task of copying of all the Devonshire files onto the new drive.

Feeling a little bit paranoid, I rejected the idea of placing an ad for someone to index the files in a spreadsheet. If they were watching me and saw my ad, one of them might end up sitting at my computer— whoever "they" were. Instead, I went to Craigslist and OregonLive.com and scanned the ads for people seeking employment and was able to find half a dozen promising candidates. I left email messages asking for résumés and qualifications.

CHAPTER 21

THURSDAY JUNE 30

I read through the cover letters and résumés that had shown up in my email. I ruled out two applicants on the basis of bad grammar and spelling—if they're that careless with their own résumés, I could hardly expect them to do any better in their work for me.

One applicant included a photograph of herself—one of those Glamour Shot photos, showing lots of cleavage. Her qualifications were obvious—both of them. Another seemed interested and enthusiastic, but her experience was pretty light. The final applicant had plenty of experience but, in twenty years on the job, had never stayed with one employer for as long as two years.

I phoned "Interested and Enthusiastic," and invited her to come in for an interview. She showed up on my doorstep in the middle of the afternoon. I guessed her age to be around forty-five. She was slim, wore her long hair straight, and wore a loose, floor-length dress. In short, she looked like an aging Jerry Garcia groupie. She introduced herself as Martha Hoskins, and I invited her in.

"I know I don't have a lot of employment experience," she told me, "but that's because I was a stay-at-home mom. Then my husband left, and now I need a job."

"What do you know about Microsoft Excel?" I asked.

"Oh, I've used spreadsheet programs *forever*," she said.

"I used Lotus and Quattro back when computers ran on DOS, and then when Windows came out, I started using Excel."

"Were you using the spreadsheet programs in your volunteer work?" I asked, looking at her résumé.

"That was the *main* thing I did," she told me.

Despite my first impression, I was actually starting to like her.

"I'm doing an investigation, and I have over five thousand documents that need to be indexed and cross-referenced in a spreadsheet. I'm guessing that the job will take at least a month, full time. Is that something you can do?" I asked.

"Well, sure," she said enthusiastically.

"I'm willing to pay twenty dollars an hour, but there won't be any benefits since it's a short-term job."

Her eyes went wide. "That would be great," she said.

Obviously, she'd never been paid that much before.

"If it works for you, I'd like you to work for a week at ten dollars an hour. At the end of the week, if I don't like your work, I'll give you a check. But if your work is good, your check will be for twenty dollars an hour, and we'll continue at that rate until the project is finished."

"Oh, that sounds perfect," she said excitedly. "When can I start?"

It's usually the employer who asks that question.

"I'd say 'right now,' but I don't expect—"

"Right now would be great!" she said.

I showed her the spreadsheet I'd started. "The documents you'll be indexing have already been given sequential file names, and they are in column A." I opened the first of the scanned documents on the left hand monitor. "The first thing to do is look for a date on the document."

She pointed at a notation in the upper right corner. It read, "July 26, 1980." She typed that into column B and then read the header on column C, "Type of Document."

"This looks like a phone log," she said and proceeded to type that in. I didn't need to say much more. Martha was off and running. I sat down at my computer number 1 and started going through my email. From time to time, Martha stopped work to suggest adding another column or changing column formats.

"You know," Martha said after about an hour's work, "this really should be done in Access, not Excel."

"Oh?" I said, moderately surprised.

"Definitely. The database program will be a lot more functional than a simple spreadsheet," she said.

I had actually wondered about that, but I hadn't used database programs much and didn't especially want to take the time to learn new software. But Martha was insistent, and I let her have her way. She opened

Access, which was on the computer as part of the Microsoft Office Suite, and set up the basic database, imported all of the data she had entered on the spreadsheet, and went back to the evidence files.

By five, Martha had burned through about fifty pages of evidence— pretty good for her first day. I was truly impressed with her work.

"Mr. Corrigan," Martha began.

"Just 'Corrigan.' Mr. Corrigan is my dad," I corrected.

"Okay, Corrigan. I was wondering…" She hesitated. "I was wondering if I could get an advance on my pay. I'm not sure there's enough gas in my car to get me home and back here tomorrow."

"You really cut it close," I told her, handing over a couple of twenties.

"I didn't have any choice."

"Yeah, but what if—"

"I don't know what I'd have done if you hadn't given me the job. But I don't have to worry about that now. Thank you, Mr. Corrigan. I mean, Corrigan."

"No, you don't have to worry about that."

She drove away in her '90s vintage Subaru. The sticker on the back bumper said, "Coexist," spelled out in a variety of religious and secular symbols.

"Hey, who's the lady?" Bud called out.

"She's going to be working for me," I told him.

"Oh, yeah? She gonna be working here?" He sounded hopeful.

"This is the only office I have."

"Just wondering."

"Have time for a beer?" I asked, knowing that Bud *always* had time for a beer.

We sat on the porch sipping our beers. Well, I was sipping. Bud was gulping.

"You see any strange cars around here the last couple days?" I asked him.

"That lady's Subaru," he said. "And then there's a little black Jap car with blacked-out windows and one of those smart-ass-looking oversized chrome tail pipes."

If nothing else, Bud was observant.

"When did you see that one?"

"Several times. Got another beer?"

I went in and got another. "Last one in the house," I lied.

"First time I saw the black car was night before last, when you were up late. He came by twice. Shut off his headlights when he turned onto Water Street. That's kinda strange, ain't it? Anyway, he came by again last night. Just cruised on by real slow, lights off."

"Do me a favor, Bud. If he comes back, you let me know."

"Who is it?"

"Find that out, and I'll give you a six-pack."

He grinned and said, "I'm on the case."

Kim drove up and parked in her usual spot at the corner of my house. Bud took his beer and vanished before she was out of the SUV.

"Didn't mean to break up the party," she said.

"Bud develops a rash in the presence of uniforms," I explained.

CHAPTER 22

FRIDAY JULY 1

Right on schedule, the 7:00 a.m. Cascade train provided my wake-up call. I shared a quick shower with Kim while the coffee brewed, and then we had toasted bagels and cream cheese for breakfast.

Over our second cup of coffee, I asked her, "You know anything about a couple of deputies named Hammond and Turner?"

"There's nobody by those names in our department," Kim assured me.

"No, I know that. They were on the original Mendelson-Devonshire investigation, thirty years ago."

"Way before my time, Corrigan."

"Thing is they both died while investigating the case, and after they were gone, it seems like nobody picked it up. Doesn't that seem kind of strange?"

"Okay, now that you say he's dead, I *do* know something about Gary Turner. He's one of the names on the plaque in the lobby. But Hammond— I don't recognize the name."

"Word I have is that Hammond died of a heroin overdose. Turner was killed in a car wreck."

"So what's this about?"

"Don't play dumb. You're not dumb, and you're no good at pretending to be."

"Look, Corrigan, I told you I can't comment on the Mendelson-Devonshire investigation," she insisted.

"I'm not asking about Mendelson-Devonshire. I'm asking about Hammond-Turner," I pressed.

"And if it's connected to Mendelson-Devonshire, I have nothing to say. But—and this is only because you're good in bed—I'll do some quiet checking and let you know what I find out." Kim winked and said, "Gotta go."

Martha showed up punctually at eight and went straight to work on the files. On my computer, I started making a list of things I had gleaned from my reading of Gary Turner's copy of the Mendelson-Devonshire murder book, things I'd learned from old newspaper articles and Leslie Charleston, and facts from the most recent investigation.

1. The original call to West Linn Police had been made by Wilson Landis Devonshire at 2:58 a.m. on July 26, 1980.

2. In that call, Devonshire said that his stepdaughter had not returned home from a date.

3. At 3:20 a.m., Devonshire appeared at West Linn PD and stated that he did not know with whom Jessie had gone out nor did he know where they had gone.

4. At 10:45 a.m. on 7/26, Oregon City Police notified CCSO that Randy Mendelson, who had been doing landscaping at the Devonshire home, had been reported missing by his mother.

5. At 1:30 p.m., Mr. Devonshire was interviewed by CCSO investigators at his West Linn home at 1525 Rosemont Rd. Devonshire stated that the missing girl had been dating Randy Mendelson.

6. Phone records show a call from Devonshire's house to his office at 4:21 p.m. on 7/25.

7. In canvassing the neighborhood, detectives interviewed a witness who said she had seen two white cars in the Devonshire driveway at around 6:00 p.m. on 7/25.

8. Another witness reported seeing a black El Camino parked at the curb in front of Devonshire's home in the afternoon of 7/25.

9. No witnesses ever reported seeing Randy Mendelson and Jessie Devonshire together on 7/25 or anytime before that date.

10. Over the next few weeks there were several witnesses who reported seeing the missing pair, but all turned out to be false leads.

11. On Tuesday, 9/2, the CCSO announced that they were suspending active investigation because they had followed all leads to their conclusion. The case would remain open, and detectives would follow up on any new leads, but in the absence of such leads, detectives Gary Turner and Richard Hammond would be assigned to other cases.

12. On Friday, 9/19, Richard Hammond was found dead in his car in a furniture store parking lot on SE 82nd Ave. in Portland. Cause of death was determined to be a heroin overdose.

13. On Monday, 10/6, Gary Turner was found dead in his wrecked car in a ravine alongside Highway 212 outside Estacada.

14. Mendelson had sustained a single gunshot wound above and behind the left ear.

15. Devonshire had sustained a massive fracture in the top-rear portion of her skull, plus a gunshot wound in the back of her head.

16. A Ruger New Model Single Six .22 caliber revolver had been found in the El Camino.

17. The El Camino transmission was in Drive, and the ignition switch was on when the car went into the river.

On the basis of these facts, the case had been declared solved by Sheriff Kerby, with the conclusion that Mendelson abducted Devonshire, killed her, drove into the river, and shot himself while the car was sinking. All reports of sightings after July 25, 1980, were dismissed as mistakes or hoaxes.

In comparing that conclusion with the wrap-up of the 1980 investigation, there was one glaring difference, and no explanation had been offered. In 1980, it was concluded that Devonshire had gone on a date with Mendelson. For some reason, Sheriff Kerby now believed that Mendelson had abducted Devonshire. I could find nothing in the information released to the media to support that change.

The logical conclusion was that something found in the car and not reported to the public had caused Kerby to change the official explanation of the crime. What could it be? Had the girl been tied up or handcuffed? If so, why suppress that information? Whatever the evidence was, it probably was behind Cal Westfall's slip-up when he referred to "at least" one homicide.

All of this led me back to my theory that political pressure had been applied to prevent damage to the reputation of the only viable alternate suspect in the crime, Wilson Landis Devonshire. I could find no other explanation for the abrupt closure of the case and the news media's apparent inability—or unwillingness—to see the obvious.

"Corrigan," Martha interrupted my thoughts, "can I ask you a question?"

"Sure, what is it?" I responded.

"Well, I'm wondering why you're investigating this. I mean, it's obvious what happened to Jessie Devonshire, and even the Sheriff's Office says the case is closed."

"I think—and more importantly, my client thinks—that the official explanation may be wrong."

"Are you working for one of those right-wing extremist groups that are always making up false accusations and trying to stir up scandals about Democrats?"

"Scandals—like what?"

"You know, like the way they were always after Bill Clinton, and then the way they attacked John Kerry's military record. And now they're after Wilson Devonshire."

"Ah, you mean Hillary's vast right-wing conspiracy theory?"

"Mr. Corrigan," she said, reverting to formality, "I'm a lifelong Democrat, and I don't like hearing you make fun of Hillary Clinton! She was *right* when she said that people were trying to destroy Bill Clinton's presidency, and the same people are trying to destroy Barack Obama today, and if you are working for those people, I'm afraid I can't work for you."

"Our client," I said, deliberately using the plural pronoun to include her, "is Randy Mendelson's mother. You may be assured that she is not a right-wing extremist. She has no political agenda. She just wants to know why her son is dead."

Martha paused a moment. More calmly, she asked, "But isn't it all pretty clear? Why doesn't she believe what the sheriff's office says happened?"

"I'm sure she has plenty of personal reasons for believing her son innocent. But we—you and I—aren't dealing with beliefs or feelings. We're dealing only with facts, and we'll follow those facts wherever they lead, even if our conclusions are the same as the official version of events."

"Well, I suppose it's okay if you put it that way," Martha said, somewhat meekly.

"I don't just 'put it that way,' it *is* that way."

Martha went back to work on the files, which she was processing with remarkable speed. Toward the end of her work day, I asked her to show me how to use the database to retrieve files.

"I'm creating a form for each of these files," she explained, waving toward the external hard drive containing the documents from Gary Turner's boxes. "I start by copying the PDF file from the hard drive into the Access database. That becomes the first entry in the form."

"That's good," I said. I hadn't thought about actually making the PDFs part of the database.

"Then I look at the PDF over here." She motioned to the left-hand monitor. "I look for names, dates, subject matter, and keywords, and I enter that into the appropriate fields on the form. When I've typed in all of the data, I press Enter, and that saves the form. Then I start the next form."

"I like that," I said. "How will we search the database?"

"You click here to start what is called a query. You'll use a crosstab query." She showed me how to fill in the fields. "If, for instance, you want to pull up all witness statements, you click here. Or if you're looking for all statements from a particular witness, you type in the name here. You can do a keyword search by typing in the word here, and that will search all of the forms and pull up the ones that have that keyword."

"That's brilliant," I said. "Give it a try. Type in keyword *El Camino* and see what comes up."

She did, and immediately we had a list of about a dozen documents that mentioned the El Camino. She then did a new query, this time calling up all of the names of investigating officers mentioned in the documents. This produced a list of about a dozen names, along with the associated documents.

As Martha was preparing to leave for the day, I asked her if she had anything special planned for the three-day holiday weekend.

"No, I'm not doing anything," she said. "In fact, if it's possible, I'd really prefer to work."

Kim would be out on river patrol all weekend. I'd been planning to immerse myself in the wiring project aboard *Annabel Lee*. But the opportunity to do something that would *make* money rather than *spend* it trumped my plans.

"Well, if that's what you really want to do, I'm up for it."

"Oh, thank you," she said. "And Corrigan? Forget what I said earlier."

I gave her another advance on her pay, figuring that if she had filled her gas tank, there probably wasn't much left of the forty dollars I'd given her the day before. This time, I gave her a one-hundred-dollar bill. I didn't want to find her standing out by a freeway exit with a Will Work for Food sign.

After she was gone, I sat down and made a query of my own in the Access database. I entered keyword *carpet*. One form came up. It was a note by one of the detectives who had visited the Devonshire home at 1:30 p.m.on July 26, 1980, the day Jessie was reported missing. I read that the detective had noted a large stain on the carpet near the front door of the Devonshire home. The stain matched the color of the freshly painted front door. Devonshire said he had spilled the paint the previous evening.

That had to be the carpet that had interested detectives Hammond and Turner. But there was no other document to indicate that anyone had done a follow-up investigation on the stained carpet. Then again, there were still thousands of documents yet to be entered into the database. Surely there would be additional documents relating to the carpet. I'd just have to wait for Martha to enter the data.

I then made another query. This time, I entered keyword *paint*. That brought back the same form that I'd just been looking at, plus three other forms. The first was a colored photograph identified as the entry hall in the Devonshire home, taken on July 26, 1980. I looked closely at the photo, which appeared to have been taken from the front porch, looking into the house. There was tile or vinyl flooring just inside the door.

On the left was a door to what probably was a coat closet.

The walls of the entry were done in a gold foil wallpaper overprinted in black with a brocade pattern that looked vaguely medieval. There was a piece of furniture against the right wall, a wooden cabinet or stand of some kind; on it there was a table lamp and what appeared to be a statue of an eagle.

About four feet beyond the entry door, the tile floor ended and light-gray wall-to-wall carpet started. Near the right-hand wall, and about a foot back from the gold colored strip that separated the carpet from the tile, a large reddish-brown stain was visible on the carpet.

Except for the lack of a victim's outline in tape on the floor, it looked to me like a photo of a crime scene.

The second form was a receipt from the True Value Hardware store on Willamette Falls Drive, showing that Devonshire had purchased a paintbrush and a gallon of brick-red exterior latex enamel at 6:15 p.m. on July 25, 1980.

The third form was the transcript of Richard Hammond's July 26 interview with Wilson Devonshire. The portion of the interview that related to the paint read:

> Hammond: Tell me about that stain on the floor.
>
> Devonshire: I knocked over a can of paint last night.
>
> Hammond: How did that happen?
>
> Devonshire: I had just finished painting the front door--my wife went to a class with a bunch of the women in the neighborhood. It was all about some kind of Chinese superstition—kung fu or some crap like that.
>
> Hammond: Feng shui?
>
> Devonshire: Yeah, anyway, it's supposed to be good luck to have a red door. Look around. People all over town have painted their doors some kind of red. My wife's been bugging me to paint ours, so yesterday I decided to do it.
>
> Hammond: And that's when you spilled the paint?
>
> Devonshire: I just finished painting the door, and I was picking up the newspapers that I'd spread out to catch any drips when the phone rang. I didn't realize that the paint can was sitting on the piece of paper I had hold of, and when I jumped up to get the phone, I yanked the paper and dumped

```
the paint. My wife is pissed off. That
carpet is almost new.

Hammond: Where is your wife?

Devonshire: She's asleep. She was attending
a conference out at the coast at that new
resort—Salishan. I called her early this
morning, and she drove back home. She got
home a couple of hours ago. She took some
Valium and went to bed. I have a receipt
for the paint.

Hammond: A receipt?

Devonshire: Yes, for the paint.
```

That part seemed really out of place. Why had Devonshire felt compelled to offer a receipt for the paint? It didn't seem relevant to anything. Nobody was investigating the source of the paint. It just seemed strange for Devonshire to offer the receipt out of the clear blue.

To me, it implied that Devonshire was expecting, and had prepared for, an investigation into the paint spill. His eagerness to proffer evidence to substantiate his story suggested that he was excessively eager to have the detective accept his story. And the whole feng shui thing seemed contrived.

If so, the implication was obvious. The only reason to fabricate a story about the spilled paint was that perhaps it hadn't been spilled by accident, and if the paint spill had been deliberate, then the only logical reason for it was to cover something else on the carpet—most likely blood. Was this what Hammond and Turner had been investigating?

❧

Kim and I sat in the shade of a huge ash tree, on the deck at McMenamin's pub in Oregon City. Across the river, *Annabel Lee* looked stately, lying at her moorage. It was hard to find slower service or better hamburgers than those at McMenamin's.

"Martha thinks I'm part of a right-wing conspiracy to bring down Wilson Devonshire," I commented.

"Sounds right to me," Kim said.

"Which part? The right-wing conspiracy or bringing down Devonshire?"

"Devonshire."

"Do you want to hear what I've found so far?"

"I can listen. I just can't comment."

So I described the photo that showed the stain on the carpet and Devonshire's explanation for it. "When you read the transcript, it just doesn't ring true," I concluded.

"Just playing devil's advocate here. None of that *proves* anything."

"No, but I think it shows why Hammond and Turner were interested in carpet. By the way, were you able to find out anything about them?"

"Yes and no. The no part is that nobody had anything to say about it. The yes part is that it is highly unusual for a law-enforcement officer to have nothing to say about the death of one of their own. And I got the impression that it would be best if I just dropped the whole thing."

"Let me put together a theory," I began. "Suppose the spilled paint covered a bloodstain. Devonshire is on record saying that he spilled the paint by accident. That implicates him directly in covering up evidence of what we now know was a murder."

"You're supposing something you can't prove," Kim pointed out.

"That's true. I can't prove it *yet*. But if Devonshire did kill the girl, he had all the right connections to apply political pressure on the investigators. The kind of political pressure that could shut down an investigation and—by the way—might cause CCSO to swear its deputies to silence."

"You really *are* a conspiracy theorist. Maybe you can tell me what happened on the grassy knoll while you're at it."

"Nice try, Deputy Stayton, but I can see that you agree with me." I raised my glass in salute.

Our food finally arrived, and I ordered another round of drinks. All conversation was suspended in favor of sweet potato fries and a fully loaded hamburger sandwich. While enjoying McMenamin's overly generous portions of food, it is best to avoid thinking about the starving masses in Somalia.

"I was thinking today about Kerby's statement to the press. His official conclusion is almost exactly the same as what was determined in 1980," I began.

"So maybe the 1980 investigation got it right," Kim said.

"Not so fast." I waved my finger at her. "There's one glaring difference. In 1980, they said that Randy went out on a date with Jessie. Now they say he abducted her."

"Once again, you've demonstrated your superior powers of observation," Kim teased.

"The thing is I think you found something in the El Camino that conflicted with the date theory."

Kim said nothing but just kept looking at me in a curious way.

"What?" I asked.

"I was just wondering," Kim mused, "if you ever went out on a date with someone wearing a see-through nightie and satin negligee."

"Are you saying that Jessie was dressed for the bedroom?" I asked.

"I'm saying nothing of the kind," she insisted. "I just asked a simple question."

CHAPTER 23

SATURDAY, JULY 2

I t was impossible for me work with any efficiency until Martha was finished indexing all of the evidence files. Despite my eagerness to jump straight into the Mendelson-Devonshire investigation, I decided instead to work from the other end and see what I could find out about the deaths of Hammond and Turner.

Thus far, the files that Martha had indexed had been largely chronological. I had scanned the files in the exact order they had been stored in the boxes. Since it appeared that Gary Turner had arranged the files chronologically, it seemed possible that by going to the last files scanned, I might be able to find out what he was working on when he died.

Most of the final pages had been handwritten notes in a pocket-sized spiral notebook, and many of the notes were not dated. Searching for a starting point, I clicked through the PDFs until I found a reference to Hammond.

Dick found O.D. 10:30 last night.

It was a note scribbled on Turner's home phone pad. The handwriting was not Gary's—probably Leslie's. The note had been inserted between the pages of the spiral notebook. I looked at the PDF files immediately before and after the phone-pad note.

The first note following Leslie's said,

Who is Trayborn? Body found M. Brighton PPD. In front seat—syringe, spoon, Bic lighter, baggie. Nelson Furniture.

The next note said,

Sept.23. Time of death. Who did PM?

Most of what was in the first note was consistent with the newspaper article that I had printed from the microfiche files at the *Chronicle* office. Marion Brighton was the Portland Police patrol officer who had discovered the body. But the article contained no mention of anyone named Trayborn. The second note hints that Turner had questions about the time of death and wanted to know who had performed the autopsy.

Several files later, I came across a scribbled note, apparently written by Gary Turner, that said,

> *Barrington is closing the book on D.H. Official ruling is accidental O.D. Heroin taken from evidence. Barrington says D.H. had been under investigation. Not true!*

Barrington—as I already knew—referred to Ralph Barrington, who, in 1980, was Clackamas County sheriff. I was unable to find anything else that was definitely related to the death of Deputy Hammond.

My interpretation of Turner's notes was that Barrington had closed the internal investigation of Hammond's death with the conclusion that the deputy had stolen heroin from the evidence vault and that he had been under suspicion for some time.

If I could find an autopsy report on Hammond, it might shed light on Turner's question about the time of death. But if Turner couldn't find one in 1980, my chances three decades later were pretty slim. I'd like to see the official file on Hammond, but that would be just about impossible. Even if it still existed, it would be buried deep in the archives where no civilian could gain access.

And then there was the question of Trayborn. Who was Trayborn? I worked backward from Leslie's note but found no reference to anyone named Trayborn. Perhaps Martha would find the name as she went through the files.

Using the resources I had available, I went to my favorite people-search website and looked up *Trayborn*. I found several people named Trayborn, but none in the Portland area. I couldn't draw any conclusions from that, however, because it was entirely possible that the Trayborn mentioned in Turner's notes had moved away or died sometime since 1980. I needed a 1980 phone book.

A Google search for a 1980 Portland phone directory led me to the Washington State Library website. They listed 1976 and 1983 Portland directories. That might be close enough. Unfortunately, the directories were not available online. I'd have to drive to Olympia to see them. For now, Trayborn was a dead end.

I went back to people search and typed in *Marion Brighton*. I found a Marion Brighton, age seventy-one, living in the Sellwood District in Southeast Portland. That looked promising, but no phone number was listed. The trend from land lines to cell phones is great for mobility, but it sometimes makes it difficult to find phone numbers.

I left Martha working on the database and drove north on SE Seventeenth until I came to Umatilla Street. I turned left and found Brighton's address in the 1200 block. It was a well-kept 1920 era bungalow with a detached single garage. A ten-year old Buick LeSabre sat on the driveway.

I handed my card to the elderly woman who answered the door and said, "I'm looking for Marion Brighton."

"Why on earth is a private investigator looking for me?" she asked, studying my card.

"Then you *are* Marion Brighton?"

"Of course I am. Who else would I be?" she snorted.

She hardly looked like someone who'd been a uniform police officer, so I asked, "Are you the same Marion Brighton who was with the Portland Police Bureau in 1980?"

"I am, and you still haven't told me what you want."

"Your name came up in a case involving a Clackamas County Sheriff's deputy who was found dead in September 1980."

"You might as well come in." She led me to a chair in her living room table and asked, "Would you like a cup of tea?"

"No, thanks just the same," I said, impatient to get to the point.

She sat on the sofa opposite me and said, "I was the one who found the body."

"What can you tell me about that?" I asked.

"I got the call on a 10-54 in a car parked in a furniture store parking lot on Eighty-Second Avenue. I found the car and saw a white male apparently unconscious in the front seat on the passenger side. I tapped on the glass and got no response."

"Someone had called it in?" I asked.

"Yes, sir. A citizen called from a phone booth and said the man in the car looked dead. The driver's door was unlocked, so I opened it and reached across the seat to check vitals. There was no pulse, the victim's skin was cool to the touch, and rigor was beginning. I called it in and stayed on scene until the detectives arrived. That was about it."

"Was it a cold night?"

"No. I was in short sleeves, so the temperature was probably in the seventies."

"How advanced was the rigor?"

"It was apparent in the neck when I felt for a pulse. There was stiffness in the arms as well."

"Do you remember who the detectives were?"

"No, I wasn't familiar with them. Homicide investigation was pretty far removed from patrol duty."

"Did you have any further involvement in the case?"

"Not really. There was a Clackamas County detective who called me a few days later. I told him the same thing I told you."

"One other thing. Were you familiar with the store where you found the body?"

"Nelson Furniture," she answered. "Big name around town—they did a lot of advertising. I guess you'd call them a high-volume store."

"Do you remember their store hours?"

"Instant credit, shop and sign, every day from nine to nine, Nelson Furniture, " Marion sang their advertising jingle with an amused twinkle in her eye.

"Ha! They were still using that jingle when I moved here ten years later! Can you describe the parking lot and where the car was parked?"

"It wasn't a big parking lot. There was a row of parking spaces facing the store and a row facing the street, with an aisle for driving in between. The victim's car was parked in the row nearest the building, facing the wide sidewalk that ran across the front of the store."

I pondered what she'd told me. The key thing was her description of the body—cool skin, partial rigor. That's why Gary Turner had questioned the time of death. It was a warm evening. The body would have cooled slowly. For his skin to be cool to the touch when she found him, Hammond had to have been dead for a while. The presence of rigor mortis to the degree that she described implied that the time of death was at least three or four hours before the body was found.

"Did you wonder why nobody had noticed the body before the store closed?" I asked.

"I would assume that the car wasn't there until after dark."

"What time did it get dark?"

"I think sunset was about seven fifteen or seven thirty. Darkness would have been around eight thirty."

"Seems like a pretty tight timeline," I suggested. "He arrives at eight, immediately shoots up and dies, and nobody notices for two hours, by which time the body is cold and in partial rigor."

"I didn't do the investigation," she reminded me. "I just found the body and reported what I found."

"But does it sound plausible to you?"

"I didn't give it any thought at the time, but later, after talking with the Clackamas County detective, it seemed kind of shaky. But like I told you, it wasn't for me to say."

I thanked her for her time and headed back toward Oregon City.

Given what Marion Brighton had told me, I would estimate the time of death to be around six thirty. If Hammond had been dead in the furniture store parking lot that long before dark, surely someone would have seen him. Time of death was critical. If he was dead before dark—which seemed probable, given the state of rigor mortis—then he was very likely murdered somewhere else and moved to the Nelson Furniture parking lot post-mortem.

But then, any competent investigation would have reached the same conclusion. There had to be something else. The body was found in Multnomah County inside the Portland city limits, so the investigation would have been done by the Portland Police Bureau and the autopsy by the Multnomah County Medical Examiner's Office. Neither office was likely to share their records with a private investigator.

My best chance, it seemed, was that the answers would be found somewhere in the documents that Martha was indexing. It may be that Turner had the facts, but once again, I'd have to wait for Martha to finish her project.

It was my standard practice to backup all of my computer files every weekend. But given the volume of work that Martha was doing, I decided to do a daily backup. In the safe under my bathroom floor, I kept an external hard drive just for backup files. After Martha left for the day, I retrieved the drive and ran the backup program on both computers.

CHAPTER 24

SUNDAY JULY 3

R ōsemont Road in West Linn runs along the ridge that separates the Willamatte River basin from the Tualatin River basin. Much of Rosemont Road is still rural land, although the housing boom of five to ten years ago spawned dozens of new developments. The Devonshire home was near the eastern end of Rosemont, in what was an upscale neighborhood when it was built in the 1950s and 1960s.

I had driven up there in hopes of seeing something that would give me some new insight into the events of July 25, 1980, though admittedly the chances of finding anything of value were remote beyond calculation. Still, I've found that when you stand on the site of an event you can gain a clearer understanding of what took place there.

1525 Rosemont Road was a stately two story brick home on a sloping lot that gave a panoramic view that included downtown Portland and the great mountains of the Cascades, Hood, Adams, St. Helens, and Rainier. While a few of the homes in the neighborhood were showing their age, most were well kept and some, including the former Devonshire house, showed signs of recent work.

The garage was on the left, and a slate-tile sidewalk led to the covered front porch at the center of the house. There was a new-looking brickwork fence across the front of the lot, with five-foot columns on each side of the driveway topped by white globe light fixtures. The lot was freshly landscaped, and there was an old fashioned fountain—probably a reproduction—that made the yard look like an old town square. It was all very tastefully done, but probably bore little resemblance to the yard that Randy Mendelson had maintained.

I picked up the envelope containing photos taken during the original investigation, including the one showing the entry hall. As I thumbed through them, the front door opened.

"Can I help you?" came a woman's voice from the porch.

I wasn't prepared for that. In the back of my mind I'd concocted a phony story about having an interest in the restoration of historic buildings. My thought was to tie it in with my restoration of *Annabel Lee* and somehow use that to get a look at the entry hall. But I was caught flat-footed.

"Maybe," I said. "My name is Corrigan." I walked up to the porch and handed her my card.

"An investigator? What are you investigating?" she asked.

I evaded her question by asking, "Are you Sara Huntington?" I'd found the names of the current owners of the house in the county tax records.

"I am," she confirmed, looking confused.

"How much do you know about the history of your home?"

"What is this about?"

She'd put me on the spot. "You've probably seen the news about the car that was pulled out of the river last month—"

"You mean the one with the bodies inside?"

"That's right. Are you aware that one of the victims used to live here?"

"Well, yes, I'm aware that the Devonshire family owned this place back in the seventies and eighties. But what does that—"

"The thing is, whatever happened to Jessie Devonshire probably started right here."

"They say that the gardener kidnapped her."

"There are plenty of unanswered questions about that," I said. "I'm trying to pin-down exactly what happened." From the envelope, I pulled out the photo that Dick Hammond shot on July 26, 1980 and handed it to Mrs. Huntington.

"What's this?" she asked, and then immediately answered her own question. "Was that taken *here*?"

"It was taken by detectives the day after Jessie Devonshire disappeared."

She continued staring at the photo and pointed at the reddish stain on the carpet. "What is that?" she asked, her voice cracking.

"Mr. Devonshire told the investigating officers that he spilled paint there."

She exhaled. "Oh! I was afraid it was—I mean, it looked like—"

I had to lay it on the line. "Well, that's the big question. Was it really paint, or was it something else?"

"Oh, no. I'd hate to think that it was—could it really have been, you know, blood? Is that what you're thinking?"

"I simply do not know," I said.

"There were stains on the hardwood," she said.

"It was carpet," I corrected.

"No, I mean the hardwood that was underneath the carpet."

I gasped, "Wait. Hardwood under the carpet—are you saying that you actually *saw* the stain?"

"Well, yes. We've been renovating the house ever since we bought it last year. We took out all of the carpet and found solid oak flooring underneath. Most of it was in good condition, but we couldn't do anything about that stain."

"So what did you end up doing?"

"The only thing we *could* do. We tore it out and re-did the entry hall with slate tile."

She stepped to the side and let me look inside. The new tiled flooring extended from the threshold to the end of the entry hall about ten feet beyond the doorway. I spotted an electrical outlet on the right-hand wall which in the 1980 photograph was directly above the red stain. If only I could have seen that stained hardwood!

All I could say was, "The tile looks really nice."

"Well, would you like to come in and see what else we've done? I just made some fresh coffee."

I'd come to the house without expectations, so there really was no reason I should feel such a letdown. Maybe a cup of coffee would ease my disappointment.

"This was a bank-owned fixer when we bought it. It's still a work in progress, but it's getting there."

"I know how that goes," I commented. "I'm involved in a big restoration project of my own."

She laughed and said, "Then you have my sympathy. Where do you live?"

"I live down by the river in Canemah, but my restoration project is my ship, not my house," I clarified.

"Your ship?" she looked at me quizzically.

"You know the big schooner down by the arch bridge? That's mine. I'm restoring her."

"I *love* that ship!" she exclaimed. "You own it, really?"

"Yeah, I call her my lifetime project."

She laughed. "I know the feeling. Hey, I don't suppose you could give me a tour sometime—"

"Sure. But it's a long way from finished."

"That's okay. I'd just like to see it. I've never been on an actual sailing ship."

"A tour for a tour. Sounds like a fair exchange," I said.

She led me through the front door, and I paused on the spot where the stained carpet had been. I looked again at the old photo. The foil wallpaper was gone, replaced by white wainscoting beneath pale beige painted plaster walls. I wondered if there was any chance of there being any trace evidence behind the wainscoting, but immediately dismissed the thought.

The entry hall ended in an open area with the living room to my right. It featured a brick fireplace with a room-width raised hearth. Built-in oak bookcases filled the walls on both sides of the fireplace. The oak flooring gleamed like new, but around the edges, I could see the telltale tack-strip marks revealing where the hardwoods had been carpeted over.

"When was the house originally built?" I asked.

"1952—it was a doctor's house. We saved as much of the old woodwork as we could, trying to retain the original character," she explained. "The bookcases, the mantle, the floors—but the wainscoting and crown moldings aren't original."

She gave me the full tour before settling at the kitchen counter, where she poured the coffee. We continued talking about the renovation, and I was not stretching the truth when I said, "You've done a magnificent job with this home. It isn't easy to update a home while still retaining its character."

"Well, I love hearing that. Sometimes the project seemed hopeless. The house had been 'modernized' sometime in the 1970s, and a lot of what we did consisted of *undoing* what was done then."

"So when you bought it, it was still in 1970s style?"

"Dreadfully so—right down to the amber sidelights by the front door, the foil wallpaper and, of course, the wall-to-wall carpet. Can you imagine carpeting over all this hardwood?"

"I just wish I could've run some tests on the flooring that was under the stain. You know, to find out if it really was paint."

"Oh. Well maybe you still can."

"What do you mean?" I asked.

"My husband kept the wood he took out—he hates to throw anything away. He used some of the clean pieces to repair a place in the living room where someone let a leaky planter ruin the wood underneath."

I let my excitement show. "Are you saying that you might still have some of the stained wood?"

"Let's go out to the garage and see what we can find."

On a rack along the west wall of the garage Sara found a small stack of tongue-and-groove oak flooring. She started picking through the boards.

"Let me see that one," I said, pointing to a three-foot length of wood, part of which was heavily stained a rusty brown. I tried to contain my excitement when she handed me the board. We looked through everything on the rack without finding any others with the telltale stains.

Before leaving, I got her phone number and promised to call next time I was aboard *Annabel Lee*—though God only knew when that would be. This investigation was really cutting into my project time. All the way home, I marveled at my incredible good luck.

Sitting on the floor of my car was the evidence that I was sure would prove that Jessie had been murdered in the front hall of the Devonshire home and that her stepfather had deliberately concealed the evidence. I had found what Gary Turner and Dick Hammond were looking for in 1980.

I concealed the piece of wood under the carpet in the back of my Yukon, which I then locked in my garage. I'd take the board to a private lab in Portland on Tuesday, where I would have it tested. If blood was present, I'd have an ABO test done and, if possible, get a DNA profile. Of course, without Jessie's DNA for comparison, the DNA profile from the flooring would be useless, but I wanted to be ready for anything.

Martha was still busy on the computer. Looking over her shoulder, I noted that after two days on the project, she was working on file number 714. That seemed like pretty good progress. I did some quick mental calculations. At the rate of 350 files a day, it would take her twenty-one more days to finish the project.

Damn! Martha's indexing project had to be completed before I could work the evidence files with any degree of efficiency. Three to four weeks was a long time to wait. I gave some thought to hiring someone to help her with the data entry but quickly rejected the idea. For one thing, I didn't have room for another person to work. For another, I didn't have a computer for someone else to use. And most importantly, I didn't want to take Martha off the task for the time it would take her to train an assistant.

I'd never seen anyone so focused on her work. The only time she'd allowed herself to be distracted from the job was late Sunday afternoon when Bud came around looking for some conversation—and, of course, a beer.

"Working on Sunday," Bud observed when I opened the door. "Must be important."

"What's important is paying the bills, and this is what pays the bills." I introduced Bud.

"Nice to meet you, Bud," Martha said with a coy smile.

Bud smiled at Martha and accepted the beer that I offered.

"One for you?" I asked Martha.

"Well, yes, thanks," Martha said.

I'd have never figured Martha for a beer drinker. She seemed more like the organic-vegetable-juice type.

"Why don't we wrap it up here and take our drinks down to the dock?" I suggested.

Martha logged off, and then the three of us crossed the railroad tracks and went down the wooden steps to the ramp that led to the dock. I pushed some chairs around so that we'd be able to watch the boats out on the river. It was a busy afternoon on the water.

On the neighboring docks, people were enjoying the holiday weekend weather. Jet skis and ski boats were tearing up the river, and somebody's barbecue smoke drifted deliciously through the air.

"So you live down here too," Martha said to Bud.

"I'm one of the originals. This whole strip was owned by Union Pacific—beach, houses, and all. They had a plan to demolish the houses so that they could straighten out the bend in the rail line. But then the city passed some historical preservation laws and wouldn't let 'em tear down the old houses."

Bud pointed downstream toward the headquarters of Pacific-Western Diving. "So when the dive company approached UP about buying some of the property to expand their yard, UP said they'd have to buy the whole thing. That was about twenty years ago."

He took a good, long drink and then continued, "The dive company held onto the lots they wanted and sold the rest off. Most of it went to employees, like Big Dan, or their friends. I got that one—a real bargain too. I've been here ever since."

"Seems like a nice place to live," Martha said.

I'd been looking at Bud throughout the conversation, trying to figure out what was different. Finally, it struck me that he was wearing clean clothes. And damn! *He* was clean too. It left me wondering—had he taken his annual bath to celebrate Independence Day, or did he do it to impress Martha? I was pretty sure it was the latter. More amazing than that was the fact that it seemed to work! Martha seemed to actually *like* Bud.

CHAPTER 25

MONDAY, JULY 4

Martha insisted on working the holiday. I told her I would pay her time and a half for anything over forty hours a week, and she was thrilled about that.

Trying to stay humble, I said, "It's not just a good idea. It's the law."

And even at thirty dollars an hour, Martha was a bargain. I was already wondering if I'd be able to find something for her to do when this project was finished. Maybe she knew how to refinish hardwood on an antique schooner.

Halfway through the morning, Martha said, "This is really looking bad for Mr. Devonshire."

"What do you mean?"

"Well, I started out thinking that he had nothing to do with Jessie's murder. But it just looks more and more like he was involved somehow."

I'd just been typing up a summary of what I'd found out in the last three days and what it might mean, and I was having exactly the same thoughts.

"What are you looking at?" I asked.

"Well, I think it's strange that he went to the police station in the middle of the night while Jessie was missing. He phoned in the initial report, and then he drove down to the station—that doesn't seem right."

"What do you think that means?"

"I don't know. It just seems like he'd want to be at home in case she came home or called. What would be more important than finding his daughter?"

She was right. "Do you know whose idea it was for him to go to the West Linn Police station?" I asked.

"I haven't found anything about that."

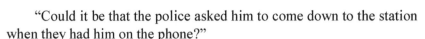

"Could it be that the police asked him to come down to the station when they had him on the phone?"

"Would they do that? I mean, it just seems that they'd go to his place."

"I think that would be the normal thing, but maybe they didn't have anyone on duty in the middle of the night who could go up to his place."

"Well, maybe..." she said hesitantly.

Or, I thought, maybe he volunteered to go to the station because he didn't want them to see the fresh paint on the carpet. Martha's instincts were dead-on. It was extremely odd behavior for any parent confronted with the disappearance of his daughter—or stepdaughter—to leave his home and phone unattended. A normal parent would be seated by the phone, and no force on earth could make him leave.

"Do you have a data field in your database for strange behavior?" I asked half-seriously.

"No," she said, "but I'm making a list."

"What else is on the list?" I asked.

"Well, there's the thing about Jessie going out with Randy. When he first reported her missing, Devonshire didn't say anything about Randy. In fact, he didn't say anything about Randy until the next day, after the police in Oregon City made the connection."

I agreed. That was a pretty big mistake. An innocent man would have searched his memory for anything that might help explain what had become of Jessie. It was hard to imagine that he could have overlooked someone as obvious as the landscaper, especially if it was true, as he later claimed, that Jessie had previously dated Randy. On the other hand, if he was guilty—and I believed he was—he should have anticipated that Mendelson would be connected to the case and included him in his story.

"And you know what else is weird," Martha continued, "is the way Jessie's mother acted. I mean, she learns that her daughter is missing and then loads up on Valium and goes to sleep? That just doesn't seem right."

"So if Devonshire had a role in Jessie's disappearance," I speculated, "you're implying that his wife must have had a part in it too."

"Either that or he drugged her just to keep her from being questioned."

"Excellent observations."

 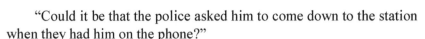

CHAPTER 26

y trip to Olympia the day after the July 4 weekend was a bust. In the state archives, I searched the 1976 and 1983 Portland phone directories for anyone named Trayborn and came up empty. That left me back where I'd started, with the same question Gary Turner had: who was Trayborn? Maybe I'd find out when Martha was finished with the Mendelson-Devonshire database.

For most of the next three weeks I worked on other things while Martha labored at the keyboard. Near the end of July, with the indexing nearly complete, it was time for me to focus on the 1980 case, starting with the question that had taken me to Olympia.

"What can you find in the database for the name Trayborn?"

"I have two files showing that name," Martha told me after a few seconds. "One is a page from Gary Turner's notebook."

That was the one that had first raised the question, "Who is Trayborn?"

"The other is a phone memo," Martha said. "It doesn't say who wrote it, but the memo pad matches other notes from Gary Turner's home phone—most likely written by Leslie Turner."

I looked over her shoulder at the image on her computer screen. It was the familiar pink While You Were Out form. It was dated September 19 and showed a call from Hammond at 1:15 p.m.. It said simply,

6:00 meeting with Trayborn about Devonshire ride.

Hammond had called Turner to say that he was meeting Trayborn to talk about a "Devonshire ride."

Since the meeting was at six on the day Hammond's body was found in the furniture store parking lot, it seemed very likely that Trayborn had been the last person to see Hammond alive.

Strangely, the note from Hammond seemed to imply that Turner knew who Trayborn was, yet Turner had scribbled his own note, wondering, "Who is Trayborn?" If Trayborn was somebody unknown to Turner, wouldn't Hammond have explained to Leslie who he was? The best clue I had about the murder of Richard Hammond—and I had little doubt that Hammond's death was murder—was this note identifying the probable killer as Trayborn. But who the hell was Trayborn, and what was the "Devonshire ride" that Hammond was going to talk with him about?

I had far better luck with the analysis of the piece of flooring from the Devonshire entry hall. The preliminary report had come back the day after I took the board to the private lab in Portland. Blood was found on the tongue-and-groove area of the board, and the blood was definitely human. It was blood type B, Rh Positive. Developing a DNA profile would take more time, possibly a couple of months, since the samples would have to be sent to a more specialized lab in Seattle.

Martha searched the data base for *blood type* and turned up the transcript of an interview with Barbara Devonshire, on August 20, 1980. A Jane Doe had been found outside Salem, and state police were trying to match the remains to known missing persons.

In the course of the interview, the interrogator asked Jessie's mother if she knew her daughter's blood type. Because Jessie had undergone appendix surgery a couple of years earlier, Mrs. Devonshire knew that Jessie had B positive blood. That ended the interview, because the Jane Doe had a different blood type, but it was critical information for us in the current investigation.

Now we had confirmation that the blood found on the flooring matched Jessie's blood type. Only 8.5 percent of the US population have that blood type, so it seemed highly likely that it was hers. DNA might prove it one way or another, but only if I could find an exemplar—something to compare my sample with.

I had no access to any physical evidence from either the original investigation or the recent one. Certainly, the remains found in the El Camino would have contained Jessie's DNA, but since the body had been positively identified through dental records, a DNA profile was not needed, and as far as I could tell, no DNA testing had been done.

My options were limited. I could think of no legal way to get my hands on anything from the El Camino. If Barbara was willing to cooperate with me, I could ask her if she still had anything from her daughter that might contain DNA—something like a hair brush. Lacking that, we could compare Barbara's DNA with that from the flooring and look for a family match.

But there were problems with that. During the 1980 investigation, Barbara had supported her husband on all points, so it seemed unlikely that she would be willing to help me find evidence that would pin a double murder on her husband.

At this point, I didn't want to show my hand by talking with Mrs. Devonshire. Maybe later, but for now, I'd have to try to find Jessie's DNA elsewhere.

"Martha, do you have anything in there that would identify Jessie Devonshire's friends?"

"I think so," she said as she started a new query. After a few minutes, and two or three more queries in the database, Martha said, "During the initial investigation, Turner and Hammond interviewed several of Jessie's school friends, trying to establish a connection between her and Randy—they came up empty on that, by the way—but here's a list."

"Only three names?" I observed.

"Yeah, it seems she didn't hang around much with school friends."

"Seems odd—a pretty girl like that. Why weren't boys all over her?" I wondered.

The three names were Cory Gibbon, James Disston, and Melissa Richland. It was doubtful that the two girls would still be using their maiden names, so I started my search with James Disston. I found a James R. Disston listed among the 1983 graduates from West Linn High, but nobody by that name currently living in the area.

I looked through the 1987 graduating classes of Oregon State University and University of Oregon and came up empty. However, I did find a James R. Disston living in Bellingham, Washington. I also found someone by the same name among the 1987 graduates of the University of Washington. Jessie's friend was a Husky.

"Yes, I graduated from West Linn High," the voice on the phone confirmed. "Why do you ask?"

"I'm trying to find people who knew Jessie Devonshire back in the 1970s, and your name came up," I told him.

"Jessie Devonshire. Wow!"

"So you did know her," I prompted.

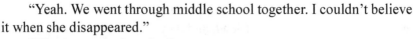

"Yeah. We went through middle school together. I couldn't believe it when she disappeared."

"They recently found—"

"I know," he interrupted. "I heard about it on the news last month."

"How close were you with Jessie?"

"Not as close as I wanted to be. I had a real crush on her, but she wasn't interested. The whole time I knew her, I never saw her with a guy."

"You think she was—"

"A dyke? Not a chance," James said emphatically. "She had some mysterious boyfriend who didn't go to our school—I don't know were he went—but he was older than me."

"How do you know that?"

"Oh, Jessie was always telling me—you know, when I'd ask her out—that she preferred someone 'more mature,' whatever that meant."

"Did Jessie ever give you anything—or send you a card, anything like that?"

"I suppose maybe we passed notes in the hallway between classes— kid stuff, you know."

"You wouldn't have kept any of those?"

"Oh, heck no. I mean, she hadn't ever been interested in me. She was just another girl I couldn't get a date with."

"Do you remember Cory Gibbon or Melissa Richland?"

"Sure. I knew both of them better than I ever knew Jessie."

"Any idea what ever became of them?"

"We had a twenty-fifth-year class reunion a couple of years ago. Cory wasn't there, but Melissa was."

"I'd like to get in touch with them."

"Hold on. They printed a directory for the reunion. Let me find it." After a couple of minutes, he came back to the phone. "Melissa lives in Salem. Her name is Vale now. Cory's married name is Lear, and she lives in Atlanta."

James read me the addresses and phone numbers from the directory. I thanked him and hung up. I called Melissa first and got voice mail. I left a message and then dialed Cory's number.

"Hello, this is Cory," came the cheerful response.

I introduced myself and asked if she remembered Jessie Devonshire.

"Oh, poor Jessie," she said. "Sure, I remember her."

"Would you call her a close friend?"

"Funny thing about Jessie, she didn't have any really close friends at school. But she had a boyfriend, and they were pretty serious."

"What do you mean?"

"Well, once she showed me a packet of birth-control pills."

As far as I knew, that hadn't ever been mentioned in 1980. "When was that?" I asked.

"Oh, I don't know. It must have been about a year before she disappeared."

"She was awfully young for that."

"You bet! We were only in eighth grade, and most of us didn't have a clue about sex. I guess you'd say that Jessie was an early bloomer. I remember she had boobs in sixth grade," Cory explained. "We were all pretty envious."

"Did she seem promiscuous?" I asked.

"No, that was the funny thing about Jessie. She never showed any interest in the boys in school. She was always saying that they were 'too immature' for her."

"What do you think she meant by that?"

"She was dating someone older. She wouldn't say who, but it was nobody in our school."

"Did you ever exchange mail with Jessie?" I asked.

"Christmas cards, birthday cards, anything like that?"

"No, we never did anything like that."

After we hung up, I made a few notes. This was the first time anyone had ever mentioned that Jessie Devonshire was sexually active—and had been for at least a year before she disappeared. Put together with Kim's hint that Jessie had been dressed for the bedroom, a whole new scenario came into focus, offering a possible motive for the crime.

Had Wilson Devonshire caught Jessie in bed with Randy? That was something that could have sent him into a blind rage and could explain why he would commit murder, even though I still had no evidence that Jessie and Randy had ever dated.

My phone rang, interrupting my thoughts.

"Corrigan," I said.

"Uh, this is Melissa Vale," the voice on the line said. "I believe you called?"

"I'm looking into the death of Jessie Devonshire in 1980," I explained. "I believe you knew her?"

"I thought they'd determined that Randy Mendelson killed her. That's what they said in the news."

"I'm just making sure the investigation got it right. How well did you know Jessie?"

"Oh, you know. We were just friends in school—seventh, eighth grade."

"Did you ever hear her talk about anyone she dated?"

"Not specifically. She was dating someone who didn't go to our school, but I don't know who."

"Did you ever hear that she was sexually active?"

"I'm not sure that she ever said it directly, but she had this *attitude*, you know—like she knew something we didn't. I'm sure she hinted that she was having sex, whether she actually said it or not."

"Do you think she might have been dating Randy Mendelson?"

"That's what they say, isn't it? But it's funny. I mean, Jessie was all about *status*. It's always seemed out of character for her to date a *gardener*."

Her emphasis on the word *gardener* clearly implied that she felt that Randy was beneath Jessie's social station.

"So you don't believe she was dating Randy?"

"I don't know. She always talked about education, like that was the most important thing—for a guy to go to a prestigious college and get a degree. But Randy just mowed grass, you know," Melissa explained.

"How much did you see Jessie during the last few months she was alive?"

"Oh, not at all. We moved to Salem almost a year before Jessie got killed. I never saw her after that."

"Did you ever hear from her after you moved?"

"I got a Christmas card from her, but it didn't say much—just 'Merry Christmas and Happy New Year' or something like that."

"I don't suppose you'd still have that card?"

"Funny," Melissa began, "the Christmas after Jessie disappeared, her card showed up among the previous year's Christmas stuff—that's how we decided who to send cards to every year. Anyway, I thought it was so sad to find that card when she was probably dead."

"Do you know what became of the card?" I asked, hopeful.

"I could never bring myself to throw it out. It just seemed wrong, you know—like throwing away the last piece of *her*."

"So you still have it?" I was holding my breath.

"Sure. I got it out and looked at it when they found her body last month."

"And the envelope?"

"It's still in the envelope."

"Would you mind if I borrowed the envelope? I'd like to have it tested for DNA."

"What for? They already know who did it."

"Well, like I said, we just want to be sure."

"I guess that would be okay—as long as I can have it back."

I got her address and arranged to meet her that evening. The envelope had the potential to prove beyond any doubt that Jessie had been killed in the front hall of the Devonshire home. We already knew that her stepfather had actively covered up the evidence.

CHAPTER 27

I sent Melissa's Christmas card envelope to the Seattle lab that was working on the DNA profile from the blood on Devonshire's flooring. I offered to pay a premium to get the results more quickly, but they told me that law enforcement always had priority in their scheduling. I'd just have to wait.

It was time to give Larry Jamieson a heads-up. Even though he had been the lead detective on the recent investigation, I believed that he wasn't in agreement with the official findings. Why else would he have sent Lila Mendelson to me? I had no desire to blindside Deputy Jamieson with a report that would contradict the sheriff's official closure of the case.

"This is Jamieson," said the voice on the phone.

"My name's Corrigan," I said. "I'm working for Lila Mendelson."

"What can I do for you, Mr. Corrigan?"

"Just 'Corrigan'—please," I said. That's half a million and one times—and counting.

"Okay, Corrigan, what can I do for you?"

"Last month you sent Lila Mendelson to me," I reminded him.

"That is not quite correct. I merely told her that her best bet for further investigation of her son's death would be to contact a private investigator. Your name came up."

"Okay, fine. I'm calling today to advise you that I've found hard evidence that I think will disprove the official version of events."

"I'm listening."

"I believe that I'll be able to prove that Jessie was killed in the entry hall of the Devonshire home."

"And how can you prove that?"

"I have a board removed from the entry-hall floor. It has already tested positive for human blood, and it matches Jessie's blood type—B positive. DNA is pending," I told him.

"How will you match DNA with Jessie?"

"I have an envelope—a Christmas card she sent in 1979. It's being tested now."

"And if it matches, how does that prove Mendelson didn't kill the girl?"

"It proves that Wilson Devonshire acted deliberately to cover up key evidence—the whole 'spilled paint' incident was contrived. I don't have to tell you, that's a pretty strong indication of guilt."

"What 'spilled paint incident' is that?" Jamieson asked.

"Devonshire told a deputy on the day after Jessie disappeared that a large brownish-red stain on the carpet was caused by a paint spill," I explained, "and the board with the blood came from directly beneath the stained carpet."

"How do you know what Devonshire told investigators?"

"Gary Turner's widow gave me his notes," I said, not revealing the extent of the material Leslie had given me.

"What are you planning to do with this, if the DNA comes back a match?"

"Only thing I *can* do. I'll have to take it to the DA—unless you guys reopen the investigation."

"Let me explain something to you, Corrigan—off the record. There is a lot of heat to keep the lid on this case. It comes from someplace a lot higher than me. Higher than my boss. Higher than the DA."

"So what are you saying? That I shouldn't turn my evidence over to you *or* the DA?"

"I'm saying I never should have gotten you into this," Jamieson said flatly. "To be honest, I didn't figure you'd be able to come up with anything. Lila Mendelson begged for help, so I gave her your name. Now I wish I hadn't done that."

"Here's what I think. I think you reached the same conclusion I did, and I think you have evidence to prove it—maybe in the pathologist's reports or maybe something else—but you don't believe any more than I do that Randy Mendelson killed Jessie."

"So what? My advice is to drop it. Just drop it."

And then the line went dead. I don't know what I'd been expecting, but that sure wasn't it. I guess I thought he'd thank me or something.

A few days later, on the last Friday in July, I gave Martha a check for all of her work to date. I told her to take the weekend off and come back on Monday to talk about what she might do for me in the future. After she was gone, I went back to my notes to see if there were any loose ends I could tie up now that the database was complete. The first thing I found was Leslie Turner's note about the phone call from Dick Hammond.

"Devonshire ride." What the hell did that mean? Did it mean Devonshire's car—did people use *ride* as a synonym for *car* in 1980? And if so, what was it about Devonshire's car that interested Hammond? Or did Devonshire get a ride with someone—or give a ride to someone? I entered query after query, trying to get Martha's database to give up a hint.

I finally thought to search the database for the word *taxi*. Had Devonshire taken a ride in a taxi? I came up with half a dozen documents, including two that were the call logs on July 25, 1980, from the two cab companies that served West Linn at that time. In the left margins, someone—presumably Turner or Hammond—had penciled asterisks next to the following entries:

* 2:55 p.m. Pick up 1620 Willamette Falls Dr./ Drop 5725 K St. WL

* 6:10 p.m. Pick up Mark's Tavern, 12th St & WF Dr./ Drop 2530 SW Hillcrest Dr. Ptld

* 8:20 p.m. Pick up 870 5th Ave. WL/ Drop at PDX

* 10:45 p.m. Pick up corner of Ostman & Dollar/ Drop 1548 Garden St. WL

* 11:30 p.m. Pick up Clyde's Bar & Grill, 15th & Willamette Falls Dr./ Drop 4330 Kelly St. WL

* 1:10 a.m. Pick up Clyde's Bar & Grill, 15th & Willamette Falls Dr./ Drop 1002 Jefferson St. OC

* 2:00 a.m. Pick up 13th and Willamette Falls Dr./ Drop 5660 Sinclair St. WL

There were many other entries in between these, but only these had been marked. What did it mean? A quick glance at the addresses revealed that they were all in the Willamette District of West Linn.

Devonshire ride. Taxi rides. *Of course!* Whoever drove the El Camino to the boat ramp needed a ride back. It was four miles from the West Linn Boat Landing to the Devonshire house, all uphill. It would probably take ninety minutes to do that on foot. Even if he wanted the exercise, there would have been way too much risk of being seen.

If Devonshire had driven the El Camino into the river, he'd have needed a ride home. He wouldn't want a cab to pick him up at Willamette Park because that would have been too obvious. But he could walk the quarter mile up to Willamette Falls Drive and call a cab without raising suspicion.

The other four documents that contained the keyword *taxi* turned out to be Hammond's notes from his follow-up investigation of the taxi trips that started after dark. It was clear that he didn't believe the El Camino would have been dumped during daylight hours. Each of the papers had a name written next to the address, and each gave an explanation for the cab ride. All appeared to have been dead ends, but I double-checked that by searching the database for each of the four names. Nothing came up other than the notes I already had.

Even though this line of inquiry had reached a dead end, it had produced one major insight—that Devonshire had an accomplice. Someone had to have given him a ride home from the boat landing in the middle of the night. Devonshire's ride. Hammond had gone to talk with Trayborn about that and wound up dead. Trayborn knew who Devonshire's accomplice was and had killed Hammond to keep the secret. The pieces all fit.

When she came in on Monday, I put Martha to work compiling a file of newspaper clippings about Wilson Devonshire, circa 1980. I wanted everything I could find out about Devonshire. I hoped that we'd be able to build a list of his friends and social contacts. The elusive Mr. Trayborn had to be among them somewhere.

"Where will I find that kind of information?" She asked.

"Best place to start is the *Chronicle* office. They'll have an index, but you'll still have to find the articles on microfiche. Search the society pages, and search the news pages during the time he was appointed to the supreme court. There'll probably be background stories there. And you might have some luck at the city library too," I said.

CHAPTER 28

WEDNESDAY AUGUST 3

In the middle of the morning, a FedEx truck stopped in front of my office. I signed for a thick envelope from the DNA laboratory in Seattle. The first page contained a summary of the methods used and the results of the tests on blood from the floorboard taken from the Devonshire home. Most of the blood on the surface of the boards was not usable because of the age of the sample and the attempts to dilute it with water and then to camouflage it with paint. But much better samples were found in the tongues and grooves on the sides of the boards.

The second page dealt with the extraction of nuclear DNA from the stamp and envelope flap on Jessie's Christmas card to Melissa Richland. The extraction and amplification protocol was described in great detail. The stamp had produced poor results because it appeared to be a reused stamp, one that had been removed from another envelope and then adhered to the Christmas card envelope using Elmer's Glue.

But the glue on the flap was undisturbed—the envelope had been opened with a letter opener that slit the flap without affecting the glue, which contained saliva and the DNA of the person who had sealed the envelope. Using the thirteen DNA markers commonly used in criminal investigation, the lab's first test found a definite match on twelve markers, with the thirteenth described as ambiguous. On a second sample, the test matched all thirteen markers.

With near-astronomical certainty, the blood on the Devonshire flooring was from the person who had licked the envelope. No surprise. I now had the physical evidence that proved Wilson Devonshire had participated in the cover up of Jessie's murder. And that, by default, made it highly likely that he was the murderer.

I was holding material evidence in a criminal investigation. I was obligated by law to turn it over to the authorities—either the sheriff's office or the DA. But Larry Jamieson had made it quite clear that my evidence would not be graciously received. What was the point of giving them my DNA evidence if they were going to simply bury it the way they'd buried the evidence found in the El Camino?

On the other hand, Lila Mendelson deserved to know what I'd found. I gave her a call, and when she arrived at my office, I handed her a summary of what I'd found.

"You've done it!" she exclaimed happily. "You've proven that Devonshire killed Randy and Jessie."

"No," I corrected, "this proves nothing about Randy. It proves only that Jessie was probably killed in the Devonshire home, but it doesn't prove who did it. It proves that Devonshire deliberately tried to hide the evidence, but it doesn't prove he killed anyone."

"But if he covered up the evidence, he *must* have done it," Lila protested.

"I agree. That's a reasonable inference. And a jury might see it that way too, but it still isn't proof."

Obviously disappointed, Lila said, "Well at least they'll have to reopen the investigation."

"I wouldn't count on that. There are indications that political pressure is being applied to keep the case from going any further."

"But with this new evidence—"

"Lila, I don't like telling you this. It's all wrong. But I believe that there was hard evidence in Randy's El Camino that proved the same thing. And the case was closed anyway."

"But they can't *do* that!"

"They *shouldn't* do it," I corrected, "but they did. Listen, Lila, I'm still working on this. There are some leads that I'm chasing down, and it's still possible that I can find out exactly what happened if you want me to continue.

"Of course, I want you to continue."

"This is a good time to mention how much this investigation is costing. I've already gone way over the five-thousand-dollar benchmark we agreed on when I started."

"That's okay! I want you to get to the bottom of this. I don't care what it costs!"

"There is one more thing you need to know," I said tentatively. "I've spoken with some of Jessie Devonshire's friends—schoolmates. They all say that Jessie had been involved in a long-term relationship with someone quite a bit older. Now I know that you don't believe that Randy knew Jessie, but we have to consider the possibility."

"That's nonsense," Lila scoffed.

"I'm just asking you to think about it. Did Randy go out on dates?"

Lila nodded, so I asked, "Did he always tell you who he was going out with?"

"Well, no, but he wouldn't have dated a fifteen-year-old girl!"

"You've seen pictures of Jessie. She looked older than she was. Dressed right, and with the right makeup, she could have easily passed for eighteen. Maybe Randy didn't know her age."

"But he *talked* about the girls he dated," Lila protested, "and he never said anything about anyone named Jessie."

"Well, let me toss in something else I've learned. Jessie's friends say that she was sexually active. Now if Randy was going to bed with Jessie, maybe he wouldn't want you to know about her."

"Mr. Corrigan, I'm no fool. Of course, there were things that Randy didn't tell me. But sleeping with Jessie Devonshire? That's impossible. For one thing, where would they do it? Not here. Not likely at her house. And when? Randy worked fifty to sixty hours a week. He didn't have time for what you're talking about."

"I believe you, Lila. But if we went to trial with what we know right now, Devonshire's attorney would almost certainly build an alternate-suspect defense around Randy. We need to close that door before we start doing things that might lead to an indictment."

"Oh dear," Lila said, finally seeing my point.

Later in the day, after spending two and a half days in Portland, Martha came back with a sheaf of newspaper clippings and a list of about a hundred people who had been associated with Wilson Devonshire around 1980. There was nobody on the list named Trayborn.

"How about Devonshire's media contacts?" Martha suggested. "He might have been pretty close to them—maybe even closer than to people in his own office. After all, he depended on them to keep the mayor's public image bright and shiny."

"We can go back to the newspaper archives and look for names on the publisher's page. Radio and TV will be harder."

"I was thinking about that. I could go to the TV stations' public-affairs departments and get the names of reporters in 1980," Martha volunteered. "I'll just tell them I'm documenting history for the Portland Museum of Broadcasting."

"That might work," I mused.

"And there's a website with a page all about Portland radio history. I'll start a thread in their forum and see how many names come up."

"Have at it."

The key to proving Devonshire's role in the murder of his stepdaughter still lay in finding his accomplice—the elusive Trayborn.

CHAPTER 29

SATURDAY, AUGUST 6

While Kim showered and dressed, I made breakfast. When she reappeared, she was dressed in her short sleeved uniform, ready to head out onto the river. "Have you decided what to do with your DNA evidence?" she asked, continuing our conversation from the previous evening.

"I can't just sit on it. But I don't want to put Jamieson's ass in a bind, either."

"I think Jamieson can take care of himself."

"Kim, there's something really bad with this case," I said seriously. "Two detectives died—almost certainly were murdered—before the case was suspended in 1980. And their deaths weren't even investigated. Doesn't that tell you something?"

"But that was over thirty years ago."

"So what did Sheriff Kerby do with the current investigation?" I didn't wait for an answer. "He clamped a lid on it and closed it before the evidence was even processed—ordered you and everyone else to keep quiet or lose your jobs. And that isn't thirty years ago—it's now."

"That doesn't mean—" Kim started.

"It seems pretty clear that Kerby ordered Jamieson to spike the investigation. He does not want new evidence, and if I give this stuff to Jamieson, he'll have to pass it along to Kerby. I'll guarantee you, he doesn't want to do that."

"So we're back to the original question. What are you going to do with it?"

"I'll go down to the courthouse and put it into the DA's hands. It's the only thing I can do."

"Then what happens?"

"I expect that shit's going to hit somebody's fan. I just hope it isn't mine."

After breakfast, we went down to the dock and motored across the river. I dropped Kim off at the marine unit dock, next to her patrol boat. It took two minutes to get there by boat, instead of the twenty it would have taken to get there by car.

Five minutes later, my boat was back at my dock, and I was on my way up to the house. I looked up to see Lila Mendelson getting out of her red Sentra.

"Mr. Corrigan, I've done a terrible thing," she cried, "and now I don't know what to do."

"Why don't you come inside, and we'll talk about it. Would you like a cup of coffee?"

"No, thank you," she said wearily.

She sat down on the chair I kept for visitors, a thick manila envelope on her lap.

"Now tell me—what's the trouble?" I asked.

"I stole this." She held up the envelope. "I took it off of Detective Jamieson's desk."

"Why don't you start at the beginning," I suggested.

She took a deep breath. "After I talked to you on Wednesday, I called Detective Jamieson. I told him what you had found out, and he invited me to meet him in his office on Friday—yesterday.

"When I went into his office, he closed the door behind me. I let him read the report you gave me, and then he said he was glad that you were finding new evidence, but then he said, 'The truth is we have a lot of evidence.' And that's when he showed me this."

She held up the envelope. "He said that this was everything they found in Randy's car. And then he suddenly asked to be excused, and just like that, he left me alone in his office—and he left this sitting right there on his desk. I know I shouldn't have done it, but I picked it up, just to look inside. Then before I could open the envelope, he came back and said that he had something urgent he needed to do. I had the envelope in my hand, but I guess he didn't notice. I just kind of hid it with my purse, and the next thing I knew, I was outside. I didn't really mean to steal it— it just happened."

"Did you look in the envelope?"

"I started to," she said, tears flowing. "But there were pictures. They were awful, and I just couldn't look at them."

She offered the envelope to me. I was dying to see the contents, but red lights were flashing in my brain.

I held up my hands and said, "I can't take that from you. You committed a crime by taking it from Detective Jamieson's office. If I were to accept it from you with the knowledge that you had acquired it illegally, I would then be a party to the crime."

Lila burst out in tears and cried, "But what can I do?"

I fished around in my desk drawer until I found William Gates' business card. On the back, I wrote the private phone number that I used to call him when his office wasn't open.

"I'd like you to call Mr. Gates. Tell him you want him to represent you in whatever criminal or civil proceedings come as a result of this investigation. Give him a check—can you afford a thousand dollars?"

She nodded.

"Good. That's called a retainer. That means that you are his client, and nothing that passes between you and him after you hand him that check can ever be used against you in court. Do you understand?"

Again, she nodded. It also extended a certain amount of attorney-to-client privilege to me, but I didn't need to tell her that.

"Then—after you've given him the check—tell him about the envelope," I said. "Tell him that you would like him to make arrangements with Detective Jamieson for the return of the envelope. He'll take care of it from there."

"There's just one thing," Lila said. "I thought about this all night, and the more I thought about it, the more it seemed like Detective Jamieson *wanted* me to take the envelope. I mean, he told me what was in it, he put it on the desk in front of me, and then he left the room. It's like he was *inviting* me to take it."

It struck me the same way, especially in light of the conversation I'd had with Jamieson. He had made it clear to me that he could go no further with the case, no matter what. And yet he had sent Lila to me. That said that he wanted the case investigated, even though he couldn't do it. So it really wasn't a stretch to believe that he might "accidentally" leave the file where Lila would be tempted to take it.

"I still can't take that from you," I explained. "I can't assist you in the commission of a crime. On the other hand, if I were to go into my kitchen to make a pot of coffee and you were to do something without my knowledge or consent, something like…oh, I don't know…like placing a stack of papers in that tray and pressing that green button, I wouldn't have committed a crime."

I pointed at the document feeder on my scanner, and while I spoke, I keyed in a few commands on my computer. Lila's face brightened.

"You know, Mr. Corrigan, I think I *would* like that cup of coffee you offered me."

"In that case, I'll make a fresh pot," I said as I got up.

When I got back from the kitchen with two cups of coffee, I found Lila sitting with the closed envelope on her lap and a smile on her face. My computer screen said that fifty-six pages had been scanned.

"Have you decided what you're going to do?" I asked.

"Just like you suggested, I'm going to call Mr. Gates."

"Would you like to use my phone?"

CHAPTER 30

After Lila left, I started looking through the documents she had scanned. There were pathology reports on the human remains, a report from the Oregon State Police Weapons Lab on the gun, and a series of detailed notes and photos taken during the search of the El Camino. I spent the next two hours studying what Lila had brought me, and it took my breath away.

First, there were the photos showing Jessie's remains still wearing the pink satin negligee and sheer babydoll lingerie. As Kim had hinted, these were hardly the clothes anyone would wear on a date. In fact, they really weren't something a person would casually wear around the house. They were seduction clothes, worn for the sole purpose of engaging in sexual play.

Then I read the report from the weapons lab.

```
Upon initial examination, it was determined
that there was live ammunition in the weapon.
After prying the loading gate open, it was
determined that the cylinder was seized and
could not be rotated. The base pin was
forcibly extracted, and the cylinder was
released by tapping with a plastic hammer,
revealing four live Remington .22 LR
cartridges and two expended shell casings.

The cylinder was initially positioned with a
live cartridge under the hammer and the two
expended cartridges in the two positions
immediately clockwise from the firing
position. The firing pin marks on the rims of
the expended shell casings were positioned in
```

```
approximately the 2 o'clock and 7 o'clock
positions relative to the radius of the
cylinder, indicating that the shells had been
removed from the cylinder after firing and
subsequently reinserted.
```

That was the proverbial smoking gun. It proved beyond any doubt that Randy Mendelson had not shot himself while his car was sinking into the Willamette River. If he had, there would have been an expended cartridge under the hammer and he would have been dead. A dead man couldn't have rotated the cylinder.

And the firing-pin marks on the expended shells should have been at the outer edge of the cylinder—that is, in the twelve o'clock position. Someone had removed the shells, perhaps to wipe off fingerprints, and put them back in without paying attention to the position of the firing-pin marks.

The report stated that no ballistics tests had been conducted because the weapon was too badly rusted to be fired safely and, in any case, the bullet fragments taken from the victims did not offer adequate markings for comparison purposes.

A note attached to the back of the weapons-lab report said, "CCSO indicates that their personnel examined the weapon before it was sent to the lab."

What? Did someone tell the state weapons lab that the gun had been tampered with after it was taken from the El Camino? If true, that would invalidate the evidence!

I reread the notes regarding the discovery of the weapon and its removal from the car. Photos supported the statement that the gun had been lifted from the floor pan using forceps and was placed directly into a tub of distilled water, which was then sealed with evidence tape.

Going back to the weapons-lab report, the preliminary paragraph describing the receipt of the weapon, it was noted that the evidence tape was intact. That didn't add up. Nor did the fact that the weapons lab had found the cylinder seized in place. For someone at the CCSO to remove and reinsert the expended shell casings, the cylinder would have to have been either rotated or removed. If that had been done, it wouldn't have been seized when received by the weapons lab.

Leaving that mystery for another time, I turned to the pathologist's reports. The descriptions of the head injuries sustained by the victims were entirely consistent with what the detectives observed when they removed the skulls from the El Camino.

Randy had a single gunshot wound above and slightly behind his left ear. Aside from the difficulty he would have had holding the gun in position to inflict that injury on himself, Randy was right-handed. If he were to shoot himself, he would logically have held the gun in his right hand.

Regarding Jessie's injuries, the report described the bullet entry wound in the right occipital region of the skull. The description of the skull-fracture injury was more detailed. It gave the dimensions of the injury and speculated as to the weapon that had inflicted it.

```
Due to the very straight edges of the
impact fracture, coupled with the complete
lack of foreign material--such as wood, or
stone—it is probable that the weapon was
smooth metal and likely quite heavy. At the
point of impact, it was a rectangular
instrument measuring 9 cm by 3.5 cm.
```

The photos that accompanied this description showed a perfectly defined rectangular hole in the top of Jessie's skull.

My mind drifted to another photo—the one taken by Dick Hammond showing the entry hall of the Devonshire home. I went to my computer and pulled up the image. There on the table next to the stain on the carpet stood a bronze statue of an eagle. The base of the statue appeared to be of exactly the right size and shape to have caused Jessie's injury.

It had been right in front of everyone from the very first day!

That afternoon, I was down on my dock when Kim brought her patrol boat in for the day. I took my boat across the river to pick her up, and as we walked up toward the house, we heard what seemed like a heated argument between Duane and Sharon Dexter, who lived two doors up Water Street.

Upon investigation, we found Duane—trying to park a new pop-up travel trailer in the narrow driveway between his house and Daryl's next door.

"I'm betting he takes out the fence," I told Kim.

"Nope. I don't think he'll ever get in far enough to hit the fence."

Kim and I took seats on my porch to watch the drama unfold.

"No, you have to turn the wheel the other way!" Sharon shouted.

"That's the wrong way—it'll put me on the railroad tracks," Duane protested.

"But that's the way you're going now! You need to turn the other way."

"I'll just pull forward and give it another try."

It was at least the third time he'd done that. Obviously he'd never backed a trailer before and had not the slightest idea how to do it. This time, taking Sharon's advice, Duane got the trailer to break in the direction of the driveway.

"Hold it! Hold it!" Sharon shouted just before the cracking sound of breaking plastic.

The trailer jackknifed against the back of Duane's Volvo, and pieces of tail light fell to the pavement below.

"I knew that was wrong," Duane whined.

"You were supposed to straighten it out," Sharon tried to explain.

"Shouldn't you go over and help him?" Kim asked.

"He'll never learn if I do it for him," I told her.

"I'm pulling forward," Duane announced.

"Not too far," Sharon advised. "Right there! Stop!" Sharon shouted. "No, that's too much!"

Duane put the Volvo in reverse and started backing up again. This time, without enough turning angle, the trailer missed the driveway, knocked over a potted plant, and rolled onto Daryl's lawn.

"Why didn't you tell me to stop?" Duane complained.

He got out of his Volvo and walked around to the passenger side to see what he'd done. One wheel of the trailer was sitting on the overturned geraniums, and the trailer tilted at a peculiar angle. After thoroughly studying the situation, he got back into the Volvo and pulled forward about ten feet.

"Now what are you doing?" Sharon asked him.

"I'm going to unhitch it,"

"But it's in the middle of the street."

"Well, I'm not going to leave it there," Duane said defensively.

He disconnected the electrical plug and the safety chains. He cranked the tongue jack down until its wheel reached the ground, and kept on cranking until the back of the Volvo had been lifted several inches. When he tried to lift the lever on the coupler, it wouldn't budge—because it was under strain from lifting the Volvo.

"Can you get me the hammer?" Duane asked Sharon.

He used the claw to pry up on the lever until it grudgingly released, the Volvo dropped about eight inches, landing hard and bouncing dangerously close to Duane's foot. He then grabbed the tongue jack and pushed it off to his right, steering the trailer toward the driveway. Once he had it aimed in roughly the right direction, he started pushing the trailer backward, which worked fine until he reached the slight uphill grade of the driveway.

"Sharon," he called urgently, "I need help pushing!"

She joined him, and the two of them together managed—with great effort—to push the trailer up the slight incline into the driveway.

"You win," I said to Kim, forking over a dollar.

"You have a mean streak, Corrigan. You really should have helped him."

❧

After dinner, I showed Kim a printout of the documents that Lila had scanned.

"How in hell did you get your hands on that?" Kim asked in amazement.

"I can't answer that question. The important fact is that I have it."

"But as soon as Kerby finds out you have it, he's going to assume that I gave it to you," she protested.

That thought had been on my mind all day. "I'm going to do everything I can to keep Kerby—or anyone else—from knowing I have this until after everything has become public knowledge. Then it won't matter how I got it."

"And how is it going to become public knowledge?"

"I don't know yet. But for now, there's no reason for Kerby to know that I have any of this." I tried to sound more confident than I felt. "If I can find enough evidence from other sources to support my theory of the crime, this file won't be an issue until the case goes to trial. Nobody will ever know that I have a copy."

"Okay, so what *is* your theory of the crime?"

"The crime starts with sex. Jessie's lingerie tells us that. Her friends have said that Jessie was having sex with an older man. Maybe Randy, but I doubt it. I think it was Devonshire—it would hardly be the first time a stepfather let his affections stray from the wife to the daughter.

"Somewhere in the middle of his sexual encounter, an argument breaks out. Jessie heads toward the front door, and Devonshire grabs a weapon of convenience—the bronze eagle—and knocks her to the carpet. When he realizes she is still alive, he gets the Ruger and puts a bullet into the back of her head.

"Randy, working in the yard, hears the gunshot and goes to the door to investigate. Devonshire gets him into the house and kills him. He probably goes through a period of total panic before figuring out how he might get away with his crime.

"First, he had to put Randy's El Camino into his garage out of view. Then he loads both bodies into the cab. He's already decided that he's going to run the car into the river, but he can't be sure that it won't be discovered, so he takes the bullets out of the gun and wipes off any fingerprints. When he puts the bullets back in, he neglects to pay attention to the positions of firing pin marks, and he accidentally rotates the cylinder one notch from where it should have been. He puts the gun in the car.

"Then he tries to clean up the mess, using household cleaners and water. When he realizes that he can't get all of the stain out of the carpet, he comes up with the 'spilled paint' idea. He drives down to the True Value Hardware store and buys the paint. The receipt for the paint says he bought it at six fifteen. He had to have spent a couple of hours trying to clean up the mess before resorting to the paint idea. That fixes the time of death at sometime around four.

"Back home, he paints the door and then spills the rest of the paint on the carpet. After dark, he drives the El Camino to the boat ramp. He sets the parking brake, gets out, and moves Randy's body to the driver's seat. Standing next to the car, he pulls the transmission into Drive, releases the parking brake, and slams the door as the car heads toward the water.

"The next part is the big question mark. How did he get back home? The original investigators searched the taxi logs and accounted for all the cab rides that night. If he didn't take a cab, someone else had to have given him a ride. Hammond and Turner were in communication with someone named Trayborn who had information about Devonshire's ride, but they both died."

"What about Mrs. Devonshire?" Kim asked. "If all you say is true, she had to have been an active participant in the cover-up. Could she have been there to give her husband a ride home?"

"I think that's possible. I've heard of other cases where a mother facilitated a sexual relationship between her husband and her daughter. It comes down to the question of when she left Salishan. We know she was there Friday evening, but so far, I haven't found anything to support her claim that she drove home Saturday morning after Devonshire reported Jessie missing. If she did drive home in the middle of the night to help Devonshire dispose of the El Camino, it would explain why she was asleep the next day."

"That's a pretty good theory," Kim mused. "I really can't see any holes in it."

"The only problem is Trayborn. Hammond seemed sure that Trayborn held the key to the case, but I have been completely unable to find out who Trayborn was. Martha spent most of the week compiling a list of everyone who worked with Devonshire, and there's nobody named Trayborn. I've been through old phone directories, county real estate records, genealogical websites, and public records for births, deaths and marriages, and I've come up empty."

"Maybe Trayborn wasn't someone Devonshire knew—maybe he was someone who had seen Mrs. Devonshire leave Salishan in the middle of the night instead of in the morning," Kim suggested.

"Good point. I hadn't thought of that. I'll have to broaden my search for Trayborn to cover that possibility. More work for Martha."

We sat in silence for a few minutes, sipping our wine.

"There's another angle to this that you have to watch out for," I told her.

"What's that?"

I showed her the note attached to the weapons lab report. "Someone's going to be made a scapegoat here. In order for the murder-suicide theory to hold water, it is necessary to blame someone for tampering with the gun—someone who was present when the gun was found."

"There's no way! I saw Elkton take the weapon out of the car and put it directly into the Tupperware box. Nobody put a hand on that gun."

"I believe you. But if Kerby ever gets pressured on this point, somebody is going to have to take the blame."

"We all saw the same thing. Nobody messed with the gun, and there's no chance that anyone there will ever say otherwise," Kim insisted.

"I hope you're right, babe. I hope you're right."

CHAPTER 31

MONDAY, AUGUST 8

Martha was spending her day in Portland again, beating the bushes in search of anyone named Trayborn among the broadcasting personalities of 1980. When I went out to get my mail I saw Bud approaching from down the alley.

"You remember that little black Jap car?" he asked. "It came back."

"Really? When?"

"Yesterday afternoon, while you were gone. They got out and knocked on your door, and then they hung around on your porch."

"What were they doing?"

"I couldn't tell. Their car was in the way."

"How long were they there?"

"One beer," Bud said, "then they got in the car and left."

As a unit of time, one beer was about ten minutes, the average time a can of beer lasted in Bud's hand.

I didn't think they had tried to break in, because if they had, they'd have triggered the alarm. My security system was far better than what the average home burglar would ever encounter. So what had they done on my porch for ten minutes?

There were really only two possible explanations for the ten minutes the men spent at my place. Either they were looking for a way to defeat my security system or they were planting a listening device—a bug. The likelihood that their visit had been an innocent social call was too small to even consider.

They were pretty good. After forty-five minutes, I still hadn't found so much as a hint that they'd been there. That told me that they weren't inexperienced. And they weren't amateurs. If they'd planted a bug, it wouldn't be something from Radio Shack. It would be something worthy of their demonstrated skills at concealing their work.

After Bud left, I went down onto my dock and made a phone call to a shadowy character who knew more about electronic intelligence gathering than most of the people who did it for a living. He offered to come out and do a sweep.

"If there's anything there, I'll find it," he said confidently.

An hour later, he drove up in a Comcast Cable company van.

"Do you really work for Comcast?" I asked.

"Sure. And you're going to get a bill for this service call too." He got out a hand held multiband scanner. "You have a good stereo?" he asked. And without waiting for an answer, he said, "Go turn it on—loud."

"I hope they like Elvis," I said.

I switched on *Elvis' Golden Records Volume 3* and cranked up the volume. A sophisticated listening device would be sound actuated. It would transmit a signal only when there was sound in the house. Elvis would take care of that.

By the time I walked back outside, the Comcast technician was kneeling on the porch, pushing a round-headed pin into the siding about a foot above floor level. He continued his scan, walking around the side of the house, waving his wand up and down as he went. He pushed another pin into the siding below my bedroom window.

"Pretty good transmitters," he commented. "State of the art. High band VHF. You pick your enemies well. Now go turn down the volume— slowly, so I can see how sensitive these things are."

A few minutes later, he signaled me to turn it back up and join him outside.

"They're *very* good units. They'll pick up a whisper from ten feet. What do you want to do with them?" he asked.

"I think I'll leave 'em there for now," I said. I saw the disappointment on his face. "Don't worry. They're yours when I decide to take 'em out."

"Cool," he said, almost drooling.

"What do you figure their range is?"

"A hundred, maybe two hundred yards, if their receiver is as good as their transmitters."

"What would it look like?"

"Oh jeez. It could look like anything—a birdhouse, a mailbox, an electrical junction box—who knows? If you find it, can I have it too?" he asked.

I nodded, and he said, "Far out!"

Then he walked around to my cable box, opened it up, and fiddled with the wiring for a few minutes. "Now you have Showtime, HBO, and the NFL Sunday package," he said. He scribbled out an invoice and handed it to me. "Hope you enjoy them."

He climbed into his van and drove away. I went inside and turned Elvis down to a normal level. I pulled up my address on Google Maps, zoomed out enough to show the surrounding blocks, and pressed the print button. Knowing that all of the lots in Canemah were fifty by one hundred feet, it was easy to get the scale.

I opened the drawer that contained my long-obsolete drafting instruments and found a compass, with which I measured and drew a two-hundred-yard arc centered from my house. The receiver could be anyplace within that radius. It was a lot of ground to cover, but then again, logic would rule out a lot of it.

For example, it wasn't likely that the receiver would be on my side of Highway 99. It was simply too small a community with too little traffic. Someone would have to periodically change out the memory cards and batteries. They'd be too easily spotted in our neighborhood.

After waiting several minutes for a break in the traffic, I loped across the highway. Starting at the western end of my search radius, I walked the sidewalk along the highway, looking for any kind of box that could conceal the receiver. When I reached the eastern edge of my search area, I turned the corner and walked a block south to Third Avenue.

Looking at telephone poles, trees, houses, and sheds, I walked back to the western perimeter, finding nothing. I never assumed that it would be easy to spot. I turned and walked the same route in the reverse direction—sometimes things are visible from one direction, but not from the other. I walked up and down each of the cross streets that ran between the highway and Third Avenue.

When I was nearly back to where I started, I stood looking at the neighborhood eyesore. The Captain Cochran House was built in 1869 and was a protected historical structure. But it was in a serious state of neglect, and the current owner—an old coot named Herb Goble—had shown no inclination to perform even the most basic maintenance. The roof shingles were curling, the paint was peeling, and the landscaping was badly neglected. A weathered real-estate sign barely showed above the blackberry brambles that had invaded the front yard.

Back before I bought my cottage on Water Street, my real estate agent, Kaylin Beatty, showed me two newly constructed homes that she had just listed. They faced Third Avenue and shared their rear property line with Herb's place. They were nice houses and modestly priced for new construction, but they weren't what I was looking for.

"What the hell?" Kaylin remarked when we walked out into the backyard.

A garden hose was connected to the back of the new house and strung across the bare ground of the yard into the weeds behind Herb's house and disappeared through a basement window. Next to it was a yellow ten gauge extension cord, plugged into the patio outlet on the new house. It too vanished through the window of Herb's house.

Kaylin walked over and pulled the plug. The radio that had been playing went silent, and a moment later, Herb peeked out a back window. The instant he saw us, he ducked back out of sight. Next, Kaylin turned off the water faucet, and I helped her unscrew the hose.

We walked over, and Kaylin pounded on Herb's back door, nearly dislodging it from its hinges.

"Who is it? What do you want?" came the grumpy voice from inside.

"It's Kaylin Beatty, your neighbor. I'm a Realtor."

The door creaked open to reveal a fat, bald old man wearing a dirty undershirt. Seeing Kaylin, he turned on the charm.

Scratching his substantial belly, he asked, "What can I do for you, little lady?"

"I'm afraid you're going to have to get your water and electricity somewhere else, Herb," Kaylin told him.

"What's it matter to you?" Herb asked.

"I represent the builder," Kaylin explained, "and I'm pretty sure he doesn't want you using his water and electricity."

"Hell, those guys don't give a shit," Herb complained.

"We can find out," Kaylin offered cheerfully, pulling her cell phone out of her purse.

"Forget it," Herb grumbled. "It was only for a couple of days."

Within the next week, Kaylin's builder had a six-foot fence constructed across the back property line, effectively cutting off Herb's access to free utilities.

Having lost his source of water and electricity, Herb had finally moved out, and the Cochran House had been unoccupied ever since. Vacant and neglected, the house continued to deteriorate. Windows were broken out by vandals, and a greenish patina of moss covered the siding on the east and north sides of the house.

That's why the telephone junction box on the east side of the house caught my eye. The gray metal box was faded and weathered, but it was completely free of moss. Taking a closer look, I could see where someone had recently waded through the tall grass from the alley to the side of the house where the box was mounted. No doubt about it. I'd found the receiver.

I could have easily removed the box—and made my Comcast friend happy—but I felt it was better to leave it in place. Whoever installed it would come back, probably within the next couple of days, to collect the memory chip and check the batteries.

Back home, I dug through some boxes in my garage until I found the components of a simple wireless remote security system—something I'd picked up cheap on eBay to catch the teenage reprobate who'd been stealing things from the docks.

With a cordless drill and screwdriver, I mounted the solar-powered motion detector on a tree, where it would be triggered by anyone approaching the gray box. The English ivy that covered the tree trunk provided the necessary camouflage for the motion detector. I switched it on and then walked over toward the gray box and immediately heard the chirping sound from the receiver that I'd left on my back porch.

By the time I got back across the highway, Bud was out in the alley looking for the source of the sound that had interrupted his morning sleep. It wasn't quite noon.

"Sorry about the noise," I apologized.

"You put a new alarm on your SUV?" Bud asked.

"No, just testing the security system."

"Think it'll catch the dudes in the black car?"

"I'm working on that," I said evasively.

It took a few minutes and a can of beer to get myself free from Bud. I had another call to make. My plan wasn't to catch the guys who planted the bugs. It was to determine who they were. I really wanted to know who was so interested in what I was doing that he would spend several thousand dollars on surveillance equipment.

I next placed a call to my favorite gadget guy. After explaining exactly what I had in mind, I asked him if he could come up with something to do the job.

"Corrigan, believe it or not, you aren't the first person on earth who wanted to do that," he said.

"Then you have what I need?" I asked.

"I have a couple of options. Come over and take a look."

An hour later, on the other side of the Columbia River, I pulled up in front of Jerry Midland's pawnshop. He greeted me at the door and led me into his storeroom. Rows of steel shelves contained everything, from engagement rings to Fender guitars, each item identified by a pawn ticket. In the back of the room was a long workbench cluttered with tools and electronic equipment.

"This is the cheapest," Jerry told me, holding what appeared to be a spring-loaded lever. "Only problem is that it's pretty easy to see after it's been triggered." He showed me a different device and said, "Now this one is harder to set up, but after it's triggered, it retracts back into the ground, so it's almost impossible to see."

I nodded. "That's the one I want."

"Okay, here's what you do. You dig a hole about a foot deep, so that the entire cylinder is buried in a vertical position. The transmitter fits onto the end of the push rod."

The cylinder looked like one of the things that hold up the tailgate glass on a station wagon. It was about ten inches long and an inch in diameter. The stainless steel push rod protruded about half an inch from the top of the cylinder. A flexible plastic tube led from the bottom of the cylinder to what Jerry called the actuator block.

"You screw a CO_2 cartridge into the block. That'll puncture the seal and arm the actuator. When you transmit the trigger signal, the actuator valve opens, releasing the compressed gas into the cylinder. The push rod extends and raises the transmitter up to the bottom of the car. There is an alnico magnet attached to the transmitter housing so it sticks to the car. After one second, the pressure is released and the push rod retracts back underground."

"That's pretty slick," I said with true admiration.

"Next question is, what kind of tracker do you want to install?" Jerry asked.

"Well, I need real-time tracking, but I doubt that I'll be able to retrieve the transmitter, so I'll need something cheap."

"You understand that you're really going to sacrifice capabilities and performance."

"I know, but I don't want to throw away an expensive GPS device."

He showed me a miniature circuit board. "Here's a simple ten-dollar GMRS transponder. It's the same thing that people use to track their model rockets. You install this on your target. It receives a signal on one GMRS channel, and retransmits it on a different one."

"What good will that do?"

"Ah, Grasshopper, it is my magic box that makes the system useful," he said, holding up a plastic case about the size of a Walkman. It had a pair of suction cups on one side and a coiled cord with a cigarette-lighter plug on the end. A short antenna protruded from the top.

"You stick this little box on your windshield. It contains three components," Jerry explained. "First, there's a GMRS transmitter that sends out a 1 kHz beep every half second. That is the signal received by the transponder, which then returns it on a different channel.

"The second component is a radio direction finder—an RDF. It measures the time lapse between the original outgoing signal and the return signal from the transponder and calculates how far away the transponder is. It also pinpoints the transponder's direction relative to your location, giving you both range and azimuth.

"But it's the third component that makes the whole thing work. It reformats the range and azimuth data and sends it to your iPhone mapping system. With the RDF app installed, the location of the transponder is superimposed on the iPhone's map display."

"Sounds good," I said. "Can I install the transponder with the CO_2 cylinder?"

"Give me two minutes," Jerry answered.

He used Super Glue to attach a plastic socket to one side of the transponder box and a rectangular magnet to the other. The socket was sized to fit the end of the push rod.

"That magnet will hold the transponder so tight you'll probably have to pry it off with a screwdriver. GMRS range is about a quarter mile. The

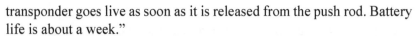

transponder goes live as soon as it is released from the push rod. Battery life is about a week."

"Perfect," I said. "What's it going to cost?"

"The whole system, including the iPhone app and the CO_2 cylinder," Jerry said, "comes to about six hundred fifty dollars. Or I'll rent it to you for one hundred dollars."

I couldn't think of any other way to install an electronic tracker that didn't involve a significant risk of being seen. With Jerry's device, I could install the transponder by remote control. I put the hundred on my Visa card and talked Jerry into throwing in an extra CO_2 cartridge so that I could test the system one time before the real thing.

That evening, I sat on the porch with Kim while the Beatles played on the stereo. When she had finished her second glass of Merlot, I said I needed her help for a few minutes.

She looked at me suggestively and asked, "What do you have in mind?"

Well, that too," I said, "but first I need you to drive me across the highway and around the block."

"Is this a new kind of foreplay?"

"No, it's a science project."

"So why do you need *my* help?" Suspicion was clouding her pretty face.

"If I drive over and park next to Herb's place, somebody might call the cops. But if *you* drive me over, they won't call the cops because you *are* the cops."

She looked at me warily. "Something tells me that this could blow up under my ass."

"I'll be finished in five minutes. Even if someone calls it in, we'll be long gone before the city cops arrive," I assured her.

"Are you going to tell me what this is all about?"

"You remember the guys in the black Acura?" I began.

She nodded.

"Well, they came back yesterday and installed a couple of listening devices in the house," I continued. "I located their receiver up on old Herb Goble's house. They'll have to come back within in a couple of days to change memory cards and batteries. While they're doing that, this little button will install a tracker on their car."

My persuasive charm won out, and Kim let me load Jerry's gadget and a post hole digger into the back of her marine unit Explorer.

"This better not cause me any trouble," she groused.

"Nobody's even going to see us. And if they do, they'll just assume it's official business," I assured her.

We drove around the block and down the alley from Third Avenue. Next to Herb's house, I found the tracks where the black Acura had been parked on their last visit. Fortunately, there was only one parking spot—everything else was overgrown. I could count on my friends to park in the same place on their next visit.

Kim stopped next to the parking spot, and I got the post hole digger out of her Explorer. I picked a spot that I figured would be under the floor pan of the Acura when it was parked there and plunged the post hole digger into the ground. It was soft, and digging was easy. Within five minutes, I had a neat hole deep enough for the push rod assembly.

I adjusted the depth of the hole until the push rod would sit with the transponder just below ground level, and then I carefully packed dirt around the unit. When the hole was half full, I sent Kim back to my place to press the button. This test would verify that the triggering unit had adequate range to activate the push rod.

My phone chirped, and Kim said, "All ready."

"Okay, let's see if this thing works," I said. A moment later, there was a click and a hiss. The push rod rose up to full extension and then slowly withdrew. "Works fine. I'll be down in a few minutes."

I installed the new CO_2 cartridge and then placed the actuator block back in the hole, with only the antenna wire sticking out above ground level. Carefully, I packed dirt around the cylinder and actuator block until the hole was almost completely filled. I placed the transponder on top of the push rod and nestled it into the hole. A handful of pea gravel over the top concealed the whole setup.

"Now what?" Kim asked when I returned home.

"When they come back, I'll push that button and then follow them home."

"No, I mean now what are *we* going to do?" she persisted.

"Whatever we want to do."

"Not with those people listening!" Kim protested.

I showed her how I'd turned my stereo speakers toward the walls where the bugs were planted. "They won't hear anything but the Beatles—and that's assuming that I haven't already run their batteries dead.

These things are made for intermittent use, and I've kept them transmitting all day."

Kim was skeptical, so I poured her another glass of Merlot.

"Maybe we could watch *Bridges of Madison County*," I suggested.

"And then listen to some heavy metal," Kim said.

CHAPTER 32

TUESDAY, AUGUST 9

Crime investigation is mainly a process of elimination. Even as more and more evidence pointed at Wilson Landis Devonshire, I still had not conclusively eliminated Randy Mendelson as a party to the crime. All three of Jessie Devonshire's schoolmates had indicated that she was involved with an older man, and there were good reasons to believe that the relationship was sexual.

It was Wilson Devonshire who had first made the claim that Jessie had been dating Randy. I went to my database and keyed in a query based on the keyword "dating" and several variations, hunting for any corroborating witnesses to Devonshire's claim. No mater how many ways I queried the database, the only document that came up was Hammond's interview of Devonshire on the day after the disappearance.

I pulled up the transcript of that interview to take another look. It was the same interview where Hammond had asked about the paint stain on the carpet. Last time I looked at the document, I'd been so focused on the part about the paint I hadn't paid much attention to the part about the date.

Hammond: When you reported your daughter missing this morning, you indicated that she had gone out on a date.

Devonshire: Yes. That's correct.

Hammond: Did you see her leave the house?

Devonshire: No. She was already gone when I got home.

Hammond: You didn't see her at all last night?

Devonshire: No. Like I said, she was gone before I got home.

Hammond: How do you know she went out on a date?

Devonshire: I talked to her on the phone. She called me in my office and said she was going out to dinner with her boyfriend.

Hammond: Do you have any idea who she went with?

Devonshire: No. I should have asked, but I was in the middle of something and just said okay.

Hammond: Isn't she a little bit young to be going out?

Devonshire: Jessie is a precocious girl. She's quite responsible for her age.

Hammond: Let me change the subject, okay? What do you know about Randall Mendelson?

Devonshire: Huh? Randy? He's the gardener. He works here sometimes, takes care of the yard.

Hammond: When was the last time he was here?

Devonshire: I'd have to check my calendar to be sure.

Hammond: Mr. Devonshire, are you aware that Randy Mendelson was also reported missing last night?

Devonshire: I hadn't heard anything about that.

Hammond: Did Jessie ever meet Mendelson?

Devonshire: Um, I guess, well yeah, sure. I mean, he's around here several times a month.

Hammond: Did she ever go out with him?

Devonshire: She talked about him.

Hammond: Could she have been going out with him last night?

Devonshire: She might have, I guess. That's possible. I mean, they'd dated before.

Hammond: They dated before?

Devonshire: I don't know the details.

Hammond: He's quite a bit older than her. Didn't that worry you?

Devonshire: Yeah, well like I said, she's precocious. She's always been a handful.

Hammond: What do you mean?

Devonshire: Oh, you know. She's just headstrong--has to have things her way.

Hammond: But you don't know if she went out with Randy last night?

Devonshire: If I had to guess, I'd say she did.

Hammond: Based on what?

Devonshire: Oh, just that they were friends. I can't think of anyone else she dated.

Hammond: Nobody else?

Devonshire: He's the only one I know of.

I read through the transcript three times. At the beginning of the interview, Devonshire didn't have any idea who Jessie had gone out with. Two minutes later, he was almost sure it had been Randy Mendelson. But he had never mentioned Randy until after Hammond brought up the name.

It looked to me like he changed his story right in the middle of the interview. But once Devonshire made the connection between Randy and Jessie, it became one of the defining "facts" of the case. If you were to ask anyone about the case, even in the sheriff's office, they'd say that Randy had been dating Jessie. Yet as hard as I tried, I could find no support for Devonshire's claim.

 ∂∞∽

When the motion detector alarm started chirping, I rushed out into the alley and looked up toward the Captain Cochran house. The black Acura was parked in the turnout. I hurried back inside and grabbed my keys and the actuator button.

I pressed the button as I climbed into my Yukon. I inserted my iPhone into its cradle and brought up the mapping function. It showed a red dot in the alley on the other side of Highway 99E. The transponder was active. I backed out to Water Street and drove a block east before turning toward the highway. While I waited for a gap in the traffic, the Acura started to move.

It was impossible to see through the car's darkened windows as it pulled onto the highway, heading north. A few moments later, I saw a small gap in traffic and bolted across the southbound lanes to drop in a hundred yards behind the Acura. My big Yukon is not the ideal vehicle for tailing someone in terms of keeping a low profile. I'd have to stay as far back as I dared to minimize the risk of being spotted.

We went north, past the Willamette Falls viewpoint, through the tunnel, and out along the Oregon City riverfront. Traffic was relatively heavy, which was good. With a lot of other cars around, there was less chance that my subject would notice me. I settled in about four or five cars back, and we crossed the green bridge over the Clackamas River into Gladstone.

At Jennings Road, the traffic signal changed to yellow just as the Acura went under it. The next two cars sneaked through on yellow, but the driver in front of me stepped on the brake. On my iPhone map display, I watched the red dot move north.

"Come on, come on," I growled, attempting to influence the behavior of the traffic signal.

Helplessly, I sat there waiting for the light to change while the Acura disappeared up the highway. Thumping impatiently on the steering wheel, I watched the RDF receiver lose its signal. The red dot vanished from my iPhone. And still the traffic light stayed red.

By the time the light finally turned green, the Acura was at least half a mile away, well out of range. And I was trapped behind a dirty Oldsmobile driven by a white haired geezer, who appeared to have misplaced his gas pedal. Cars in the left lane zipped past, leaving no gap for me to change lanes, and I contemplated pressing the four-wheel-drive button and driving right over the top of the Oldsmobile.

In my left side mirror, I saw a lady in a mini-van. She wasn't quite keeping up with the Chevy that was going past me. When the Chevy was half an inch past my front bumper, I held my breath, hit the gas, and pulled left in front of the mini-van, hoping it had good brakes. It did. And a good horn too.

I made an apologetic wave to the mini-van lady as I accelerated past the Oldsmobile, whose driver was still plodding along at fifteen miles an hour, totally oblivious to the quarter-mile line of frustrated drivers behind him. I pressed as far beyond the forty-mile-per-hour speed limit as I dared, changing lanes several times, to get past slower cars.

The Acura was no place to be seen. I drove past the Bomber, a World War II B-17 that had been mounted on poles above a gas station, the wings providing shelter for the gas pumps. The gas station had closed down years before, but the B-17 was still there, a local landmark. But all I cared about was the Acura.

North of the Bomber, the city of Milwaukie slows traffic to thirty miles an hour with a notorious speed trap. I could only hope that the Acura would get held up by the traffic signals ahead. Impatiently, I plodded along with the surrounding traffic until I got past the Highway 224 interchange.

The next couple of miles consist of the last remnants of the fabled Super Highway. In the 1930s, while Germany was building the autobahn, the Oregon Highway Department built the Super Highway, a four-lane concrete thoroughfare that ran from Portland to Oregon City. There were no traffic signals on the fifteen mile length of the Super Highway, so drivers in their Model A Fords could make the entire trip at full speed—about sixty miles per hour.

North of Milwaukie, in sections of the limited-access divided highway, it is still common for cars to reach sixty or more, even though the posted speed is forty-five. I went as fast as the traffic would allow. As I approached Holgate Blvd., the red dot on my iPhone flashed back to life, indicating that the Acura was about five blocks ahead.

I pressed my luck, running a couple of signals on yellow and weaving past slower cars. Just north of the SE Powell overpass, the dot on the map exited to the right. I hurried to catch up. The Acura went a couple of blocks east and then turned right again. A block later, it made another right turn onto Powell, heading west.

The driver led me across the Ross Island Bridge and took the exit toward downtown Portland, then north on Corbett Ave. I had him in sight as he drove beneath the huge freeway interchange where I-405 joins I-5. He made a left turn onto Caruthers Street, and at the end of the block, he stopped.

On my iPhone screen, I could see that Caruthers was a dead end, so instead of turning, I found a place to park. From the back of the Yukon, I grabbed a yellow hard hat, an orange vest with an Oregon Department of Transportation logo, and a clipboard—not much of a disguise, but most people will focus on the uniform, not the face.

Walking up Caruthers Street, I found a concrete block building with a pair of garage doors on the front. On the left, there was a window and an entry door. The glass was edged with a metallic ribbon, indicating the presence of a security system. Above the door was the number 21. The right-hand garage door was open, and the Acura was inside. Simultaneously, the right-hand garage door started down and the left-hand door started to rise.

Ducking behind some brush at the end of the street, I watched a man appear briefly in the doorway. He was not the gangsta drug dealer you might expect to see driving a black Acura with dark-tinted windows. He was a fifty-five to sixty-year-old man with gray hair worn in a crew cut. He was dressed in blue jeans and t-shirt, and he looked remarkably fit. He carried himself like a marine as he walked around the back of a gray Ford Taurus parked in the second bay.

There must be thousands of gray Ford Taurus sedans in Oregon, but I couldn't help believing that this was the same one that had followed me the day I went to visit Leslie Turner Charleston. I jotted down the plate number as the Taurus backed out onto the street. As it pulled away, the garage door started down. When the Taurus turned out of sight, I sprinted over and waved my clipboard under the nearly closed garage door.

The clipboard interrupted the photoelectric sensor, and somewhere, a relay clicked, reversing the motor and sending the door back up. I quickly searched inside the Acura but found nothing of interest. I knelt down and used my Leatherman tool to pry the transponder loose from the floor pan.

There was little else to see in the garage. The door to the partitioned-off office area on the left was locked, and I didn't want to take a chance on triggering the security system. I went out front to look in the window but found it covered by a mini blind. Back in the garage area, I looked around for the overhead-door buttons.

I found them on the wall between the two overhead doors, and on hooks beneath each button was a remote control—apparently spares. I tested one, and the open door started to descend. This was an unexpected piece of luck. I hurried back to my Yukon with the garage door remote and used it to program one of the buttons on my overhead console.

I drove up in front of the concrete block building and confirmed that my programmed button worked, and then I returned the remote to its hook, closed the door, and left. If I ever needed to get back into that building, I would be able to do it with the push of a button. I love modern conveniences.

Back home, I dug out a bottle of King's Hill Pinot Noir and walked over to Kaylin Beatty's house. I traded the wine for some quick work on her computer. She looked up the Multnomah County property-tax records for 21 SW Caruthers St. in Portland.

"The property is owned by RTE Consulting LLC. The property-tax bill goes to Richard T. Elgin at 2530 SW Hillcrest Drive in Portland," she told me.

"Consulting—isn't that another word for *unemployed*?" I mused.

After a few more keystrokes, she said, "RTE Consulting has no other real estate in Multnomah County." A few seconds later, she said, "Mr. Elgin bought his home in 1977, for $155,000. The property is currently assessed at $810,000. Nice piece of real estate. Looks like he also owns a pair of duplexes in Beaverton. He bought those in 1989."

"Is there any way you can find out more about RTE Consulting?"

"No, this is about the limit of my access to public records."

After printing all of the records she'd found, she led me back to the door. I went back to my office and clicked on my computer. While it booted up, I went outside to where my Comcast friend had located the listening devices. Under my front window, I noticed that the bug had been planted adjacent to the end of a strip of siding. I worked a putty knife under the end of the board and easily pried it out enough to see that a hole had been drilled through the sheathing underneath.

A wire hung out of the hole, and when I pulled on it, a small cylindrical object came out of the wall. That was the listening device that Richard Elgin and his friend had planted. I went around to the side and found the same situation under my bedroom window and an identical device inside the wall.

I took a few tools across the highway, where I used a screwdriver to open the gray box on the side of Herb's house. Inside was a plastic box containing the receiver and digital recording device. I took it out and replaced it with something given to me as a gag gift many years ago—a carved wooden hand with the middle finger extended in a well-understood gesture.

CHAPTER 33

WEDNESDAY, AUGUST 10

The Comcast van arrived shortly before eight. When I showed my friend the electronic devices I'd removed from my walls and the gray box attached to the Cochran House, his eyes went wide.

"Dude, those are *radical*!" he exclaimed.

I thought that term had gone out of fashion about thirty years ago. Nevertheless, I handed him the box containing the components. "They're yours as promised. No instruction manuals, however, and I think the batteries might be dead," I told him.

"Oh wow, thanks man!" he said with the gratitude of a kid receiving his first bicycle.

"I may ask to borrow those sometime," I ventured.

"No, problem. Hey, I gotta get going—service call in Gladstone."

As the Comcast van pulled out, Martha's Subaru took its place.

"Cable trouble?" Martha asked.

"Nope, just checking the connection," I said evasively as we walked inside.

"Well, let me show you everything I found out downtown," Martha said, holding out her empty hands. I handed her a cup of coffee, about one-third cream, the way she liked it.

"This Trayborn guy is a ghost. I've searched everywhere I can think of, and there is no record of anybody named Trayborn. I even tried different spellings and still came up empty," Martha explained.

"That's disappointing," I said. "I've really been counting on finding him."

"Right now, I don't know where else to look."

"Okay, well, that's how it works sometimes. Let's just put that aside for now. Maybe we'll find him through some other lines—I mean, Trayborn is a key figure in this whole thing. He's bound to come up again. Meanwhile, I have another name for you. And this one is no ghost. I'd like to know everything you can find out about a Richard T. Elgin."

I gave her his address and his company's name and address, along with the license plate numbers for the Taurus and Acura. On the computer, I showed her half a dozen websites where she could go to gather personal information about anybody.

"Can I ask how he's connected to all of this?" Martha asked.

"He planted listening devices in my walls." I pointed to the place where I'd removed one of the transmitters.

"What?" she said in astonishment.

"Yeah. Sunday evening, Bud saw him here with a friend. I found the bugs, and I followed him to his company headquarters."

"Why on earth would he bug your office?"

"Not just the office. He bugged my bedroom too. As to why, that's what I hope to find out by learning more about Mr. Elgin."

We were interrupted by the chirping of the motion detector alarm. Someone was approaching the gray box on Herb's house. The fact that he was back so soon probably meant that I'd been successful at discharging the batteries. I turned off the alarm and strolled out into the alley just in time to see a man open the metal box.

Upon seeing what was in the box and realizing that his secret was blown, he looked abruptly around. When he looked straight at me, I saw that it was not Richard Elgin. This man was shorter and had dark hair. He took my gift, slammed the box shut, and stormed back to the Acura. Gunning the engine and throwing up a cloud of dust, he shot out onto the highway and was nearly run down by a northbound Dodge Ram pickup.

The pickup's horn and screeching tires brought Bud charging out of his shack. He gaped out at the highway, but the drama was already over.

"Sounded like a close one," he observed.

"Pretty close," I agreed.

"Wasn't that your old friend's car?" he asked, referring to the rapidly disappearing Acura.

"Yeah. I think he could use some counselling on impulse control."

"What's he doing over at Herb Goble's place?"

"Who knows, maybe he wants to buy it."

"Who the hell is he?"

"Damned if I know, but I'll bet he comes back here next time I'm gone," I said—and that made me ponder. Just how in hell did Elgin and his buddy *know* when I was gone?

If they had another listening device, my Comcast friend would have found it. Did they have a tracker on my Yukon? Damn! That's how they followed me home from Leslie Charleston's place! No wonder I lost sight of the gray Taurus. They'd simply pulled back out of sight and kept track electronically. And ever since then, they had been able to tell whether or not I was home.

I went out to my garage. Shining a flashlight under the Yukon, I found a tracking device inside the frame rail near the rear bumper. I recognized it as a Spark Nano Plus—quite possibly the best real-time GPS tracking device you could buy.

It was considerably larger than the little GMRS transponder I'd planted on the Acura because it had a six-month battery. It would start transmitting with any movement of more than a couple of feet. I pried it loose and lowered it to the floor directly beneath where it had been. I opened it up and switched it off before carrying it over to my workbench.

I sat down and tried to think of all the places Elgin would have tracked me. They almost certainly had been right behind me when I went to the storage unit and retrieved Gary Turner's hidden files. That's why they kept coming around that night—they wanted to get those boxes of documents. If I'd gone to bed that night, I'd probably have been dead by morning and they'd have gotten the evidence that had caused them to stalk Leslie Turner for thirty years.

I really doubted that Elgin had the resources to keep watch over me in real time, but the Spark Nano transmitted everything to a data center with a website where Elgin could go anytime and see every move I'd made.

That meant that Elgin knew of my visits to Marion Brighton's place in Sellwood, to Sara Huntington's house on Rosemont Road, to the State Library in Olympia, Washington, the DNA lab in Portland, and to Salem to get Melissa Vale's Christmas card from Jessie.

None of that was good news, but still there were two good reasons to believe that Elgin was not doing full-time surveillance. Number 1, if he'd seen me take the piece of flooring out of Devonshire's old house, he'd have stopped at nothing to prevent me from taking it to the DNA lab. Number 2, if he'd been monitoring his tracker in real time when I was following him, he'd have known I was there and would not have led me to his little shop on Caruthers Street.

But if he had logged on and downloaded my travel history, he'd know that I'd followed him. And if he hadn't downloaded it already, he'd do it as soon as his partner reported that I had found his eavesdropping devices. It seemed likely that these things would force him to do something. Maybe he'd try to install new listening devices—there were ways to make it more difficult to find them—or maybe he'd find some other way to find out what I knew.

My phone rang, and the display screen identified the caller as William Gates.

"Corrigan," I answered.

"Lila Mendelson came to see me," Gates said.

One of the things I liked about Gates was that he didn't waste time on small talk. He got right to the point.

"Did you take the job?" I asked.

"She asked me to deliver a package to Larry Jamieson at CCSO."

"How did that go?"

"I called Jamieson and told him that my client had accidentally removed something from his office and now wanted me to return it. Pretty sure he knew what I was talking about because he didn't ask who my client was. Anyway, he told me not to take it to his office. Instead, we agreed to meet at Shari's Restaurant. The meeting took place this morning."

"Did he ask if Lila had shown it to anyone?"

"Nope. It was a very short meeting. He took the envelope and left. Didn't say a word."

"What's Lila's exposure?"

"None. Jamieson has the envelope back, and on the record he doesn't know who had it or what was done with it."

"Perfect," I said.

"Just wanted to keep you in the loop," he said before hanging up.

CHAPTER 34

n the middle of the afternoon, Martha handed me a print-out containing a summary of everything she had been able to find out about Richard T Elgin:

Born July 20, 1949, Portland, Oregon

Graduated Madison High School, Class of 1965

Enlisted USMC September 22, 1965 Assigned to 5th Regiment, 3rd Battalion

Served Vietnam May 1966-August 1969

Separation from Active Duty Sept.21, 1969

Honorable Discharge September 1971

Employed by Portland Police Bureau May 1970, Retired June 1995

Registered Business Name "RTE Consulting" June 1982

Address since 1977: 2530 SW Hillcrest Drive in Portland

Married August 29, 1981, to Alicia Crabtree, Divorced September 10, 1985

Married January 11, 1986, to Carrie Whitney, Widowed March 26, 1994

Married April 6, 1996, to Kathy Saginaw, Divorced January 13, 1998

Married May 23, 1998, to Christie Brogan, Widowed July 17, 2004

Married November 20, 2004, to Jennifer Crane, Separated February 20, 2009

```
Children: None
Registered Vehicles: 2008 Cadillac
Escalade, 2011 Mercedes SLK 300
Criminal History: None
Credit Score: 780
Acura & Taurus are registered to RTE
Consulting LLC
```

"I don't see anything here that connects Elgin to our case," Martha observed.

"The connection is that RTE Consulting had somebody watching Gary Turner's widow. When I went to see her, they latched onto me," I told her.

"Yes, I know. But the question is, why?"

"Elgin was anticipating that someone might pay a visit to Leslie Turner," I speculated. "My best guess is that he was tipped off by one of the former CCSO deputies I visited—Odell, Haines, or Buxton. They didn't know who I was because I showed them fake media credentials, so Elgin couldn't come straight to me, but he could anticipate that I would end up visiting Gary Turner's widow."

Martha nodded slowly and said, "That would establish a connection between Elgin and one of the former deputies, but not to Mendelson-Devonshire."

"When you get a chance, search the database for any contact between the sheriff's office and the Portland Police during the 1980 investigation since Elgin was a Portland cop at the time."

Martha scribbled a note.

"We also need to follow-up on Elgin's wives. Locate the living ones and find out what happened to the dead ones," I said.

Still making notes, she commented, "Isn't it pretty unusual for a man to be widowed *twice*?"

I nodded. "Very. That's why I want to know how Carrie Whitney and Christie Brogan died. I'm betting that it wasn't natural causes."

"You think he might have killed them?"

"I don't know enough to answer that question, but irrespective of that, I'm starting to think that this investigation is pretty dangerous."

Looking startled, Martha asked, "What do you mean?"

"Well, you remember where the *Trayborn* name first came up?"

Martha nodded. "It was in Leslie Turner's note—Hammond was going to meet Trayborn."

"And Hammond was murdered, probably by Trayborn."

"Yes, but—"

"Then two weeks later, Turner was dead too," I reminded her.

"But that was thirty years ago!"

"Listening devices, late-night visits, tracking devices—these things all tell me that someone is very interested in what we're doing here—and they're willing to spend a lot of money to find out."

"Elgin," she said simply.

"Not just him. We know that Elgin has at least one accomplice, the other guy in the Acura, and I'm pretty sure that there's another—the person who tipped him about my inquiry."

Martha nodded.

"Now, there's no way to tell if they have any idea what *you've* been doing here or how much you might know," I continued. "They were unsuccessful at bugging the office to find out. But it is not impossible that they were watching you in Portland."

"Then they'd know that I was looking for Trayborn."

"Yes, but they'd also know that you came up empty."

"So does that mean I'm safe?" she asked plaintively.

"It might. But the minute they start to think that we're a threat, we'll *both* be in serious danger."

"I see."

"I think you're safe while you're here, but once you're alone, anything could happen."

"So what should I do?"

"The safe thing would be to get out now before things get ugly."

She pondered that for a few moments before saying, "But I *like* working here, and I really *need* the job!"

"Well, I have to say I think you are way too vulnerable by yourself in your apartment—and maybe even on the road."

"So what can I do?"

"I've been thinking about that, and as I said, the safest thing would be to get out now before you're marked."

"But you don't know that I'm not already marked," she objected.

"Unfortunately, that's true. If I had an extra room, I'd happily let you stay here, but—"

"Maybe someone else in the neighborhood has an extra room."

"I've been thinking about that too," I said, "but I don't feel good about sharing our troubles with someone else."

Martha sighed. "No, that wouldn't be right."

Then an idea came to me. "You probably haven't met Bud's son, Daryl Tiernan—he lives next door. He has a live-aboard that nobody's using right now. I'll bet you could rent it pretty cheap. That way, you'd be right here in the neighborhood—and not much happens here without someone seeing it."

"What's a live-aboard?" Martha asked.

"In this case, it's a thirty-four-foot Sea Ray with a blown engine."

"A boat?"

"Want to take a look?"

She nodded, so I went to the refrigerator and pulled out three cans of beer. I led Martha over to Bud's shack, handed her a beer, and knocked on the door. I got a glimpse of Bud peeking through a gap in the blind.

"Hold on a second," Bud called.

"We were taking a break, and I thought you might like to join us for a beer," I said loudly.

"It'll just be a minute."

"We'll be down by the river."

Martha and I walked across the railroad tracks and down the steps to the beach. I pointed to Daryl's Sea Ray tied up at his dock.

"Daryl neglected to drain the engines last winter, and they froze. When he started her up last spring, one of the engines went up in smoke. She's been sitting there ever since."

Bud arrived, his hair wet and freshly combed. He wore clean clothes for the second time in less than a month, and I was pretty sure it was not to impress me.

"We were just admiring Daryl's boat," I said. "Has he made any progress toward getting it running?"

"Naw, he's going to have to replace the engines," Bud replied.

"Wow. That's too bad," I sympathized. "Hey, you don't suppose he'd be willing to let Martha live aboard for a month or two?"

Bud looked stumped for a moment and then broke into a grin. "I don't know why not—he isn't using it for anything."

"Could we take a look?" Martha asked.

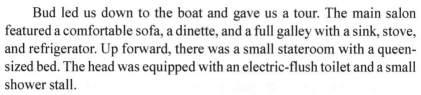

Bud led us down to the boat and gave us a tour. The main salon featured a comfortable sofa, a dinette, and a full galley with a sink, stove, and refrigerator. Up forward, there was a small stateroom with a queen-sized bed. The head was equipped with an electric-flush toilet and a small shower stall.

"All the comforts of home," Bud extolled.

"Is she connected to water and sewer?" I asked.

"Not at the moment, but it won't take but a few minutes to hook it up," Bud said.

"What do you think Daryl will want for rent?" Martha asked.

Bud scratched his head and said, "Don't know. But if you like, I'll talk to him about it tonight."

We finished our beers and sauntered back up to my front porch. When Martha and I went inside, Bud went back into his shack. Martha was pretty excited about the prospect of taking up residence on Daryl's boat.

"If that works out," I said, "I think you'll be pretty safe there."

"It'll save me a *ton* of gas and travel time."

"Well, let's call it quits for today. I'll call and let you know what Daryl says."

After Martha left, I got Elgin's tracker and snapped a couple of pictures of it with my phone. I left it on the workbench in my garage and backed out. As long as it was turned off, the tracker would make it appear that I was home and thus discourage a visit by my adversaries while I drove to Jerry Midland's pawnshop in Vancouver.

I handed Jerry the box containing his tracking system and said, "That did the job. I especially like the way the cylinder system worked. And the interface with the iPhone is great! But a stronger transmitter would have been useful."

"Yeah," Jerry said, "that's the problem with GMRS. I could give it a more powerful transmitter, but it wouldn't be legal."

"What can you tell me about this unit?" I asked, showing him the photo of Elgin's tracker on my phone.

"Sweet! A Spark Nano Plus. Where'd you get that?"

"Someone planted it on my Yukon."

"And what would you like to know about it?"

"Well, first, is there any way to erase data from its server?"

"You'd need to have the owner's user name and password to log on."

"Would you be able to get that data if you had this unit?" I asked, indicating the unit in the photos.

"Not likely. I would expect the transmitter to have a built-in log-on algorithm—something completely different from the user log-on."

It was what I figured. "In that case, can I reprogram the transmitter and use it myself?"

"Not without the current owner's help. He'd have to transfer his account to you."

"So this is just scrap?" I asked, picking up the photos.

"You got it."

"That's what I figured. Thanks."

That evening, when Daryl Tiernan got home, I broached the subject of renting his boat. "The lady who works for me would like to find a place to live down here," I began.

Daryl said, "I don't know of any vacancies—unless she wants to rent one of the houseboats."

"Actually, I was wondering if you'd entertain the idea of renting your boat to her for a couple of months."

"Never thought about it," Daryl mused. "It wouldn't hurt to have a little extra money coming in."

"What do you figure it'd be worth then?"

"Well, I know that Kaylin gets five hundred dollars a month for her downstairs apartment."

Bud appeared and said, "Daryl, you can't expect that lady to pay five hundred dollars a month for your boat."

"Why not? The houseboats go for five hundred a *weekend*," Daryl objected.

"Yeah, but the houseboats are twelve hundred square feet," I said.

Bud said, "I think two hundred dollars would be about right."

"It's got to be worth four hundred dollars," Daryl shot back. "Three fifty at the minimum."

"Come on, don't be greedy," Bud protested. "You try to get three fifty, you'll end up with nothing."

"What do you know about it anyway?" Daryl demanded.

Bud said, "I know that lady, and two hundred is what she can pay. Any more than that, forget it!"

"What the hell?" Daryl asked, looking at me.

I shrugged. "Bud likes her."

"I just don't want anyone taking advantage of her," Bud said defensively.

"Well, shit," Daryl said in surrender. "Tell her she can have it for fifty dollars a week—but only until I get the new engines."

"All right!" Bud and I said in unison.

With the negotiation finished, I invited Bud and Daryl to join me for a beer. Daryl declined, but Bud followed me over to my porch. While we drank our beers, I called Martha to tell her the good news.

"Fifty dollars a week!" Martha said happily. "That's what I spend for gas driving back and forth from Beaverton."

CHAPTER 35

THURSDAY, AUGUST 11

O nce she had finished moving her things aboard Daryl's boat, Martha and I discussed our plans for the day.

"I think we should focus on the wives," I said. "An ex-wife can be a great source of information."

Martha said, "I was thinking that I could search for information on the wives using the same websites I used yesterday to find out about Mr. Elgin."

I nodded. "And, of course, enter anything you find in the database—"

"It needs a name," Martha interrupted.

"Huh?"

"The database. It needs a name. We can't just keep calling it the database. It needs a name."

"Okay, what do you want to call it?"

"I think we should call it Merlin," she said without hesitation. "You know, like the magician?"

Obviously, she'd given it some thought. "Sure. Merlin it is."

She patted the external hard drive and cooed, "Nice, Merlin."

"While you work on the internet searches, I'm going to go down to the *Chronicle* office and see what was published at the time Elgin's two wives died."

In the garage, I looked at the Spark Nano sitting on my workbench. If I left it turned off too long, Elgin would know that I'd found it. I decided that it wouldn't hurt to have him know that I was visiting the newspaper office, so I put the unit on the floor in my backseat and switched it on.

When I walked into the *Chronicle* archives, I had two names and two dates of death: Carrie Whitney Elgin, died March 26, 1994, and Christie Brogan Elgin, died July 17, 2004.

On the front page of the Metro Section for Monday, March 27, 1994, I found this article, accompanied by a photo of Christie Elgin. She was a strikingly attractive blonde.

Clackamas River Takes Life

A 28-year-old Portland woman died Sunday after falling from a raft on the Clackamas River approximately 12 miles southeast of Estacada.

Carrie Whitney Elgin was floating the river with her husband, Portland Police Sergeant Richard Elgin, when she fell from the raft in a rapid known as the Toilet Bowl. She was pulled from the river a mile downstream by kayakers, who performed CPR until rescue personnel arrived. The victim was pronounced dead at the scene.

Although wearing a lifejacket, the victim sustained multiple injuries, which may have contributed to her death. The cold water in the Clackamas River may also have been a factor, although the cause of death has not yet been determined.

Elgin said that the couple had launched their raft at Big Eddy just half a mile above the scene of the accident. He said that they thought there were no major rapids in the river below that point. Elgin said that upon rounding a right-hand bend in the river, they found themselves in a long, steep rapid. Before they could get to shore, the raft dropped into the Toilet Bowl, where Carrie Elgin was ejected.

Elgin lost track of his wife in the rough water and paddled to shore a short distance downstream, where he summoned a passing motorist to go for help. Elgin remained at the scene, walking downstream in hopes of finding his wife. He came upon the group of kayakers a short distance downstream from a popular kayaking spot known as Bob's Hole.

Chris Wendling, one of the kayakers, said that they spotted Carrie Elgin floating facedown in the river at Bob's Hole. He said that he paddled downstream to catch up with the victim and was able to attach a rescue line to her lifejacket and pull her to shore. There, another member of the group, who is a volunteer with the Mount Hood Ski Patrol, started CPR.

Estacada Fire Department rescue personnel and EMTs arrived on scene about 40 minutes after the accident. They reported that the victim showed no vital signs, and continued efforts to revive her were unsuccessful.

There seemed to be nothing in the story to indicate that the death was anything but an unfortunate accident. I was familiar with that stretch of river, and I knew that the Toilet Bowl was a rapid that could take a person by surprise. It was one of the few rapids in the area that was not easily visible from the roadway, and it had a violent drop hidden in the middle of a seemingly innocuous wave train. There was a follow-up article on the inside pages of the Metro Section two days later.

Clackamas River Death Victim Wore No Helmet

Twenty-eight-year-old Carrie Whitney Elgin died last Sunday while rafting with her husband on the Clackamas River approximately twelve miles southeast of Estacada. The cause of death was determined to be head trauma resulting in drowning.

At the time of the accident, Mrs. Elgin was wearing a Type 3 life jacket, but no helmet. It is believed that her head struck a rock in the riverbed after she was ejected from the raft in a rapid known as the Toilet Bowl.

The victim's husband, Portland Police Sergeant Richard Elgin said that the couple had launched at Big Eddy, a quarter-mile above the Toilet Bowl, believing that there were no major rapids downstream.

The victim was pulled from the river by a group of kayakers a mile downstream from the accident. They performed CPR without success. One of the kayakers was quoted as having said that the raft the couple was using was "a piece of crap that was totally unsuitable for whitewater."

The yellow four-man raft had been purchased by Elgin just a few days before the fatal trip. Elgin stated that he had prior rafting experience but was not familiar with the stretch of river where the accident occurred. When asked to comment on what the kayaker had said about the raft, Elgin said, "The problem was not the raft. The problem was that we were taken by surprise."

Both Elgin and his wife were wearing shortie wetsuits in addition to Coast Guard–approved personal floatation devices.

Nothing jumped out at me except the statement that Elgin had prior rafting experience. If he were really an experienced rafter, he should have known that a four-man raft was not suited for whitewater. But then again, he said that he didn't know there was a class 4 rapid just down from where he launched. If he thought it was a lazy flat-water float, the little raft would have seemed okay. Still, an experienced rafter should have been able to see that there was significant whitewater ahead while there was still time to paddle to shore.

Those were small points—hardly enough to build a case for murder. Finding nothing else about the untimely death of Carrie Elgin, I turned my attention to the untimely death of Christie Elgin. Perhaps because Christie's death occurred out of state, a hundred miles north of Portland, she didn't make the front page.

Scuba Lesson Turns to Tragedy

A 29-year-old Portland woman died Saturday while scuba diving in Puget Sound about ten miles north of Shelton Washington. Christie Elgin was diving with her husband, Richard Elgin, at a popular dive site known locally as Octopus Hole when the accident occurred.

According to Elgin, the couple entered the water and swam on the surface to a point about 100 feet off shore before going down. Elgin said that they started to descend together, but that his wife's rate of descent was too fast, and he quickly lost sight of her. Visibility was estimated to be fifteen feet.

Believing that his wife may have returned to the surface, Elgin went up to look for her, but when he did not find her there, he descended to the bottom.

Depth at that point is about 40 feet but quickly drops to over 100 feet. Elgin said that he searched the bottom for about fifteen minutes before surfacing and swimming to shore.

He used a mobile phone in his car to contact emergency services. The 911 call was logged at 2:19 p.m. First responders arrived at the scene about 15 minutes after the call. An underwater search-and-rescue team started a grid search at 3:25 p.m., and the body was recovered at 4:45 p.m. Attempts at resuscitation were not successful.

Elgin stated that he had been giving his wife scuba lessons, and this was her first open-water dive. He said that she was a good swimmer and had practiced using scuba gear in a swimming pool. Elgin is certified as an advanced diver, but not as a scuba diving instructor.

The story was on page 3 of the Monday paper and was not accompanied by a photo. Three days later, there was another story. This time there was a photo of Christie Elgin, and it was startling how much she resembled Carrie Elgin.

Questions Raised About Scuba Death

When Christie Brogan Elgin entered the cold water of Puget Sound last Saturday, she had no prior scuba-diving experience. The 29-year-old wife of Portland Police Sergeant Richard T. Elgin drowned, apparently as a result of equipment failure.

When the body was recovered, it was noted by rescuers that her air tank was empty. Her tank was not equipped with a pressure gauge, but it did have a J-valve emergency reserve. The J-valve

had been pulled, indicating that Christie knew that she was low on air.

Skip Rome, spokesman for the Mason County Sheriff's Office, said that Christie Elgin was wearing "very old" scuba gear and may have been the victim of equipment failure. Rome said that the release valve on Mrs. Elgin's buoyancy compensator appeared to have stuck open. Rome explained that the buoyancy compensator is an inflatable vest that divers use to adjust their buoyancy while in the water. A diver wishing to descend presses the release valve to let air out of the vest. When he wants to return to the surface, he presses a different button to inflate the vest with air from the scuba tank.

With the release valve stuck open, it would have been impossible to get air into the vest to bring the victim to the surface. Rescue divers on the scene also said that they had difficulty releasing the weight belt from the victim. One diver told reporters that he had to pry the buckle open with his knife because he couldn't open it by hand. Dropping the weight belt for an emergency ascent is a routine part of scuba training.

The Mason County Sheriff's Office is conducting an inquiry into the events surrounding Christie Elgin's death, focusing on the condition of the equipment she was using. Richard Elgin declined to be interviewed.

There was plenty to chew on there. Elgin was an advanced diver. He should have known to check the operation of every piece of equipment. I could see no way that an experienced diver could put an untested buoyancy compensator on someone. If Elgin was giving his wife lessons, he should have taught her that the first thing you do in the water is a full equipment check. Obviously, that wasn't done.

And the use of a submersible pressure gauge on scuba tanks has been standard procedure for sport divers since the early 1970s. Even with a J-valve reserve, it is a serious compromise of safety to dive without the ability to check your air supply while under water.

Christie's weight belt buckle had to be pried open with a knife. These buckles are supposed to be easy to open—in fact, I've known divers to lose their weight belts by *accidentally* flipping the buckle loose. If Christie's buckle had to be pried open, it probably had to be forced closed. That should have been a huge red flag. I found one more article, which seemed to close the books on Christie Elgin.

Faulty Equipment Blamed for Scuba Death

Christie Elgin drowned on her first open-water scuba dive July 17, 2004, in the Hood Canal area of Puget Sound. This is an area popular with Oregon scuba divers because of its calm, relatively warm water and good visibility. On July 17, however, the visibility was only ten to fifteen feet because of a recent algae bloom.

Ms. Elgin drowned when she was unable to surface from a depth of 110 feet. Multiple problems were noted in the equipment she wore. Her tank was long past due for an inspection. She had no pressure gauge on the tank. The release valve on her buoyancy compensator was defective. And the buckle on her weight belt was stuck so she could not release it.

When questioned by Mason County Sheriff's Office deputies, Richard Elgin, who is a Portland Police sergeant, said that he had purchased the equipment from a private party at a garage sale. He said that he was told that the gear was in good working condition.

Elgin also told investigators that he had been giving his wife diving lessons for several months in public swimming pools. The fatal dive in July was Christie Elgin's first open water dive, and apparently the first time she had ever worn scuba gear.

It turns out that Christie is not the first person married to Richard Elgin to die in a recreational accident. Ten years ago, Richard Elgin's second wife, Carrie Whitney Elgin, died in a rafting accident on the Clackamas River east of Estacada. Christie Brogan Elgin was Elgin's fourth wife.

"Lightening can strike twice in the same place," Mason County Sheriff's Office spokesman, Skip Rome, said. "Richard Elgin must be the unluckiest man in the world."

I'm a guy with an imagination. If Elgin wanted to kill his wife, all he had to do was convince her to go scuba diving with him. He went out and bought old equipment that shouldn't have even been used. Without current inspection markings on the tank, it wasn't legal for anyone to fill it. But maybe Elgin didn't care.

He could have intentionally put his wife in the water with an air tank that was already on reserve. She wouldn't know because her instructor—Elgin—had never taught her to check her air pressure and J-valve before going into the water.

The weight belt buckle could have been jammed by threading the loose end of the belt through the buckle crooked, so that one edge of the thick web belt jammed against the side of the buckle. That sometimes happens by accident, but it doesn't go unnoticed. It takes some hand strength to squeeze the buckle closed against the wedged belt—and it would be equally difficult to release.

Then to make the whole thing happen, all it would take is a bent shaft on the buoyancy compensator release valve. After wading into the water, Elgin would have inflated Christie's buoyancy compensator for the surface swim. He probably had shown her how to press the release-valve button in order to descend. Once pressed, the bent shaft would prevent the spring-loaded valve from re-closing.

A novice diver, Christie would not have immediately understood that she was sinking too fast. Then she would have been preoccupied with equalizing the pressure in her ears. The deeper she sank, the more her wetsuit compressed and the less buoyancy she had. So she sank faster.

She would have tried to swim against her free fall, exhausting herself and consuming a lot of air.

She'd have been in full panic by the time she reached the bottom. A more experienced diver might have been able to collect enough composure to realize that ditching the weight belt would save her life. But even if Christie did have that thought, the buckle was jammed. She died terrified, confused, and alone.

I didn't believe for an instant that her death was an accident. It was a coldly calculated murder. With that conclusion in mind, I took a second look at Carrie Elgin's rafting "accident."

If you wanted to stage a death to look like a rafting accident, how would you do it? First, you'd pick a place where you could plausibly claim that you didn't know about the rapids—a rapid that cannot be seen from the road. Then you'd use a raft that was too small for the rapid so that you could plausibly claim that your victim had been ejected.

Elgin bought the raft especially for this trip. He had decent life jackets and wetsuits. These things would show his "good intent," even with the inadequate raft. Elgin and Carrie paddled away from the beach at Big Eddy on smooth water. At the point where the rapids came into view, Elgin most likely coached Carrie to help paddle the raft to shore.

Elgin probably had visited the scene a few days before the raft trip. He knew exactly where to pull ashore, and he would have an appropriate weapon—a pipe, a branch, a baseball bat—stashed in the rocks. He would call Carrie's attention to some feature out in the river, and while she focused her attention on that, he would deliver the blow to her head.

Then he'd just have to roll the body into the water and let the river do the rest. He'd toss the weapon into the deep water and then show up wet and legitimately exhausted at the side of the road—to all appearances, he was the lucky survivor.

So that's the kind of man I was dealing with. Calculating. Ruthless. Dangerous. If I needed a candidate to be Devonshire's accomplice in the killing of Randy and Jessie, Richard T. Elgin had a pretty good résumé.

CHAPTER 36

t was time to see where Richard Elgin lived. I switched off his Spark Nano and then keyed Elgin's address into my GPS navigator. From downtown Portland, I drove south on Broadway, crossing over I-405. I wound my way up Broadway Drive to Vista Avenue, turned right and went up Vista to Hillcrest Drive.

I made the right turn onto Hillcrest Drive and found Elgin's home on the left side of the street. The three-story house at 2530 Hillcrest Drive was a classic mid-century contemporary clinging to the steep hillside, with a panoramic view of downtown Portland and Mount St. Helens beyond. This is one of Portland's most desired neighborhoods—hardly the kind of place you would expect to find a petty criminal living.

It was hard to imagine how Elgin could have bought this place—even at 1977 prices—on a police officer's pay. I made a note to follow up on that question. While driving back downtown, I contemplated what to do with Elgin's tracking device.

I returned to the *Chronicle* office and switched on the tracker. Again driving south on Broadway, when I reached I-405, I took the southbound on ramp. Staying right on I-405 led me onto I-5 northbound, across the Willamette River and up to the I-84 interchange. I got onto I-84 heading east and settled into the center lane.

Twenty-five miles east of Portland, I arrived at Multnomah Falls and took the exit into the parking lot. Multnomah Falls is a compulsory stop for every tourist driving through Oregon. Slowly driving up and down the rows of parked cars and RVs, I finally found what I was looking for. I pulled into a vacant parking space and carried Elgin's Spark Nano over to a large Itasca motorhome with South Carolina license plates.

I loitered around until I was pretty sure nobody was looking, and then I slipped beneath the Itasca. I placed the tracking device inside the left-hand frame rail. I figured that by the time Elgin figured out that his Spark Nano was no longer attached to my Yukon, it would be a couple of time zones away.

It was doubtful that he would ever get the device back, but for the next six months or so, he could monitor the travels of the retired couple from South Carolina. With a smile on my face, I drove back to Oregon City.

When I turned onto Water Street in Canemah, I knew that something was wrong. There were two Oregon City Police cruisers and an unmarked county car crowded around my cottage. A German shepherd in the back of one of the cruisers barked and scratched at the window.

I squeezed past the parked cars and got the Yukon into my garage. Martha appeared and frantically said, "I tried to call you, but I couldn't get through."

Damn! I'd turned my phone off when I went into the newspaper office and hadn't turned it back on.

"What's going on here?" I asked.

"They showed up about an hour ago. They have a search warrant."

"A search warrant," I dumbly repeated. "For what?"

"I don't know. They told me, but it didn't register. I was too upset," she cried. "They took the computers."

"*What?* I need to find out what this is all about," I said, striding toward the house.

"Who's in charge here?" I demanded as I went inside.

"I am," said a man in a brown sports jacket. "Are you March Corrigan?"

"I'm Corrigan," I said impatiently. "Who are you, and what's going on here?"

"My name is Roger Millican. I'm Clackamas County District Attorney. I have a warrant to search your property and seize your computers."

"What are you looking for, and why?"

"We are searching for certain electronic devices that were reported stolen from a vehicle parked at the Fred Meyer store in Oregon City. We are taking your computers to look for evidence that you sold such devices online."

"I assume you had to present some 'probable cause' in order to get your warrant," I challenged.

"Of course, but we're not at liberty to tell you what that is," Millican explained.

"What are these 'certain electronic devices' that you are looking for?"

Millican showed me a list of brand names and model numbers, and I recognized the first three items as the eavesdropping equipment that I'd given to my cable guy.

The fourth item was the Spark Nano that was on its way to South Carolina.

"And what have you found?" I asked.

"We've taken your computers."

"What else?"

"That's all," Millican said. And then he added, "So far."

"Fine," I said. "Now if you will excuse me, I'm going to phone my attorney."

I went back outside and found Martha. "You know what they're looking for? They're looking for the listening devices that RTE Consulting planted in the house! Can you believe that?"

"But how would they know about the bugs?" Martha asked.

"There's only one way. After Elgin found out that I'd discovered his listening devices he—or one of his gnomes—reported them stolen. He even reported the tracking device that he put on my Yukon!"

"But they planted them illegally."

"Sure, but once I removed them, that will be hard to prove."

"Where are they?" she whispered.

"There are no electronic devices here," I said emphatically. "They will not find anything."

"They took the computers," Martha reminded me.

"And I can't help but wonder if that's what they were really after."

"But they didn't get Merlin," Martha said with a conspiratorial smile. She opened her large purse just enough to give me a glimpse of the external hard drive.

"Excellent! That makes me feel a whole lot better about all of this. But I do still hate being a neighborhood spectacle."

A small crowd was gathering. Bud was there. Daryl's wife, Joanie, was there. Kaylin Beatty was there. Rosie was there, with a large glass of mystery wine; Sharon Dexter was there. This was not really the kind of publicity I needed for my business.

I called William Gates and told him what was going on. Five minutes later, Gates joined the party.

"I am representing Mr. Corrigan in all matters pertaining to this investigation," he told Roger Millican.

"I want a copy of your warrant."

"I'll have to have a copy made," Millican stalled.

"Now would be a good time," Gates insisted.

"Would your client mind if I use his copier," Millican asked superciliously.

"I'm sure that would be fine, assuming that your office will reimburse him for the cost."

In obvious frustration, Millican slapped a five-dollar bill on the table. "Will that cover it?"

I nodded to Gates, who asked, "Would you like a receipt?"

"Okay, I'll play your little game," Millican complained. "Yes, I want a receipt!"

I wrote a receipt while Martha assisted Millican in making a copy of the warrant. I assumed that Millican would put the five bucks on his expense report and get reimbursed by the taxpayers of Clackamas County.

"Is it normal for the district attorney to be this involved in a car-prowl case?" I asked Gates when we were back outside.

"It is *not* normal," he said. "In fact, it is decidedly *abnormal*. There has to be something bigger in play here."

"Like what?"

"You tell me. What have you been involved in that could possibly warrant this kind of attention?"

"Like I said on the phone, the items listed in their warrant are surveillance devices planted on my property by someone working for RTE Consulting. RTE started looking at me when I went to visit the widow of Gary Turner, who was one of the original detectives on the Mendelson-Devonshire investigation."

"You're sure about that?"

"Quite sure, but I don't yet know how RTE is connected to the case."

"It's a reasonable inference, and it's also reasonable to infer that this little sideshow is the result. Assuming all that to be true, I would further infer that what they're really after is the data on your computer. They're trying to find out what you've been doing and what you know."

"Well, that's too bad for them because I don't think they'll find anything at all on those computers."

Gates raised an eyebrow and gave me a curious look.

"The data is stored externally," I explained, "and they don't have it."

"Will they find anything else?"

"Nothing that's on their warrant, but if they're snoopy—and I assume they are—they'll read documents that are on and in my desk. That will include a DNA lab report stating that Jessie Devonshire's blood was found on a board taken from the entry of the Devonshire home."

"Material evidence in a criminal investigation. When did you get this report?"

"It was delivered a few days ago. I told Larry Jamieson what I had, and he made it clear that he didn't want anything to do with it."

"Irrelevant," Gates said flatly. "If Millican is out to get you, he will come after you for withholding material evidence—unless you can turn over the evidence before he has a chance to do anything."

"Can my attorney handle that?" I asked.

"I thought you'd never ask."

I went inside and found the FedEx envelope in my desk drawer. I held it up for Millican to see. He nodded, so I carried the envelope outside and gave it to Gates, who headed downtown to the county courthouse.

Half an hour later, Millican wrapped up his search and left. He never found the removable floor tiles in my bathroom or the safe hidden beneath it. He had my computers, but they wouldn't tell him much. I spent a few minutes straightening up. The searchers had not destroyed the place the way they do in the movies—if anything, they'd taken great pains to leave it looking as they'd found it, except for the missing computers.

I drove to Fry's Electronics in Wilsonville and bought two new computers to replace the ones taken by Millican. There was no telling when I'd see them again or what kind of spyware would be installed on them before they gave them back.

Using my Norton backup utility, I was able to easily turn the new computers into precise clones of the ones Millican had taken. Martha and I would be back in business the next day. I went to work changing the user names and passwords on all of my online accounts.

If Millican's computer geeks were able to penetrate my security they'd be unable to do anything worse than reading my browsing history. I was just finishing that task when Kim pulled in.

"How was your day?" she asked innocently.

"I don't even know where to start," I told her.

"New computers?" she asked, spotting the pile of boxes and packaging foam in the corner.

"Yes. Roger Millican, the district attorney, borrowed my old ones—indefinitely."

"He borrowed your computers?" she asked with a quizzical expression.

"It's a long story best told over a glass of wine."

CHAPTER 37

FRIDAY, AUGUST 12

"I'm really glad you were able to get out of here with that hard drive," I told Martha.

"Well, I couldn't just let them take Merlin," she said.

"How did you manage it?"

"Well, after you left yesterday, I got to thinking what I'd do if those guys in the little black car showed up while you were gone. I figured Merlin was the only thing here they could use, so I fixed it up so that I could get the hard drive out without them seeing."

She showed me how she put the hard drive in her purse on the floor next to the CPU, with only the USB cable in sight. Picking up her purse would pull the USB plug, and she could walk away. Slick. I showed her the microfiche prints of the newspaper articles I'd found the day before.

"Do you think he killed them?" Martha asked.

"It sure looks that way," I said. "And what did you find?"

"I was able to track down the two ex-wives and the estranged wife. I have current names, employers, addresses, and phone numbers for all of them. I also found contact information for the families of the two dead wives. I figured they might have something to say."

Martha printed three pages containing all of that information and handed them to me. I decided to start at the top and dialed the number for Alicia Jefferson, Richard Elgin's first ex-wife.

"This is Alicia," the voice on the phone said.

I introduced myself. "My name is Corrigan. I'm investigating the business activities of your former husband, Richard Elgin."

There was a pause, and I heard her inhale a deep breath. "So?"

"I was wondering if you'd be willing to talk with me about that."

"I'd hoped that I'd never have to think about him again," Alicia finally answered.

"Could we meet somewhere, maybe for coffee or lunch?" I asked

"Lunch at McCormick & Schmicks on Beaverton-Hillsdale Highway," she said. "Eleven thirty."

"It's a deal. See you there." If nothing else, Alicia was decisive.

It may be a symptom of my age, but I don't think so. My first thought when I saw Alicia Jefferson was, *This* must the wrong woman. The one I'm looking for is *fifty-two years old.* A fifty-two-year-old woman should look like an old lady. Alicia looked good. Note that I did not say she looked good for someone her age. She looked good. Period.

Her blond hair was medium length, she was well dressed, and she filled her dress well. We sat across from one another in a comfortably private booth, and we had just finished ordering lunch.

"Now what is it that you'd like to ask me that's worth the price of lunch?" Alicia asked.

"Richard Elgin. You were married to him for four years. Can I ask why you split up?" I began.

"He had a permanent wardrobe malfunction," Alicia told me. "His zipper wouldn't stay up."

"Anything else?"

"Isn't that enough?" she said with a raised eyebrow.

I changed the subject. "You lived up on Hillcrest Drive?"

She simply nodded.

"I've seen that house," I said. "I couldn't help wondering how he could afford it on a cop's pay."

"He had other sources of income."

"His consulting company?"

"Actually, he invented the consulting company so that he could bill the city for his freelance work while he was on the city payroll."

"What kind of freelance work did he do?"

"A lot of different things. He always billed it as 'security' work, but what he was really doing is billing the city for favors that he did for powerful people in city government."

"What kind of favors?"

"He called himself a fixer. If someone had a problem, he'd fix it. If someone needed something, he'd get it."

"What kind of things are we talking about?"

"Any kind. But mostly the female kind, I think."

"He got women for city officials?"

"And more importantly, he made sure that nobody would ever find out. That was his specialty. That's what his 'clients' paid the big money for."

"How many 'clients' did he have?"

"Not many. But he had the *right* ones—the ones with the money—"

"Or the ability to get the city to write the check," I finished for her. Changing the subject again, I asked, "What was his job with the police bureau?"

"Oh, I thought you knew," she said with true surprise.

"He drove the mayor's limo."

"Alan Blalock?"

"You got it. Blalock had lots of money to throw around, and he threw a lot of it Richard's way."

"In exchange for—"

"Services, cash for services. But when there got to be too much cash to handle without raising questions with the IRS—and others—he opened up RTE Consulting."

"To launder the money," I said matter-of-factly.

"That sums it up," she agreed.

"Your husband procured women for the mayor?" I clarified.

"*Young* women," she corrected.

"What about Wilson Devonshire?"

"Sure. He was the mayor's top aide. He was the go-between. Richard and Devonshire worked together to make sure that the mayor always had smooth sailing."

Our conversation was temporarily interrupted when the waitress delivered our lunches, refilled our coffee cups, and asked if there was anything else we wanted.

I got back to the questions. "Did you know Richard's second wife, Carrie Whitney?"

"Not really," she said. "I mean, we met a couple of times, but she was just the 'new young chick' as far as I was concerned."

"Funny you should say that. I noticed that Richard's been married five times, but never to a woman over twenty-nine years old."

"Women and cars—when they get too old, trade 'em in for a newer model."

"He liked his women young?"

"You bet. Thirty was over the hill as far as Richard was concerned."

"What do you know about Carrie's death?"

"I know what I read in the newspaper. She died while rafting with Richard. The newspapers got one thing wrong, though."

"What's that?"

"They said that Richard had never rafted that river before, but that wasn't true," she said. "Richard and a bunch of his cop buddies used to float the Upper Clackamas every spring when the water was up."

"You're sure it was the same stretch of river?" I pressed.

"Of course! Sandstone Creek to the Memaloose scaling station," she insisted. "That was their standard run."

"Did it make you suspicious when the newspaper said that Richard claimed he'd never floated that stretch of river before?"

"Not really. I just figured the newspaper got the story wrong—they do it all the time. But then after Christie died, I got to wondering."

"Did you know Christie?"

"Sure. She was the daughter of our neighbors!" Alicia exclaimed. "I babysat her when she was five years old for Christ's sake!"

"Neighbors?"

"Yes, right across the street. He watched her grow up from infancy, and as soon as she was twenty, he married her," she said contemptuously.

"You said that Christie's death made you think again about Carrie's death," I reminded her.

"I never believed that Christie's death was an accident. I read what they said in the newspaper, and even *they* were suspicious."

"What made *you* suspicious?"

"It was the old equipment. He'd have *never* bought old, used equipment unless he *intended* for it to fail. He was what they call a gear nut. He was *fanatical* about anything mechanical—it had to be perfect, or he didn't want anything to do with it. When they said that he put old, used gear on Christie, I knew that he did it to kill her."

"For what it's worth, it struck me the same way, and I didn't even know him."

"I guess I didn't either," she said wistfully.

We finished our lunch, and I thanked her for her time. While I was driving back to the office, I pondered what she'd said. Elgin's attraction to young women was interesting. I tried on a new theory. Suppose Jessie Devonshire's older boyfriend had been Richard Elgin?

Maybe he, not Devonshire, had killed Jessie and Randy. But then, why would Devonshire help cover up the crime? Something didn't fit.

My phone chirped, and I pressed the button on my Bluetooth earpiece.

"Corrigan," I answered.

"Gates. I delivered your DNA report to the district attorney's office yesterday. They didn't seem surprised by it or even interested in it. They simply logged it in and said thanks," he said.

"Think there'll be any trouble over it?"

"Doubtful. If they were going to nail you for withholding evidence, they should've done it yesterday. Now they don't have a case."

"Were you able to find out what was their probable cause for their search warrant?"

"They won't tell me that unless they get an indictment. But my guess is that Roger Millican and the judge who issued the warrant belong to the same 'country club,' if you know what I mean."

"So probable cause wasn't necessary?"

"Oh, if they ever have to show documentation, they'll have something," he explained. "They probably had an eyewitness who saw you breaking into the car and stealing the electronics. More than likely, an anonymous tip."

"What about my computers?" I asked.

"Nobody's talking. They've sent the computers to a forensics lab somewhere. You may not see them again for months."

"I guessed as much. I bought new ones last night, and we're back up and running."

"Glad to hear it. I just wanted to bring you up to date."

"Thanks," I said as the line went dead.

CHAPTER 38

"I found something odd," Martha said.

"What's that?" I asked.

"Well, I was going back and reviewing some of the documents I scanned, looking for things that have never been explained, you know. Anyway, I was looking at the transcripts of interviews with Devonshire's neighbors the day after Jessie disappeared."

"I don't remember seeing anything in those interviews."

"This one wasn't filed with the others," Martha said.

"It was mixed in with the 'sighting' reports, where people said they'd seen Randy and Jessie after they disappeared."

I nodded, so she continued, "Gary Turner was talking to a neighbor— Mary Drewsey—and she saw something that nobody else had mentioned."

Martha handed me a copy of the scanned document.

Turner: Did you see or hear anything unusual around the Devonshire's house yesterday?

Drewsey: No, nothing unusual.

Turner: Did you notice anyone visiting them?

Drewsey: Well, the gardener was there. I saw his little truck parked by the road when I went out to get my mail.

Turner: What time would that have been?

Drewsey: I guess maybe about two thirty or three. He's always late on Fridays. Why is that?

Turner: The gardener is late?

Drewsey: No! The mail man. He's always late on Fridays.

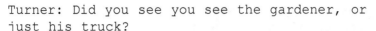

Turner: Did you see you see the gardener, or just his truck?

Drewsey: No, just that little black pickup.

Turner: Did you notice when the pickup left?

Drewsey: It was gone when I took my dog out.

Turner: And what time was that?

Drewsey: She always goes out at a quarter to six.

Turner: Why a quarter to six?

Drewsey: Well, I don't know. She can't talk. She always wants to go out at a quarter to six.

Turner: And the gardener's truck was gone?

Drewsey: That's right. The little black pickup was gone, and there were two big white cars in the driveway.

Turner: Excuse me?

Drewsey: There were two big white cars.

Turner: Didn't you say that you hadn't seen any visitors at the Devonshire house?

Drewsey: Oh, these weren't visitors. One was Mr. Devonshire's car, and the other was Mrs. Devonshire's.

Turner: They were both there?

Drewsey: Well, yes, and there were people standing by the cars.

Turner: Did you recognize them?

Drewsey: I didn't have my glasses on.

Turner: How many people did you see?

Drewsey: There were two. Or maybe three. I'm not sure.

Turner: What were they doing?

Drewsey: I couldn't tell. Then I saw Mrs. Devonshire drive away.

Turner: And what time was that?

Drewsey: Oh, it was only a couple of minutes after I went out.

Turner: Did you see who was driving?

Drewsey: Mrs. Devonshire was driving. Who else would be driving her car?

Turner: So you saw Mrs. Devonshire?

Drewsey: Well, I didn't actually see her, but it had to be her.

Turner: What about the other car?

Drewsey: Mr. Devonshire's car.

Turner: Did you see Mr. Devonshire?

Drewsey: Yes. He drove away a few minutes after Mrs. Devonshire left.

Turner: Anything else?

Drewsey: Later, I saw Mr. Devonshire painting his door.

Turner: Pardon?

Drewsey: Mr. Devonshire was painting his door.

Turner: Do you remember what time that was?

Drewsey: Seven. <u>Jeopardy</u> was just coming on TV, and I saw him out my front window, painting his door that red color.

Turner: Did you see anything else?

Drewsey: I can't think of anything.

I remembered having seen something in Gary Turner's murder book notes about two cars, but it hadn't registered. Was it actually possible that Mary Drewsey had seen Mrs. Devonshire at home Friday evening?

"Martha, does Merlin have anything to document when Barbara Devonshire left Salishan?" I asked.

"That's the strange thing," Martha said. "Barbara Devonshire was still at Salishan when Mary Drewsey claims she saw her in West Linn."

Martha handed me another document. It was Barbara Devonshire's bill from Salishan. Martha had highlighted a portion of the list of charges to Mrs. Devonshire's room.

```
16:08  Long Dist Phone $2.18
16:37  Attic Lounge $6.50
17:09  Attic Lounge $6:50
19:25  Prime Steakhouse $31.75
21:30  Room Service $8.50
```

At the bottom of the document was a note that appeared to be in Gary Turner's handwriting, which said that Barbara Devonshire's signature for all of these charges had been confirmed by hotel staff.

"See what I mean?" Martha asked. "Mary Drewsey *couldn't* have seen Mrs. Devonshire."

"Yet there was a car like hers in the driveway around six on Friday," I said. "Do we know what kind of car Barbara Devonshire drove?"

"I checked on that. According to Turner's notes, she drove a white 1978 Cadillac Fleetwood."

"And what did Wilson Devonshire drive?"

"He drove a white 1980 Oldsmobile Royale—city owned. Mary Drewsey saw two white cars, so she just assumed they were Mr. and Mrs. Devonshire's cars."

"Still, two white cars on the driveway clearly put someone else at the crime scene," I observed.

"Someone driving a car that looked like Barbara Devonshire's Cadillac," Martha concluded.

Late that night, I was still thinking about the puzzle of the two white cars, and it wouldn't let me sleep. If the second car wasn't Barbara Devonshire's, whose was it? And how did it fit into the murders of Jessie and Randy?

I'd already established a timeline for the murders that indicated that the victims probably had been killed at about four in the afternoon, based on when Devonshire had purchased the paint to cover up the bloodstain on the entry carpet. Mary Drewsey said that she'd seen the two white cars on Devonshire's driveway at five forty-five and that both cars had driven away a few minutes later.

The timing of the departure of Wilson Devonshire's car dovetailed nicely with the purchase of the red paint, and Mary Drewsey's observation that Devonshire was painting his door at seven further reinforced the timeline. Aside from the question of who drove the second car, the other big issue was when Wilson Devonshire had left his office.

In his statements to police on July 26, he had said that he left his office after four thirty. In order to place Devonshire at the scene when the murders occurred, I'd have to find evidence to refute that claim. Even Gary Turner's summary of "known facts" included the notation that Devonshire was in his office at four thirty.

But the only thing I found that appeared to support Devonshire's timeline was the phone records. Devonshire's home-phone records had been obtained by investigators in 1980, in hopes of finding proof of a relationship between Jessie and Randy. No such evidence was found, but there had been a four-minute phone call to Devonshire's office at 4:21 p.m. on July 25.

This was the phone call that Devonshire had said was Jessie calling him to say that she was going out on a date that evening. But in reality, the call probably was placed after Jessie and Randy were dead. Had Devonshire placed the call after the murder to help establish his alibi?

Or suppose he had been calling someone to help him cover the crime. That could explain the presence of the second white car. The city had a fleet of white Oldsmobiles. Mary Drewsey easily could have mistaken an Oldsmobile for Barbara Devonshire's Cadillac. So who might Devonshire have called in his own office to drive out to West Linn to help with the clean up?

If Devonshire had been out of the office when the call came in, his secretary would have picked up the call, yet I could find no record that the secretary had ever been interviewed. That probably was because investigators had accepted Devonshire's word that he had been there to take the call. But if Devonshire had *made* the call, he could have asked his secretary to send someone to his house. Who would it have been? Trayborn was the first name that came to my mind.

Trayborn could have been dispatched to the Devonshire home shortly after the 4:21 p.m. phone call. He'd have arrived sometime around five. That gave him at least forty-five minutes to help Devonshire carry the bodies to Randy's El Camino, clean up the crime scene, and come up with the idea for the paint spill. The only problem was that for Trayborn to have access to a city vehicle, he had to have been a city employee, and Martha had spent three days in an unsuccessful attempt to find anyone by that name among former city employees. Maybe it was a mistake to focus on Trayborn.

Devonshire's helper, *whoever* he was, apparently had used a city car. There should have been a motor pool record. Would the motor-pool records still exist? That was something to pursue. If I could find someone who checked out a city car at about four thirty on July 25, I might have Devonshire's accomplice. Whoever that was could have met Devonshire at the boat ramp at a prearranged time to give him a ride home after running the El Camino into the river.

Things to Do:

1. Find out who was Devonshire's secretary.

2. Look for motor pool records.

3. Look for a list of city employees who had permanently assigned city cars.

4. Check city payroll records for someone claiming overtime pay on 7/25/80.

None of these things would be easy. The city records would be available to a private citizen only through a successful Freedom of Information Act request. And that assumes that the records still exist. The city has file retention rules that dictate how long files of each specific kind must be retained and thus, in effect, when they are destroyed. There was a good chance that the files no longer existed.

The first step was the direct approach. Martha could go downtown and simply ask for the documents. Sometimes that worked. At the very least, it would establish the basis for the FOIA request. There was nothing I could do about it before Monday, so I gave myself the weekend off to work on the Project.

CHAPTER 33

MONDAY, AUGUST 15

I sent Martha down to Portland City Hall to work on getting the records that could be the final pieces in the Devonshire puzzle. I was busy with Merlin, trying to find anything that would document when Devonshire had left his office on July 25, 1980. It was obvious that he'd been at home at four, but it was difficult to prove.

I was interrupted by a blue PT Cruiser pulling up next to my front porch.

"Are you March Corrigan?" the girl from the PT asked.

"I'm Corrigan," I said, "and you are?"

"Oh, I'm sorry. I'm Amy Powers," she said, extending her hand. "I'm with the *Oregon City Journal*."

I shook her hand. "What can I do for you, Ms. Powers?"

"Your name appeared on some documents that were delivered to the courthouse last Thursday."

Unwilling to volunteer anything, I asked, "And?"

"The documents were delivered by an attorney named William Gates."

"And?"

"You aren't being very helpful, Mr. Corrigan," she observed.

"Corrigan," I said, "Just Corrigan."

"The documents were logged in as evidence in the Mendelson-Devonshire investigation," Powers revealed.

"Are you working on that case?"

"I'd rather not comment on that."

Powers took a deep breath and said, "Okay, I'll just tell you what I know. The documents were lab reports that linked Jessie Devonshire's

DNA to blood found on a piece of flooring taken from the Devonshire home in West Linn."

Hmmm, she had it right. Someone in the district attorney's office had spilled the beans, and that really surprised me. I'd expected them to bottle this up tight.

"Like I said, I'd rather not comment on that."

"Let me help you," Powers offered. "I understand that you submitted these documents in confidence, so, of course, you don't want to comment on them. But let me tell you what happened. The clerk in the DA's office who received the envelope from your attorney—"

"You don't know who that attorney was representing," I interjected.

She quickly corrected herself. "The clerk who received the envelope from *the* attorney made copies of its contents. She apparently left a copy in the tray on a copy machine, where it got mixed in with some legal notices that were being copied for publication in the *Journal.* When our courier picked up the legals, he also got a copy of the documents, which stated—among other things—that the DNA lab work was done for you."

"If you can write that down as well as you just recited it, you'll be a candidate for a Pulitzer Prize." I sounded a little more sarcastic than I'd intended.

"Are you confirming what I just said?"

"No, I'm complimenting you for your good work."

"I've spoken with Sara Huntington, and she confirmed that she gave the piece of flooring to you. How did you know she had it?"

I sighed. "This is something I *can* talk about. When I went to the Huntington home, I had no idea that the wood scrap existed. I was merely looking at what I believed was the scene of the Mendelson and Devonshire murders."

"What made you think it was the crime scene?" she asked.

At this point, I was forced to consider a strategy for dealing with the information contained in Gary Turner's file boxes and Larry Jamieson's envelope. The answer to Powers's question came directly from the Turner files, without which, I'd never have known about the blood in the Devonshire's entry.

In the big picture, it probably would be best if all of the investigation files could be made public. That, if nothing else, would force a reopening of the investigation. But I still couldn't reveal everything I knew without it becoming apparent that I possessed files that were supposed to be locked up in the sheriff's office evidence room, and that would be very bad for Kim and probably Larry Jamieson as well.

On the other hand, if I mentioned one solitary fact without revealing my source, it might cause certain people to wonder where I got my information, but it wouldn't look like a major security breach. Amy Powers's appearance at my door provided me with a golden opportunity to crack the wall of secrecy that had been built around the case.

"The day after Jessie Devonshire disappeared, a detective observed a large dark-red stain on the carpet in the entry hall of the Devonshire home. Devonshire's explanation for the stain was spilled paint, but I was skeptical about that. I didn't go there expecting, or even hoping, to find anything. But Sara Huntington invited me in to see her newly remodeled home. I was admiring the work she and her husband had done, and in the course of our conversation, we talked about the tiled floor in the entry. She said they were forced to replace the hardwood there because of a large stain that couldn't be sanded out. It was just a stroke of luck that she had retained one of the stained pieces of wood. She gave it to me and I sent it in for analysis."

"Where did you get Jessie Devonshire's DNA for comparison?"

"There was a Christmas card that Jessie had sent to a friend. DNA was taken from the stamp and the flap on the envelope."

"And the DNA was a match?"

"It's all in the report."

"So what do you think happened to Jessie Devonshire?"

"I don't have all of the answers on that. But here's what you need to know: Wilson Devonshire told investigators that he had accidentally spilled paint on the carpet on the night Jessie disappeared. It now has been proven that the paint covered a pool of blood. Maybe Mr. Devonshire can explain that to you."

"You're suggesting that Wilson Devonshire deliberately concealed evidence!" she exclaimed.

"No," I corrected, "I'm only telling you what Devonshire told investigators."

"Why are you investigating this?"

"My client is Lila Mendelson, Randy Mendelson's mother. She believes that her son is as much a victim in this crime as Jessie Devonshire."

"But the sheriff's office concluded that Randy had killed Jessie and them himself. Are you saying they're wrong?"

"If the case is really that simple, then Wilson Devonshire will be able to explain why his paint spill covered the bloodstain on the floor."

"You know a lot more than you're telling me, don't you?"

"That's right. I know things that I can't reveal without doing harm to innocent people," I told her.

"I really want to get this story right," she said.

"Listen, Amy, you need to know, before you get too deep into it, that this investigation is extremely dangerous. But if you decide to go ahead with it, I'll help you get your story right. Just show it to me before you publish."

"But you still won't tell me everything you know?"

"I won't tell you anything that will put innocent people in jeopardy. And please don't quote me as a source of *anything*."

"Okay," she said cautiously, "we have a deal."

"You already have enough to write the most explosive story your newspaper has ever run. Do your homework. Dig out the old newspaper reports and gather all the information you can find about the original investigation. Then just use good sense to put the pieces together."

After Powers left, I leaned back in my chair to analyze what was happening. Had it really been an accident that the copy of the lab reports had been given to the *Journal*? Not likely. Someone in the DA's office had *wanted* the DNA evidence made public.

This seemed like a good thing for me. It was somewhat comforting to know that I had an anonymous ally in the DA's office, and it was good to have the existence of the DNA analysis made public. Generally speaking, the more details of this case that became public knowledge, the less reason anybody would have to silence me.

But I still had to protect Kim. Even though she hadn't revealed anything to me, it wouldn't look that way if anyone found out that I had a full set of investigation files. Any reasonable person would conclude that I'd gotten them from Kim, and that conclusion would be the end of her job.

So I walked a fine line. It would be very interesting to read the *Journal* on Wednesday. That, of course, was assuming that the editor and publisher would print Amy Powers's story. If they were people inclined to protect Wilson Devonshire's reputation, they'd spike the story. If they believe Powers's story wasn't adequately documented to protect the newspaper from libel charges, they'd spike the story. If forced to give odds, I'd have put the chances of publication at no better than 25 percent.

The chirping of my phone interrupted this exercise in higher math.

"Corrigan," I answered.

"This is Bill Cheshire," the voice on the phone said.

"Uh oh," I said. Bill Cheshire was my accountant. I couldn't think of any good reason for Bill to be calling me in mid-August. Still, I meant it as a joke.

"Don't jump the gun, Corrigan," Bill said. "I haven't given you any bad news yet."

"Okay then, what's the bad news?" I asked.

"I've been notified that you've been selected for audit," he said.

"Oh, lovely," I complained. "What can you tell me about it?"

"Well, first, don't panic. I'll represent you in the audit," Bill said. "All you'll need to do is provide the paperwork to back up the deductions you've claimed."

I groaned. "How far back?"

"Seven years is the limit," Bill said.

"I was afraid of that," I said. "My records go back three years. Anything older than that is in the hands of my ex-wife."

"Will that be a problem?" he asked.

"Global warming, world hunger, thermonuclear war—these things are easy. My ex-wife is a problem," I said. "Did they say why they selected me for audit?"

"No, but anyone who files as a self-employed taxpayer is going to get extra scrutiny," he explained. "And a home office is a red flag. What's more, a lot of your clients don't file 1099s for what they pay you. Taken together, you're high risk."

"The timing sucks."

"Perhaps you know of a *good* time to get audited."

"Hmm. Good point," I conceded. "So what's next?"

"Start gathering your files. When you think you have everything together, I'll help you organize it."

"And how much time do I have?"

"Three weeks. We're scheduled to meet the auditors on September 7."

I drew a deep cleansing breath and released it slowly.

"Call me when you have your files together," Bill said.

"Right."

In my mind, the only thing less desirable than facing an IRS auditor was facing my ex-wife.

CHAPTER 40

TUESDAY, AUGUST 16

Martha was still downtown, trying to find out who could have driven a city vehicle to the Devonshire home in the afternoon of July 25, 1980, so I took some time to go back through the old interview reports from the original investigation.

In addition to Mary Drewsey, who had seen the two white cars on the Devonshire driveway, there was another witness who had seen Randy Mendelson's El Camino parked at the side of the road in front of the Devonshire house. On July 27, Gary Turner interviewed sixteen-year-old boy named James Lacomb, who had been working in his parents' yard.

Turner: Are you aware of the search for
Jessie Devonshire?

Lacomb: I heard on the news yesterday that
she was missing, but that's about all I know.

Turner: Were you around here on Friday
afternoon?

Lacomb: Yeah, I was home all day.

Turner: What were you doing?

Lacomb: I mowed the lawn and kinda cleaned up
the garage.

Turner: Did you see anything happening around
the Devonshire house on Friday?

Lacomb: There was someone there in the
afternoon. He drove a pretty sharp El Camino.

Turner: Can you give me any more details on
that?

Lacomb: Yeah, sure. The El Camino was black, and it looked like it had just been waxed. The dude parked it on the side of the road, instead on the driveway. He was a younger guy. I mean, older than me, but maybe--I don't know--college age.

Turner: Have you seen that car there before?

Lacomb: No, I don't think so. I like that El Camino, and I'd have noticed it.

Turner: What time did he arrive?

Lacomb: Must have been about two thirty or three. Something like that.

Turner: Did you see the El Camino leave?

Lacomb: Nope. Last I saw, it was backing into the driveway.

Turner: You saw the "dude" backing into the driveway?

Lacomb: It might've been someone else.

Turner: Someone else? Can you give me a description?

Lacomb: Naw, I didn't really see him, except I think maybe he had short hair. The first dude had long hair.

Turner: What did he do after he backed into the driveway?

Lacomb: I didn't watch, but I noticed a few minutes later that it was gone.

Turner: And what time was that?

Lacomb: It was around five o'clock, maybe a ten or fifteen minutes before.

Turner: Do you know Jessie Devonshire?

Lacomb: Said hi to her a few times--would like to know her, but she ain't interested.

Turner: So you never dated her or anything like that?

Lacomb: Like I said, she ain't interested.

I sat staring at the page. The Lacomb kid saw someone—probably not Randy—backing the El Camino into the driveway between four forty-five and five. Somehow that part of the interview had been left out of the case summary. This witness had probably seen Devonshire backing the El Camino into the garage so that he could put the bodies inside.

The timing fit perfectly. The phone call to Devonshire's offices was at 4:21 p.m. That would have been Devonshire calling for help. Then he parked the El Camino in the garage. Later, he backed his own car out of the garage, perhaps to give himself more room to work—it couldn't have been easy to get the bodies out of the house and into the El Camino. After awhile, the other white car—no doubt driven by Devonshire's accomplice after the fact—showed up.

So what *exactly* did the mysterious accomplice do while he was there? Mary Drewsey had seen him leave at five forty-five, and he couldn't have arrived before five. Whatever he did, it took less than an hour. Would that have been enough time to help Devonshire clean up the crime scene? And more importantly, who could Devonshire *trust* with a job like that?

Logic suggested that Devonshire had brought in someone who knew how to clean up a crime scene. Yet even knowing all that I knew about Devonshire, it was difficult to believe that he would have such a person listed in his Rolodex. Yet Devonshire's secretary apparently had been able to contact this person and get him to the crime scene in about thirty minutes—possibly in an official city vehicle.

Who would know how to clean up a crime scene? A cop—and a cop might also have access to a city vehicle. Two names came to mind: Richard Elgin and the elusive Mr. Trayborn. I knew that Elgin had been a cop, and I was acutely aware that he was a man not bothered by a conscience.

What had Alicia Crabtree called Elgin? She said he was a "fixer," someone who took care of problems. Did Trayborn work with Elgin? Had he been a cop too? So far, we hadn't found his name anywhere among the public employees of Portland, but what if he worked for Elgin?

In any case, if Devonshire had brought in an expert to cover up the crime, that person would also have figured out what to do about transportation after disposal of the El Camino. It was simply too big a loose end to have been overlooked by someone worth bringing in to help Devonshire out of his jam.

He could have done it two ways. Either he stashed a car in the neighborhood of the boat ramp for Devonshire to drive home, or he agreed to meet Devonshire at the landing at a prearranged time. The second option seemed more likely because stashing a car would have left the fixer stranded, and it would have left Devonshire with an extra car in his garage.

It suddenly struck me as curious that a fixer would have driven something as high profile as an official city vehicle out to West Linn to cover up a crime scene. It would seem more logical for him to take something inconspicuous—unless the city car was the only transportation available to him on the spur of the moment. So it was someone who did not drive his personal car to work—someone who had a permanently assigned city car. It had to be either a high-level city executive or a cop—and not just any cop. Only a select few cops were permitted to take their unmarked police cars home.

Late in the afternoon, when Martha came back from Portland, she plopped tiredly into her chair and said, "The term *civil servant* is a *double* oxymoron. They are neither civil nor are they servants. Do you have any idea how convoluted Portland city government is? There are at least twenty-five bureaus and offices in City Hall, and nobody can tell you who is in charge of what!"

"I guess that means you struck out," I said.

"No, I managed to get some stuff. I'm just saying it wasn't easy."

"What did you get?"

Martha handed me some papers and said, "There's a list of everyone who worked in the mayor's office in 1980. The mayor's office was surly about it—no help whatsoever. I got this from the people who administer the employees' pension fund."

I started scanning the list, but Martha said, "Don't bother. There's no *Trayborn* on the list. I checked."

"What else do you have?" I asked, seeing that she was still holding some papers.

"We thought we might find something useful in the city motor-pool files. Well, guess what? There is no city motor pool. I tried for two days to find out who's in charge of the city-owned cars, and I still don't know," Martha complained. "I still don't know who's authorized to drive a city car, and if you're a Portland taxpayer wanting to know how the city is spending your money, all I can say is 'Good luck'!"

"Careful there, Martha, you're starting to sound like Lars Larson," I teased, referring to Portland's well-known radio talk-show host.

Martha made gagging gestures and said, "Give me a break!" She stared me down for a few seconds, challenging me to say something. "Anyway, I got this from a police-bureau clerk who made me promise never to tell anyone who gave it to me. It is a 1980 roster that shows police assignments."

She handed me the list as she spoke. "Still nobody named *Trayborn*, but look who was assigned to the mayor's office." She pointed to the name of Richard T. Elgin. "He was the mayor's personal driver," Martha said triumphantly.

"Funny. I found out the same thing from Elgin's first wife," I said.

"The mayor was driven around by a wife killer!" she exclaimed.

"Technically, he hadn't killed any wives yet."

"I'm just talking about his character. If he was the kind of guy who would think up ways to murder his wives, he was very likely devious about other things. And clearly, his morals didn't just abandon him in mid-life. He never had any to begin with."

"No argument here. So why would the mayor have a guy like that around?"

"You said it yourself—Elgin is devious. He probably was able to conceal what he was. I'd bet that he presented himself as an upstanding citizen and all-around nice guy."

"No doubt true," I conceded. "But doesn't it seem that somebody should have caught on—at least after his second wife died?"

"Maybe that just shows how good he was at schmoozing," Martha suggested.

"Yeah, or maybe they kept him around, not *in spite* of his character flaws, but rather *because* of them."

"That's pretty cynical."

"Sure, but look at what we're dealing with here. We have the mayor's top aide involved in a double homicide, while at the same time, we have a future wife killer driving the mayor's limo. That's way too much criminality in one place to be a coincidence."

"You're implying that the mayor deliberately packed his staff with murderers?" Martha complained.

"No, actually I'm not implying that," I corrected. "The *facts* are implying that."

Martha protested, "He was the governor! He's a US senator!"

"Yeah," I said. "Makes you wonder…"

CHAPTER 41

WEDNESDAY, AUGUST 17

T he *Oregon City Journal* arrived in the afternoon mail. I unfolded it to find photos of Jessie Devonshire and Randy Mendelson next to the front-page headline,
"New Evidence in Devonshire Case."

Amy's story described how the DNA evidence proved that Jessie's blood was on the floor in the entry hall of the Devonshire home. In the final paragraph, she mentioned "an unconfirmed report" that on the day Jessie was reported missing, a large stain was observed on the carpet in the entry hall, which Devonshire had explained away as spilled paint.

I was frankly surprised to see the newspaper stick its neck out and quote from Dick Hammond's interview of Devonshire. That was a good sign. The editor and publisher were not going to blindly defend Devonshire and his cronies. On the editorial page, I found more reason for optimism.

Under the headline, "Why No Investigation?" Amy castigated the authorities for having failed to adequately investigate the stained carpet when they observed it in 1980. She went on to speculate that Devonshire's political connections may have been the force behind the cover-up.

It would remain to be seen whether anyone else would pick up the story. Over the years, the Portland news media had shown a remarkable lack of curiosity about scandals involving any politicians they supported, and Wilson Devonshire was one of their favorites. I figured they would react only if the story got too big to ignore. The thing I had to do was help keep the story alive, so I logged onto Merlin and located Gary Turner's copy of Dick Hammond's handwritten notes from his Devonshire interview. I attached that image, along with the full transcript of the tape recording of that interview, to an email to Amy Powers.

Amy,

I applaud the courage that you and your newspaper have shown in publishing your article and editorial in today's paper. I am attaching documents that will support the "unconfirmed reports" that you quoted. If you are ever forced to prove the authenticity of these documents, I can provide other samples of Dick Hammond's handwriting.

You might already know that Dick Hammond died while working on the original investigation of the Mendelson-Devonshire case. Within two weeks, his partner, Gary Turner, also died. The investigation was suspended almost immediately thereafter. There's a story in that, and I can provide some help. But it will also underscore the risks I spoke of in relation to the Devonshire case.

I urge you to take those risks very seriously. Feel free to call me at anytime.

Corrigan

I had mixed feelings about taking Amy's story off on a tangent. I'd rather have stayed focused on the Devonshire case, but I could give her everything I knew about the deaths of Hammond and Turner without jeopardizing Kim's position in the sheriff's office. None of what I knew about their deaths had come from files that I wasn't supposed to have. And of course, Amy—and the general public—needed to know the character of the people who had been stifling the Devonshire investigation for three decades.

My phone started ringing at the very instant I pressed the Send key for the email.

"Corrigan," I answered.

"This is Lila. They're talking about Randy's case on the radio."

"What station?"

"It's on *The Lars Larson Show*. There's someone saying that Wilson Devonshire may have killed Randy and Jessie!"

"I'll call you back," I told her as I switched my radio on.

Lars was saying, "I haven't seen that article, so I can't really comment."

"It's the *Oregon City Journal*, front page story," the caller said, "Jason, do you have access to a fax machine?" Lars asked.

"Sure," Jason said, "I'll send that article right over."

Jason disconnected, and Lars said, "I'm not challenging what Jason said was in the article, but you have to understand that my stations are liable for anything they broadcast, so I need to be very careful with unconfirmed reports. Callers can say anything on the phone, but I need to have some documentation to protect myself, my producers, and my stations."

After a string of commercials, Lars came back on and said, "Before the break we were talking about an article in the *Oregon City Journal*. We now have Amy Powers, who wrote the article, on the phone. Ms. Powers, thank you for coming on the show today."

"Well, Lars, my phone hasn't stopped ringing since the newspaper hit the mailboxes today," Amy said, "and please call me Amy."

Lars got to the point. "You have written an article for the *Oregon City Journal* that contains blockbuster news about the famous—or infamous—Mendelson-Devonshire case. Amy, how confident are you about the validity of the DNA evidence that indicates that Jessie Devonshire may have been killed in her own home?"

"One hundred percent. We have confirmed the source of the blood sample, and we have confirmed that the DNA analysis was done by a highly respected lab using the latest processes."

"You said that the evidence that led to this DNA match was found by a private investigator."

"Yes, that is correct. He does not want his name publicized, but he did say that he is working for Lila Mendelson—Randy Mendelson's mother."

"Mrs. Mendelson has always maintained her son's innocence. Do you think this will exonerate him?"

"You know, Lars, that's hard to say. It certainly changes the way we have to look at the crime. If Jessie was killed in her home, you can't ignore the possibility that a member of her household was involved."

"Wilson Landis Devonshire," Lars said.

"It would be normal to look at family members in a case like this," Amy confirmed.

"You said that you have an 'unconfirmed' report that an investigator saw a large red stain on the carpet in the Devonshire home."

"That is correct. We have a copy the investigator's handwritten notes, saying that there was a large stain on the carpet just inside the front door of the house. We're trying to authenticate that note through handwriting analysis. The deputy who we believe wrote the note is no longer alive."

"So how did Wilson Devonshire explain the bloodstain on the carpet, and why wasn't it investigated at the time?"

"In the investigator's notes, it said that Devonshire had told him he had spilled a can of paint on the carpet. Apparently, the sheriff's office didn't see the need to investigate further."

"I'm not a criminal investigator, but that seems like a pretty serious oversight."

"I agree. I can only speculate why the carpet stain wasn't investigated. Maybe it was out of respect for Devonshire's position in the Portland mayor's office."

"I might expect that kind of respect for a major political figure, but Devonshire was aide to the mayor. That doesn't strike me as the kind of position that warrants a great deal of deference by law enforcement."

"I don't know how else to explain it, Lars," Amy concluded.

"Well, let me ask you this," Lars began. "Don't you have to wonder how it is that Devonshire 'just happened' to spill his paint over the very spot where Jessie's blood was found?"

"Of course," Amy said. "But remember, we don't know when Jessie's blood got on the floor. For all we know, it could have been years before—and there might be a perfectly innocent explanation. I'd like to ask Justice Devonshire about that, but he declined to speak with me."

"Somehow, that doesn't surprise me. So where do you go from here?"

"Well, like I said, we're working on authenticating the investigator's notes, and we have some other avenues to explore as well. There's more to this case than has ever been made public."

Lars ended the call with thanks to Amy, and then he took a succession of calls demanding Devonshire's scalp. With each caller, the charges against Devonshire escalated. There are no rules of evidence on talk radio, so callers were free to base inference upon inference until they had proven to their own satisfaction that the Oregon Supreme Court justice was guilty of a double murder and cover up.

While I agreed with their conclusion, I knew quite well that there wasn't enough evidence to get an indictment and conviction. But it was very useful to have Lars talking about it with his huge radio audience.

My phone rang again, and this time it was Amy Powers.

"This thing is exploding!" she exclaimed.

"Yeah," I said. "That was pretty gutsy talking about Devonshire's paint spill."

"I trusted that you'd come through with the evidence."

"You took a big chance. What if I didn't have it?"

"I'm pretty good at reading people," Amy explained. "If you didn't have the evidence, you'd have never brought up the subject. Now I'm trusting that you'll give me those handwriting samples."

"I have my assistant working on that. She'll get them to you this afternoon."

"Now what can you tell me about the deaths of Richard Hammond and Gary Turner?"

"We have copies of the newspaper articles relating to their deaths. We'll get copies of those to you."

"What made you look for those?"

"Lila Mendelson told me about Gary Turner's death. Then his widow told me about Hammond's death."

"How can I get in touch with the widow?"

"Don't. She lives in fear for her life, and whether her fear is justified or not, there's nothing she can tell you that you can't get from me."

"Okay…" she said slowly. "Anything else?"

"Marion Brighton," I said. "She's in the Portland phone book. She was the cop who found Hammond's body. Read the *Chronicle* articles, and then go talk to Brighton."

Martha gave me a wave.

I told Amy, "We're e-mailing the handwriting samples and the newspaper articles right now."

CHAPTER 42

THURSDAY, AUGUST 18

The morning *Chronicle* hit my porch at five, and I couldn't get back to sleep, wondering if there'd be a front page story about the Mendelson-Devonshire case. A quick glance confirmed that as expected, the paper was going to try to ignore or bury the story. But since I was up, I made coffee and sat down to go through the entire paper.

There was no mention of the news story that had broken in the little Oregon City weekly. I searched the radio and TV station websites, and the only station that had a story about the DNA match was the station that carried Lars Larson, and their coverage was pretty restrained. Unlike the *Oregon City Journal*, the radio station would not go out on a limb and mention Devonshire's paint spill—at least not until they could find independent confirmation.

Verification of the handwriting on Dick Hammond's notes would go a long way toward validating the evidence, and Amy Powers was working on that. No doubt, whatever she found out would not be mentioned until the *Journal's* next issue. It was disappointing, but we'd have to wait another week before shaking the major media loose.

At noon, when *The Lars Larson Show* came on, the first topic of discussion was the Devonshire case. Lars was still acting on the side of caution with regard to Devonshire's statement about the paint, but his callers wouldn't leave it alone. It sounded like the public—certainly the part of the public that listens to Lars Larson—was determined to see the investigation reopened. This was encouraging because it would keep the pressure on the mainstream media to get onboard with the story.

"Well I'll be damned!" I muttered to myself.

"No doubt," Martha agreed. "But to what do we attribute this sudden insight?"

"I just found Devonshire's ride!" I exclaimed.

Martha jumped up and came to look over my shoulder at my computer screen. "I've been cross-checking everything I can find about Richard Elgin," I explained, "and I got to thinking that Merlin might have something about his luxury home up there overlooking the city. So I queried the street name, Hillcrest, and look what came up!"

"The taxi logs?" Martha asked.

"Exactly! And look at this." I pointed at the screen.

✳ 2:55 p.m. Pick up 1620 Willamette Falls Dr./ Drop 5725 K St. WL

✳ 6:10 p.m. Pick up Mark's Tavern, 12th St & WF Dr./ Drop 2530 SW Hillcrest Dr. Ptld

✳ 8:20 p.m. Pick up 870 5th Ave. WL/ Drop at PDX

✳ 10:45 p.m. Pick up corner of Ostman & Dollar/ Drop 1548 Garden St. WL

✳ 11:30 p.m. Pick up Clyde's Bar & Grill, 15th & Willamette Falls Dr./ Drop 4330 Kelly St. WL

✳ 1:10 a.m. Pick up Clyde's Bar & Grill, 15th & Willamette Falls Dr./ Drop 1002 Jefferson St. OC

✳ 2:00 a.m. Pick up 13th and Willamette Falls Dr./ Drop 5660 Sinclair St. WL

"The second entry—someone took a cab ride from the Willamette District to Elgin's house at 6:10 p.m. on July 25. Mark's Tavern was right up the hill from the boat ramp!" I explained.

"Oh my god!" Martha exclaimed. "He left a car there for Devonshire to drive home after dumping the El Camino."

"And that was probably the second white car that Mary Drewsey saw on Devonshire's driveway. At the very least, it shows that Elgin was somehow involved."

"It was right there the whole time while we were looking for Trayborn! So maybe Trayborn was someone who saw the white car at Mark's Tavern."

"Maybe. But that doesn't fit with the idea that Trayborn lured Dick Hammond to his death. There has to be something we're still missing."

"Okay, let's say Devonshire killed Jessie and Randy. Then he called his office and arranged for Elgin to drive to West Linn to help with the cover-up. The two of them put the bodies into the El Camino and make a plan to dump it into the river. Elgin drops off his car at Mark's Tavern so that Devonshire has a way to get home in the middle of the night and then takes a cab home. Maybe *Trayborn* is just a name that Elgin made up to lure Hammond into a trap when he thought that he was getting too close," Marta speculated.

"That would explain why we've never been able to find anyone named Trayborn," I mused. After a little more thought, I said, "There's something wrong here. Elgin was catching his cab at Mark's Tavern at almost exactly the same time that Devonshire was buying his paint just a couple of blocks away. Seems like they'd have just parked Devonshire's car at Mark's Tavern. That way Elgin could simply drop off Devonshire at his house and drive on home."

"I see what you mean," Martha said. "There must have been some reason that Devonshire didn't want his own car parked at Mark's Tavern."

"Could be he was afraid that someone would recognize his car. That wouldn't have looked good if the El Camino had been discovered right away."

"But if Elgin was driving a city car, it would've looked just like Devonshire's. So what would be the point?"

"And it also leaves Devonshire with two city cars in his garage after he dumps the bodies."

"Could there have been something in the cars that Devonshire had to clean up—something that would take some time?" Martha wondered.

"Maybe, but they still could have done that before Elgin took the second car home," I pointed out.

Martha shrugged. "Maybe they just weren't thinking clearly. I mean, they had to be under a lot of stress."

"You're right, of course. We tend to think as though people always act rationally, even though we know it isn't true." Then another possibility came to mind. "Martha, suppose there was *another* person at Devonshire's house, and *he* needed the second car to get home?"

"If there was, I'll bet his name was Trayborn."

"Could be. But then, why wouldn't he and Elgin have simply gone together in the second car?"

"I don't know, maybe they were going opposite directions."

"It has to have something to do with timing. For some reason, Elgin had to get home. The other guy—Trayborn or whoever—may have needed more time to help Devonshire clean up the crime scene."

"I guess that means we have to keep looking for Trayborn," Martha said resignedly.

CHAPTER 43

FRIDAY, AUGUST 19

The red numerals on my digital clock said two thirty-eight. I listened carefully, attempting to determine what had awakened me. There it was—footsteps crunching in the gravel right outside. I quietly slipped out of bed and pulled on a pair of sweat pants. On my dresser lay my holstered Model 1911 Colt .45 automatic—not as fashionable as a Sig Sauer or a Glock, but damn effective. I hesitated for only a second before snatching it up.

The noise had come from someplace very close to my back door, so I tiptoed to the front. Quietly, I slipped out onto the porch, where I peeked around the corner. The outline of a small dark-colored car was visible in the blackness. I went to the opposite side and peered down the gap between my house and the fence, just in time to see the silhouette of a man appear from behind the house.

He was dressed in dark clothing and moving slowly and deliberately. I pulled the Colt from its holster and leveled it at the figure.

"Don't do anything stupid," I advised him.

The man froze for an instant, but then bolted to his right, back toward the alley and the parked car. I charged up the gap between the house and the fence and paused at the corner of the house. A car door slammed, and an engine started. I bolted from cover and ran to the alley, just as the car—which I now recognized as a black Acura—accelerated toward the highway, spraying gravel in every direction.

The Acura blasted from the alley onto the highway, straight into the path of a Kenworth double. Heading south at just over 40 mph, the driver of the rig had the throttle wide open in anticipation of the uphill stretch of highway ahead. He barely had time to lift his foot off the accelerator pedal before slamming into the Acura. Seventy thousand pounds of tractor-trailer mauled the Acura, grinding it into the pavement.

With the remains of the Acura wedged under the Kenworth, and all sixteen wheels locked up, the rig screeched to a stop half a block past the point of impact. Flames flashed over the twelve gallons of gasoline that spilled from the Acura's ruptured fuel tank. The gasoline flowed to the gutter at the side of the pavement and ran toward the storm drain.

The truck driver jumped down from the cab onto the highway and backed away from the fireball. He could see the same thing I saw. There was no helping the driver of the Acura. If he wasn't already dead, he was dying an excruciating death, pinned in his burning car.

Kim, having hastily thrown on her uniform, was on her hand held VHF calling for fire and rescue. Within thirty seconds, the sirens could be heard from Oregon City. Three minutes after the radio call, the first units arrived. The fire in the gutter now ran the full length of the tractor-trailer, creating a high curtain of flames between the wreck and the buildings along the highway.

"Back away!" Kim was shouting at some people who were approaching the wreck. "*Get back!* There's a hundred gallons of diesel fuel in that truck!"

She turned to some of the neighborhood people who were gathering in clusters on the sidewalk. "Somebody start knocking on doors. Get everyone out of those houses!" She gestured toward the structures nearest the fire.

City police were the first to arrive, and once they determined the futility of any rescue attempt, they set up a roadblock to stop northbound traffic from approaching the scene. The first fire engine arrived, and crews brought out chemical fire extinguishers and fired them at the burning wreckage beneath the Kenworth.

Great clouds of white exploded into the air, suppressing the flames that curled out of the demolished Acura. The orange flames darkened and turned into heavy black smoke, while the firemen continued to blast away with their fire extinguishers. Firefighters worked their way around the front of the Kenworth toward the wall of flames still burning along the curb.

Their prime focus was extinguishing the flames beneath the truck to prevent the big rig's fuel tanks from igniting. Each time they stopped spraying the Acura, the fire would flare up again. Gradually, the flames along the curb diminished as the fuel there was consumed.

The red-hot mass of crumpled steel crackled as it began to cool, and gradually the smoke diminished. More fire units arrived, and firefighters connected hoses to nearby fire hydrants. Once they were sure that all of the burning fuel had been extinguished, they started to spray water on the smoldering wreckage, sending up clouds of steam. About the only identifiable part of the Acura was the oversized chrome exhaust pipe.

Since I was wearing only my sweat pants and still carrying my .45, I took the occasion to hurry back inside and get dressed. By the time I got back, the panic had settled into ordered chaos. The highway was closed to all traffic, and spectators were urged to go back inside.

Rescue workers set to work figuring out how they were going to extract the remains of the Acura from beneath the semi. They directed the huge Peterbilt tow truck to back up to the front of the Kenworth, where they'd attempt to lift it off the Acura and allow rescue workers to remove the body of the driver.

I joined Kim at the edge of the scene.

"How did this happen?" she asked me when things settled down.

I said, "Something woke me up. I went outside to investigate and found a guy right next to where we were sleeping. He bolted for the Acura and neglected to look before pulling out onto the highway. The rest you can see."

"Was that the same Acura that's been here before?"

"Can't say for sure, but it's about 99 percent certain."

We were interrupted by the emergency tone from Kim's radio.

"This is Stayton. Go ahead," she said.

"There's a report of a boat drifting toward Willamette Falls. How soon can you get there?" the radio dispatcher said.

"I'll be on the river in five minutes," she said, waving to me. She signed-off and turned to me. "Come on," she commanded. "I need a ride across the river!"

I grabbed my keys and a portable spotlight and rushed with Kim down to my dock. Glancing to my right, I noticed that Daryl's boat was missing.

I shouted to Kim, "It's Daryl's boat! Martha is onboard."

I stepped into my boat and gave the primer bulb a few squeezes before climbing behind the wheel. Kim quickly untied the mooring lines.

The old Mercury outboard grumbled to life, and I pushed the control lever forward and felt the transmission engage. I eased away from the dock and then pushed the lever all the way forward. The Tigershark leapt forward and accelerated across the river toward the entry to the locks.

∂∘ᖆ

Martha half-awoke to the sound of a passing train. The boat jiggled, and the roar of the train went on and on. It gradually dawned on Martha that this must be the longest freight train she'd ever heard. Suddenly, she sat upright wide awake. Something wasn't right.

Peering out the starboard porthole from the bow stateroom, Martha was horrified to find herself staring over the brink of Willamette Falls. She bolted into the main salon, where the tall windows revealed a panoramic view of the thundering forty-one-foot falls.

Rushing out onto the after deck, she got a full view of the situation. The boat was flat against the flash boards atop the dam that runs around the rim of the falls. The low dam had been constructed over a hundred years earlier to provide a stable water level for the operation of the first hydroelectric plant in the nation.

The boat had floated a quarter mile downstream from Daryl's dock and drifted up against the dam midway between the spillways and the abandoned Blue Heron Paper Mill. The water level stood about six inches below the top of the flash boards, so there was no immediate danger of being swept over the top of the dam, but as Martha looked over the side of the boat, she realized that it was slowly moving away from the mill, toward the spillways.

The nearest spillway was open, and a great green tongue of water gushed into a frothing cauldron of whitewater that crashed down onto the rocks below. If the boat were to be sucked into the spillway, it would be shattered in an instant.

Martha rushed back into the salon and switched on the lights, thankful that they still worked. She found her phone and hurriedly punched the buttons.

"Nine-one-one, what's your emergency?"

Martha said, "I'm on a boat, and I'm right at the brink of the falls."

"What falls, ma'am? What is your location?"

"Willamette Falls," Martha yelled. "I'm looking right over the brink of the falls!"

"Ma'am, please be calm. Does your boat have power?"

"Yes, the lights are on," Martha replied, misunderstanding the question.

"Is the engine running?"

"No! The engines are dead."

"So you are without power?" the dispatcher clarified.

"Just the lights," Martha said, still confused.

"Ma'am, I've called for assistance. Do you understand? Help is on the way."

"Yes, yes! Tell them to hurry! I'm moving toward the spillway."

"How far away are you right now? From the spillway?"

"I don't know. Fifty feet, I guess, but the boat is moving."

"How fast is it moving?"

"Not fast. Maybe three or four feet a minute."

"That's good. There's time. You aren't in immediate danger. Can you tell me your name?"

"Martha. Martha Hoskins."

"Okay, Martha, are you wearing a lifejacket?"

"No, I was sleeping."

"If you have a life jacket, I want you to put it on. Do you understand?"

"Yes. I know where the life jackets are. Hold on." She put the phone down in order to get a lifejacket out of the compartment under one of seats in the salon. "Okay, I have it."

"Good. Martha, I want you to put it on and fasten all of the buckles, okay?"

"I'm doing it."

"Is the boat still moving?"

"Yes. I can hear it rubbing against the dam."

"Does your boat have an anchor?"

"I don't know."

"Okay, don't worry about that."

"I think I see someone coming!" Martha said suddenly.

"You see a boat?" the dispatcher asked.

"Yes! I can see lights on a boat."

"Where are you seeing the boat?"

"I see it out the front windows. It's going across the river. Why isn't it coming here?"

"It's okay, Martha. Help will be there soon. Just stay calm."

As we raced across the river, I sneaked a quick glance downstream. I spotted Daryl's boat up against the dam off to the right of the three spillways. Because of the angle, I couldn't tell how close it was, but it looked dangerously close.

I raced up to the sheriff's dock, and Kim hopped out. While I tied up my boat, Kim got aboard her Jetcraft patrol boat powered by a 454 Chevrolet V-8. She switched on the engine-room fan and pulled on her type V lifejacket. She tossed another one to me.

"You've just become a deputy," Kim said. "We can't wait for the cavalry."

The rumble of the big engine echoed across the water while I cast off the mooring lines. I put on the lifejacket while Kim pulled away from the dock. She switched on the overhead lights and lifted the microphone from the dash.

"Marine One to dispatch, Marine One to dispatch," she said.

"Dispatch. Go ahead, One."

"I'm en route to Willamette Falls. I'll be on scene in three minutes."

"We have confirmation that there is one person onboard."

"Ten-Four."

It took only about two minutes to recross the river and race downstream to a point adjacent to Daryl's boat. I could see lights on in the salon, but I didn't see anyone aboard. The boat was about forty feet to the right of the spillway, a frighteningly small distance.

Kim picked up the mic and said over the PA speakers, "Attention, Sea Ray, Attention, Sea Ray. Is anybody aboard?"

Martha appeared on the afterdeck and waved frantically.

"Okay, Martha, we're going to get you out of there. Are you injured?"

Martha shook her head.

"Is the boat taking on water?"

Again, Martha shook her head.

"Good. Now just stay where you are and hold on."

We were within twenty feet of the Sea Ray, and I could feel the cross current pulling us left toward the spillway. Hanging from a cleat on the port bow, I could see a dock line dangling into the water. Having assessed the situation, Kim shifted into reverse and backed away from the Sea Ray.

I could see the panic in Martha's eyes as we backed off about three boat lengths. Kim spun the Jetcraft into a quick 180-degree turn.

"Corrigan, if I back in there, can you grab that dock line?" Kim shouted.

"Get me close enough, and I can," I told her.

"Good! I want you to grab it and belay it on the pylon."

The roar of the spillway filled my ears, and I could see the Sea Ray creeping ever closer to it. Kim kept backing toward the Sea Ray, but the cross current was pulling us faster than it was moving the other boat. She had to pull forward and make another run. This time, she took aim at a point further aft. Martha started to climb up on the port rail, preparing to jump onto the Jetcraft.

I held up my hands and shouted, "No! Stay where you are!"

The cross current carried us toward the bow, and reaching as far as I dared, I managed to get a hand on the dock line. Quickly, I pulled it in and gave it two quick wraps around the pylon. A reverse loop over the top finished the belay.

"Okay, take it up," I shouted.

Kim eased the throttle forward, and the line went taut. The belay held.

"It's good!" I shouted. "Go! Go!"

The rumble of the 454 increased, and the Sea Ray started to move. The dock line strained.

I kept shouting, "Still good. Still good. She's coming around."

The bow of the Sea Ray slowly pulled away from the dam, and Kim pushed the throttle a little further. The boat turned and started following the Jetcraft crookedly away from the dam. Five feet. Ten feet. The roar of the engine matched the roar of the falls. Twenty feet. The pull from the spillway decreased.

I'd been watching my end of the dock line, making sure the belay didn't slip. I looked up toward the boat and saw that the other end of the line was coming loose from the cleat. Someone was going to have to teach Daryl how to tie up a boat!

"Ease up! Ease up!" I yelled.

Kim eased back on the throttle.

"We're losing her!" I shouted. "Stop!"

The line fell away from the cleat, and in an instant the Sea Ray was twenty feet behind us. I grabbed a coiled line from a stanchion on the Jetcraft's starboard rail and climbed out onto the swim platform. Kim backed in toward the bow of the Sea Ray, while both boats were drawn back into the current leading to the spillway. I ducked my head as we went in under the anchor pulpit.

I reached the bow eye and threaded the line through it. I pulled some slack and tied it off with a spilled-hitch bowline. I dived back into the Jetcraft and wrapped the line around the tow pylon.

"That's it!" I shouted. "Take it up."

Again, Kim pushed the throttle forward. The line went tight, and the Sea Ray fell in line behind us. I gave the towline a couple more wraps for good measure and belayed it with a loop.

"We're secure!" I shouted. "Let's get out of here!"

Kim towed the Sea Ray straight toward shore until we were safely out of the current, then she turned upstream toward Canemah. She brought the Jetcraft up alongside Daryl's dock, and I stepped off with the dock line. As the Sea Ray came alongside, I threw an overhand loop in one end of the dock line and fed it through the cleat, looped it over the ends, and pulled it tight.

I pulled the boat in and tied it off to a cleat on the dock. Meanwhile, Kim gave me some slack on the towline so that I could untie it from the bow eye. She gathered in the line and then tied up the Jetcraft at my dock. While she reported on the radio, I helped Martha onto the dock.

She started to walk toward shore, then wobbled and crumpled. I guided her fall into a chair on the dock, where she slumped with her head between her knees. She assured me that she was okay but didn't seem to be in any hurry to go anywhere. I went back and secured two more dock lines on the Sea Ray.

That's when I noticed the severed drain hose lying on the dock. Next to it was the cut end of the shore power cord, black with soot. A few feet away was a bolt-cutting tool, its jaws burned and pitted. That was when it became clear that this was no accident.

"Maybe you should spend the rest of the night up at the house," I suggested.

Kim and I walked with Martha up to the house. There were still emergency vehicles and flashing lights all over the highway.

"What's going on here?" Martha wondered.

"Hey, you people!" someone shouted. "What are you doing there?"

I turned to see a state police officer, waving us toward himself.

"What's going on?" I asked.

"This area is evacuated. You have to get out of here," the officer said.

"Evacuated?" Kim repeated. "What for?"

Seeing Kim's uniform, the officer adopted a peer-to-peer attitude. "Explosives. There's a big brick of Semtex in that wrecked car up on the highway."

"What?" I exclaimed.

The officer ignored me and asked Kim, "What are you folks doing here?"

"We just pulled this lady's boat away from the falls. It was a boat length from the spillway when we tied onto it," Kim explained.

"Busy night," the officer said.

"How far is the evacuation zone?" Kim asked.

"Six blocks," he said. "Basically all of Canemah."

Kim knew better than to ask how long it would take to reopen the area. She used her portable VHF to request someone to pick us up. We started walking up toward the Willamette Falls viewpoint. When we arrived at the police barricades, there was a sheriff's office patrol car waiting for us.

"Let's go to my place," Kim suggested and gave the driver her address.

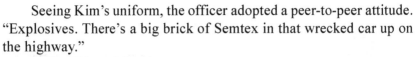

"Would either of you like something to drink, or am I going to have to drink alone?" Kim asked when we got to her place.

"Make mine Bushmills," I said.

"Same for me. Whatever," Martha said in a quavering voice.

CHAPTER 44

It was 4:45 a.m. and already getting light. There really wasn't much point in trying to get any sleep—we were all too keyed up. So we sat around Kim's table comparing our experiences.

"I just don't understand how the boat came untied," Martha said.

"It didn't do it all by itself," I told her.

"You mean…"

"The sewer hose and power cord were cut," I said matter-of-factly. "Someone intentionally untied the boat."

"But who…and why?" Martha asked.

"The same person who came to visit me with a brick of Semtex," I speculated.

"Do you think it was Elgin?" Kim asked.

"I got only a glimpse of him before he ran," I said, "but it didn't look like Elgin—wasn't tall enough. I think it could have been the guy I saw over at Herb Goble's place after I pulled his eavesdropping equipment. He drove the same way. You remember he almost got creamed that day when he pulled out into traffic without looking."

"I think he should've taken a class on anger management," Kim commented.

"The Acura belongs to Eglin—or rather to RTE Consulting, which is Elgin's company, so we can reasonably assume that whoever was driving it was working for Elgin," I figured.

"Then he'll send someone else to try again," Martha said.

"Maybe, but I'll bet he lays low for a while," I told her. "He might be able to talk his way out of this one, but if there's another incident traceable to him, he'd be in trouble.

"So he'll make sure it isn't traceable to him."

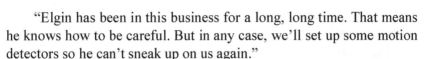

"Elgin has been in this business for a long, long time. That means he knows how to be careful. But in any case, we'll set up some motion detectors so he can't sneak up on us again."

We switched on the television and found a morning newscast on Channel 8. They had their helicopter circling over Canemah, and we could see that the tractor-trailer rig was still there. The reporter said that the bomb squad was still working to remove the explosives from the Acura. The victim had been removed but had not yet been identified.

"I wonder if it's safe to go pick up my boat," Kim asked.

"I think you'd be pretty well sheltered from the blast down at river level, but you could still get hit by airborne debris," I speculated.

"Yeah, that's what I figured." Kim sighed. "I guess I'd better call in and explain the situation before Cushman shows up and finds your boat parked where mine should be."

"That ought to be fun," I teased.

She phoned in and told the dispatcher that the patrol boat was unavailable as long as the Canemah evacuation order was in effect. She explained how she had ended up in Canemah after rescuing Martha from the brink of the falls. The dispatcher agreed to notify Kim as soon as the evacuation order was lifted.

With nothing else to do and no way to go anywhere, Kim suggested, "I'm going to take a shower, and then I'll make us some breakfast."

An hour later, we sat down to an extravagant breakfast. The TV was still on, but we'd long since tired of the endless repetition of the few facts known to the reporters, so the volume was turned low.

We were just finishing breakfast when we saw on the TV a live shot of a state police vehicle towing a trailer with a blast-containment vessel. Turning up the sound, we heard the reporter say that the explosives had been safely removed from the wrecked car.

Figuring that the evacuation would soon be lifted, Kim called for a patrol car to come to her condo and give us a ride down to my place so she could get her boat. When we arrived at the roadblock on Highway 99, we were told that the highway would remain closed for at least four more hours, but that residents were being allowed back into Canemah.

We seemed to be the first people back—or at least I didn't see anyone else around. I made a quick check of my house, which I hadn't had a chance to lock up, and found everything untouched. Martha went down to the Sea Ray to change clothes, while Kim and I took the marine patrol boat back to the sheriff's dock.

I hopped into my boat and motored back across the river to my dock. Up at the house, I made coffee and then sat down to plan my day. The morning news on the radio was filled with coverage of the wreck in Canemah and the subsequent bomb scare. There was also a brief story about the marine unit's rescue at the falls, but of course, details were sparse and no connection was made between the two incidents.

The knock on my door was followed by Bud's voice.

"Hey, Corrigan, was that your friend in the Jap car who got barbecued out there?" Bud asked.

"Come on in, Bud," I said. "How about a cup of coffee?"

Bud came in. "What happened out there? Do you know?"

"I got up because I heard someone outside," I told him.

"The guy ran to the car—which I'm pretty sure was the same one that's been coming around—and he bolted out onto the highway. Didn't bother to look for cross-traffic."

"I heard the crash, and when I looked outside, all I could see was fire."

"I guess the truck driver got out okay."

"Hey, where did *you* go? I saw you racing out onto the river in your boat."

"So you didn't hear that Daryl's boat almost went over the falls?"

"What! Are you kidding me?" Bud exclaimed.

"Someone cut it loose—probably the guy in the Acura," I told him. "I took Kim over to get her patrol boat, and we went down and towed the boat back away from the falls."

"I heard that a boat nearly went over the falls, but I didn't know—Hey! Was Martha still onboard?"

"She got a view of the falls that she'll never forget."

"But wait. Why would that guy cut the boat loose?" Bud asked.

"Good question," I said. "Martha's going to need some help getting the drain hose and power line reconnected. I'm afraid you'll have to splice them."

"Okay, I'll take care of that, no problem. Maybe I'd better go take a look—see what it's going to take to fix it."

My phone rang, so Bud excused himself and headed out the door.

"Corrigan, this is Amy Powers."

"Good morning, Amy."

"Hey, I hear you had some excitement down there."

"Enough to last me for a week or two."

"Were you involved?" Amy asked.

I told her the highlights of the story, leaving out for the time being the fact that I knew who owned the Acura. That would come out soon enough, along with the identity of the dead man.

"Would you let me come down with a photographer?" Amy requested.

"The person whose picture you need is Deputy Stayton—she's the one who made the rescue on the river. All I did was tie a knot, but if you can get down here quickly, you can get some pictures of the wreckage on the highway. Just tell them at the roadblock that you live down here—they won't know the difference," I told her.

"Great! We'll be right down."

Amy and her photographer arrived about ten minutes later and went straight out to the highway to shoot pictures of the efforts to clean up the wreck. By then, all of the other media people had talked their way past the roadblocks, so the area was crowded with reporters and cameramen. I showed her where the Acura had sped out of the alley into the path of the semi.

"What was he doing in the alley?" Amy asked.

"You know Martha Hoskins, my assistant? She was sleeping aboard the boat she rents down here when someone cut the boat loose. That happened right about the time our now-crispy friend came to visit," I said.

"Are you saying he cut the boat loose?"

"I can't say that for sure. But *someone* cut the boat loose, and he seems to be the most likely suspect."

"So that was the boat that almost went over the falls, Amy speculated.

"Right now, you're the only news people who know that," I confirmed.

Over the next hour, I told Amy the full story, starting with the prowler outside my house and finishing with the rescue of Martha from the falls. When we'd exhausted that subject, Amy asked what I could tell her about the deaths of Dick Hammond and Gary Turner.

I showed her the notes the two had written during the final weeks of their investigation—and their lives. Then I told her about my visit with Leslie Turner Charleston and explained how I had come into possession of the Mendelson-Devonshire investigation documents.

"Corrigan, I'd like to see those files," Amy said.

"Listen, somebody is serious about killing everyone who has seen those files," I reminded her.

"What difference does it make whether you show the documents to me one piece at a time or all at once?" she challenged.

"The problem with that is that the Sheriff will see only one possible way that we could have gotten those files. He'll assume that Kim Stayton took them illegally from the file room. That will be the end of her job."

"Won't he assume the same thing about the documents you're giving me?"

"No, the documents I'm giving you were never in the official file. All of this was in the personal files that Turner locked in his storage locker before he died."

"But sooner or later, you'll have to reveal the other files, won't you?"

"Here's the thing. Sheriff Kerby is an elected official. That makes him more a member of a political party than he is a member of law enforcement. I think he spiked the Devonshire investigation because the people at the controls of his political machine don't want to see Devonshire harmed. I don't know if Kerby can ever be separated from his political cronies, but that's what has to happen before it'll be safe to show everything we have."

"That kind of limits what we can do," Amy objected.

"I know, but there's still plenty for you to publish. If you can convince your readers that Dick Hammond was murdered to suppress the Devonshire investigation, there'll be too much public pressure for the sheriff to keep the lid on this."

"We're still just a small-town weekly newspaper," she reminded me.

"That's right, and your small-town weekly newspaper is going to shame the mighty *Portland Daily Chronicle* into doing its job," I said emphatically.

After Bud finished reconnecting the sewer and electrical service to the boat, I told Martha to take the day off and get some rest. Bud found a piece of chain and a padlock and chained the boat to the dock. At the very least, that would make it a bit more difficult for anyone to cut the boat loose.

I was walking up from the dock when I saw Kim drive up, not in her marine-unit SUV, but in her personal Mustang.

"You're off duty early," I commented.

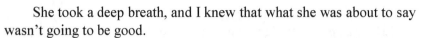

She took a deep breath, and I knew that what she was about to say wasn't going to be good.

"Yeah. Maybe permanently. They've suspended me," she said.

"What for?" I asked.

"They're going to review the way I conducted the rescue last night. They think I took unnecessary risks by taking a civilian onboard."

"That's a load of crap. If you hadn't done it the way you did, Martha would be dead."

"Well, that's the way I see it. We'll see if I can convince the review board."

"When will that be?"

"I have no idea. If Kerby wants to, he can drag it out forever."

"He won't do that. Once the news hits the air, you'll be the biggest hero on the job. Kerby won't be able to keep you suspended."

"I don't even know if it's going to make the news. So far, there's been no press release. I filed my report and got the call from Kerby."

"Okay then, if Kerby isn't going to do a press release, I will."

Martha joined us in the office, and while I wrote up a detailed report of what Kim had done, she searched for the email addresses for all of the major news outlets in Portland. The one thing we agreed not to reveal was that Martha's boat had been cut loose. That could wait. At the bottom of the press release, I signed Corrigan Investigations, and my phone number.

Five minutes after Martha sent her email, my phone rang. It didn't stop ringing for the next hour. And then for the rest of the afternoon, Kim, Martha, and I posed for pictures and gave video interviews. We even took a group of reporters for a ride up to the Willamette Falls Viewpoint to point out exactly where the rescue took place.

I shuttled Kim and a couple of camera teams across the river in my boat to shoot video of the marine-unit Jetcraft, and Martha did a great job of describing what it was like to wake up looking over the brink of the second biggest waterfalls in the US.

By three, the radio stations were already on the air with the story and all of the TV crews were racing back to their studios to put together their stories for the evening news. Before seven that night, Deputy Kim Stayton was the biggest celebrity in Oregon. There's no telling what kind of response any of the news media people got if they contacted the sheriff's office, but we didn't hear any mention of Kim's suspension.

"Kerby is really going to be pissed," Kim lamented.

She was probably right, but I said, "He should be grateful. This is the best publicity the sheriff's office has had in years."

"That doesn't mean he won't be pissed."

"Yeah, but all of the press releases came from me. It was all beyond your control."

She knew better. "He won't fall for that. I gave the interviews and posed for the pictures."

Kim's phone rang, and she listened for ten seconds before saying, "Seven thirty. I'll be there. Thanks." She turned to me and said, "Cal Westfall has called a press conference over at the marine-unit dock at seven thirty—wants me to be there. That means we have just time enough for a glass of wine—providing we go by boat instead of by road."

"Does that mean you're un-suspended?" I asked.

"Cal didn't say. I guess I'll find out when we get there."

CHAPTER 45

SATURDAY, AUGUST 20

Cal Westfall's press conference could best be characterized as damage control. It was Kerby's best attempt to salvage appearances in a media fiasco. He was indeed pissed—at Kim, at me, and at the world in general, or so it appeared. He had little choice but to reinstate Kim to active duty, even though she would still have to face the review board. I carefully stayed out of his way.

Saturday morning, Kim left my place at 7:00 a.m. Over a quick breakfast, we read the two stories on the front page of the *Chronicle*.

Willamette Falls Rescue

An Oregon City woman was rescued from near-certain death in the predawn hours Friday morning, when the boat she was on got loose from its moorings and was nearly swept over Willamette Falls. Martha Hoskins was sleeping aboard a 30-foot Sea Ray cabin cruiser that had been tied up at a dock about a quarter mile above the falls. She awoke to find the boat sideways against the dam at the brink of the 41-foot falls and drifting toward the spillway.

Clackamas County Sheriff's Deputy Kim Stayton performed a dramatic rescue using a 22-foot jet boat. Stayton is head of the Sheriff's Office Marine Unit, and was assisted in the rescue by a civilian, identified as March Corrigan.

According to witnesses, Ms. Hoskins' boat was "within a boat-length" of the spillway when the rescuers secured a line to it and pulled it toward shore. Asked why a civilian was aboard the Sheriff's Office rescue boat, Deputy Stayton said, "I couldn't make the rescue alone, and if I'd waited for another deputy to arrive, we would have been too late. If we had been one minute later, the boat would have gone over the falls."

Ms. Hoskins said she had no idea how her boat got loose, but that she was "very grateful for the quick and courageous actions of Deputy Stayton."

In a fortunate coincidence, Deputy Stayton was able to respond almost immediately to the distress call from Hoskins because she was on the scene of a fiery crash on Highway 99E, less than a hundred yards from the dock where Hoskins' boat had been moored. Corrigan, who also lives in the area, gave Deputy Stayton a ride in his own boat across the river to the Sheriff 's Office moorage at the Willamette Falls Locks before joining her on the Marine Unit jet boat for the rescue.

The runaway boat was towed back to its original mooring place and was reportedly undamaged. Immediately after tying up the two boats, Stayton, Hoskins, and Corrigan were ordered to evacuate the area because explosives had been found in the wrecked car on the highway. A Beaverton man died in that crash.

The first paragraph of second article contained the surprise of the day.

Explosives Found After Fiery Crash

A 57-year-old Beaverton man died in a fiery crash involving his compact car and a tractor-trailer rig early Friday morning on Highway 99E south of Oregon City, in the Canemah National Historic District. The victim was identified as Trey Bourne, driver of a 1999 Acura that apparently entered the highway from an alley into the path of a southbound semi driven by Thomas Dundee of Missoula, Montana. Dundee escaped without injury.

The small car was crushed beneath the semi and immediately burst into flames, igniting gasoline from the ruptured fuel tank and creating a block-long wall of fire along the curb. Witnesses were unable to approach the wrecked car to attempt a rescue because of the intense heat.

Off-duty Clackamas County Sheriff's Deputy Kim Stayton was first at the scene and called emergency services at 2:40 a.m. First responders immediately called in a second alarm upon seeing the extent of the fire. Firefighters used chemical fire extinguishers to suppress the flames and then used water to cool the wreckage.

The entire community of Canemah was evacuated at 3:30 a.m. when explosives were found by rescue workers in the car driven by Bourne. Oregon State Police bomb-disposal experts worked for more than three hours to safely remove the device, which was described as a two pound brick of plastic explosive armed with an electric detonator. The bomb was removed from the scene and taken to a remote location for safe disposal.

Stephen Troy, spokesman for Clackamas Fire and Rescue, said that the bomb was spotted by firefighters who were working to remove Bourne's body from the wreckage. Troy said that the partially burned brick of explosive material was lying in the passenger seat foot well of the Acura.

An explosives expert told the Chronicle that the quantity of Semtex found in the Acura could have leveled everything within a hundred-yard radius had it exploded. He also said that

Semtex cannot be detonated by fire and will simply burn if ignited. "That," he said, "is why the bomb did not detonate during the fire following the car crash."

Investigators declined to speculate on why Bourne was carrying the explosive device or what he was doing in the Canemah area. The Clackamas County Sheriff 's Office and Oregon State Police are continuing the investigation.

Trey Bourne—we finally knew who Trayborn was! When Leslie Turner took the phone message, she wrote the name the way she heard it. Now we had a name we could work with, and we'd be able to find out who he really was, even though I already had a pretty good idea. He worked for Richard Elgin. That much was certain. I don't know what his job title was, but I sincerely doubted that he had a written job description for the work that he did. He was what is called a mechanic, someone who does the dirty work—like killing inquisitive deputies, planting listening devices, and blowing-up private investigators.

But tracking down the details of Trey Bourne's life would have to wait. My first priority was to set up some security systems to discourage anyone from making another attempt to kill Martha and me. I used the same wireless motion detectors on Daryl's dock that I'd used to catch Bourne opening the receiver box on Herb Goble's house. I gave Martha a remote control for turning the system on and off.

I set up a similar system to trigger an alarm if anyone came prowling around my house, and augmented it with a motion-activated, low-light video recorder. While I was installing the sensors, I made a curious observation about where Trey Bourne had been when I interrupted his attempt to plant his bomb. If it had been his intention to simply blow my house and anyone in it sky high, he could have easily pushed his bomb into a foundation vent that was quite visible on the side of the house next to the alley. If he'd done that, I'd have never heard him.

Instead, Bourne chose to creep around the house, across the loose gravel that made the sounds that woke me up. There was really only one good reason to do that. The place where he was preparing to plant the bomb was directly adjacent to the location of my hidden safe. But how could he have known that?

Only two possibilities came to mind. Either he got the information from the contractor who installed the safe two years earlier or he got it from someone who had found the safe during the district attorney's search for Elgin's allegedly stolen surveillance equipment. It made me wonder if that wasn't the real reason for the search.

Elgin knew I had Turner's files because he'd followed me to the storage unit. Unless he had seen me carry the boxes into the bank, he would have assumed that I still had them at home. So while Roger Millican's squad searched for surveillance equipment, someone there was looking for Turner's files—and found the location of my safe. The logical assumption would have been that the files were in the safe.

That would explain the excessive amount of Semtex Bourne was trying to plant. He wasn't just trying to kill me. He was trying to destroy my safe and its contents. Someone on that search team was connected to the same fraternity as Trey Bourne, Richard Elgin, and Wilson Devonshire. The logical suspect would be Roger Millican himself, though I couldn't definitively reach that conclusion without first excluding the other possibilities.

"This is Gates," came the answer to my phone call.

"Corrigan here. Can you get me a list of everyone who was here during the DA's search?"

"No problem. I probably already have that information.

Anything else?" he asked with his customary brevity.

"Any update on what's happening with that investigation?" I asked.

"Nothing new. I'll let you know if anything breaks. And I'll email that list of names."

"Great, thanks," I said to the dead phone.

৯৵৶

Devonshire was an important person, but it was hard to imagine that he had the kind of network it would take to influence the county sheriff, the district attorney, and the city police. The man at the top of the machine was Alan Blalock, the godfather of Oregon politics. There were hundreds, if not thousands, of people ready to do just about anything for Blalock simply to gain his favor. Compartmentalization was the key to making a thing like this it work. It didn't function as a single grand conspiracy, but rather as dozens of small tight conspiracies, all reporting to one person—the godfather's "business manager." Could that be Devonshire's role? As Blalock's personal aide in Portland City Hall, that was precisely Devonshire's job. Was it possible that he still served in that capacity?

The best way to track a network was to read telephone records. I was already pretty sure that Trey Bourne got his orders from Richard Elgin. If I could get my hands on Elgin's phone records, I'd probably have the phone number of the business manager.

Of course, there was no way I could get the phone companies to hand over Elgin's phone records. The next best way to find out who Elgin was talking to was to pick up his trash. With Portland's compulsive obsession with recycling, citizens were perpetually urged to sort their bottles, cans, papers, and garbage and put them in separate containers at the curb. I needed to find out when Elgin's trash was collected.

My next call went to Kaylin Beatty. Real-estate companies maintain lists of everyone who provides services to homeowners for the benefit of people moving into a new neighborhood. Kaylin was able to tell me that Consolidated Recycling & Waste served the neighborhood where Elgin lived.

Next, I called CRW and asked when they collected trash on SW Hillcrest Drive. They told me that trash and recycling should be put out Monday night because collection would be early Tuesday morning every week. I knew where I'd be at dawn on Tuesday.

CHAPTER 46

MONDAY, AUGUST 22

Monday morning, I put Martha on the task of finding out everything she could about Trey Bourne. As she'd done with Elgin and attempted to do with "Trayborn," she got on her computer and searched the online databases, picking up bits of information wherever they were available.

Trey Bourne had grown up in San Jose, California. After graduation from high school, he joined the Marine Corps in 1973. In the post-Vietnam era, Bourne was stationed first in South Carolina and later in Hawaii. He was honorably discharged in 1978. In January of 1979, Bourne enrolled in the Portland Police Academy. He was a patrolman for the Portland Police Bureau at the time Jessie Devonshire and Randy Mendelson disappeared. Bourne got married in 1981 and bought his first house, a modest bungalow in southeast Portland, a few months later. He resigned from the police force in 1984 and went to work for RTE Consulting, where he worked until his death. In 1988, he bought a house in a new subdivision on Cooper's Mountain.

He was divorced at the time he bought that house, but the date of the divorce was not known. His ex-wife got custody of their two children and apparently moved out of state. Bourne made child-support payments until 2005.

He made the news as a member of a mountain climbing party that was reported lost on Mt. Hood in 1990, but they found their way off the mountain without assistance after spending the night in a snow cave. Bourne was praised for having the survival skills that saved the rest of the group.

He had arrests for assault in connection with a barroom brawl in 1987 and for discharging a firearm in a residential neighborhood in 1992. In the latter case, he shot a neighbor's dog, which Bourne claimed was attacking him. The neighbor said the dog was pissing on Bourne's car tire. Bourne paid restitution in an unknown amount, and the firearm was confiscated.

Bourne had two cars, a 1958 Corvette and a 2007 Corvette. He also had a twenty-five-foot Allegro Class C motorhome. All in all, Bourne appeared to have led a rather unremarkable life. Nothing in the record suggested that he was the kind of person who would lure Dick Hammond to a clandestine meeting and then kill him with heroin.

But we knew that he *was* the kind of person who would plant two pounds of Semtex under someone's house and who would try to send someone over Willamette Falls, so the idea that he had murdered Dick Hammond was pretty easy to believe.

CHAPTER 47

TUESDAY, AUGUST 23

With a big cardboard box in the back of my Yukon, I was off before dawn, heading to SW Hillcrest Drive to pick up Richard Elgin's trash. I drove slowly up his street past dark houses, seeing trash cans and recycle tubs sitting on the curb. Two blue tubs overflowing with Elgin's papers sat next to his driveway.

I stopped next to the tubs and pressed the hatch-release button. Quickly, I hopped out and lifted the rear hatch. Elgin's recycle tubs were stacked tall with old newspapers, weighted with bricks to keep them from blowing away.

Knocking the bricks aside, I hurriedly tossed all of the paper into the box in the back of the Yukon. I put the empty tubs back on the curb, quietly closed the hatch, and was driving away within twenty seconds. It seemed highly unlikely that anyone had seen me.

Back home before six, I emptied the box onto the floor in my garage and started to understand how lucky I'd been. It was obvious that I was looking at more than one week's worth of paper. In fact the first newspaper I picked up was from late June, and mixed in with all of the newspapers, I saw all kinds of bills.

Digging through the heap, I set aside all of the newspapers until all that was left was a stack of junk mail and bills. People really should get into the habit of shredding their bills instead of relying on the integrity of anyone who might pick through their recycle bins.

I hit the jackpot with Elgin's July and August bills from CenturyLink and Verizon. I threw everything else into my own recycle bin. As might be expected, most of Elgin's phone activity was on his cell phone. All I needed to do was use a reverse directory service that I subscribe to, and I'd have the names of everyone Elgin had talked to in the previous month.

Martha went to Portland to see what she could find in the newspaper archives and library about Trey Bourne. It was the same search she'd done before, but now she had the right name. Despite my desire to dig into Richard Elgin's phone bills, I got busy on the Xycon work that I had intended to do the previous Friday. I didn't want to neglect my bread-and-butter clients.

The heavy pounding on my door startled me out of my online snooping.

"Hey, Corrigan," the rough-edged female voice demanded, "you in there?"

I got up and said, "Hold on, Rosie. I'm here."

Rosie Bly, dressed in a short and well-worn bathrobe, stood on my porch with her arms crossed and a look of ferocious anger on her face. It was perhaps the first time I'd ever seen her without a glass of cheap wine in her hands.

"Someone trashed my trailer," Rosie blurted.

My first thought was, *How would she know?* But setting aside housekeeping issues, I asked, "When did this happen?"

"While I was asleep. Sometime after the Leno Show last night."

"Why don't you tell me the whole story," I suggested.

She snorted and said, "I went to bed last night, and when I got up this morning, the door was open, and there was stuff all over the floor, and my kitchen looks like a tornado hit."

"Is anything missing?"

"Damn right!" Rosie exclaimed. "They took a whole box of wine—well, it wasn't quite full, 'cause I opened it Sunday—and what they didn't drink, they dumped on the floor!"

It didn't sound to me like a burglary. More like teenage vandalism. We did have a neighborhood reprobate who had been caught spray-painting obscene words on the sides of garages, but trashing Rosie's trailer while she was in it seemed like a major escalation.

"Let's go take a look," I suggested.

Rosie led the way up the railroad tracks, past Big Dan's place, to the slab where her trailer was parked. As we approached her front door, Rosie bent down to pick up her morning paper, and I was momentarily subjected to a sight that no person should ever have to see. Oblivious, she opened the screen door and pointed inside.

The scene of destruction that greeted me went far beyond Rosie's normal state of disarray. The small refrigerator stood open, and everything in it had been swept onto the floor. A half-eaten head of lettuce, broken jars of mayonnaise and grape jelly, a package of chicken wings, and several Chinese take-out boxes were all stirred together with half a loaf of bread, a bag of potato chips, and a five-liter box of Burgundy.

"You slept through this?" I asked in amazement.

Rosie shrugged, "I'm a heavy sleeper."

Now the truth is that I was hoping to find something that I could pin on that teenager who made a habit of stealing things off of people's docks—except Big Dan's—and who intermittently ran a shake-and-bake meth lab in his parents' garage. But the carnage in front of me simply didn't fit any pattern of teenage vandalism that I'd ever heard of.

"Look at that!" Rosie exclaimed, pointing at something in the middle of the floor. "They shit in my kitchen!"

Seeing what she was pointing at changed my whole perception of the crime. I backed out the door and studied the ground around the trailer and the path leading across the railroad tracks and down to the river. There I found the footprints of the culprit.

"Rosie," I asked, "did you have your door locked last night?"

She snorted. "I just had the screen door closed last night. It was too damned hot to lock up."

I opened and closed the screen door, confirming what I suspected. The latch was broken so that only a weak spring held the screen door shut.

"Take a look at this, Rosie." I pointed to footprints on the dirt path coming up from the river.

"What the hell's that?" Rosie asked, squinting at the ground.

"I believe those are raccoon tracks."

"What? What the hell are raccoons doing here?"

"Actually, they are pretty common along the edge of the river. Usually, they eat crawdads and berries, but it looks like a family of them paid you a visit last night," I explained.

Rosie calmed down a bit. "Raccoons, huh? Never heard of 'em raiding a house before"

This wasn't the sort of investigation I could charge for. I'd write it off as pro bono work for the general good of humanity. Besides, Rosie would need her money to replace the wine taken by the animals. My only worry was what kind of havoc might be wrought by a family of wine-drunk raccoons.

When I told the story to Kim that night, she howled with laughter.

"I don't know which is scarier. A drunken raccoon or a sober Rosie," I said.

"It was sweet of you to help her out," Kim said.

Changing the subject, I asked, "How are things going between you and Kerby?"

"He's not going anywhere with his review board thing. He's still pissed off at me, though, and he's none too happy about your press-release stunt."

"I'm not surprised. But it did put an end to your suspension," I reminded her.

"Still he'll be looking for any excuse he can find to nail me—or you, for that matter. How's your big investigation coming?

"I think we have Devonshire in a box. With the pathologists reports on the bodies from the El Camino and the report on the gun, we can prove not only that both Jessie and Randy were murdered, but also that Devonshire lied about just about everything when he reported Jessie missing. We have the DNA evidence, and we can prove that he covered up the bloodstain on the carpet. We can show that Elgin left a car at Mark's Tavern for Devonshire to drive home after dumping the bodies and have the phone call showing when Devonshire called for Elgin's help. We even have a photo of Devonshire standing next to the bronze eagle that probably crushed Jessie's skull."

"That's all just fine, but those pathology reports and the ballistics lab report are still not public knowledge. The second you reveal that information, I'm toast. If Kerby's looking for a reason to dump me, that'll give it to him."

"I wonder what would happen if your lab techs saw a copy of the note attached to the back of the weapons lab report—the one that said, 'CCSO indicates that their personnel may have inspected the weapon before it was sent to lab.' Would they force the issue?"

"They probably would, but that could still blowback at me."

"I don't think so. As long as no tracks lead back to me, Kerby doesn't have anything on you."

"I hate this!" Kim growled.

"No, listen," I insisted, "I can make a copy of the weapons-lab report with the note on the back. I can make it show up in a mailbox, and nobody will know where it came from. When the people who handled the gun after it was taken out of the El Camino see that they've been branded as incompetent, they'll go ballistic."

Kim dug in. "I still think it's just the kind of thing that Kerby would use to burn me."

"But there's no connection to you. I'll tell you what. I'll take the letter to Salem and mail it from there, so it'll look like it came from someone in the weapons lab. There have to be people there who know that the official CCSO conclusions are bullshit. Why would Kerby—or anyone else—doubt that someone down there would tip off the techs that they're being used as scapegoats."

"Damn! I know you're right. But I still don't like it," Kim said resignedly.

CHAPTER 48

WEDNESDAY, AUGUST 24

Not wanting to wait for the mail delivery, I drove up to the office of the *Oregon City Journal* and bought an early copy over the counter. The entire front page was given over to reports of Kim's rescue at Willamette Falls and the wreck on Highway 99E and subsequent discovery of the Semtex bomb.

The articles were accompanied by photos of the wreckage, an official CCSO portrait of Kim, photos of Daryl's Sea Ray and Kim's Jetcraft, and photos of Martha and me. I could have done without seeing my own photo there, but it was hardly unexpected.

On the editorial page, I found a long, detailed article entitled "The Strange Death of Richard Hammond," written by Amy Powers. She first gave the known—albeit sparse—history of the discovery of Hammond's body and the subsequent dismissal of his death as an accidental overdose by a junkie. But what Amy did that had never been done before was to tie Hammond to the Devonshire investigation and the death of Gary Turner. These connections led directly to the evidence found in Turner's personal files, most notably the whole scenario surrounding the bloodstained carpet, Devonshire's attempt to conceal it, and the recovery of Jessie's DNA from the flooring.

On the facing page, I found another editorial. This one was entitled "The Unanswered Questions about Trey Bourne." Here Amy reviewed the events surrounding Bourne's death, the likelihood that his bomb was intended for me, and his probable involvement in cutting loose Daryl's boat.

With that connection established, she then revealed that Bourne's two intended victims, Martha and me, had been involved in a private investigation of the Devonshire case. She then tied Bourne to RTE Consulting and Richard Elgin, which connected them to Wilson Devonshire through the Portland Mayor's Office circa 1980.

Amy Powers was taking this to the wall. I reread both articles, and I could see no way that the major media in Portland could ignore this. Everything in the articles was documented, and all of Amy's logic was sound. It would be fun to see who'd get onboard first.

Setting the *Journal* aside, I got to work on my major task of the day. I put on a pair of white cotton gloves and opened a fresh package of printer paper. I loaded it into my laser printer and then printed a two-sided copy of the Oregon State Police Weapons Lab report that described the position of the cylinder and shell casings in the gun from the El Camino.

On the back side of the sheet, I highlighted the Post-it note that said someone at the Clackamas County Sheriff's Office had told the weapons lab that the technicians had tampered with the gun before sending it to Salem. Still wearing the gloves, I folded the sheet and put it in a business envelope. It wasn't likely that anyone would ever check the copy for fingerprints, but if they ever did, they wouldn't find mine.

Pocketing the gloves, I took the envelope out to my Yukon. It took me about forty-five minutes to drive to the headquarters of the Oregon State Police on the capitol mall next to the Oregon State Capitol Building. In the reception area, I found applications for employment, and I made a show of sitting down and filling out the form.

After a while, I went up to the desk and asked, "Do you have an envelope that I could use to mail this in? I have to get out of here before my parking meter runs out."

The lady at the counter helpfully gave me an envelope, which I was careful to hold by the edges. I took the envelope down the hall to a restroom. There, I put on the cotton gloves and transferred the weapons-lab report into the official Oregon State Police envelope. I used a dampened paper towel to seal the envelope and then peeled the preprinted address label from its backing and stuck it onto the envelope.

I walked up to the second floor and went into the first office I came to. A helpful lady looked at my visitor's badge and asked if she could help me.

"Yeah, can you tell me where the personnel office is?" I asked.

"Just go downstairs to the lobby. They'll be able to help you," she said.

"Okay, thanks. Hey, could you drop this in the mail for me?" I asked without explanation.

She took the envelope and said, "Sure. No problem."

If anyone ever tried to track the source of the lab report, it would carry the postage-machine imprint of the State Police Headquarters. Nobody could ever connect it to me or to Kim. The envelope was addressed to David Elkton, CSI criminalist at the Clackamas County Sheriff's Office in Oregon City.

What happened after Elkton opened the envelope was beyond my control, but I doubted that he'd simply shrug it off and toss it into the trash. Somebody in a position of authority had accused him and his co-workers of gross incompetence, and he'd want to find out who and why.

Back at the office I sat down to finally start looking up the phone numbers from Richard Elgin's phone bills. My phone rang, and the caller ID said Bill Cheshire. Damn. I knew what that meant.

"It's been ten days, Corrigan," Bill started. "When can I expect those records?

I groaned. "You wouldn't believe the condition they're in. I swear, my ex-wife must've put the whole mess in the clothes dryer. There's ten years worth of records all shuffled into a disorganized mass."

"Better bite the bullet, my friend. The meeting with the auditors is scheduled for next Tuesday. I'll need those records organized so that I can defend your deductions."

"I'll get it to you in time," I told him, though I couldn't figure out how.

"Can you get it to me by the weekend?" Cheshire asked.

"I'll give it my best," I assured him.

I set Eglin's phone bills aside and went to the front closet where I'd stashed the boxes of paper the night I brought them home from Marie's place. There were four cardboard boxes, all from the liquor store. I randomly selected one box and took it to my desk.

I laid out a tray for each year from 2004 through 2007. The first receipt I selected was for dental work I had done in 1999. Great. Anything older than 2004 went straight into the trash. The task of locating the date on each of perhaps ten thousand scraps of paper was tedious beyond belief.

I'm pretty sure that the people who design cash register receipts take malicious pleasure in making the date as obscure and unreadable as possible. Sometimes I could stare at a stinking piece of paper for five minutes without finding the date. And with every receipt I picked up, I cursed the preposterous system we have that requires us to keep all this damned paper.

At least 90 percent of the papers in the box were completely irrelevant. There was a receipt for a set of wind chimes that we'd sent Marie's mother for Christmas in 2001 and a receipt for a 1998 stop at the Trees of Mystery on the Oregon coast. So that was how this project was going to go.

CHAPTER 49

THURSDAY, AUGUST 25

The morning *Chronicle* and my channel surfing on the radio and TV yielded no mention whatsoever of the revelations made in Wednesday's *Oregon City Journal*. The media were fixed in their determination to shield their anointed one from any challenge to his integrity. In the minds of the news directors, Devonshire was a saint. But even if he was a crook, he was *their* crook.

Martha had finished her search for information about Trey Bourne without finding anything that shed light on who he really was. There were no newspaper articles and only a few public records, and they did nothing more than confirm what we'd found out on the internet. I think Martha had been hoping to find something that would help her understand the creep who tried to kill her.

"Well, that's the way this business is," I lamented.

"There are a lot more dead ends than there are clues. You just have to wade through a lot of crap to find the one piece of information you can use."

Martha sighed. "Oh, I know. It's just that after looking so long for Trayborn, I really hoped we'd be able to make the connection and wrap this thing up once we found him. Instead, we don't know much beyond his name."

"I have another project for you," I said, handing her Richard Elgin's phone bills. "Go to the reverse directories, and find out who Elgin talks to on the phone. When you attach a name to a phone number, see what you can find out about person behind the name."

Martha brightened up. "That sounds like the kind of job you usually keep for yourself."

"It is," I said glumly. "But I have to dig through this." I pointed at the three remaining whiskey boxes filled with wrinkled, faded receipts.

"Ugh," she concluded.

I started picking papers off the top of the second box. What was this? Marie had spent $430 in the petite shop at Nordstrom in June of 2007—right when she had been berating me about quitting my job at Pacific-Northern Mutual Insurance. She was telling me that we were on the verge of having to forage for food from the dumpsters behind Safeway while at the same time spending $430 at Nordstrom!

I'd bet she deliberately put that receipt in there just to aggravate me. I took time to wad it into a ball before spitefully pitching it into the trash. Glancing at my one-thousand-tablet bottle of antacid tablets, I again wondered how long it would last. Turning on TV, I found the classical music channel and switched the audio over to my stereo in an effort to buffer the misery.

Mozart, Chopin, Schubert, and the rest did in fact make it somewhat less tortuous, but no less tedious. I cursed the Sixteenth Amendment, I cursed the government, I cursed the IRS, and I cursed the faceless individual who ordered this audit. It was outrageous that anyone should have to go through all this to keep the government from taking their money and giving it to some third-world socialist dictator on the far side of the earth.

Martha quietly worked at her job while I labored over Marie's diabolical whiskey boxes, and she discretely avoided questioning the cause of any of my frequent outbursts of frustration and anger. In the middle of the afternoon, I tossed aside the second empty box. Break time.

I walked out into the rain to get my mail and found an envelope from the State of Oregon Department of Public Safety Standards and Training. That was odd. It wasn't time to renew my license. Back at my desk, I slit the envelope open and pulled out the folded letter informing me that I was being investigated for unethical or unlawful activities in association with my investigations.

There was a litany of charges ranging from vandalism to breaking and entering, stalking, theft, misrepresentation, and fraud. The specifics associated with the charges made it clear that they all had come from one source, and that source could only be Richard Elgin.

I was invited to answer each of the charges in writing within ten days or face suspension or revocation of my license. Elgin was beginning to irritate me.

I faxed the letter over to William Gates and waited for him to call. He'd be able to help write answers that wouldn't dig a deeper hole than I was already in. The theft and vandalism had to do with Elgin's lost eavesdropping equipment. Stalking was what he called it when I followed him to his secret lair—something he wouldn't have known about if he hadn't put the tracker on my Yukon. The breaking and entering was a pure shot in the dark. There was no way he could know I'd been in his shop. Misrepresentation and fraud were just blanket accusations relating to the little fibs that every PI tells in order to get information.

It would have been gratifying to point out that Elgin had illegally trespassed and bugged my house, had planted the GPS tracker and followed me from Leslie Charleston's house to Gary Turner's storage unit, and had sent his goon to blow me up and send Martha over the falls. But none of that would answer the charges he had leveled against me. And *he* had no license to challenge.

Richard Elgin was a guy who knew how to work the system. He was probably pissed because I sent his Spark Nano to South Carolina. But there was more to it than that. He was feeling threatened, and this was his second preemptive strike—the first was Trey Bourne and his Welcome Wagon gift.

When Gates phoned, he had already read through the accusations that I was required to address.

"What is the truth behind these accusations?" he asked.

"The theft and vandalism relates to listening devices that he planted in my home and office. I removed and disposed of them. The receiver-recorder for the listening devices was in a metal box illegally attached to a vacant house. I opened the box and removed the electronics, which I disposed of along with the transmitters. He'll have to admit to illegal trespass in order to even have a case," I explained.

"That won't trouble him—the Department of Public Safety Standards and Training has no power over him. You, on the other hand, depend on them for your license and your livelihood."

"So what's your suggestion?

"Neither admit nor deny the charges. The one thing you absolutely don't want to do is get caught in a lie,"

Gates told me. "If they have evidence, make them show it to you. If they don't have evidence, they don't have a case."

"Okay. Then how do I answer their letter?" I asked.

"I'll write the answers for you. But don't expect that to be the end of it. Even if they don't have any evidence, they could call you in for a hearing. Then they'll try to intimidate you into admitting some kind of wrongdoing. Don't fall for that. Insist on confronting your accuser or at least knowing who he is. If it's who you think it is, then you can demonstrate to the hearings officer that he harbors a grudge against you to the degree that he was involved in an attempt on your life."

The Department of Public Safety Standards and Training would have to get in line behind the IRS. I spent the rest of my Thursday afternoon and evening plowing through the third box of receipts. When Kim came down after work, she observed my periodic tantrums and discretely stayed out of my way. It was almost dark when I tossed the third empty box aside. I had a headache, and I was feeling sick from eating too many antacid tablets. Kim was out on the porch reading a book, so I poured a couple glasses of wine and joined her.

"Three down and one to go," I said.

"I hope you can get it done soon," she said. "You're kind of boring when you work."

"That isn't work. That's torture."

CHAPTER 50

FRIDAY, AUGUST 26

I dug into the final box of receipts, determined to get that pain-in-the-ass project off my desk once and for all. While I cursed and fretted over barely readable cash-register tapes, Martha quietly worked away on Richard Elgin's phone bills. From time to time, she would find something that she knew was important.

"Oh—my—god," she mumbled.

"What'd you find?" I asked.

She hastily said, "Oh, it doesn't matter now—sorry I disturbed you."

There were several exchanges like that during the day, and each time, Martha told me, it was nothing. I knew better, but I had to stay focused on sorting out the receipts for the IRS. By noon, I could almost see the proverbial light at the end of the tunnel—though it may have been an oncoming train.

At exactly three thirty, I crushed the final empty box and tossed it in the general direction of the overflowing wastebasket. In front of me were four stationery boxes labeled 2004, 2005, 2006, and 2007. Each contained receipts for all of my deductible expenses in that year and would substantiate everything I had claimed on my tax returns. Or so I hoped.

I put lids on the boxes lest a gust of wind send them flying, and carried them out to my car. With no sense of satisfaction whatsoever, I delivered the boxes to Bill Cheshire's office on the far side of town. Cheshire, on the other hand, greeted my delivery as if I had brought him boxes of gold.

"I live for this stuff," he said, knowing perfectly well how much I hated it.

"That's pretty twisted," I told him. "You really ought to see someone."

"If it weren't for people like me, where would you be?" he challenged.

"Okay, that's a good point," I conceded. "It's all yours."

I hurried back to my office to see what Martha had found in Elgin's phone bills. She handed me a printout of the calls that she felt might be related to what we were doing. A quick scan of Martha's list showed a correlation between significant events in the investigation and Elgin's phone calls

It confirmed everything that we had suspected about Richard Elgin and revealed even more than we had imagined. The first surprise was a call from Sheriff William Kerby at 1:44 p.m. on June 11, the day that Randy Mendelson's El Camino was first identified. What was it that compelled Kerby to call Elgin that day?

Then on the twelfth, thirteenth, and fourteenth of June, Elgin received more calls from Kerby and then placed calls to a restricted number in area code 202— Washington, DC. It was easy to speculate that Elgin was getting updates from Kerby and passing them along to someone in DC.

On the fourteenth, fifteenth, and sixteenth, the pattern reversed. Elgin received calls from Washington and then turned around and made calls to Kerby. So was Elgin relaying orders from the godfather back to Sheriff Kerby? It sure looked that way. On the sixteenth, Sheriff Kerby declared the case closed.

As I read the phone log, it seemed logical that the calls to Washington had probably gone to Senator Alan Blalock, but since the restricted number was not shown on the bill, there was no way I could prove that. Then I looked at the log for Elgin's land line, where I found a series of calls to a nonrestricted number in Washington, DC. This number proved to be a fax machine, and the bill went to Alan Blalock. The dates of the fax transmissions to Blalock corresponded to the publication of the *Oregon City Journal*'s news articles and Amy Powers's editorials.

There was no longer any question that Elgin was in contact with Blalock. The log showed several calls to and from Wilson Devonshire, but it appeared that Elgin had far less reason to talk with him than with Blalock in Washington, DC.

My interpretation: when Devonshire found himself in trouble, he had gone to the godfather for help—help that came in the form of Richard Elgin. Elgin got his instructions from Washington, DC, not from Devonshire. I continued scanning the phone logs. June 27 was the day I visited former deputy Mickey Odell. At 2:16 p.m., just minutes after he slammed his door in my face, Odell called Elgin, no doubt to report that someone was asking around about the Mendelson-Devonshire investigation.

Right after he received that call, Elgin contacted Bourne, most likely telling him to put a watch on Leslie Charleston's house. August 9 was the day Elgin picked up the memory card from his eavesdropping receiver on Herb Goble's house. Assuming that he listened to the recordings, this was when he found out that his eavesdropping wasn't going to work because I'd found his bugs. All he had managed to learn was that I have a good collection of Beatles and Rolling Stones.

His response to that was a series of calls on August 10, including calls to Trey Bourne and Mickey Odell, a call to the Department of Public Safety Standards and Training, and two calls to Roger Millican in the Clackamas County DA's office. Following those calls, Millican came and raided my office with his bogus search warrant, and the DPSST was challenging my license.

There was more at stake here than protecting Devonshire from prosecution for his involvement in his stepdaughter's murder. If Devonshire went down, it would have serious repercussions on his entire political network, including Blalock, Elgin, Millican, Kerby, and all of their political allies.

In light of what I'd learned from the phone logs, I decided that it was time to start paying more attention to the activities of Richard Elgin. He'd done his best to conduct covert surveillance on me. I needed to return the favor. I phoned Jerry Midland and asked if he could get me a good GPS tracking device, and he said that he could sell me a Spark Nano Plus—the same model that Elgin had put on my car.

The money would have to come out of the account that I'd set aside for *Annabel Lee*. I hated to do it, but Elgin was too dangerous to ignore. Saturday morning, I drove to Jerry's pawnshop in Vancouver. He had already set up the user account and given the battery a full charge, so the Spark Nano was ready to go. All I had to do was install it on Elgin's car.

I drove to Portland and threaded my way down onto Corbett Street. When I got to Caruthers Street, I found a place to park that was within a hundred feet of Elgin's building, but out of sight to any hidden surveillance cameras Elgin might have. I put on my ODOT vest and hard hat and carried my clipboard up Caruthers Street.

Keeping my head down to shield my face from any cameras, I walked up and knocked on Elgin's door to see if anyone was there. When nobody answered, I went back to my Yukon and pressed the garage door button that I'd programmed when I first visited this building. The door went up.

I'd expected to find Elgin's gray Taurus inside, but instead I found a silver-colored Subaru WRX parked in the bay where Elgin used to keep his black Acura. Like the Acura, the WRX had dark-tinted windows and looked like something that a drug-dealing kid would drive. It was interesting that Elgin would choose such a highly visible car for undercover work. I could only guess that his theory was that it would misdirect any interest in the car toward a whole different class of people.

Here was a dilemma. I'd planned on installing the tracker on Elgin's Taurus. Now that he had replaced his Acura with this WRX, I had to guess which car's movements would be more worth following. I should have bought two trackers. In the meantime, I could track only one, and the WRX was the one I had access to, so I went ahead and tucked the Spark Nano up under the Subaru's rear bumper. I was finished in less than two minutes.

Back in my Yukon, I logged my laptop onto the tracker's website and confirmed that the device was functioning, and then I pressed the button closing the garage door. As I drove away, I wondered if Elgin had a replacement for Trey Bourne to go along with his replacement for the wrecked Acura.

CHAPTER 51

SUNDAY, AUGUST 28

L ooking forward to spending the day on *Annabel Lee*, I got up early and made coffee. While it brewed, I went outside and found the *Sunday Chronicle* under my porch. It was a daily challenge to see where the paper carrier had tossed it in his drive-by delivery.

Back inside, I tossed the paper onto my desk and went to fill my coffee cup. I settled into my chair and picked up the *Chronicle*. As I scanned the front page, I passed over the article about the president's latest proclamation about ending the war in Afghanistan and took a quick look at an article about the latest idea for a new Columbia River bridge. I almost passed over the editorial that started in the lower corner of the front page and overflowed onto page A-10.

A Master of Misinformation
Tibbett Gaylord

Right-wing talk radio in Portland this week has been overflowing with outrageous and vicious allegations against Oregon Supreme Court Justice Wilson Landis Devonshire. During his twenty-five year tenure on the court, Devonshire has been known as a man of the highest integrity and is considered one of the nation's most thoughtful jurists.

Justice Devonshire has written the majority opinion for some of Oregon's most challenging cases, but because some of his decisions have ruled against right-wing orthodoxy, he has long been a target for attacks from the far right. So it is to be expected that the usual suspects on right-wing talk radio would jump all over the opportunity to use the sad news of the discovery of Wilson Devonshire's murdered daughter to stir up a furor over "evidence" that only they can see.

And what is this so-called evidence? There is DNA extracted from a piece of wood that supposedly came from the house that Jessie Devonshire lived in for five years prior to her death. That

DNA allegedly matches DNA from a thirty-two-year-old postage stamp that may have been licked by Jessie, although that cannot be proven.

Even if one accepts the rather spurious notion that this DNA match proves that Jessie's blood was present on the piece of wood, it only proves that she was there—and we already knew that. She lived there. It pushes the bounds of credulity to believe that never once, between the ages of ten and fifteen years, did Jessie Devonshire ever have a nosebleed or a skinned knee. In reality, it would be more of a surprise if one didn't find a trace of blood.

What is more questionable than the evidence itself is its source. The scrap of wood and the postage stamp were found by Oregon City private investigator March Corrigan and processed by a private lab in Seattle. There is no chain of custody to prove the validity of the evidence. There is nothing to prove that the wood and the stamp were properly handled or that thirty-some years of deterioration and contamination haven't tainted the DNA test. All we have is March Corrigan's word. The *Chronicle* sent a reporter to talk with Corrigan at his office in a seedy corner of Oregon City, but he was conveniently "unavailable for comment."

Our reporter has discovered that Corrigan is currently under investigation by the Clackamas County District Attorney and Oregon City Police Department in a case involving the theft of electronics from a vehicle in the parking lot of the Oregon City Fred Meyer store. A search warrant was executed at Corrigan's office in June, and several electronic devices were taken into evidence.

It has also been determined that Corrigan faces revocation or suspension of his private investigator's license by the Oregon Department of Public Safety Standards and Training, pending an ongoing investigation into his business practices and charges of his involvement in criminal activities.

On top of all this, it is reported that Corrigan is under investigation by the US Internal Revenue Service on a matter of possible tax fraud. All in all, it appears that March Corrigan may not be a "reliable source" for evidence pointing the finger at a man whose reputation for integrity is untarnished in his three decades of service to the people of Oregon.

March Corrigan made the news on August 19 when he participated in the rescue of a runaway boat above Willamette Falls. Corrigan presented himself as the hero in that event, but now there is some question as to whether the drifting boat—which was occupied by Corrigan's assistant—was ever in any actual peril.

Conveniently, the only witnesses to the so-called rescue were Martha Hoskins, Corrigan's assistant, and Deputy Kim Stayton, who also participated in the event. Our reporter has found out that when the boat allegedly got loose, Deputy Stayton was spending the night with Corrigan in his riverside cottage—a nice, neat little circle of friends all backing up each other's stories. It is difficult not to wonder if the whole event was staged just to lend substance to Corrigan's outrageous "discoveries" about Jessie Devonshire's death.

Authorities also believe that there is a connection between Corrigan and Trey Bourne, the Beaverton man who was leaving Corrigan's office with a bomb made of plastic explosive when he was killed in a traffic accident. The nature of Corrigan's relationship with Bourne is not yet known nor is the intended target of the bomb that Bourne may have just picked up from Corrigan. That investigation is ongoing.

It seems that there are many things about March Corrigan that are currently under investigation. And since all we have is March Corrigan's word on the validity of the so-called "new evidence" in Jessie Devonshire's murder, it seems prudent to give the evidence the same credibility as its source. And at this time, that is zero.

I threw Section A across the room in disgust. I had seen similarly sanctimonious pieces on the *Chronicle*'s pages before, but this was the first time I was the target. I stomped around the office for several minutes trying to get my blood pressure back under control. It was appalling that the *Chronicle* would publish such a collection of lies, and I wondered what legal recourse I had to make them pay for their recklessness.

My phone rang, and before I could even say hello, the caller started shouting invectives and threats. After two more such calls, I switched my phone off in disgust. I've always marveled at how vicious these good liberals who flock around people like Devonshire and Blalock can be, while characterizing themselves as intellectually and morally superior.

Instead of spending the day on *Annabel Lee*, I went to the Town Center Mall and bought a disposable phone with what I hoped would be enough minutes to last until the furor over the *Sunday Chronicle* died down enough to let me use my regular phone. When I gave him my name, it became obvious that the young guy behind the counter had read the *Sunday Chronicle*. He eyed me curiously as he tapped the computer keys, and I knew he was wondering if I really was the criminal that the newspaper had portrayed me as being. That was something I was going to have to get used to.

I spent half the afternoon giving my new phone number to people I might want to talk with. After twice emptying the hate messages off of my regular voice mail, I decided instead to just let it fill up. That would deny my critics the satisfaction of sounding off.

CHAPTER 52

MONDAY, AUGUST 29

The dark, rainy morning matched my mood. I'd spoken with William Gates about filing a libel suit against the *Chronicle*, but he advised against it. In the first place, libel suits were almost impossible to win, and in the second place, the only thing that was guaranteed was that it would keep the lies alive through the course of any legal proceedings. It was better to just let it die a natural death. Fine. I knew he was right, but that didn't mean I had to like it.

With nothing happening on the river, Kim went up to spend her day at the sheriff's office. Martha came in complaining that she'd left the hatch open under clear skies Sunday evening, only to be awakened in the middle of the night by rain pouring through onto her bed. Nobody was happy.

At noon, Kim called to say that people weren't too happy up at the sheriff's office, either. The letter I had mailed from the State Police Headquarters had arrived on Saturday, and David Elkton had gone ballistic. He had taken the page showing that Sheriff Kerby had told the OSP ballistics lab that the Mendelson-Devonshire weapon had been mishandled by the county CSI criminalists directly to his union representative.

"I'll say this for you, Corrigan, when you stir up a hornet's nest, you really do it right," Kim told me.

"You're brightening my day," I said.

An official grievance was immediately filed, and within an hour, everyone in the office knew the content of the OSP ballistics-lab report. After talking with Kim, I phoned Amy Powers and suggested that she try to get the story from Elkton's union representative.

"If you're lucky, they'll give you a copy of the lab report before Kerby has a chance to put the clamps on it," I told her. "If they don't volunteer to give it to you, press them. This will be your best chance to get it."

"I'm on my way," she said. Who am I looking for?"

"The union rep is a lady named Billie Austin. I think she'll be your best shot. David Elkton could lose his job for giving it to you, but the union rep has some protection because of her position."

"I don't want to get anybody fired."

"As soon as the reports are made public, there'll be such a stink over what Kerby did that he'll be too busy swatting flies off his own ass to do anything to anyone else," I said optimistically.

"That doesn't sound like a sure thing."

"Even if Kerby does make trouble, the deputies will have the union behind them. I'm sure this will come out okay in the end," I assured her. "And one more thing. If you do get the ballistics lab report, come down here and I'll give you the reports on everything else found in the El Camino."

"What's all this going to prove?"

"At the very least, it will prove that Randy Mendelson didn't shoot himself. The implications of that fact alone will tear the whole 'official conclusion' apart."

"You bet it will! I'll see you in a while," she said before clicking off.

Forty-five minutes later, Amy showed up on my porch, waving several sheets of paper. They were copies of the OSP ballistics-lab report and the note that had been attached to it.

"I couldn't get Billie Austin to say anything about the grievance, but she gave me copies of the report. I read it in the car before I drove down here," Amy said. "This is amazing!"

As promised, I handed her copies of the rest of the material that Larry Jamieson had let Lila take from his desk. When Amy saw the photo that showed the way Jessie Devonshire was dressed, her eyes opened wide.

"My god!" she exclaimed. "She didn't go out on a date—she was having a sex tryst."

"Exactly," I agreed. "And that's why she was killed."

"You think Devonshire caught her with Randy and killed them both?"

"That's a possibility. But Jessie was hit in the head before she was shot. I think she had an argument with her lover. He lost his temper and whacked her with the nearest blunt object. My guess is that Randy heard something and was killed for trying to be a good samaritan."

Amy looked at me, eyes wide. "You're suggesting that Wilson Devonshire was Jessie's lover?"

I shrugged. "It would explain a lot."

"If you have anything to support that, you'd better give it to me now," Amy said firmly.

I produced copies of the witness statements that Gary Turner and Dick Hammond collected during the first few days of the investigation, including Wilson Devonshire's. I gave her copies of my interviews with Jessie's friends, saying that Jessie had been sexually involved with "an older man," and had been for at least a year before she died.

"Who had better access to Jessie than her own stepfather?" I asked rhetorically.

Martha made copies of the timeline we had put together showing that Jessie and Randy had probably been killed around four in the afternoon and the phone logs that show the call to his office at 4:21 p.m.

"I can't believe the *Chronicle* is treating this slime ball like some kind of a saint," Martha grumbled.

I looked at her with an eyebrow raised in surprise.

"Well, I'm entitled to change my mind," she said sheepishly.

"This is the same information that Gary Turner and Dick Hammond had, and it is probably what got them killed. You've already seen what they tried to do to Martha and me down here. You really should think about getting some protection," I said to Amy.

"A bodyguard?" she asked.

"Think about it," I insisted.

On a sudden impulse, I then showed her a printout of the GPS tracker's report on Richard Elgin's WRX. I had been in the process of showing Martha how to retrieve the data from my Spark Nano when Amy arrived. We hadn't yet had a chance to analyze the report, but something that jumped out at me was that Elgin—or his new Trey Borne—had driven the WRX to several locations in Oregon City Saturday evening.

"What's this?" Amy asked as she studied the printout of the map with Elgin's path superimposed in red.

"I have a tracker on Richard Elgin's car," I explained.

Amy suddenly went pale and pointed at the subdivision called Land's End near the southern fringe of Oregon City.

"I live there!" she exclaimed. "He drove right past my house!"

"Damn!" was all I could say. "Do you recognize any of the other places he went?"

Amy followed the red line and quickly said, "That's the *Journal* office!"

I had already observed that Elgin made a round of the Canemah neighborhood, coming in the back way, down South End Road to Fifth Avenue and winding down to Third. He had stopped on Third where he'd have had a view overlooking my place. At the time he was there, he'd have seen Kim's sheriff's office SUV parked at the side of my cottage.

"I don't know what he might be planning," I told Amy, "but none of this is good news. It definitely proves that you and the *Journal* are on his radar."

Obviously rattled, Amy left to go talk with her publisher about the new ominous turn that this story was taking. I hoped she didn't get cold feet because at this point, it wouldn't do any good to back down. She'd already been targeted.

CHAPTER 53

TUESDAY, AUGUST 30

"You're not going to be happy," I warned Kim.

"Damn it!" she exclaimed when she saw the vandalism. During the night, someone had spray-painted "Lying Bitch" and several other, more obscene names on the sides of her marine-unit SUV. Similarly articulate comments were painted all over the alley side of my cottage—the side not protected by my motion detectors. I couldn't put motion detectors on that side because they'd sound off whenever anyone moved in the alley, and there was too much legitimate traffic there.

Was this Elgin's handiwork? It seemed out of character. He was more comfortable with two-pound bricks of Semtex. It seemed more likely that it was done by one of the good, open-minded progressive readers of the *Sunday Chronicle*—conscientiously exercising his free speech rights.

Officer Durham came down and wrote up the complaint. He took pictures and explained what I already knew—that the only way the perpetrators of this kind of crime ever got prosecuted was if they were caught in he act. After the photos were taken, I tried to clean the paint off of the SUV, but no solvent in my garage would do the trick. Kim had no choice but to drive it to the sheriff 's garage.

With that kind of a start, your day can only get better, right? Wrong. In mid-morning, while I was painting over the graffiti on the side of my house, my new phone rang. I hadn't programmed any of my contacts into it, so I answered blind.

"Corrigan, this is Bill Cheshire. I've been entertaining your IRS auditors this morning."

"Wonderful," I said flatly. "How'd it go?"

"Well, I have good news, and I have bad news. The good news is that your receipts backed up all of your expense claims."

I groaned. "Then what's the bad news?"

"They're challenging your home-office deduction. They're going to disallow it unless you can prove to them that you don't use it for anything other than business," Cheshire said.

"What do you recommend?"

"I got the sense that they're determined to nail you. They'll look at your office, and they'll find something that isn't related to business—a John Grisham novel on a shelf, a boating magazine on the end table—anything. And that'll invalidate your deduction."

"That's a bunch of crap!" I protested. "What am I supposed to do—I mean, the office is part of my house—how can I *not* use it for personal space sometimes?"

"I don't know, but that's what the tax code calls for. Usually, auditors will be reasonable, but my impression is that these two aren't going to cut you any slack."

"What's it cost me to lose the deduction?"

"For three years, you've written off a fourth of your house as office space. On top of that, you've claimed a fourth of your electric, gas, water, and sewer bills, along with maintenance and repair costs. If you lose the deduction, you'll owe at least eight thousand in taxes, penalties, and interest."

"I don't have an extra eight grand sitting around for them!"

"That's okay with them. They'll just take your car or your house—both if they can find a way to do it."

"Bill, can you come down here and show me what it will take to win this thing?"

"Sure, but I won't guarantee that these guys won't find something I miss."

An hour later, Bill was there helping me prepare for my visit by the auditors. He had me take down pictures of my family, all of the little nautical things that I'd accumulated since bringing *Annabel Lee* home, and even my key ring.

"There are keys on that ring that aren't related to business," he explained.

"But there are also keys that open my office door, my filing cabinet, my desk—" Cheshire pointed at a padlock key and asked, "What does that open?"

"It's for my dock box."

"They've got you. That key can't be in your office."

"Unbelievable," was all I could say. Together, we went through every drawer and every file in my filing cabinets. We went through my desks, and then we looked at my computers."

"Ever send an email to your mother?" Bill asked.

"Of course I have," I said.

"Then they've got you twice. Not only do you lose your office deduction, you also lose your capital-expenditure deduction."

I was starting to appreciate the pervasive tenacity of the tax code.

"Okay, I can go through the computers and try to purge anything that doesn't relate to business," I said, "but I don't know how to erase hidden files and—oh, shit!"

"What's wrong?" Bill asked.

"The district attorney has my computers. These are clones. I can purge these, but if they look on the computers the DA has, they'll find whatever is there."

Bill thought that over. "I'd *like* to say that the odds are against them ever even learning about those computers. Normally, auditors won't go to that much effort. But if these two are serious—and I think they are—they'll keep digging until they find something."

"Well, I can't just roll over," I complained.

"No, you can't," he affirmed. "The best you can do is try."

So I spent the rest of the day deleting any files that might be considered "personal" or transferring them to an external drive. There weren't very many, but it was tedious and time consuming to find them. I was sitting on my porch when Kim drove up in her Mustang.

"Have room in your garage?" she asked.

"You bet," I said. "Let me get my keys."

I went inside and grabbed my key ring, and I was halfway to the garage when I remembered that this was my IRS key ring. My personal keys were in the kitchen. So I went back and got the right keys, fuming the whole time at the absurdity of the IRS and the tax code.

"So I guess this means they couldn't clean the paint off the Explorer," I said to Kim after she was parked in the garage.

"No, I think they got it cleaned off okay," Kim said, "but Kerby took advantage of the vandalism to declare me a liability to the office. I'm on suspension—and this time, it'll stick, thanks to that mealy-mouthed editor at the *Chronicle*."

There wasn't any kind of press release I could issue to undo this suspension. More than ever, I wanted to crush Devonshire and the entire Blalock machine that was supporting him, *including* Sheriff Kerby. The problem was that I didn't know how to do it.

I felt that we had more than enough evidence for an indictment of Devonshire, but nobody was going to issue that indictment with the sheriff having declared the case closed, and apparently, nobody in the County DA's office showing any interest in what I had.

After dinner, Kim and I sat on the porch sipping wine and watching the river go by.

"The good news is that the suspension is with pay—at least until the *Chronicle* finds out and adds that to their holy crusade," Kim commented.

"Will the union stand behind you?" I asked.

"They'll try. I guess this will test the union's strength."

"Anything happening with Elkton's grievance?"

She shook her head. "I don't know. I was too wrapped up in my own troubles to even wonder about that."

"Well, I haven't heard anything from Amy Powers today, but if she doesn't back down—and I don't think she will—there's going to be hell to pay at the sheriff's office tomorrow," I said.

"Yeah, I'm almost glad I won't be there to see it."

We were interrupted by the appearance of a white Ford Focus with "News Radio KXL" in bold red letters on the hood and doors. I shook my head. The last thing I wanted was an interview with a reporter.

"I have nothing to say to you," I told the man who climbed out of the Focus.

"Are you March Corrigan?" the man asked, ignoring my statement. And then before I could correct him on the name, he added, "I'm Frank Manning, producer of *The Lars Larson Show*."

Knowing that Lars had been the only person on the air in Portland who had shown any interest in the truth about Devonshire, I said, "I'm Corrigan."

Manning stuck out his hand and said, "We tried to call you, but all we got was voice mail, and your mailbox is full. So I decided to drive down and see if I could find you."

"You found me. Now what makes that worth the drive to Canemah?"

"Have you listened to our program the last couple of days?"

"No, I've been pretty busy here."

"I understand that. I'm sure you can understand that after Sunday's *Chronicle*, you've been the topic of a lot of discussion on the show."

"I can only imagine," I said.

"Lars would like to have you on the show to tell your side of the story," Manning said.

I had listened to *The Lars Larson Show* enough to know that he wouldn't sandbag me. He would argue relentlessly if he didn't agree with what I had to say, but he wouldn't set any traps, and he would give me every opportunity to state my case whether he agreed with it or not.

"My side of the story is pretty simple," I told Manning. "There wasn't a grain of truth in the editorial in the *Sunday Chronicle*, and I can prove all of the accusations that have been made against Wilson Devonshire."

Manning smiled. "That's exactly what Lars would like to hear you say on the air."

I looked at Kim and, to my embarrassment, realized that I hadn't introduced her. Belatedly, I said, "This is Deputy Kim Stayton."

Manning shook her hand. "Very happy to meet you. You know, Lars would probably like to have you on the air too."

"No chance," Kim said, "I'm on suspension, but I'm still bound by the rules of the sheriff's office. I can't talk to the media."

Manning looked surprised. "Suspension? May I ask for what?"

"Because I have been determined to be a liability," Kim said.

"I don't get it. What did you do?"

She shrugged. "I'll let you know when I find out."

Manning turned back to me and asked, "Well, what do you say. Will you come on the show?"

"By phone or in person?" I asked.

"Lars would prefer that you come to the studio, but we could do it by phone if that's easier for you."

"Let me think about it. I'll call you in the morning."

We exchanged cards, and I wrote the number of my new phone on the card I gave him.

CHAPTER 54

WEDNESDAY, AUGUST 31

Sleep didn't come easily that night. Every little noise woke me up. I couldn't help thinking of Elgin sitting up there on Third Avenue looking down at my office. If he'd been there when the KXL car pulled up, he just might have put two and two together. In fact, it wasn't beyond the realm of possibility that he could have had a long-range listening device.

Either way, if he thought I might show up on *The Lars Larson Show*, he just might feel the need to make a preemptive strike. That's what made me decide that I had to go on the show. The other decision I made during my sleepless night was to turn over all of Gary Turner's files to the *Oregon City Journal.*

Over breakfast, I talked with Kim about that decision. My thinking was that since Kerby had already suspended Kim, there was nothing to lose by making the files public.

"Kerby will still think that I took the files," Kim said, "and he'll just add it to the list of charges he's already made."

"Kerby's going to be dealing with troubles of his own because of Elkton and his grievance. Once the *Journal* comes out today, he's going to be on the hot seat. He'll be pissed, but he's going to have so many fires under his fat ass he won't be able to deal with all of them."

"Yeah, but there's a fire under my ass too, and this isn't going to put it out," Kim argued.

"Here's the thing. We can suggest that the *Journal* have tests done to determine the age of the paper as part of the validation process. If they'll do that, it'll prove that the copies were made when you were in grade school."

"Do you think the *Journal* will do that?"

"They will if I attach that as a condition to turning over the files."

"All right, if they'll do that—and you're sure they can prove that the files are thirty years old—then I'm okay with it."

I called Amy Powers, and she got her publisher, Gerald Banks, on the line, and I made my offer.

"Before he was killed, Gary Turner put all of his Mendelson-Devonshire files and notes in a storage unit. Turner's widow gave me the key, and I retrieved the files from storage back in June," I explained. "Are you interested?"

In unison, Amy and Gerald both said, "Of course, we're interested."

"Just one condition. I'd like you to have whatever kind of test is needed to prove the age of the paper. That'll be important for you to prove their validity and very important to all of us to prove that the files weren't acquired illegally."

"We'll do that," Banks said.

"Then we have a deal. The files are in safe-deposit boxes at the US Bank down on Main Street. What time would you like to meet me there?"

"I assume they open at nine," Banks said. "We can meet you then, if that works for you."

With nothing better to do with her time, Kim came along. We met Amy and Gerald in the lobby, and he handed me an advance copy of the latest issue of the *Journal*. I gave it to Kim while the teller led me into the vault to unlock the safe deposit boxes. The others joined me in the private cubicle, where we transferred the files from the safe-deposit boxes into cardboard boxes that we'd brought along.

"We have cataloged everything we're giving you in an Access database, all cross-referenced and set up for searching. I'd be happy to give you a copy of that if you want to put the originals in a secure place," I proposed.

"I'd like to take you up on that offer," Banks said.

"What'll it take to get that database?"

"Just send someone down to my office with whatever USB device will hold about twenty gigabytes of data,"

I said. "I do have a question for you, though. Have you taken any steps toward providing security for yourself, the newspaper, and your employees?"

"We're working on that. There are proposals from a couple of firms, and we're comparing our options."

"Don't take too long," I urged. "These guys will do anything to get their hands on these files."

"I understand. You're making me feel like we should have brought an armored car down here."

"That's not so far from the truth. I suggest that you do what you need to do to confirm that our database truly was made from these files, pull a few random pages out for age-testing, and put the rest back in here."

"You're making me nervous," he said.

"You *should* be nervous," I answered.

I helped carry the boxes out to Gerald Banks' car, and as we put them in the trunk I looked up and down Main Street for anything that looked out of place—like a silver WRX or a gray Taurus. I didn't see anything, but I still worried about the security of the files.

Half an hour later, a courier stopped at my office and waited while Martha copied Merlin onto the *Journal*'s portable hard drive. I attached a note to Banks offering any help needed in the use of the database.

"The *Journal* is really going all-out with this," Kim commented.

She'd been reading Amy's front page article about the OSP ballistics-lab report and the resulting union grievance filed on behalf of David Elkton. She included reproductions of the lab report and the note saying that CCSO had, in effect, invalidated the evidence by mishandling the weapon.

She gave a detailed and convincing explanation of how the weapon had been handled from the time it was uncovered in the mud on the floor pan of the El Camino until it was sent to Salem for analysis. This was backed by "several witnesses, who wish to keep their identities confidential." I knew that those witnesses included just about everyone who had been present.

"It's all or nothing now," I said. "If the *Chronicle* is going to keep defending the sainthood of Wilson Devonshire, they're going to have to destroy the *Journal* to do it."

"Honestly, I think that's exactly what they'll try to do,"
Kim said.

"Which is precisely why the *Journal* needed the files we gave them this morning."

I took my copy of the *Journal* along when I drove into the KXL studio in Portland. Getting there an hour before Lars Larson was scheduled to go on the air allowed some time to go over what we would talk about. In addition to Frank Manning and Lars, the meeting was attended by the station manager and an attorney.

In order to keep the presentation focused, we agreed to concentrate on the evidence recovered from the El Camino—basically, the content of the *Journal*'s article.

"When we start taking calls, you can expect to be attacked," Lars told me. "We have what we call the naysayer's line, and that's where we invite people who don't agree with us to call in. Are you prepared for that?"

"I can take care of myself," I assured him.

"Good. We don't often have guests in the studio," Manning explained. "The way we'd like to do this is, first, Lars will give you an introduction, and then he'll ask you questions. They'll generally be open-ended questions, so you'll be able to answer in detail."

"That sounds good to me," I said. "I trust you'll signal me if I talk too long?"

"How much time do you think you'll need?" Lars asked.

"It won't take long to tell what was found in the car," I said. "Explaining what the key pieces of evidence mean is pretty easy too. The part that gets sticky is explaining why the sheriff's office claimed that the evidence supported the murder-suicide theory."

That's when the attorney spoke up. "Don't mention any specific individuals, and don't try to attach a motive. Stick only to the provable facts, and don't speculate—not even when the callers try to bait you, which they will do."

Manning reinforced the point. "You'll be fine as long as you state only the facts. Let the listeners draw the conclusions, and then you can discuss their ideas. If you give them the right facts, they'll tell you what they think happened. You can agree or disagree, just make *them* draw the conclusions."

The Lars Larson Show went on the air right after the noon newscast. He introduced the topic and then asked me what the latest news was. I talked about what had been covered in the *Journal*, explaining that this was the first time the evidence discovered in the El Camino had been made public. By prior agreement, Lars diligently avoided asking me how I had come into possession of the OSP ballistics-lab report and photos.

When Lars introduced the subject of those files, he had been talking about the union grievance regarding the ballistics report. The natural inference would be that the files had come out because of that, even though he never said so, and in fact, it wasn't the case. But that's what I needed everyone to believe in order to protect Larry Jamieson and Kim.

Lars focused entirely on the firearm evidence. He was very knowledgeable on the subject and was quite familiar with the specific weapon found in the car. Looking at the photos, he instantly saw the same things that the technicians in the ballistics lab had seen—that the cylinder had been rotated after the last shot had been fired.

On the air, he said, "I'm reading from the official Oregon State Police ballistics-lab report, where it talks about the removal of the cylinder from the weapon. 'Upon initial examination it was determined that there was live ammunition in the weapon. After prying the loading gate open, it was determined that the cylinder was seized and could not be rotated. The base pin was forcibly extracted, and the cylinder was released by tapping with a plastic hammer, revealing four live Remington .22 LR cartridges and two expended shell casings.' It turns out that this is critical."

I took the cue and said, "That's right, Lars. Everything was stuck together. They had to pry the loading gate open, forcibly extract the base pin—"

"The base pin is like an axle running through the center of the cylinder," Lars interjected.

"Right. And then they had to strike the cylinder with a hammer to break it loose from the frame. Keep that in mind."

"Now here's why it's so important," Lars said. "Reading again from the report, 'The cylinder was initially positioned with a live cartridge under the hammer and the two expended cartridges in the two positions immediately clockwise from the firing position. The firing pin marks on the rims of the expended shell casings were positioned in approximately the two o'clock and seven o'clock positions relative to the radius of the cylinder, indicating that the shells had been removed from the cylinder after firing and subsequently returned.' Now I know—because I'm very familiar with the Ruger New Model Single Six—that the firing pin strikes the rim of the cartridge at the twelve o'clock position."

"That is extremely critical information," I said. "There was a live cartridge under the hammer. That means that the cylinder was rotated after the gun was fired. And that means that a third person was involved in the shooting—a dead person couldn't have rotated the cylinder."

"Yes," Lars agreed, "and then there's the position of the expended shell casings. They had to have been removed from the cylinder and reinserted after the gun was fired."

"And the only reason I can think of for someone to do that would be to wipe off fingerprints."

"And again, that couldn't have been done by a dead person. At the moment the second shot was fired, both Jessie Devonshire and Randy Mendelson were dead. So who removed the shells and rotated the cylinder?"

"That's the big question."

"But the official sheriff's office conclusion was that Randy shot Jessie, drove into the river, and then shot himself while the car was sinking. How could they possibly reach that conclusion?"

"That's where this gets ugly. Someone—I don't know who—attached a Post-it note to the lab report, saying that the cylinder had been removed from the weapon by someone in the Clackamas County Sheriff's Office before the weapon was sent to the lab in Salem."

"That, in effect, invalidated the evidence that the lab found when they took the weapon apart."

"And it was only by disregarding the weapons-lab report that the 'official' conclusion of murder-suicide could be reached," I continued for him.

"So a Post-it note trumped the entire ballistics report?" Lars sounded incredulous.

"That's right. Only thing is, what the Post-it note says couldn't have happened. Remember how much trouble the lab technicians had taking the weapon apart? If the Clackamas County investigators had taken it apart first, it would have come apart easily for the technicians in Salem."

"Now I remember somewhere later in the ballistics report it describes how the shell casings were so firmly stuck in the cylinder that they had to be pushed out with a hydraulic press."

"And yet somebody—and we don't know who—claimed that the shell casings had been removed and reinserted by someone in the Clackamas County Sheriff's Office."

"But if the shell casings had been removed before the weapon was sent to Salem, they wouldn't have still been seized in place, would they?" Lars asked.

"No. Of course not," I said firmly.

"So we have to decide whether to believe the ballistics lab report or the Post-it note attached to it. Sounds like an easy choice to me."

"I agree. But the sheriff's official conclusion goes the other way."

At that point, Lars opened the phones for listeners to call in. The rest of the hour was filled with questions and comments. Those on the naysayers' line for the most part just regurgitated what Tibbett Gaylord had fed them in the *Sunday Chronicle*. The more they said it, the more pathetic they sounded.

I left the studio after the first hour but continued to listen to the show while I drove home.

"Carl from Salem, welcome to *The Lars Larson Show*," Lars said.

"Good afternoon, Lars. I work in the State Police Ballistics Lab, and I was there when that weapon was brought in," the caller said.

"I'm sorry to interrupt, Carl, but I have to ask, are you going to get in trouble for talking to me on the air?"

"No, I'm actually on vacation this week."

"Well, I just want to make sure that you aren't going to lose your job. You know that some state agencies—Department of Transportation for sure, and maybe others—have standing orders that their employees are not allowed to speak on this program."

"I've heard that, but there hasn't been any order like that where I work."

"You're sure of that?" Lars pressed.

"Quite sure," Carl affirmed.

"Okay then, go ahead."

"Well, like I said, I was there when that weapon was brought in, and I witnessed the whole process of disassembly."

"Can I ask what is your job there?"

"I'm a photographer. I took the pictures that were in the report," Carl explained. "Anyway, the gun was delivered to us in a Tupperware tub filled with distilled water—that's standard procedure with a gun that's been in the water for any length of time. It prevents it from rusting up."

"What was the condition of the gun when you first saw it?"

"Well, it was caked with mud. There was mud packed all around the cylinder and frame."

"That doesn't sound much like a gun that had been taken apart before it was sent to you," Lars commented.

"No, that's the thing," Carl said. "There is no way anyone could have taken it apart. I mean, our guys had to use Vise-Grips to pull the base pin out. Maybe there was some other gun in the car, but the one I saw had definitely not been tampered with."

"So what did you think when you heard the Clackamas County Sheriff's Office announce that the evidence found in the car supported their original murder-suicide conclusion?"

"I didn't think anything of it. I did not know how the weapon we had fit into the picture—we didn't have any of the facts about the case. If anyone in our lab had been told that Randy Mendelson was supposed to have shot himself with this weapon as the car was sinking, we'd have said that it simply wasn't possible."

"Now you've heard that the CSI folks in Clackamas County have lodged a formal grievance over the accusation that they tampered with the gun," Lars began.

"Yeah, I don't blame them," Carl said. "It's the same thing as calling them incompetent idiots. And I can tell you, it's a total lie."

"Will you say that if you're called to testify in their hearing?"

"Of course I will. So would anyone else in the lab."

By the time the evening news came on television, the protective wall that the media had built around Wilson Devonshire was starting to crumble. Channel 12 was the first to give objective coverage to the revelations contained in the *Journal* articles during their five o'clock newscast. By six thirty, Channel 8 had picked it up, and on the eleven o'clock news, all of Portland's television stations were talking about the ballistics-lab report and its implications.

CHAPTER 55

THURSDAY, SEPTEMBER 1

I wanted to see the *Chronicle* eat crow after their steadfast defense of Devonshire, but I was disappointed to see no mention of the case on the front page. It wasn't until page A-8 that I found a small article under a headline stating, "New Interpretation of Old Evidence." The article played down the significance of the ballistics-lab report and dismissed the facts as being "one interpretation of the evidence."

But everywhere else, the story was exploding. I even heard it mentioned on ABC Radio's national feed. I could only imagine how things were going in Devonshire's inner circle. I was just starting to visualize a gratifying scene where Richard Elgin was telling Wilson Devonshire that it's all over when my phone rang.

"This is Bill Cheshire," I heard. My day suddenly turned to crap.

"What's happening?" I asked warily.

"Milo and Otis are heading your way."

"Who?"

"The two IRS auditors—they're on their way to do an inspection of your office."

"Milo and Otis?"

"Those are their names—Stewart Milo and Mattie Otis."

"You can't be serious. Milo and Otis?" I scoffed.

"I'm sure some supervisor got a big charge out of matching those two up."

"Great. Looks like they're here now," I said, watching a gray Chevy Cobalt drive slowly up Water Street. Milo and Otis got out of the car, clipboards in hand, and came up to my door. They entered without knocking. My guess was that they were testing whether I'd upbraid them for walking into my house. If so, I disappointed them.

Milo was about six-two and probably weighed no more than 140 lbs. He had buzz-cut hair and wore a pair of those terribly fashionable glasses with lenses about half an inch tall. Otis was about a foot shorter than her partner and, if anything, was even skinnier. Her straight brown hair was pulled back severely and fastened into a knot at the back of her head. Between them, they displayed about as much charm as a drive-by shooting.

As they introduced themselves, their eyes darted around the room, no doubt searching for anything that looked remotely personal. It seemed they took that particular failure as a challenge.

Displaying a grimace that I think was intended to look like a smile, Otis commented to Martha, "Oh, it's so nice here. It looks like a wonderful place to sit back and read a good book."

Without looking up, Martha said simply, "I wouldn't know."

Cheshire had warned us to watch out for that kind of seemingly innocuous question. If Martha had been the least bit conversational, there was any number of things she might have said that the auditors could have interpreted to be an admission of "personal use" of the office space.

Milo and Otis went through a whole litany of questions about the contents of my filing cabinets, desk drawers, book shelves, and cabinets. Milo snooped around, looking like a pigeon in search of bread crumbs.

Otis challenged me, "When you carry things to and from your boat, do you ever come through the front door?"

Of course, I did.

I said, "I go in and out through the back door." *Nice try, mousey.*

Milo looked at his clipboard and said, "I see that you are claiming a deduction for depreciation on a Hoover vacuum cleaner. Can you show that to me?"

I led him to the broom closet in my kitchen, where the Hoover was stored. Triumphantly, he said, "Looks like you keep this here for both business and personal use."

"Nope," I corrected, pointing to a broom and dustpan, "that's what I use back here."

"Mr. Corrigan, are you telling me that you *never* use this vacuum cleaner outside your office?" he scoffed.

"Yes. I am," I said with a straight face.

He angrily scribbled a note on his clipboard. He inquired about every piece of office furniture, every piece of computer hardware and software, and all of the little business machines that were on my list of capital assets that were being depreciated. When he got to my computers, he triumphantly declared that they didn't match what was on his list, certain that he had finally caught me in a lie.

"No," I explained, "these are new. They'll be on my next tax return. The old ones are gone."

I didn't want to tell him where the missing computers were, lest he feel compelled to search the files. Otis, in the meantime, was sitting at my desk snooping through the files on my computer, hoping to find an email from my mother or a recipe for brownies—anything that wasn't business.

The two auditors spent over three hours, and I could tell that they were becoming angry. They weren't used to going away empty-handed. Finally, Milo picked up my phone—the one I'd stopped using after Gaylord's editorials. He scrolled through the numbers stored in the phone's directory.

"Aha," he said, with a smug look of triumph. "Some of these names on your contact list aren't business contacts!"

No kidding.

I showed him my new prepaid phone. "This is the phone I use to make personal calls. I have no control over who calls me on that phone. I keep the names in the contact list on there so that they'll show up on my caller ID."

Milo scribbled on his notepad. Apparently, it is a federal crime to keep family names on your phone. I felt pretty good that this was the best the two of them could come up with. But then again, maybe they were happy just for having wasted half my day.

After they left, I sat down at my computer and logged on to see where Richard Elgin's Subaru had been lately. I noted that he had made a trip to Salem the previous afternoon.

"Oh, Richard, you've been exceeding the speed limit. Eighty-three miles an hour is a bit excessive for Interstate 5, don't you think?" I scolded.

The GPS tracker had all kinds of interesting little features. Not only did it tell me how fast he drove, it showed when, where, and for how long he stopped.

"Martha, can you find out what's at 275 Commercial Street Southeast in Salem?" I asked.

After a few minutes, she said, "It's a place called Magoo's—a sports bar."

Elgin—or at least Elgin's car—had spent thirty-five minutes at Magoo's and had driven back to Portland. It seemed very odd that anyone would drive forty miles to grab a quick snack at a sports bar just to turn around and drive back home. Nobody's hamburgers are that good.

He had some other reason for going there. I took a look at a Salem map and quickly determined that Magoo's was about eight blocks from the Oregon Supreme Court building. If Elgin needed to have a quick face-to-face meeting with Devonshire, the sports bar would be an ideal place. Clearly, they had things to talk about.

Kim came up from the dock, where she'd been lounging in the sun and reading a book. When she reached for the screen-door handle, I said, "Wait! Are you here on business?"

"Huh?" she asked.

"I can't let you come through that door unless you're here on business. Milo and Otis said so."

"What are you talking about?"

"Milo and Otis, the IRS auditors, they told me that we can't use that door except for business."

"Milo and Otis?"

I handed her their business cards. She took one look and rolled her eyes meaningfully.

"Who wants to go water skiing?" I asked.

Kim raised her hand, and I raised mine.

"Too bad, Martha, you're going to have to come along," I said.

"I don't know how to water ski," she objected, "besides, I need to work."

"No you don't—we almost have Devonshire on death row."

I succeeded in breaking down her resistance, and she finally agreed to ride along as spotter. After changing clothes, I went out to the garage and got Kim's ski. Mine was already in the boat. We spent the rest of the afternoon tearing up the river and generally putting Devonshire, the IRS, and Richard Elgin out of our minds.

CHAPTER 56

FRIDAY, SEPTEMBER 2

By Friday, even the stubborn *Chronicle* editors were beginning to bend. They were willing to concede that there "may be" cause to take another look at the evidence. Meanwhile, others in the media were demanding an explanation from Devonshire. A few were even calling for his arrest.

I phoned Lila Mendelson and told her that my investigation was over. I'd found the evidence to clear Randy, and whatever happened beyond that was in other people's hands.

"I can't even begin to tell you how much I appreciate everything you've done," Lila said.

"Oh, sure you can," I kidded, "after I send you my bill."

"Corrigan, I don't care how much your bill is—it's worth it to see Randy's name cleared."

"Seriously, Lila, I don't want you to have to take anything out of your pocket. If Randy's insurance policy doesn't cover the bill, you tell me—I want you to promise you'll do that."

"Okay, but I know you've earned every cent."

It felt good to close the book on Devonshire. The problem was, though, the book wasn't closed on Richard Elgin. I didn't know exactly what his role had been in the murders of Jessie and Randy, but I knew for certain that he had been part of it. And I also knew that he was involved in the murders of Deputies Hammond and Turner—not to mention the attempted murders of Martha, Kim, and me.

Elgin was simply too dangerous to ignore. I went back to the contact list that Martha had compiled for Richard Elgin's wives. I still considered the ex-wives to be a potentially good source of information, but after I talked with Alicia Jefferson, Elgin's first wife, I'd somehow gotten sidetracked and had never contacted the others.

I was unable to reach Elgin's most recent wife, Jennifer Crane. The phone numbers Martha had found were out of service, and I could find no new listings for her. It looked like she might be in hiding. I had better luck with Kathy Saginaw, whose current name was Weingard. After I had explained who I was and what I was doing, Kathy invited me to stop by and have a glass of wine at her place near Wilsonville.

After she gave me the address, I asked, "Eilers Road—which side of the road?"

"The north side," she said, "on the river."

"In that case, I think I'll make the trip by boat and get some recreation out of the deal. What time works for you?"

"How about two?"

"That sounds perfect."

"Just look for the dock with the blue-roofed boat shelter," she said.

Then I made a call to John and Emma Whitney, parents of Carrie Whitney Elgin. John Whitney snorted contemptuously at the mention of Richard Elgin.

"That son of a bitch killed my daughter," he growled. "What's your connection with him?"

"I'm investigating the business dealings of a consulting firm he owns," I told him, using my standard noncommittal line.

"Consulting firm, my ass!" Whitney spat.

"That's just about the same thing Elgin's first wife had to say about it," I said, hoping to establish some rapport.

"All that so-called consulting firm is, is a way for Elgin to get the taxpayers to pay for the dirty work he does to keep Alan Blalock on top of his political shit pile!"

"That's exactly what I'd like to talk to you about. Pick the place, and I'll buy breakfast tomorrow—if that works for you."

"Tell you what. If you're trying to nail that bastard, I'll buy *you* breakfast! You know Elmer's Pancake House in Clackamas?"

"I know the place. Pick a time."

"Seven thirty too early for you?" he asked.

With that settled, I hung up the phone and wandered out to the front porch, where Kim was working on a crossword puzzle.

"How'd you like to go for a boat ride?" I asked.

She looked up and said, "What, and interrupt all this fun I'm having?"

"I located Richard Elgin's third wife. She lives on the river, just this side of Wilsonville—said she'll talk to me about her ex."

"Sounds good. I'm going nuts with nothing to do!"

I put a bottle of Chardonnay on ice in a little soft-sided cooler and carried it down to the boat. After warming the engine, we cast off the dock lines and idled out to the middle of the river. I pointed us upstream and pushed the throttle forward. In a matter of seconds, we were skimming along the glassy-smooth surface of the river at a speed just over fifty miles an hour.

We passed through the narrow passage at Rocky Island, raced past Forest Cove, and made the big right-hand turn where Hollywood Video mogul Mark Wattles's mansion has stood unfinished for fifteen years. Passing Peach Cove, I had to slow down while the Canby Ferry crossed in front of us. We passed the mouth of the Mollala River and, a few minutes later, spotted the blue roof on Kathy Saginaw's boat house.

I pulled back on the throttle and eased up alongside the dock, where an attractive blonde woman in a yellow bikini sat in the shade of a large umbrella mounted on a round glass-top table. She looked to be in her mid-twenties, even though I knew her actual age was thirty-eight. That's four for four. Elgin had a real knack for finding attractive blonde women. Kathy got up and strolled our way while Kim and I got out and tied up the boat.

"Didn't I see you skiing up here yesterday?" Kathy asked.

I nodded and said, "I'm Corrigan. This is Kim Stayton."

We shook hands all around, and I offered Kathy the chilled bottle of wine.

"I can see that we're going to be good friends," Kathy said. "This is better than what I have open, but would you like a glass anyway?"

"Would love it," I said.

Kathy waved us to seats at the glass-top table while she poured the wine.

"So you're the guy who's been raining on Wilson Devonshire's parade," she observed.

"You've been following the news?" I asked.

"It's pretty hard to ignore."

I got down to business. "Did you know Trey Bourne?"

"Yeah, I knew the stinking little weasel. Richard paid him to do the dirty work so that he could keep his own hands clean."

"You heard how he died?"

"If anyone ever deserved to be burned alive, it was Trey Bourne. It's just too bad it didn't happen about thirty years ago."

"Do you know anything about the work that Bourne did for your husband?"

Kathy looked at me for a few seconds, appraising me, and then said, "He killed a couple of cops back in the 1980s. They were investigating something that Richard wanted covered up, so he had Bourne kill them and make it look like accidents."

"How do you know that?"

"Bourne told me. He'd get drunk sometimes and start hitting on me, bragging how he'd killed the cops and gotten away with it."

"Did he say how he did it?"

"He said a lot of things—most of it, I've managed to forget. But he said something about killing them with heroin. He said he screwed up the first one and almost got caught, so he sent the second one off a cliff in his car after he was dead."

"And he did it for your husband?"

"That's what he told me. He thought I'd be impressed," she said with contempt.

I decided to change the subject. "You were Richard's third wife, right?"

She nodded.

"What do you know about the others?" I asked.

"I know I'm lucky to be alive. When I met Richard, he seemed like a dream come true. He had looks, he had money, he was charming, and he was well connected. He was easy to fall for."

"Did you know that his second wife had died?"

"At first, I didn't even know he'd been married before. It wasn't until after I was hopelessly in love with him that he mentioned his previous marriages. By then, I didn't care."

"His second wife, Carrie—what did he tell you about her death?"

Kathy took a sip of wine and said, "He told me a heartbreaking story about how they had gone rafting and Carrie drank too much and fell out of the raft in a rapid. He said he jumped in and swam after her, finally getting her ashore a mile downstream. He said he performed CPR for two hours. Later, I learned that it was someone else who pulled

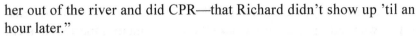

her out of the river and did CPR—that Richard didn't show up 'til an hour later."

"Did you ever have reason to suspect that it wasn't an accident?"

"Not really. I just figured he embellished the story to make himself look good, but I didn't start wondering if he killed her until after Christie died. That really woke me up."

"How so?"

"Well, Richard had bought scuba gear for me and promised to teach me how to dive. But we split up before he ever got around to doing it."

"Why did you split up?" I pressed.

"The usual reason, I guess. I found out that he was messing around, so I packed up and walked out," she said.

"Smartest thing I ever did. Otherwise I'd have been the one at the bottom of Puget Sound."

Kathy opened my bottle and poured us another round, even though it was becoming clear that she'd already had plenty.

"What do you know about Richard's consulting company?" I asked.

She uttered a hollow laugh. "What a joke! All that was, was a bank account where he could deposit checks from the city for 'security work' that he never did."

"He must have done *something* to warrant the pay."

"Oh sure! He earned his pay, all right—but not doing security work. He was the official driver for, I think, four different mayors in Portland. He made it a point to exploit that position, doing whatever special favors he could and then sending the city an invoice for security work."

Special favors—those were the same words Alicia had used. "What kind of 'special favors'?"

"Whatever sleazy thing they couldn't do for themselves. He got them women and then covered for them. One of the mayors—I don't remember which one—got drunk and ran into another car in a shopping center parking lot. Richard got him out of there and then fixed it up with the cops and the other driver so that it never made the news."

"What do you know about his relationship with Wilson Devonshire?" I asked.

"That was way before my time—back when Alan Blalock was mayor. Now there's a piece of work. He's the one who really got Richard into this line of work," she said. He *always* needed some kind of favor."

I'd have stayed around and talked some more, but I worried that Kathy was getting to a point where she was going to embarrass herself. I made some kind of excuse, so that Kim and I could make an exit. She didn't have the look of a chronic drinker, though. I wondered if it was just the result of thinking about Richard Elgin. It often made *me* want to drink.

CHAPTER 57

SATURDAY, SEPTEMBER 3

As was my standard practice, I placed my miniature Sony audio recorder on the table. John Whitney nodded his approval. I recited my standard lame joke, "This is just in case Mr. Alzheimer has sneaked up on me during the night."

The fact was I'd never been much good at memorizing entire conversations.

"So what are you trying to do here?" Whitney asked.

"I want to find out everything I can about Richard Elgin. On the phone you indicated that you believe that Elgin killed your daughter."

Whitney was emphatic. "There's no question about that. How much do you know about her death?"

"Initially, it looked to me like an accident—until Elgin's first wife told me that he lied about being unfamiliar with the river," I answered.

"Elgin had floated that river at least a dozen times. He killed her and then passed it off as an accident," Whitney insisted.

"It sure looks that way to me. Was their marriage in trouble?"

"Not in the usual sense. I don't think Carrie ever did see Elgin for what he was. She just had a starry-eyed crush on him."

"So what do you think was Elgin's motive for killing her."

"He told her things that he shouldn't have," Whitney explained, "and when she started repeating them to other people, he had to shut her up."

That was something new. I'd held the opinion that he had gotten rid of Carrie—as he had with his other wives—simply because she was pushing thirty years old.

"What kind of things are we talking about?" I asked.

"Elgin told Carrie some of the things he had done for Alan Blalock back when he was mayor of Portland, and when word started getting around, Carrie had to be silenced."

"Do you know specifically what he told her?" I pressed.

Whitney rubbed his forehead and said, "Carrie never said anything to me, but have you ever heard the rumors about Blalock and underage girls?"

I shook my head.

"The rumors have been around for years—even before Carrie died. But in 1994, early in Blalock's campaign for a second term in the US Senate, one of the Republican challengers was Charles Arock. Somebody gave Arock's campaign people the name of a woman who had been sexually involved with Alan Blalock back in the mid-1970s—when she was only fourteen years old.

"Arock's people called me shortly after Carrie's death, trying to validate the story. They said that Carrie was the source of the tip, and they wanted to know if I knew anything about it. They also said that the lady, who by then was in her mid-thirties, was in a mental institution."

"Was Carrie campaigning for Arock?" I asked.

"No, not at all," Whitney said firmly. "She was a Democrat."

"So why would she be helping the Arock campaign?"

"I don't think she was—not intentionally. I think she was simply demonstrating that she too knew what she probably assumed her friends already knew. Carrie didn't have a job, so she spent a lot of time at the Multnomah Athletic Club, rubbing shoulders with older, more sophisticated women, and she was awfully proud of that. My best guess is that one of those ladies worked for Arock.

"Arock never went public with the accusation, presumably because he could never verify any of it. But the story has been out there ever since, with Carrie's name attached to it. Every few years someone calls, just like you did, and some have told me that the woman in the mental institution wasn't the only one."

"So you think Alan Blalock has a 'thing' for little girls?" I asked.

Whitney shrugged. "That's the buzz I get."

"So what do you figure was Elgin's role in it?"

"Elgin was Blalock's driver almost the whole time Blalock was mayor. Whatever kind of affairs Blalock had, Elgin *had* to have known about them and most likely facilitated them."

"I've been told that Elgin routinely procured women for sex with city officials and VIPs."

"You can bet on that. Listen, I've been looking at Elgin for twenty years. He's as slimy as a catfish. You find any dirtbag public figure with an embarrassing problem, you're going to find Elgin close by. The city has paid his consulting company hundreds of thousands of dollars, but nobody can tell me what the money was for. I've tried repeatedly to get copies of invoices or purchase orders, and nobody can ever find anything."

"Have you ever heard of someone named Trey Bourne?" I asked.

He thought for a moment and said, "No, I don't recall ever hearing that name."

We talked our way through breakfast, but I didn't learn anything new. The main revelation was the possibility that Alan Blalock was a pedophile. I suddenly had to consider the possibility that Blalock was the "older man" in Jessie Devonshire's life. It wasn't beyond the realm of possibilities.

Maybe Devonshire had found out that Jessie was involved with Alan Blalock, and that led to the argument that ended in Jessie's death. Had Devonshire come home unexpectedly and found Jessie dressed for an afternoon tryst with Blalock?

అంళ

I went back to my office and transcribed the recording of my conversation with John Whitney. None of what he told me could ever be used in court. It was all hearsay. But it fit the known facts, and more importantly, it offered a pretty good explanation for Elgin's prosperity.

Martha came bursting into the office, panting from her sprint up from Daryl's boat.

"Devonshire's dead!" she gasped. "I just heard it on the radio."

"Dead? How did he die?" I asked while turning on the television.

"He was found dead in his car. No other details."

I scrolled through the local channels, and all I found was Saturday morning cartoon shows. I went to the computer and Googled "Devonshire dead." Up came a KGW news report that said little more than what Martha had said. Devonshire had been found dead in his car this morning on a side street in Salem. Cause of death was not yet known. Investigation was ongoing.

"Unbelievable," I said. "There's no way he died in an accident."

"You think someone killed him?" Martha asked.

"Either that or he killed himself."

By the time Kim and I sat down to watch the evening news, a lot more was known about Devonshire's death. His wife said that he hadn't been home the previous evening. He had died of a single gunshot wound to the head. A gun was found in the car. The initial indications were that it was a suicide.

"Do you know anyone on the Salem police force?" I asked Kim, knowing perfectly well that she did.

"Yeah, I know several," she said, knowing perfectly well that I knew.

"Think they'd give you any inside information?"

"They might over a beer, but I doubt they'd tell me anything over the phone."

"When's their happy hour?"

"Damned if I know. But leave me alone for a little while," she said thoughtfully, "and maybe I can find out."

Kim went out to her car and dug a little spiral notebook out of the glove compartment. She took that and her phone down to the dock. I watched as she flipped through the pages and dialed a number, and then I went back inside to see if there was anything new on television.

CHAPTER 58

K im didn't mention that one of the Salem cops she knew was an old boyfriend. She knew better than to bring that up. Down on the dock, she looked up the number in the little notebook, but she didn't really need to. She'd dialed it too many times back in the old days to ever forget it.

"Hey Fox," Kim said when he answered.

"Well, I'll be damned!" Kevin Fox exclaimed. "It's the famous Kim Stayton, heroine of Willamette Falls."

"So you heard about that."

"Headline news, even way down here. To what do I owe the pleasure of your call?"

"Oh, hell, I'm bored. Maybe you heard, I'm on suspension."

"Hadn't heard. What'd you do? Shoot someone?"

"No, nothing that much fun. Administrative crap. They think I didn't take proper care of my SUV."

"You wreck it?"

"Not completely." She wasn't out to make up a lie, but at the same time, she wanted to stay away from the full truth. "It'll blow over," she assured him. "But 'til it does, I have too much time on my hands."

"Are you prospecting for a job with Salem's finest?"

"Well"—she drew it out until it sounded like a tease—"maybe that. And maybe…a beer, for old time's sake."

"I'd love to see you again," Kevin said.

"Hey, you remember that place out on Silverton Road?" Kim asked.

"You mean the Silver Spur?"

"They still hot on Saturday nights?"

"Yeah, far as I know."

"Well?" she asked, playing coy. "Want to meet me there—say around eight?" Kevin asked.

"That sounds like fun. Hey, I look forward to seeing you again."

Kim came back up at the house. "How'd you like to take me out dancing?" she asked.

"Uh…" I stumbled, taken by surprise, "sure, sounds like fun."

"Just one thing," Kim said.

I held my breath because coming from Kim—"just one thing" is never just one thing.

"I'll be dancing with someone else," she finished.

"Would that be Sergeant Fox?" I asked, dropping the pretense.

"I'll have to string him along a bit in order to get him to talk. And I'll probably need a ride home."

"Does he know anything?" I figured there was no sense doing this if there's no return.

"I couldn't ask him that up front. You know that. But I'd bet he knows every detail. That's the way things work down there."

I summed it up. "So I have to stay sober, watch you dance with your old boyfriend, not intervene when he starts getting too friendly, and then pack you home when you can't stand up anymore?"

"Sounds about right."

"I can't wait." I growled.

She headed for the door. "I'm going to have to go up to my place and get ready. I don't have any country dancing clothes down here."

Forty-five minutes later, she was back, dressed in cowboy boots, tight jeans, and a lacy top that was far too sexy to be worn in front of Kevin Fox.

"Come on, Corrigan, you want the information, you gotta pay the price," she said. "This'll help loosen him up and make him talk."

"Yeah," I groused, "it'll loosen him up all right."

"I'll make it up to you when we get home," Kim promised.

"I'm going to hold you to that, too."

∂∞∾

We took her Mustang to Salem and pulled up in front of the Silver Spur at seven thirty. The parking lot was nearly full, but Kim found an empty space at a far corner of the lot. She pulled a cowboy hat out of the backseat and put it on.

"Why don't we just stay here and make out?" I suggested.

"Because you won't find out what you want to know about Devonshire," she said.

It cost us five bucks apiece to get through the door. Inside, the place was like a high-school gymnasium, with a high girder ceiling and a huge maple dance floor. A DJ sat behind a console on stage, playing country music, and couples on the dance floor did their best impressions of a country two-step.

"I'm going to go hang out at the bar," Kim shouted over the music. "That's where Fox'll be looking for me."

"I'll see if I can get myself a table somewhere," I shouted back.

We split up, and I started looking for a place to sit. I finally managed to grab a stool at a little round table off the side of the dance floor. I caught Kim's eye, so she knew where I'd be, and then we both settled into our routine: Kim fending off horny cowboys and I suppressing the urge to dump beer over the heads of horny cowboys while trying to look inconspicuous drinking overpriced nonalcoholic beer.

Kevin Fox arrived a few minutes after eight and went straight to Kim. He gave her a hug that was way friendlier than I'd have preferred, and then he and Kim started looking around for a table. They found a booth down the side where I couldn't see. Kim slid into the booth, and then Fox slid in next to her—out of my sight.

I contemplated trying to find a place where I could watch them but decided that I was better off where I was. Kim later told me how things went.

"Fox asked me, 'How long has it been now? Five, six years?' I said, 'Yeah. It's been awhile.' Then he said something like, 'You're looking good,' so I flashed him a seductive smile, to loosen him up."

"Yeah," I grumbled. "Just what he needed."

Kim ignored my comment and continued, "Then Fox asks if I was really thinking about coming to Salem, like I'd hinted on the phone, so I said, 'I'll go where the job is, at this point.' Then he asked if I still remembered how to dance. So you saw the rest."

Yeah, I saw. Fox got up and led her out to the floor, where they stayed for the duration of the song that was playing, plus the next two. I judged Fox's dancing at somewhere in the advanced mediocre range—okay, but nothing special.

Way below Kim's class. So was I, for that matter, but I was better than Fox. Far better.

They disappeared back into their booth, where I soon saw a waitress delivering a large pitcher of beer. Kim was going to work on him. At least, that's what I hoped was going on. I ordered another pretend beer, which I pretended to like, while I pretended to enjoy myself.

I was looking the other way when Fox and Kim again appeared on the dance floor. When I spotted them, they were dancing to a slow tune. He was awfully damned friendly and not shy about where he put his hands. *That whispering in her ear better damned well be details about what happened to Devonshire*, I thought. And I noticed that Kim was showing an awful lot of cleavage—did she know a button had come undone?

They danced until I could see the perspiration glistening on Kim's breasts, far too much of which were visible. When they went back to their booth, I leaned back and took deep, cleansing breaths.

"Would you mind if we shared your table?" asked a girl who may or may not have been in there legally.

"Sure, why not?" I said.

"I'm Kara," Miss Jailbait said. Her head bobbed from side to side when she talked.

"My name is Bailey," Kara's friend said. She was cute in a sandbox kind of way.

"Corrigan," I said, trying to act sociable.

Kara wore a tight-fitting top and short skirt, and of course, she had the compulsory cowboy boots and hat. Her friend wore low-cut jeans and t-shirt that was torn off just below her breasts so that she was bare down to her belt. Nice hat too.

"I've never seen you here before," Bailey said.

"This is my first time," I replied.

"Oh," she said, as though I had revealed a great *truth*.

"What do you do?" Kara asked.

"I'm self-employed."

"Oh, wow. That must be great."

"I can't bitch about the boss."

"Oh, that's funny." Kara giggled. "So, like, what's your job? What do you, like, do?"

"I'm an investigator. I investigate."

"Like a private eye?" Bailey exclaimed, eyes wide.

"I prefer *investigator*."

Bailey leaned toward me. "Are you carrying a gun?" she asked.

"No. I'm not carrying a gun," I told her. The waitress came by, and I said, "I'll have another of these—and whatever these ladies want."

Kara ordered a watermelon martini, and Bailey ordered an Irish crème.

"Bailey's," Bailey said. "Like my name, get it?"

"That's clever. Next time I'll have a Corrigan."

"Really? I never heard of that."

"No, I was just making a joke. There's not a drink named Corrigan."

"There ought to be. I'll bet it'd be *really* strong."

The girl is hitting on me! Now what?

"Hey, what kind of things do you investigate?" Bailey asked.

"Mostly things like fraud and larceny, occasionally I find people."

She looked disappointed. "Do you ever investigate murders?"

"Sometimes."

"Wow, that's exciting!"

With every exchange, she moved a little bit closer to me until I could feel the warmth radiating from the bare skin of her belly.

"When I was a kid, our neighbor, like, murdered his wife. I think he stabbed her," Kara said.

"Really," I asked, "How long ago was that?"

"Oh, it was, like, five or six years ago."

"So what happened to the guy—the one who killed his wife?"

"He got arrested. I don't know what happened after that."

Over Kara's shoulder, I saw Kevin Fox once again leading Kim out to the dance floor. She was without her hat now, and her blonde curls kept a rhythm of their own as she danced.

"Hey Corrigan, do you dance?" Bailey asked.

"Sure," I said. "Want to give it a try?"

I went out onto the floor with Bailey and tried to lead her in a basic swing, but all she could manage was shifting her weight from one foot to the other, more or less in time with the music. I tried to give her a twirl, but she got all crossed up, so I just let her do it her way.

About then, someone bumped into my back, and I turned to apologize and found myself looking at Kim. She rolled her eyes and then turned back to Fox, who was oblivious to the exchange. I decided that it would be in my best interest to retire from the dance floor.

Kara was out on the floor when Bailey and I got back to the table, and Bailey pulled her stool over close to mine and climbed up, pressing her thigh against mine. I bought her another drink when she finished her first and just let her chatter away. She told me all about her apartment and the roommate she couldn't *stand* and her old boyfriend who was *so* immature and the time her dog puked on the carpet and on and on and on. Kara never did come back.

It must have been after eleven when Kim rushed over to my table. "Come on, let's get out of here," she said urgently.

I nodded to Bailey and said, "Nice talking to you."

"Fox went to take a leak," Kim said.

"I told him I was going to the ladies' room." She pulled me toward the exit. "Boy, is he going to be pissed when he figures out I've gone," she said when we got outside.

We hurried to the far corner of the parking lot, but before getting in, Kim went around in front of the Mustang and squatted down to pee on the ground. "I couldn't take the time to go in the ladies' room," she explained over the sound of running water.

"Okay, here's what I found out," Kim said after we were both in the car. "Fox is still single, and he has way too much testosterone."

I groaned. "I hope to hell you found out more than that."

"Oh, you mean about Devonshire," she said, feigning ignorance. "He was found on Trelstad Avenue, just east of Thirty-Sixth. Dead end road, nothing around. Body was found at eight thirty this morning by a guy who made a wrong turn and was looking for a place to turn around. Single shot to the right side of his head, no exit wound. A .25 Beretta was in his right hand. Preliminary tests showed gunshot residue on Devonshire's hand."

"Straightforward suicide?"

"Probably. But there were some things to check out. Tire tracks next to Devonshire's car indicated that someone stopped next to him and then left. The witness who reported the body said it wasn't him—he simply made a U-turn and left."

"He didn't even get out of his car?"

"Nope. Said the way Devonshire was leaning against the window and not moving spooked him. He called it in and then left. Anyway, Salem PD is looking at the tire tracks. One other thing. Fox thought that he could see a shadow in the blowback pattern. They're having a blood spatter expert look at the car."

When a bullet penetrates a person's skull, the shock wave sends a mist of fine blood droplets back in the direction of the shot's origin. The pattern of that spray is quite predictable and can help investigators determine both the direction of the shot and distance from the wound. If anything, or anybody, is present and blocks a portion of the back spray, that is called a blowback shadow.

The presence of a blowback shadow may mean nothing—or it may mean everything. In a suicide, the victim's hand and arm might cause a blowback shadow. This would be confirmed by the presence of blood spray on the victim and his clothing. Often, however, the suicide victim's gun hand jerks away and does not block the spray.

So if there is no blood on Devonshire's shooting hand, the presence of a blowback shadow could indicate the presence of someone else in the car when the shot was fired. That's what the spatter expert would try to determine.

"Anything from Devonshire's wife?" I asked.

"They interviewed her. She said that she'd expected Devonshire home by seven last night, but he didn't show up. She started calling around at eight but couldn't find out anything. She said that Devonshire was worried about what was being said in the news but hadn't seemed despondent or suicidal," Kim said.

"What about the location? Was there any reason for Devonshire to be there?"

"By all accounts, it's not a place anyone would have reason to go— even by accident, although the guy who called it in did just that—oh, there was one other thing. Sometime this afternoon, someone else reported to the police that she'd been picking blackberries last night on the other side of the field. She said that she heard a gunshot at six thirty-five."

On the basis of what Kim had found out, a determination of suicide seemed fairly reasonable. The tire tracks probably meant nothing, and the spatter analysis would undoubtedly explain away the blowback shadow. I drove Kim back to my place, upholding my end of the deal. Kim upheld her end of the deal too.

CHAPTER 59

SUNDAY, SEPTEMBER 4

I would have slept late, but Lila Mendelson woke me up with an early phone call. "I just read that Wilson Devonshire killed himself," she told me.

"Yes, I got that news last night. I did some checking with the Salem police, and it does look like it was a suicide. They're still investigating. I'll let you know if I find out anything else," I said.

Since I was up, I made coffee and went out to get the *Sunday Chronicle*. Their front page story about Devonshire's death was built around the presumption of suicide. The tone of the article surprised me because it reflected a complete acceptance of Devonshire's guilt in the murders of Randy and Jessie.

It talked about the recent media furor over what they now called "the convincing new evidence" found in Randy's El Camino, saying that Devonshire had been "living a lie for more than three decades." The clear implication was that Devonshire, driven to despair over his guilt, had taken his own life.

While it was gratifying to see the *Chronicle* finally accepting the obvious, their change of position was so abrupt that I found it difficult to accept their sincerity. Only a week earlier, the editors had been strident in their insistence that there was no substance to the accusations against Devonshire. Now they found there to be no controversy about his guilt.

There were companion pieces, most of which extolled the virtues of Wilson Devonshire and chronicled his three decades on the bench. They praised his courage for "standing up to the powerful gun lobby" in his unwavering support of gun control legislation. The *Chronicle*, even while accepting that he was guilty of murder, still wanted to preserve his legacy as a supreme court justice.

I couldn't take any more of that, so I switched on my computer, intending to refocus my thoughts in regards to Richard Elgin. I considered getting him off the street to be not just a service to humanity, but also an act of self-preservation. I had no confidence that Devonshire's death would alter Elgin's fear of what I might be able to reveal about him.

I went back and reviewed my transcripts of the interviews with Alicia Crabtree, Kathy Saginaw, and John Whitney. They all said the same things about Elgin—he made his living by helping Alan Blalock and his political cronies get away with doing illegal things, which I knew included Wilson Devonshire's murder of Randy Mendelson and Jessie Devonshire.

All three were equally certain that Elgin had murdered Carrie Whitney and Christie Brogan. I puzzled over how it would be possible to find evidence to prove his guilt, but at best, it would be a difficult task. With Devonshire, I had the benefit of Gary Turner's investigation files, but there had never been a criminal investigation into the deaths of either of Elgin's dead wives. Maybe it was hopeless.

Still, I needed to keep track of what Elgin was going to do about the files that I'd given to Gerald Banks and Amy Powers. Those files still tied Elgin to the deaths of Deputies Hammond and Turner through his connection with Trey Bourne, and he was also implicated in the cover-up of the Mendelson and Devonshire murders.

He no longer needed to protect Devonshire, but he still needed to protect himself. Banks had never told me what—if any—security measures he had taken since acquiring the Turner files, so I could only hope that he'd taken my warnings seriously.

Meanwhile, about the only proactive measure I could take was monitoring Elgin's movements with the GPS tracker—assuming that he would use the Subaru WRX. On that thought, I logged onto the tracker website and downloaded the record of the Subaru's movements since Thursday afternoon.

"Oh, holy shit!" I said out loud.

The computer screen told the whole story. On Friday afternoon, the WRX left the RTE Consulting garage and traveled down I-5 to Salem, exiting onto Kuebler Road at 6:20 p.m. It traveled a quarter mile east on Kuebler before turning left onto Thirty-Sixth Avenue and right onto

Trelstad. It stopped at the end of Trelstad at 6:25 p.m. At 6:35 p.m., it left and retraced its way back to Portland.

It was Elgin's car that left the tire tracks in the dirt next to Devonshire's Cadillac. Forget the suicide theory. Devonshire was another murder victim.

"Did I hear you singing Christmas hymns in here?" Kim asked as she wandered, naked, into the room.

"Look at this. Richard Elgin was on Trelstad Avenue when Devonshire was shot."

"You're kidding," she challenged.

"I'll bet my next paycheck that the tire tracks next to Devonshire's car match the tires on Elgin's Subaru," I told her.

By then, Kim was looking over my shoulder at the computer screen. "Oh my god!" she exclaimed. "He murdered Devonshire."

"Looks that way—unless Elgin has brought someone in to replace Trey Bourne."

"Damn!"

"What?"

"I'm going to have to call and tell Kevin Fox about this," Kim groaned. "He's going to be pissed!"

"He'll get over it once he figures out that we're handing him a murder takedown."

"Nope, he'll still be pissed."

A minute later, I said, "Uh, I personally have no complaints, but you might want to think about putting something on." I pointed out the window at Bud walking up the alley.

"Oops," Kim said and quickly scurried back to the other end of the house.

I cooked up some breakfast while Kim showered and dressed, all the while trying to figure out a plan of action that would result in Elgin's arrest and conviction. The problem was that even if we were to tell Kevin Fox that Elgin's Subaru was at the scene when the gunshot was heard, there would still be considerable doubt as to whether or not he could do anything with that knowledge.

The courts have not yet sorted out what constitutional protections apply to GPS tracking. In Oregon, it is still generally legal, but other states' courts have ruled it an invasion of privacy. In any case, I couldn't tell anyone about the Spark Nano I'd planted on Elgin's WRX without at least implying that I had trespassed on his property. And that could render the tracking record inadmissible, along with any evidence gathered as a result of the tracking record. In other words, it would make the tire tracks inadmissible. What I needed was some *other* way to call Fox's attention to the WRX. But I couldn't imagine what that would be.

Kim said, "Maybe Fox will come up with some kind of hard evidence. If we tip him off, he'll at least know where to look for a match. "

"You're right about that," I said. "It's a hell of a thing to know that a murder was committed and not be able to do anything about it."

Kim picked up her phone and dialed Kevin Fox's number.

"Yeah, this is Fox," came the answer.

"You asshole, where the hell did you go last night?" Kim demanded.

"What the hell?" Fox sputtered. "You're the one who walked out."

"I went to the can, just like I told you. When I came back, you were gone and some other people were sitting in our seats."

"Christ, you must have taken your sweet time in the can."

Kim kept the heat on. "There was a line. When was there ever *not* a line in the ladies' room?"

"I waited a long time," Fox said defensively.

"Not long enough," Kim said.

Fox finally surrendered. "Okay, you're probably right. I'm sorry."

Kim exhaled loudly. "Well, what the hell, we never did get along all that well."

"We did all right."

Kim finally got down to business. "Hey, after you told me about that Devonshire thing, I got to thinking. There's a guy in Portland who may have had a beef with Devonshire. Richard Elgin—a former cop—used to be the mayor's driver or some shit like that."

"What makes you think he had a beef with Devonshire?"

"Okay, here's the thing. It's totally inadmissible, and you can't use it to get a warrant. Elgin owns a car that was parked at the end of Trelstad Avenue at the time your witness heard the gunshot."

"How the hell could you know that?"

"I know someone who has a GPS tracker on that car. I just found out where the car had been Friday evening."

"What am I supposed to do with that?"

"I don't know," Kim admitted. "Just keep Elgin in mind if your CSI people come up with any trace evidence."

"Okay, I'll do that," Fox said. "Now, how about a 'do over' on that date."

Kim groaned. "Oh hell, Fox, we'd just end up in another scrap."

"Come on," Fox pleaded. "It's worth another try."

"No it isn't. You take care, Fox." Kim said. She clicked off the phone, looked at the ceiling, and released a sort of primal scream.

"You handled that well," I said.

"Why don't we lock up and fly to Vegas," Kim suggested.

"What good would that do?"

"In regards to Elgin, none. But it would be fun."

"Okay, let's go to Vegas."

Kim was startled. "Really?" she asked.

"On one condition…" I began.

"Uh oh."

"We get married before we come back home."

"But that'd take all the fun out of it!" she objected.

"Naw, it would only take a few minutes," I countered.

"I don't mean it would take the fun out of the trip to Vegas. I mean it would take the fun out of our relationship. I *like* living in sin."

"We live in Oregon City," I reminded her.

"Enough! I give up," Kim said.

"So we'll get married?"

"No, I mean I give up on Vegas."

We'd been having this same discussion, with variations, about once every three months, for about a year now. The result was always the same—so far.

"So maybe water ski therapy would help," I suggested.

"How would that cause me to change my mind?" she asked.

"I don't mean about that. I mean about thinking up a way to nail Elgin."

"It's worth a try."

CHAPTER 60

MONDAY, SEPTEMBER 5

The Labor Day crowd was out. The river was busy with boaters trying to make the most of the last holiday weekend of the summer. Skiing and lounging around on the beach all day hadn't resolved anything about Elgin, but it sure had felt good. Unfortunately, Elgin was still out there and still as much of a threat as ever.

On Labor Day a year before, we'd had a spontaneous neighborhood cookout. This year, Daryl had spent some time coordinating an organized neighborhood event. He had collected at least half a dozen barbecues and lined them up across his beach and mine. His wife, Joanie, had bought a huge package of ground-beef patties, and everyone else in the neighborhood brought something to contribute to the feast.

There were lawn chairs and folding tables, ice chests filled with beer and soft drinks, and everyone was having a grand time. Bud was showing Martha how to back braid an eye in the end of a dock line, Big Dan was telling Duane about some kind of raid during Desert Storm, while Rosie shared some wine with Red Harper.

The party went on all day. When people finally started drifting back home around seven, the food had been consumed down to the last few crumbs, the ice chests were empty, and there were several barrels filled with empty cans. Kim and I retreated to our front porch to put our feet up and watch the sunset.

"I miss being out on the river," she said, "but today, it was nice to be here instead."

"Seems like they ought to tell you something tomorrow," I speculated. "With Devonshire dead, all the heat should be off Kerby. He has to know that he doesn't have a case against you."

"I'm not sure that having or not having a case is as important as having or not having a grudge. And Kerby most assuredly does have a grudge."

Changing the subject, I said, "I think I'll try turning my old phone back on. Maybe the hate calls have died out."

"Good luck with that," Kim said skeptically.

I switched it on and waited for the Verizon screen to switch off. "It says I have twenty-nine new messages."

After logging in to my voice mail, I had to listen to only the first few words to know the tone of the message. One by one, I deleted the hate calls sparked by Tibbett Gaylord's editorial. Lost among all of that garbage, there were a few calls voicing support and a couple that actually pertained to business. When I had my voice mailbox cleaned out, I went to work on text messages. About five seconds after I finished that project, the phone started ringing.

"Well, here's where we find out if it's safe to leave this thing turned on," I said. "Corrigan."

"Mr. Corrigan?" came a weak female voice.

"Yes, this is Corrigan."

"My name is Barbara Devonshire," the voice said.

I was too stunned to say anything for a moment.

"Mr. Corrigan?" she finally asked.

"Uh, yes…I'm here," I said, gathering my wits. "What can I do for you, Mrs. Devonshire?"

"Are you the investigator who stirred up this whole mess about my husband?"

"I believe it was the discovery of Randy Mendelson's car that started the ball rolling."

"I didn't ask the question to challenge you about what happened. I just wanted to make sure I was talking to the right person."

"In that case, then yes, I am the one who has been investigating the death of your daughter." I was unsure where this was going.

"At first, I was convinced that you were a political operative and that you were simply creating a twisted misinterpretation of the evidence, but now I know that most of the things you said were true."

Still trying to figure out what she wanted, I said, "I'm sorry for the loss of your husband."

"Mr. Corrigan, you needn't apologize. I hold no hard feelings toward you," she said—to my surprise.

"Well...I just—"

"I have something that I want to show you. I'd like to meet with you—tomorrow, if possible."

"I don't understand. What do you want to show me?"

"I don't want to talk about it on the phone," she said firmly.

"When and where then?" I asked.

"Can you come to my house? Tomorrow morning?"

She gave me her address, and we agreed on nine.

CHAPTER 61

TUESDAY, SEPTEMBER 6

The Devonshire home was a mansion that probably dated to the 1930s in a fashionable old neighborhood on the south side of Salem. I parked on the circle drive and walked to the front door. As I raised my hand to knock, the door swung open.

Barbara Devonshire was in her mid-sixties, and it was clear that she had been a beauty in her youth. She was still a striking woman, her silver hair cut moderately short and combed back stylishly. We introduced ourselves, and she escorted me to a sitting room.

"Mrs. Devonshire," I started.

"Please, call me Barbara," she said.

"Okay, Barbara, I'm wondering why, of all the people in the world, you chose to call me."

"Because I think you're someone I can trust. You don't appear to be a person who blindly accepts what people say, and you aren't afraid to challenge 'official' conclusions."

"In spite of what I've found out about your husband?"

"Not *in spite* of it," she corrected, "*because* of it."

"Help me out. I don't understand."

She surprised me by saying, "For thirty-two years, I've wondered if my husband killed Jessie. You proved that he didn't."

"But I didn't—"

"I heard you on the radio when you said that Jessie was killed at four o'clock, and I knew right then that Wilson couldn't have done it."

"I'm not following you."

"Well, I was out at the coast, if you recall, and I was talking with Wilson on the phone at a quarter after four," she said.

I was surprised. That fact had never come up, so I told her, "The time of death was just an estimate. It could be off by as much as half an hour either way."

"I understand, but he was in his office when I talked to him. He couldn't have killed her."

"How do you know he was in his office when he called?"

"Because he didn't call me. I called him. Even if he'd left the office right after I talked with him, the very earliest he could've gotten home was five o'clock."

I was lost for words. Mentally, I was trying to force this new fact to fit with what I already knew, and the pieces just wouldn't go together. Barbara had to be mistaken.

"You called from Salishan?" I asked.

"That's right," she said. "I had some down time, so I went to my room and called Wilson."

If she called from her room, it would show up on her bill. We had a copy of that bill from Gary Turner's files. How was it that nobody had noticed? She had to be mistaken. But I saw no need to argue the point with her. I'd just double-check the hotel bill when I got back to the office.

I said, "I didn't know about your call."

"Oh, I know that. I don't think it ever came up," she told me. "Anyway, that's not why I asked you to come down here. I want to talk to you about Wilson's death."

I was relieved that I wasn't going to have to debate the timeline of Jessie's murder. "What about his death?"

"The thing is, they're saying that he killed himself, and I know he didn't."

It figured that Barbara Devonshire wouldn't want to believe that her husband had killed himself, and even though I knew he hadn't, I didn't see any point in telling her what I knew. She picked up a small note pad from the end table and stared at it.

"I heard my husband talking on the phone last Friday morning. I couldn't hear well enough to understand the words, but he sounded angry," Barbara explained. "Last night, I found this next to the phone. I could see the impressions, so I scribbled across it with a pencil—believe it or not, I saw that on *Perry Mason* on television about fifty years ago."

She handed me the notepad, and I read what appeared under Barbara's scribbling.

6:30
Kuebler E from I-5
L on 36th
R on Trelstad
End of road.

"That's Wilson's handwriting," Barbara explained. "It's instructions to the place where they found him."

Her point was immediately apparent. Nobody writes himself a note with instructions on how to get to a spot to commit suicide. He had taken notes while talking on the phone, setting up a meeting at a place his killer had carefully chosen.

"You see what I mean?" Barbara continued, "There's a man—someone my husband knew. *He's* the one who did it. Richard Elgin is his name."

I shot upright in my chair. "Did you say Richard Elgin?" I asked.

"Yes. Do you know him?" she asked meekly.

"I don't know him, but I know who he is. What makes you think he killed your husband?"

"It isn't a matter of *thinking* he did it. I *know* he did it."

"Barbara, I also know he did it."

"Really?" The surprise was obvious in her voice. "But how?"

"I'm not at liberty to say how I know, but I believe the Salem Police have some tire impressions that will match a car that belongs to RTE Consulting—Richard Elgin's company."

"Then they know about Elgin?" she asked hopefully.

"I'm afraid not. Right now, they just have the tire prints."

"I don't get it."

"What can you tell the police about Richard Elgin that might give them probable cause to obtain a search warrant for Elgin's car?"

"I can show them this note."

"Of course, but that doesn't point a finger at Elgin," I explained. "Do you have anything that would show that Elgin had some reason to kill your husband?"

She paused to think about that. "I know this sounds corny, but I think that Elgin was blackmailing my husband."

"About what?"

"I think it had something to do with Jessie."

After a pause, she continued, "Corrigan, I'm not completely naïve. I know that Wilson helped cover up evidence about Jessie's death. At the time, I believed his story about the spilled paint, but when you found Jessie's blood under the carpet, I knew it was no accident."

"Why would he conceal evidence if he didn't at least have a role in her death?"

"To protect his boss—Alan Blalock."

I shook my head in confusion.

"At the time, I convinced myself that it was just my imagination," she said sadly. "They called it internship—all the time Jessie was spending with the mayor—and I chose to believe that it was an educational experience. I didn't want to believe that my daughter was sexually involved with Blalock. *Denial* is the word that comes to mind."

I'd wondered about that possibility, but the whole idea seemed too far fetched to take seriously.

"I've thought about it for thirty-two years," she said wistfully, "wondering if Jessie would still be alive if I'd just faced the truth, but it was simply too easy to focus on what we had and avoid looking at the price—you know what I mean?"

"Wait a minute," I said. "You lost me."

"In 1977, my husband was a low-level assistant in the city attorney's office with no particular prospects for advancement. Wilson helped set up a field trip at the city hall for Jessie's class at school—she was in seventh grade. The mayor talked with the kids, and somehow, Jessie caught his eye.

"A couple of weeks later, my husband told me that the mayor had been so impressed with Jessie's interest in city government that he'd invited her to participate in a 'junior internship' program. Of course, I was pleased to think that Jessie had impressed the mayor. I didn't question the validity of the internship program.

"Anyway, it started out with once-a-week sessions. Wilson would pick her up after school and take her to the mayor's office. She'd get to watch how things worked in city hall for a couple of hours, and then my husband would bring her home. It all seemed to be above boards.

"I don't know when it turned sexual, but now I think that it's what Blalock had in mind from the beginning. Jessie was one of those girls who developed early. When she was twelve, she looked more like a sixteen-year-old. *That's* what Blalock noticed. I was naïve to think that he picked her for her intellect—not that she wasn't bright. She was, but that wasn't the first thing you'd notice about her.

"Pretty soon, Blalock recruited my husband to serve as his aide. Our income doubled, and we moved into the nice house in West Linn and became members of the Portland elite—that is, we got to attend a lot of city functions with the mayor. Sure, I thought that Jessie was spending too much time with Blalock, but I refused to let myself think that there was anything bad about it.

"Even when I noticed changes—Jessie started acting differently. She had less to do with her school friends and no longer talked much about boys. She insisted on buying her own clothes, and she often dressed more like a twenty-year-old than a thirteen-year-old—especially when she was doing her 'internship.' I let myself believe that it was normal that she'd want to 'dress older' when she was in the company of adults.

"Wilson was issued a car by the city, and he bought me a new Cadillac. He was on the fast track, and Jessie had become a personal friend of the mayor. I simply didn't consider the possibility that Wilson's sudden career success might be tied to Blalock's interest in Jessie.

"It was about this time that I first met Richard Elgin. He was a Portland cop, but he never wore a uniform. He was assigned as the mayor's driver, and that's all he did officially. Unofficially, he was the one who made arrangements for Blalock and Jessie to go to private places for sex. I saw it even then, but I refused to acknowledge it.

"Wilson knew what was going on. He knew that his main 'duty' as aide to the mayor was to facilitate Blalock's relationship with Jessie. He knowingly and willingly turned my daughter into Blalock's mistress. But I was too wrapped up in the glitter to see what was right in front of my eyes.

"I don't know exactly what happened, but Blalock was in our house with Jessie. The gun that they found in that boy's car? It came from my husband's nightstand in our bedroom. It had been there for at least a year, and then sometime after Jessie disappeared, I noticed that it was gone. Wilson said he'd sold it, but I always wondered. Then I saw the picture in the newspaper, and I knew it was the same gun. I remember the little black-and-silver emblem in the grip."

She paused, and her eyes filled with tears. She dropped her head and sobbed, not for her recently dead husband, but for the little girl she lost to a sexually deviant politician. John Whitney had been right about Alan Blalock. He was a pedophile.

I tried to console her. "Barbara, I don't think you can blame yourself."

"But I do," she cried. "I do."

"With this information, I'll go back and look at the evidence we have. Maybe I'll find something there that will make a case against Blalock."

"Then you'd better watch out for Richard Elgin,"

Barbara warned. "His mission in life is to protect Alan Blalock. If you become a threat to Blalock, Elgin will come after you."

"Do you think your husband had become a threat to Blalock?"

"Of course! If he had been tried for Jessie's murder, he'd have told the truth. So Blalock sent Elgin down here to fix the problem."

"Elgin must at least suspect that you know all of this."

"And that's why I'm telling it all to you—once I've told the story, there won't be any reason for him to shut me up. Am I right?"

"It's a good theory, but you should consider getting out of town," I advised. "At least talk to some security people and see what they can do for you."

"Can't you do something to get Elgin locked up?" she pleaded.

"The first step will be finding probable cause for a search warrant. "Do you think there might be anything among your husband's things that could help?"

"I'll see what I can find."

"And by all means, make the police aware of your suspicions about Richard Elgin," I urged. "The sooner they have him on their radar, the better."

CHAPTER 62

Throughout the drive back from Salem, I tried to get my mind around what Barbara Devonshire had told me. For three months, everything had seemed to point at Wilson Devonshire. I'd have to go back and rethink the meaning of every piece of evidence. Was it really possible that the murders had been committed by Alan Blalock—or, for that matter, *anyone* other than Devonshire?

The first thing I did after getting back to the office was have Martha pull up Barbara Devonshire's bill from Salishan.

"Look for phone calls on her bill," I told Martha. "I want to see if she made any calls on the afternoon of July 25."

A few minutes later, Martha said, "Okay here it is. She made a six-minute call from her room at 4:08 p.m. to what looks like a Portland number."

"Now cross-check that with the number for Devonshire's office."

"It's a match. She called his office."

"And she says that she talked to her husband."

"But that means…" Martha began.

"That's right. Devonshire couldn't have killed Jessie and Randy," I finished for her.

"But if he didn't do it, who did?"

"Barbara Devonshire thinks it was Alan Blalock."

"But that's ridiculous! Why on earth would he—I mean, that just can't be right!" Martha objected.

"Don't be too quick to rule it out," I advised. "I've heard from three different people—Alicia Crabtree, Kathy Saginaw, and John Whitney—that Blalock had a thing for young girls."

"Oh, that's just slander! I can't believe people would even say such things."

"Barbara Devonshire thinks it's true. John Whitney thinks the reason Elgin killed his daughter was that Carrie was repeating things her husband had told her in confidence—specifically Blalock's history of grooming young girls for sex."

"I just don't believe it."

"Let's just wait and see how it shakes out. What we need to do is go back through the evidence we have and test the theory against the facts. Can you do that?"

"I'll do it, but I think it's a waste of time," she said resignedly.

Late in the afternoon, Kim came home and parked her Mustang by the front porch. "Can you give me a ride back up to the office?" she asked.

"Sure. What's happening?" I asked

"Gonna pick up my Explorer."

"Ah, so you've been released from purgatory."

"Yeah, Billie Austin and the union challenged the suspension, and I guess Kerby figured out that he couldn't show cause. I'll be back on the river in the morning."

"That's great."

"There's more. This morning, Cal Westfall issued a press release stating, in effect, that a closer look at the evidence from the El Camino now suggests very strongly that the murders were committed by the late Wilson Landis Devonshire. The department also issued a letter of apology to David Elkton and Carrie Silverton, saying that the Post-it note was attached to the lab report in error."

"That's a pretty abrupt turnaround."

"Yeah, I guess they just gave up."

"You'll love this. Now that Devonshire is dead and everyone has conceded that he was the one who killed Randy and Jessie, I've found something that might prove he didn't do it," I said.

"What on earth are you talking about?" Kim asked.

On the way to the sheriff's office, I told Kim all about my meeting with Barbara Devonshire.

"That makes perfect sense," she commented. "Devonshire owes his career to Blalock, so he covers for him with help from Richard Elgin. I think Barbara might be right."

"I have Martha testing that theory—which she doesn't buy—against the known facts," I said. "Meanwhile, I'm focusing on Elgin."

I went on to describe the note that Barbara Devonshire had found on her husband's desk, proving to her satisfaction that Wilson Devonshire was meeting someone on Trelstad Avenue.

"When I asked her who she thought had killed her husband, she immediately said Richard Elgin. She thinks that Elgin had been blackmailing her husband. I told her to tell that to the Salem Police and give them Devonshire's note. Maybe that'll be enough to get them looking in Elgin's direction."

"It'll still be pretty hard to get a search warrant. And even if they did get a match on the tire tracks, there's no way to prove when they were made. Elgin could simply claim that he had turned around on Trelstad Avenue on Thursday, and there'd be no way to prove otherwise—unless they want to take a chance on the admissibility of your GPS evidence," Kim said.

CHAPTER 63

WEDNESDAY, SEPTEMBER 7

The *Journal* came out with what appeared to be a complete wrap-up on the Devonshire case, declaring that Wilson Devonshire's suicide was as good as a confession. I felt bad for having let Amy Powers go off in that direction, but I didn't feel that I had enough on Blalock to make a credible accusation. As to Devonshire's death, I didn't want to tip off Elgin that the police might be looking at him, so I couldn't tell Amy that I knew it wasn't a suicide.

I hoped I could make it up to her when I had the proof I needed—if that ever happened. I tried to imagine what evidence might still exist. If there had ever been physical evidence in the Devonshire home other than the bloodstained flooring, it was long gone—probably eliminated in the original cover-up. Lacking physical evidence, I'd need witnesses placing Blalock in the Devonshire home at four on the afternoon of July 25, 1980.

Gary Turner had given me the transcripts of the only two witnesses who saw anything that afternoon, and they couldn't positively identify anyone. It seemed that Randy was the only witness to the original crime, and he quickly became a victim himself. Maybe it was hopeless.

"I've run every query I can think of," Martha told me, "and I can't find a single thing in our entire database that connects Alan Blalock with the murders, other than through Wilson Devonshire. No evidence and no witnesses."

"Since Hammond and Turner had focused in on Devonshire, it isn't surprising that they might have overlooked evidence that pointed a different way," I said.

"You know, it just might be that Blalock didn't do it."

"I can't disagree with you."

But I still believed that Blalock was guilty. If there was one witness who would be able to place Alan Blalock at the scene of the crime, it was Richard Elgin. What would it take to get him to talk? To that question, I had no answer. Still, a good place to start would be nailing him for the murder of Wilson Devonshire. In the middle of the afternoon, Barbara Devonshire called.

"After you left here yesterday I called the Salem Police and told them about the note," she said.

"What did they say about that?" I asked.

"A couple of police officers came to the house this morning. I gave them the notepad and told them that I thought it proved that Wilson hadn't killed himself.

"Did they have anything to say about that?"

"One of the officers said that there was other evidence indicating that it wasn't suicide, and then he asked if I knew of anyone who would want my husband dead. Of course, I told him about Richard Elgin."

"I assume they asked why you suspected Elgin."

"Oh yes. I told them the same thing I told you—that I thought Elgin was blackmailing my husband. They asked if I would mind if they looked in Wilson's study, and I said okay. They looked through his desk but didn't find anything."

"Did the police officers give you any hint what other evidence they had?

"Not really, but they did ask about a bag of groceries—did I leave a bag of groceries in the car, or something like that."

After a moment's thought, I said, "So they found a bag of groceries in the car. People don't buy groceries if they're on their way to commit suicide."

"They asked about the gun too. Did my husband own a hand gun? I told them no. We haven't had a gun in the house since that one I told you about yesterday."

After I got off the phone, I made a mental review of what the police had. There was the blood-spatter evidence that might indicate that someone else was in Devonshire's car. To go along with that, there almost certainly would be a lack of spatter on Devonshire's hand and clothing since he hadn't fired the gun.

They had the note that Barbara found and a sack of groceries. And they had the tire tracks—but still it was only Barbara's words that could connect the case to Richard Elgin, backed by my inadmissible GPS evidence. That still wasn't enough for a search warrant.

Fox had told Kim that Devonshire's hand showed gunshot residue, but Elgin could easily have planted that—all he'd have to do is fire a gun a few times and then run a brush up and down the barrel, catch the particles that came out, and put them on Devonshire's hand after killing him.

So since Elgin had planted fake evidence to implicate Devonshire as a suicide, would it not be fair to plant fake evidence that would lead police to the truth about Richard Elgin? Certainly it would not be legal, but could it be done?

The best possible evidence would be Elgin's fingerprint somewhere on or in Devonshire's car. Elgin wouldn't have been wearing gloves when he met Devonshire—that would have been a dead giveaway on an eighty-five degree day. He probably paid careful attention to what he touched and then wiped off any prints before leaving the scene. But maybe there was a way to replace one of the prints that he wiped off. An idea began to take shape.

I did a quick check on the movements of Elgin's WRX. It was still parked in the RTE Consulting Company's garage. It hadn't moved since its return from Salem on Friday evening. That was perfect. I drove down to the corner of Corbett Avenue and Caruthers Street.

With my clipboard and ODOT hard hat and vest, I walked up Caruthers and made sure that nobody was in the RTE Consulting building. Hurrying back to my Yukon, I picked up a small plastic case with the supplies I'd need, and then I pressed the garage door button.

Once inside Elgin's building, I pressed the button to bring the overhead door back down, closing myself in the garage. I went to the Subaru and found the driver's door unlocked. I looked at the surfaces that someone would necessarily touch when driving.

The steering wheel and gearshift handle were leather textured—no good for taking a fingerprint. But the driver's door handle was smooth, and surely, whoever last drove the car had to have pulled that handle to get out of the car.

I got out a small Ziploc bag and a tube of Super Glue. After squeezing a bit of the cyanoacrylate glue into the bag, I carefully used the bag to form a small tent over the door handle. After a couple of minutes, the images of two clear fingerprints formed in white on the smooth handle. I used a high-resolution digital camera to photograph the fingerprints.

That done, I wiped the Super Glue residue off the handle and packed up my things. I wriggled under the back of the WRX and retrieved my Spark Nano. If this idea worked, I wouldn't need to track the Subaru any further. It would be in the Salem Police impound garage.

I peered out through a dusty window to make sure the coast was clear before raising the garage door and hurrying back to my Yukon. I punched the door back down, stashed my plastic case and GPS tracker in the back seat, and quickly left the neighborhood.

It was two thirty when I got back to my office. I was short of time. I downloaded the images from my camera and opened them in Photoshop. After picking the best print and scaling it to life size, I loaded a sheet of overhead transparency film into my laser printer and printed the image onto the film.

Because of the thickness of the toner standing on top of the plastic film, what I had was a three-dimensional negative image of the fingerprint of the last person who drove the Subaru. Over that image, I spread a thin layer of Elmer's woodworking glue. The glue would dry while I drove to Salem.

I changed into the clothes I wear when I go boating—shorts, t-shirt, and sandals—and selected a stick-on mustache and a good fake driver's license from the secret place where I keep such things. I grabbed a piece of fried chicken from the refrigerator, dropped it into a plastic bag, and headed out the door. I found the Salem Police impound garage and parked around the corner.

By then, the Elmer's glue had dried to a rubbery consistency. I brushed a layer of contact cement over it and also on the index finger of my left hand. After allowing a few seconds for the contact cement to become tacky, I pressed my finger against the glue on the transparency.

The Elmer's glue peeled away from the transparency and adhered to my finger. I now had a three-dimensional replica of Richard Elgin's fingerprint adhered to my left index finger.

I carefully touched the piece of fried chicken with my left hand, applying a thin film of oil to the fake fingerprint. Then I strode boldly toward the impound garage. Through the side door, I could see a few cars inside, including a blue Pontiac Grand Am.

I walked in the front door of the garage to a small counter, where I found a sign stating "Press button for service." I put on my best bubba smile and pressed the button. When a young police cadet appeared, I handed him my fake driver's license, and he dutifully studied it for a moment.

"What can I do for you, Mr. Levitt?" he asked.

"Officer, I hope you can help me out here. My buddy's car got towed, and my clothes are in it. I've got a dinner date, and I can't go dressed like this," I told him.

"I can't let you take anything out of someone else's car," he said, looking confused.

"Oh, come on, man. I'll describe my clothes. I'm not trying to steal anything, I just want my clothes back, and ol' Jim went and parked in the boat-trailer parking space. I told him he'd just get towed away, but he didn't listen. It's a black suit, a blue shirt, and it's all in a vinyl hanging bag that says Macy's," I blurted in a continuous stream.

"I'm sorry...uh...what kind of car?" the kid stammered.

"It's a metallic blue Grand Am 4-door. I don't know the license number, but I can point it out to you," I bluffed.

I'd overloaded his circuits, and the kid said, "Okay, you can take a look, but I still can't let you take anything without authorization."

The first thing I saw when he led me into the garage was the silver Cadillac belonging to Wilson Devonshire. It was draped with yellow crime-scene tape and parked at the side of the garage. The kid led me down to the blue Grand Am.

"Is this the car?" he asked. "I don't see any clothes in it."

"Sure looks like his car. You think someone might have stolen my clothes out of it? I know that's where I left 'em. Larry's car's too dirty. I wouldn't have put my clothes in there. No. I'm sure it was Jimmy's car I put 'em in."

"Well, mister, I don't see anything here. Maybe you'd better check Larry's car."

"Well, dang. You mean I came all the way up here for nothing?" I complained.

"It sure looks that way," he said as he led me back toward the front of the building. On the way past the Cadillac, I touched my left index finger to the upper corner of the window on the passenger side door. The rest was up to the Salem CSI people.

CHAPTER 64

THURSDAY, SEPTEMBER 8

The sound of automatic gunfire shattered the mid-morning quiet. Somewhere between twenty and fifty rounds were fired off in less time than it takes to write about the event. A moment later, Terrel, the teenage son of Furman Ritter came sprinting down the railroad tracks from the direction of Big Dan's place.

He leapt from the tracks up onto Water Street and continued his sprint until he disappeared around the corner onto Miller Street. The Ritter family lived in what is commonly called the Deliverance House, a nondescript bungalow facing Highway 99 that is the scene of frequent visits by the police, the fire department, and the hazmat squad.

After the meth lab in the garage blew up and set the house on fire, the garage was converted into a bedroom for Terrel, who was Canemah's "usual suspect" for any vandalism, petty theft, or car prowl that occurred within a two-mile radius. The riverbed behind the Ritter house is a collecting place for stolen bicycles from all over town. Big Dan once pulled nine bikes out of the river on a single dive.

From time to time, Big Dan finds it necessary to reinforce his image as a commando and generally scary guy. When the police arrived to ask about the sound of gunfire, Big Dan would tell them that he hadn't heard anything. Around the neighborhood, nobody would put the finger on Big Dan, but in close company, he would admit to having fired off a magazine of blanks just to make a point.

In reality, anyone with a shovel and a low regard for personal safety could dig about a pound of lead out of the ground outside Big Dan's back door, where he had made his point. The point was not lost on Terrel, who would never again be so reckless as to set foot on Big Dan's beach.

According to neighborhood lore, the success rate of Big Dan's rehabilitation program for juvenile delinquents was 100%. The only re-offender was a California sea lion that had gotten the idea that Big Dan's dock would be a fine place to rest between raids on the Salmon coming up the Willamette Falls fish ladder. The sea lion apparently had sneaked up through the locks when a barge was brought up from the lower river, and then was trapped above the falls until the Department of Fish and Wildlife captured him and transported him back to the Pacific Ocean.

I was in the middle of teaching Martha how to do some of my online snooping for Xycon. I had this idea that I could pay her to do my work so that I could spend more time restoring *Annabel Lee*. In reality, if I was going to keep Martha employed now that the Devonshire investigation was finished, I'd need another regular account. William Gates and Xycon alone couldn't provide income for both of us.

I'd done some jobs for a worker's compensation insurance provider on several occasions over the past couple of years, and I'd recently given them a proposal for a reduced rate in exchange for steady work. There was no shortage of people trying to defraud the worker's comp system. My last investigation had involved a man who was receiving total disability payments for an on-the-job back injury. I caught him on video playing hockey at a local ice arena.

The cacophonous clatter of Bud's old Pontiac drew my eyes to the window, in time to see Bud come around the corner with a stack of lumber and sheetrock lashed to the roof of the small car. The Pontiac leaned precariously as Bud made the turn, and I feared that he was going to dump his load against the side of my house. How he'd gotten all the way home from Home Depot is beyond my imagination. Curiosity compelled me to go outside and find out what Bud was up to.

"I'm remodeling my cabin," he told me. "It's time to build a real kitchen and bathroom in there, and I'm converting the shop into a real bedroom."

"That's quite a project," I commented.

"Can you give me a hand with this stuff?" he requested.

I helped Bud carry the lumber and sheetrock into the shop area of his cabin and was surprised to find that he'd cleaned the place out. The greasy remains of unfinished projects were all gone, replaced by a stockpile of building materials. In addition to what we were hauling inside, he had new windows and doors, kitchen and bathroom fixtures, and even some hardwood cabinetry.

"Looks like you're going all out," I observed.

"Yeah, six weeks from now, you won't recognize the place," he said.

"What did you do, inherit an oil well?"

"Something like that. I turned sixty-five. Now the government sends me a check every month. It's better than having a job."

This was going to be a whole new lifestyle for Bud. I wondered if I'd be able to adjust to his being civilized. That was a pretty big change.

"How about a beer?" I suggested when we finished carrying the building materials.

"Sure thing," Bud said, and then he did the most amazing thing I'd ever seen him do. He went to his own refrigerator and brought out a couple of beers. That was a first.

Since Bud didn't have any outdoor furniture—or indoor furniture either, for that matter—I invited him to pull up a chair on my front porch. He excused himself for long enough to go back and get another beer, which he offered to Martha.

"Any word on that bad guy you've been hiding from?" Bud asked Martha.

Martha looked at me before answering. "He's still out there. We don't know if he's still after us."

"But he's still dangerous, even if he isn't after us," I added.

"Can't you get him locked up for something?" Bud asked.

"I think the law is closing in on him. I'm hoping they'll round him up pretty soon."

Bud looked disappointed. "Does that mean you'll move back to Beaverton?" he asked Martha.

"I don't think so. I mean, as long as I'm working here, I'd like to keep living nearby."

"Someday, Daryl's going to buy new engines and want his boat back," I reminded her.

"I hope by then something else will open up," she said.

Bud just smiled.

CHAPTER 65

FRIDAY, SEPTEMBER 9

was starting to feel marginally comfortable. It was just a matter of time, in my view, until the Salem Police nailed Richard Elgin for the murder of Wilson Devonshire, and in my optimistic imagination, I could see that event leading to new investigations into the deaths of Carrie Whitney and Christie Brogan. But the main thing was that Elgin would be off the street.

I was startled from my thoughts by a phone call. The display on my phone identified the caller as Bill Cheshire.

"Good morning, Bill," I said cheerfully.

"Corrigan, I have some bad news. The IRS is going to disallow your home-office deduction. They're also disallowing the depreciation deductions you've taken on your computers," Cheshire said.

That took the smile off my face.

"What the hell is that all about?" I demanded.

"It seems that Milo and Otis identified some personal files on your computer and some nonbusiness email messages."

"That's impossible. There was none of that on these—uh-oh, are you telling me that they got hold of the computers the DA seized?"

"I don't know that they actually got their hands on the computers, but they definitely know what's on the hard drives."

"You're telling me that the DA's office gave the IRS what they found on my computers?" I said in disbelief.

"Looks that way," he said.

"That can't be legal! How in hell can they do that?"

"You may be right. It might not be legal. But I don't see much you can do about it."

"What do you mean I can't do anything about it? I'll challenge them in court!"

"Well, I'm not an attorney, but I can tell you that I've seen a very low success rate on cases like this in tax court."

"This is ridiculous!"

"Yes, it's ridiculous. But at this point, all I can do for you is calculate how much it's going to cost you. Maybe I can talk them into waiving the penalties, but given the agents' general hostility toward you, I'm not optimistic about my chances."

"Hostility toward me—what reason do they have for being hostile?"

"Honestly, I can't answer that. It's like they're taking it as a personal affront that you tried to cheat them out of their money."

"*Their money!*" I exploded. "It isn't *their* money, and I didn't cheat anybody!"

"They see it differently," he said, obviously trying to calm me down. And of course, I knew it was futile to debate the issue. The IRS had made its decision, and the only way to challenge it would be in court. "This whole thing stinks to high heaven," I complained.

"You should talk to an attorney," Cheshire said, "but like I said, few people win against Big Brother."

We talked a bit more without changing anything. Bill agreed to call me as soon as he knew what it was going to cost me. My next call was to William Gates.

"What do you know about challenging the IRS?" I asked.

"I'm not a tax attorney," Gates said, "but unless you owe millions, it probably isn't worth it."

"I'd *better not* owe millions."

"You'd probably spend more on attorney fees than you could hope to get back, even if you win."

"So what you're saying is that I just have to roll over and take it?"

"That's what I'm saying. You should be more careful in choosing your enemies."

"Who—Milo and Otis? I didn't choose them. They chose me."

"I'm not talking about Milo and Otis," Gates said.

"They're just worker bees. I'm talking about the guy who's *causing* all this trouble."

"You don't mean Richard Elgin," I began.

Gates scoffed. "Elgin. Hell no. He's just another worker bee. He doesn't have the juice to bring the mighty IRS down on you."

"Who then? You don't think Devonshire—"

"Corrigan, you surprise me. Can't you see where all this is coming from?" Gates challenged.

"You lost me," I said, honestly confused.

"You pissed off a US senator. This is what a pissed-off senator does."

"Who? Blalock? I asked. "I didn't do anything to him!"

"Don't be naïve. You interfered with the operation of his machine. Blalock doesn't tolerate that."

"So you're saying that Blalock is responsible for my trouble with the IRS?"

"And the DA's office, and the Department of Public Safety Standards and Training," he added.

"It was Elgin who did those," I said. "I have his phone bills."

"And tell me again who Elgin works for?" Gates asked patiently.

"Damn!" was all I could say.

"Blalock has a history. You aren't the first person he's dropped the bureaucracy on. To him, the IRS is just another weapon that he uses to win his political wars," he said.

If all that was true, and Elgin acted on orders from Alan Blalock, it wouldn't help to have Elgin locked up. If the real enemy was Blalock, he'd simply find another "worker bee" if he didn't already have one. Gates was right. I was naïve to think that my troubles would go away when Elgin was out of the picture. I changed the subject.

"How are things going on those other two things?" I asked.

"The DA's investigation is going nowhere. They've found nothing to support their alleged witness's claim that you broke into his car. That whole thing was a sideshow." Gates said.

"Not entirely," I corrected. "They found my hidden safe and told Trey Bourne where to plant his bomb. And they furnished the IRS with the contents of my computer drives."

"True, but that's history now. They don't have anywhere else to go on it."

"And what about my license?"

"They'll try to use this business with the IRS as an excuse to pull your license. None of their other inquiries panned out, but this one might stick."

"Do you have a defense?"

"Working on it. Best advice I can give you right now is bite the bullet and pay-off the IRS as quickly and quietly as possible. That'll show your good intentions—at least that's what I'll try to convince the license review board. Just don't get mucked up in anything else."

What came to mind at that instant was my breaking into the RTE Consulting garage. My guess was that a B & E charge would constitute getting mucked up.

CHAPTER 66

MONDAY, SEPTEMBER 12

The search warrant was issued by a Marion County Circuit Court judge first thing Monday morning. It then had to be certified by a Multnomah County judge before the Portland Police, acting on behalf of the Salem Police, could execute the search of the RTE Consulting LLC building on Caruthers Street. When the tires on Elgin's Subaru were found to be the same brand and have the same tread pattern as those that left the tracks next to Devonshire's car, the WRX was pulled from the garage and loaded onto a flatbed tow truck.

I learned about the raid when Kevin Fox phoned Kim, who switched her phone to speaker.

"I thought you'd like to know that the WRX your friend has been tracking is on its way to Salem," Fox told her.

"Thanks for the update," she said.

"What's your interest in this, anyhow?"

"I thought that was obvious. I pulled the car with the Devonshire girl in it out of the river, and that's what set this whole thing in motion, right up to the death of old man Devonshire."

"How does Richard Elgin fit into that picture?"

"Back when Jessie Devonshire disappeared, Wilson Devonshire was aide to Portland Mayor Alan Blalock. Elgin was Blalock's driver. In effect, Elgin and Devonshire were co-workers both reporting to Blalock. Nobody knows for sure what Elgin did in the cover-up of the Mendelson-Devonshire murders, but he was definitely involved."

"How do you know that?"

"There was a taxi log among the Mendelson-Devonshire evidence. Someone took a cab ride to Richard Elgin's house from a tavern a quarter mile from the boat ramp where the car was dumped. He most likely left a car at the tavern for the person who dumped Mendelson's car to drive home."

"You think he knew that Devonshire had killed the kids?" Fox asked.

"I'm pretty sure he knew who did it—it would be hard to be that involved in the cover-up and not know who he was covering for," Kim said.

"Barbara Devonshire thinks that Elgin was blackmailing her husband."

"Then why would he kill his golden goose?"

"That's the question I've been struggling with."

"Maybe he figured that if Devonshire went to trial for the murder, he'd be dragged into it as an accessory after the fact," Kim speculated.

"That's as good as anything I've heard yet," Fox agreed.

"You had method and opportunity. Now you have motive."

"I'm glad I called. Thanks. We'll work that taxi log angle."

"Now I have a question for you," Kim began. "How did you get the warrant to pick up Elgin's car?"

"We got lucky. Our lab people picked up a print when they processed the evidence out of Devonshire's car. We ran it through the AFIS database and came up dry. Then after your tip, we ran it against the law-enforcement database. Elgin was a match. That was enough to get the warrant."

"Good job, Fox."

"We still have to build a case that we can take to court," Fox reminded her.

"Somewhere along the way, you might want to talk to his ex-wives—the ones that are still alive," Kim suggested.

"You're hinting at something. Let's hear it."

"Two of Elgin's wives died—one in a rafting accident, one in a diving accident. Only, there's good reason to doubt that they were accidents."

"Whose jurisdiction are those cases in?"

"The scuba death was in Washington State—Mason County. The rafting death was in Clackamas County."

"So why aren't your people investigating it?" Fox asked.

"There was no real investigation when it happened and no interest now. But that could change if you guys stir it up," Kim told him.

"This guy sounds like bad news."

"The closer you look, the scarier he is. You remember the guy up here with the Semtex bomb in his car when he got creamed on Highway 99? That car belonged to RTE Consulting, and the stiff was Elgin's employee."

"Jesus, Stayton, is there anything else you want to tell me?"

"Yeah. Be careful. This guy is worse than just bad news. Connect all the dots, and keep your ass covered."

"Kim, where are you getting all of this?"

"Like I told you before, I have a friend," she said evasively.

"Would your friend be that *private*—Corrigan—the one in the newspapers?" Fox pressed.

"Yeah, it's Corrigan," Kim admitted.

"And let me guess, it was Corrigan who sent you down to the Silver Spur to pump me for information on the Devonshire death."

Kim sighed. "There's no fooling you, Detective Fox."

"Damn! I *knew* you wouldn't just call me for old time's sake," Fox complained.

"But look at the good side," she said. "Now you have the opportunity to close the biggest case of your career."

"Believe it or not, we'd have done this *without* your help—or Corrigan's. We developed a lead on Elgin in our own investigation. I know you big-city people up north think that we're a bunch of hayseeds down here in Salem, but we really *are* capable of doing good police work."

"Sorry, Fox, I didn't mean to make it sound that way."

He backed off, saying, "Forget it. Let's just call this 'interagency cooperation,' okay?"

"Fair enough. Take care, Fox," she closed.

Kim disconnected and tossed her phone onto the sofa. I was pleased that Fox had been able to get the warrant that would start the undoing of Richard Elgin. He seemed like a pretty good detective, and I was optimistic about his chances of closing the books on Elgin. I hoped that somewhere in the process, he'd stir up some interest in the deaths of Carrie Whitney and Christie Brogan.

CHAPTER 67

TUESDAY, SEPTEMBER 13

While it was good news that the arrest of Richard Eglin was eminent, I couldn't help thinking that this case was far from closed. Despite Barbara Devonshire's assertion that Alan Blalock had been sexually involved with her daughter—and was thus a prime suspect in her murder—I had found not one shred of evidence to support that charge. Furthermore, I still hadn't conclusively ruled out Wilson Devonshire.

All I had was Barbara Devonshire's assertion that her husband had been in his office at the time I had calculated Jessie Devonshire and Randy Mendelson had been killed. Her hotel bill confirmed that she had called Devonshire's office at 4:08 p.m. One of three things had to be true.

First possibility: she was mistaken about having talked with her husband—that is, she had instead spoken to someone other than Devonshire when she called his office. It would hardly be the first time that a witness had faulty recollections—three decades after the event.

Second possibility: my timeline was all wrong. It was based on Devonshire's 6:15 p.m. receipt for paint, the witness—James Lacomb—who had seen someone moving the El Camino at 4:45 p.m. to 5:00 p.m., and the time it would take to commit the murders and then formulate a plan to cover it up. Maybe Lacomb could have been off by half an hour, and maybe Devonshire could have gotten home fifteen minutes quicker than usual, and if *both* of those had happened, then *maybe* there would have been time to commit the murders.

Third possibility: Barbara was right, and somebody else killed Jessie and Randy. If so, in order for Devonshire to have any motivation to participate in the cover-up—which we knew he did—the murders had to have been committed by someone he needed to protect or by someone who could implicate him in some tangential way. Alan Blalock would fit the bill on both counts. But where was the evidence?

Some people say that intuition or instinct play as big a role in criminal investigation as does physical evidence. I don't disagree, but I would say that a lot of what is called intuition comes from having a good understanding of human nature. Gut feelings most often come from anticipating what a person would do when confronted with a particular set of circumstances.

Assuming the third possibility, my understanding of human nature told me that a person in Wilson Devonshire's situation would preserve evidence to protect himself—because that's what people do. If Devonshire didn't commit the murders himself, it was highly probable that he kept a CYA file hidden away somewhere. That file would contain proof of someone else's guilt—probably Blalock's.

As soon as that idea crystallized, I realized that I had to have another talk with Barbara Devonshire—and soon. If I could figure out that Devonshire probably kept a CYA file, so could the guilty party. I already knew what that individual was willing to do to protect his secrets.

I dialed the phone, and when Barbara Devonshire answered, I made arrangements to meet her at one. I left my place at noon and drove down I-5 to Salem. I pulled up in front of the Devonshire home at 12:55 p.m. Barbara answered the door and escorted me to her sitting room.

"Now what did you want to talk about?" she asked.

"I've been told that the Salem Police are closing in on Richard Elgin," I began.

"You didn't drive all the way down here to tell me that."

"No, I want to talk a bit about your husband. After we talked last week, I gave some thought to some of the things you said. The thing is, if what you think happened is true, I think there's a good chance that your husband kept evidence to protect himself."

Barbara looked baffled.

"From the beginning, there was always the possibility that Randy's car would be found and bring the case back to life," I explained. "Your husband knew that he'd be the prime suspect, and he almost certainly knew who did the killing. The only way he could prove his own innocence would be to prove that someone else was guilty. To do that, he would have kept evidence—proof of the other person's guilt."

"I see," she said slowly.

"I'm sorry to have to ask you this, but have you gone through your husband's things?"

She hesitated. "A little bit. There's so much…"

"And you haven't found anything like—"

"I wouldn't even know what to look for," she interrupted.

"It could be documents, physical evidence, photos—I think it would be someplace where it wouldn't be found by accident, maybe in a safe or a safe deposit box."

"Well, I'll keep my eyes open."

"Barbara," I said earnestly, "if there's a guilty party out there, he's going to have the same thought I had. And he's going to do whatever it takes to get his hands on anything your husband may have hidden."

"Do you think I'm in danger?"

"I think you need to go through your husband's things as soon as possible. Look for notes, keys, envelopes marked 'To be opened in the event…' and try to think of secure hiding places."

"I wouldn't know how to do that. Do you think you could help me?"

"I could do that, but for your protection as well as mine, I'd like you to have your attorney hire me to do the search—and be present during the search. That way anything I find will be protected by your attorney-client privilege. That could be important if I find something that implicates you," I explained.

"What could possibly implicate me?"

"I don't know. But talk with your attorney. If he agrees to what I've suggested, have him call me."

"But when—" she started to ask.

"Call him today—now!" I urged. "The longer you wait, the more likely it is that Jessie's killer will come after you."

"Corrigan, you're scaring me."

"There's a lot at stake. I'd like to start the search tomorrow."

"Let me make that call," she said.

‍❧

A couple of hours later, I was back at my desk when my phone rang.

"This is Robert Sumner. I'm an attorney representing Barbara Devonshire."

"Then may I assume that she's told you about the conversation I had with her earlier today?" I asked.

"She has," he said. "Mr. Corrigan, you've scared that poor lady out of her mind. She wants me to hire you, but I'm not sure I want to have anything to do with someone who would terrorize a person that way."

"Mr. Sumner, Barbara Devonshire is convinced that someone other than her husband killed her daughter back in 1980, and yet we *know* that he did things to cover up the crime scene. That means that he was—for whatever reason—protecting the killer, at considerable risk to himself. He had to have known that he'd be a prime suspect if the bodies were ever found. Under those circumstances, don't you think it is highly likely that he kept evidence to shift the blame from himself?"

"But that's all just speculation."

"I'll tell you something that I didn't tell Barbara Devonshire. The person who would worry about the existence of that evidence sent someone to my house in the middle of the night with a two-pound brick of Semtex because he thought I might have evidence against him."

"That's a very dramatic statement, Mr. Corrigan, but I doubt that you can prove any of it."

"We'll find out about that pretty soon. The guy with the Semtex was an employee of the man who is about to be charged with Wilson Devonshire's murder. You think that's a coincidence?"

"How could you possibly know that?" he challenged.

"I'm an investigator. It's my job to know things like that," I reminded him.

"Okay," he conceded, "assuming that's true, he'll be locked up so he can't hurt anyone."

"That's true. But he isn't doing all of this to protect *himself*. He's doing it to protect is employer—and that's the man to look out for. I think you know who I'm talking about."

"I refuse to participate in your politics of personal destruction."

"There are no 'politics of personal destruction' involved in this, except as related to the cover-up of a double murder. If Devonshire kept evidence, it needs to be found and used to prosecute the guilty party."

"That's a very noble statement, Mr. Corrigan, but it doesn't alter the fact—"

"Okay," I interrupted, "I can see that you've already made up your mind. If you have a conflict of interest in this case, you are obligated to inform Mrs. Devonshire that you cannot represent her."

"Mr. Corrigan, I don't—" he sputtered.

"What's it going to be, Sumner?" I demanded.

"Oh, for Pete's sake! You want to play your little game? Go ahead and play it."

"Tell me what that means."

"Do your search. Send me the bill," he said in resignation, "but you won't find anything."

An hour later, I was still puzzling over the certainty in Sumner's final assertion. Was he expressing his opinion, or did he know something that I didn't?

CHAPTER 68

WEDNESDAY, SEPTEMBER 14

I was on Barbara Devonshire's front porch a few minutes after eight the next morning. In the back of my Yukon, I had a stepladder and an athletic bag containing a pair of coveralls, a couple of flashlights, and a high-intensity headlamp.

I was surprised to find Robert Sumner there ahead of me. After our exchange on the phone, I hadn't expected him to participate.

Once the introductions were complete, Barbara asked,

"Where do we start?"

"The cellar and the attic are obvious hiding places."

"You want to search the attic first before it gets hot up there?"

"Will we need a ladder?"

"No, there's a pull-down stairway."

Before climbing the steps, I pulled on my coveralls and donned my headlamp. Sumner looked abashed for not having thought of such things himself. I handed him a flashlight. When I offered one to Barbara, she shook her head.

"I'm not going up there," she said. "You guys go ahead—have a good time. I'll wait here."

Sumner followed me up but stopped a couple of steps from the top, unwilling to risk getting his charcoal-gray suit dirty. The attic in the eighty-year-old house was tall enough to stand up in. The only light was what filtered in through vents in the gables. The floor consisted of utility-grade two-by-six lumber that appeared to be newer than the house itself. The undisturbed layer of dust that covered the floor told me that nobody had been in the attic for a good many years.

I swept my flashlight around the entire space. There was a stack of cardboard boxes near the stairway we had just climbed, but most of the attic was empty. I knelt down and opened the first box and found in it the first seven volumes of a 1969 World Book Encyclopedia. I pulled each volume from the box and fanned the pages in case anything had been hidden there. Two more boxes contained the remaining volumes of the encyclopedia, and I repeated the process.

The other boxes contained Christmas decorations of the style made in the sixties, and what looked like a full set of Fiesta Ware dishes. I looked inside the serving pitcher and between the plates but again found nothing. Then I walked slowly over the entire attic floor, looking for any loose boards that could conceal a hidden compartment. Satisfied that there was nothing in the attic, I climbed down the steps.

"That Fiesta Ware will bring good money on eBay," I commented.

Barbara just nodded and led us to the cellar. Typical of houses of its age, the ceiling was low—in most places barely over six feet, so the tall attorney had to stoop over to keep from bashing his head on the joists. The concrete floor was clean, indicating that the cellar was in active use. In the center was a massive old furnace with ductwork branching out from the top like limbs on a tree trunk. Against one wall, there was a row of shelves that most likely were once used for home-canned food. A few empty mason jars were the last remnants of the lost art form.

On the opposite wall was a long workbench cluttered with the residue of unfinished and forgotten projects. I searched the bench from end to end, looking in drawers full of odds and ends, jars full of screws, and cigar boxes containing a peculiar collection of small broken items that Devonshire had perhaps hoped one day to repair.

Sumner mostly watched, preferring to keep his hands clean. I noticed, however, that whenever I looked inside something, he was right there, looking over my shoulder. When I found an old key ring with half a dozen tarnished brass keys, Sumner snatched them out of my hand and turned his back to examine the keys. He handed them back to me only after satisfying himself that none was what we were looking for.

I checked the bottom side of each drawer in case Devonshire had taped a message or a key there but found nothing. One by one, I went through the cardboard boxes on the shelf below the workbench, finding them filled with Devonshire's twenty-year accumulation of items he thought he might need someday.

Shining my light upward, I searched the entire ceiling for anything that might conceal a small compartment. I belly-crawled along the floor, shining my light under the work bench and fruit shelves, but all I discovered there was the desiccated carcass of a mouse caught in a trap.

After two hours, I had no place else to search in the cellar. We went up to the enclosed back porch, where I peeled off my coveralls.

"It's lunch time," Sumner observed. "Why don't we take a break?"

"I could make some sandwiches," Barbara offered.

"I need to check in at my office. There's a good lunch spot right around the corner. My treat," Sumner said.

We took my Yukon because Sumner had driven a two seat Mercedes and Mrs. Devonshire was still without a car. She had no desire to have the Salem Police return the car in which her husband had died.

Following Sumner's guidance, I drove four or five blocks over to Liberty Street, turned north and drove toward downtown Salem. As we approached Ferry Street, Sumner told me to turn left and then make another left into the parking lot at his office.

"There's a good sports bar right over there," Sumner said, pointing the way. "I'll join you there in a few minutes."

I walked with Barbara in the direction Sumner had indicated, and when we turned the corner onto Commercial Street, I found myself looking at Magoo's—the very place visited by Richard Elgin's Subaru while I had the GPS tracker on it. I suddenly had a whole new perspective on Robert Sumner, and I no longer wanted to find anything in the Devonshire home—at least not while Sumner was around.

He cast himself as working only in Barbara Devonshire's best interest, but the probability that he was associated with Richard Elgin, together with our phone conversation the day before, left me feeling that he had some other purpose in mind. He clearly was opposed to my involvement in the search.

Sumner had been Wilson Devonshire's attorney, so apparently, Devonshire had not left him one of those "To be opened in the event of" letters telling him what to look for. My guess was that Sumner's meeting with Elgin had been to discuss a contingency plan in case Devonshire had kept a hidden file. Mrs. Devonshire's unexpected call to me had no doubt disrupted whatever plan they had concocted to deal with it.

After lunch, we returned to the house and started our afternoon search in Devonshire's study. This was the place where he spent his time, and I figured was the place most likely to contain a hidden file. The trick now would be to avoid finding it while making it look like I was doing a thorough search. If I found something, I'd need to pass over it without Sumner noticing.

Devonshire's study was fairly large, with a bay window overlooking the front-yard fountain. His massive cherry desk illogically faced away the windows toward an entire wall of built-in bookshelves filled with law books. Against the wall to the left of the desk was a pair of two-drawer filing cabinets built of cherry to match the built-in bookcases.

Next to the door through which we had just entered stood a credenza that matched the desk. On top of the credenza, there was a matched dictionary and thesaurus between a pair of polished-cherry bookends. But what caught my eye was the cast bronze statue of a bald eagle standing to the right of the books. It looked like the same statue I'd seen in Dick Hammond's photo of the entry hall in Devonshire's West Linn house the day after Jessie disappeared—the statue that had probably fractured Jessie's skull.

I made a quick judgment call, figuring that the odds were against Devonshire hiding his secrets in the law books. Though admittedly remote, there was some possibility that anything hidden in the books could be found by accident, and I didn't think Devonshire would take that chance. I instructed Barbara and Sumner on how to search the books while I went to work on the desk, which I figured was the most likely place for something to be found.

I could see Sumner's dissatisfaction with that plan, but he went along with it, though always keeping himself turned so that he could keep an eye on what I was doing. I made a show of checking the bottoms of all the desk drawers, and then I started leafing through the files. If I were to find something that looked interesting, I'd make a mental note of it and keep searching.

To maintain the charade, I stopped from time to time, extracted a file, and leafed through it page by page as though I'd found something. On every occasion when I did that, Sumner dropped what he was doing and rushed over to see what I'd found.

After ninety minutes of searching, I picked up a paperweight that appeared to be an ordinary piece of river rock. Immediately, I recognized it as one of those fake rocks with a key hidden in the bottom. I casually set it aside and focused my attention on the papers that it had been sitting on.

There were many places I would have searched had Sumner not been there, such as the lamp base and the wastebasket, either one of which could contain a hidden compartment, but I passed over them. I'd come back to those later.

It took the entire afternoon for Barbara and Sumner to go through all of the books. They succeeded in finding a few papers, including a certified copy of Jessie Devonshire's birth certificate, between the pages of the books, but they found nothing related to the murder of Jessie and Randy. Meanwhile, I searched the desk, the filing cabinets, and the credenza.

If I'd actually wanted to find something, I'd have checked for hidden compartments built into the bookcase, the fireplace, the wall paneling, the floors, the light fixtures, and the furniture. Instead, I finally threw my hands up in frustration.

"Well, I guess there's nothing here," I said in resignation. "Tomorrow we can take a look at other parts of the house."

My hope was that Sumner would have had other plans, but if he did, he seemed perfectly willing to ditch them in order to stay on top of my search. We had just agreed to meet again at eight in the morning to resume our search, when Sumner's hand came to rest on the fake rock.

Whether he suspected what it was or picked it up by random chance, I'll never know. My heart sank when he turned it over and spotted the key compartment. Quickly, he turned the rock back over and set it down. I looked away, pretending I hadn't seen anything. Now it would be a game to see who could get to it first, and clearly, Sumner had the home-court advantage.

We made our way to the front door and said our good-byes. I went to my Yukon and Sumner went to his Mercedes, and we both drove out to the street. Sumner turned left, so I turned right. I drove a quarter mile and then looped around the block and drove back toward the Devonshire house, with the intention of telling Barbara that I'd left my notebook in the study. As I approached, I saw Sumner's car already there, and he was at the door, no doubt telling Barbara the same thing I'd planned to say.

It was crushing to be that close to finding something, only to see it slip out of reach. Once Sumner had that key, I'd never have a chance of getting Devonshire's hidden files. But what could I do? The only thing I could think of was to hang back and follow Sumner when he came back out. Maybe he'd lead me to something.

Five minutes later, Sumner reappeared. I followed him to his office, where he parked and hurried inside. I found a curbside parking space on Commercial Street where I could keep an eye on the Mercedes. I phoned Martha and asked her to look up Robert Sumner's home address, which turned out to be in the Salem Heights neighborhood.

I waited for about twenty minutes before seeing Sumner getting into his car. He came out of the parking lot and turned left onto Commercial Street, heading south. I followed him up Commercial to the Liberty Street Y. He stayed right on Liberty. By then I already knew where he was going. He made a right turn onto Salem Heights Drive. The driveway he turned into was his own. I drove on past.

CHAPTER 69

"They picked up Elgin," Kim said when I got home. "It's all over the news."

She led me to the TV, where Matt Zaffino was starting his weather forecast.

"You just missed it," she said. "They arrested him at home and executed a search warrant. Other than that, the news story didn't say much that we didn't already know. By the time the TV stations found out about it, Elgin was already gone, so they were left to shoot video outside his house. One shot showed cops carrying out some bagged evidence, but I couldn't tell what it was."

While the arrest of Elgin was good news, it didn't offset my depression over having lost Devonshire's CYA file to Sumner. It looked like they'd get Elgin, but it also looked like the bigger fish was going to get away.

The sound of a power saw drowned out the weather report, and I looked out the window to see Bud carrying a stack of two-by-four studs into his shack.

"He's been working all evening," Kim said. "Sawing and hammering—he really has a project going."

"Yeah, it's pretty amazing. All this time, I've thought that beer was the only thing that could motivate Bud," I said.

At that moment, we heard doors slamming and someone shouting. Terrel Ritter came sprinting up the alley, followed a moment later by Red Harper. Harper lived in an old house facing Highway 99 and drove a big blue Dodge pickup with a large Vietnam Service Ribbon sticker on the rear window.

"You little shit!" Red shouted. "That's my medicine!"

Terrel hurdled over the low picket fence, down onto the railroad tracks, and took off in the direction of the Deliverance House. Before he disappeared from sight, I noticed that he was carrying a fistful of greenery.

"Come back here, you bastard. I need that!" Red called after him.

It was no secret in the neighborhood that the garage behind Red's house was home to a crude—but substantial—pot-growing operation. Red let everyone know that he had a state-issued medical-marijuana card, authorizing him to grow pot for his own consumption. Red claimed that it helped with the pain from his unspecified war wounds. A few minutes later, Red came staggering back down the tracks, bent over and gasping for breath.

Seeing Kim's uniform, he wheezed, "That son of a bitch stole my medicine! Arrest him!"

"You need to report it to the Oregon City Police. This isn't my jurisdiction," Kim said.

"But you gotta do something," Red pleaded. "He took a whole damned plant!"

"Now if I did anything, I'd have to evaluate whether or not the amount of 'medicine' you're growing back there exceeds what you actually need. Are you sure you want me to do that?"

Red's eyes widened, and he protested, "I got a *right* to grow that! I need it for the pain."

"You must have a lot of pain. I've seen inside your garage," Kim said.

"What do you know about pain?" Red countered.

Kim gave Red a cold stare.

"That worthless kid," he mumbled, "otta be in jail. Stinkin' little turd."

"Maybe you should lock up your garage a little better," I suggested.

"He just pried the damned lock off."

"You lookin' for this?" Big Dan asked. He held up the plant that Terrel had been carrying. "Kid tripped on a railroad tie and took a header into the blackberries. He'll be awhile getting himself out."

Red made a grab for the plant, but Big Dan held it up out of his reach.

"That's my medicine," he complained. "I gotta have that."

"What do you think, Deputy?" Big Dan asked Kim.

"Is the Ritter kid okay?" Kim asked.

"Oh, yeah, he's just ass-over-teakettle in the blackberries. He'll probably be able to get himself out," Big Dan said.

"Maybe we should get him some help," I suggested.

"Nah," Big Dan said, "This'll help with his rehabilitation."

"I'd better take a look," Kim said.

"Gimme my medicine!" Red demanded.

"This looks to me like contraband," Big Dan said.

"If anything, Dan, it's evidence for a B & E charge," Kim told him.

"You plan on filing charges?" I asked Red.

Red looked confused. I think he was in need of some of his medicine. He sputtered, "I just want my medicine back."

Big Dan handed over the plant, which Red clutched to his chest.

"Goddamn kid," he muttered as he shuffled back down the alley.

The rest of us walked up the railroad track to the point where Terrel tumbled into the blackberries. Halfway down the steep embankment, suspended in the brambles overhanging the riverbank, Terrel looked like a bug caught in a spider web. His face and arms were covered with scratches, and his clothes were hopelessly snagged on blackberry thorns.

"I can't get loose," he said helplessly.

Kim used her VHF to call the Clackamas Fire and Rescue unit.

"We have a young adult male entangled in blackberry vines on a steep embankment near the north end of Paquet Street in the Canemah district," she told the dispatcher. "He's going to need minor medical attention, but mostly he needs someone with pruning shears and a climbing harness."

A minute later, we heard the sirens, and soon there was a rescue unit and a fire engine parked next to Rosie Bly's trailer. Rosie came outside with a bottle of wine in one hand and a full glass in the other and watched Kim lead the rescue personnel to the scene. After evaluating the situation, they went back to get their equipment.

The only anchor point available for the rescue squad's climbing ropes was the railroad track. They wrapped a loop around the rail and used carabiners to connect their climbing ropes. Two firemen then rappelled down the steep gravel embankment. They had just started snipping away the brambles when we heard the train whistle.

The southbound Coast Starlight, running a couple of hours late, came through at forty-five miles an hour and sheared the climbers' anchor loop. The two rescuers slid on their bellies down the embankment until the blackberry brambles stopped them from going into the river. A chorus of cursing and shouting immediately followed.

Meanwhile, Big Dan showed up with a three-foot long piece of inch-and-a-quarter galvanized water pipe.

He threaded a loop of rope over the pipe, which he then laid down between the rails. He fed the loop under the rail nearest the river, so that the pipe and loop created an anchor that wouldn't get cut if another train came by. After extricating themselves, the firemen went back to work cutting Terrel loose.

When everyone was safely back on Paquet Street, the EMTs went to work, plucking thorns and applying antiseptic cream and Band-Aids to Terrel's many scratches. He looked like he'd just lost a fight with a dozen crazed tomcats. When the EMTs suggested that he should go to the hospital, Terrel declined. They told him that he ought to at least get a tetanus shot.

CHAPTER 70

THURSDAY, SEPTEMBER 15

The morning *Chronicle* provided no new information regarding the arrest of Richard Elgin, other than the fact that he was scheduled for arraignment at ten in the morning. No doubt, Elgin's attorney would submit a motion for bail, but it would be very surprising if bail would be granted in a high-profile capital case.

My phone rang while I was driving to Salem to continue my probably futile search of Devonshire's house. I didn't recognize the number that appeared in the caller ID window.

"Corrigan," I answered.

"Corrigan, this is Kevin Fox, Salem PD."

"What can I do for you, Detective?" I asked, trying to conceal my surprise.

"I need to talk to you—today."

After a moment's thought, I suggested, "How about lunch time?"

"McGrath's Fish House at Lancaster Mall. You know the place?"

"I'll find it."

"Twelve-thirty. You're buying," he said before hanging up.

I could only guess why Fox wanted this meeting. Maybe he wanted to see what else I knew about Elgin. In any event, I hoped that I'd be able to find out more about the case against him.

Arriving at the Devonshire mansion, I pulled into the circle drive. Predictably, Sumner's Mercedes was not there. I figured he'd be working on whatever paperwork it would take to get authorization to use the safe deposit box key that I was convinced he'd found in the paperweight.

Even though I was 99 percent sure that there was nothing left to find, I needed to finish the search—just in case. Barbara welcomed me in and led me back to her husband's study. While we were talking casually, I picked up the bronze eagle. It was fairly heavy, but not heavy enough to be solid bronze. There was an inscription in Latin on a brass engraving plate affixed to the eagle's base. Turning the statue over, I saw a coin slot in the sheet metal bottom. The murder weapon was a piggy-bank! I gave it a hard shake, but nothing rattled inside.

Next, I picked up the stone paperweight and looked at the empty key compartment on its underside, wondering what kind of key it had held. I hoped it wasn't for a storage locker, like the one Gary Turner had rented, because Sumner would have free access as I did at Turner's locker.

"Barbara, do you know if your husband ever rented a storage unit anywhere?" I asked.

"No, he wasn't a collector of things. Even if he had been, we have plenty of room to store things around the house," she said.

"I want to take some time to look for a hidden compartment in this room. Did your husband have any work done—remodeling—in his study?"

"No, we never remodeled anything. We had a cabinet maker build the cherry filing cabinets to match the woodwork in the study, but other than that, everything is the way it was when we moved in."

"In that case, let's start by taking a good look at those filing cabinets."

We spent the next three hours going over the study in search of hidden compartments in the furnishings, walls and floor. We went from closet to closet, throughout the house, removing all of the contents of each and looking for secret compartments. I checked behind all of the picture frames in all of the rooms on the main floor. I gave the parlor a careful search but still found nothing.

"I have an appointment for lunch," I finally said, "but I'll come back this afternoon and we'll search upstairs if that's okay."

She looked weary. "I'm beginning to doubt that he kept that—what did you call it? That CYA file."

"I still think it's highly likely that he did," I assured her. "I don't think we should give up now."

"Okay, if that's what you think is best."

I drove through the lunch-hour traffic and found McGrath's on Center Street just off Lancaster Drive. The place was busy, but I spotted Fox at a table not far from the entrance. I waved-off the hostess and went over and took a seat opposite Fox.

"Now what is it that you want to talk about?" I asked.

"You know that we searched Richard Elgin's building on Carruthers Street, right?" Fox replied.

"Yeah, I heard that."

"Funny thing about that place, it looked like just a place to store a car or two."

I shrugged, wondering what he was getting at.

He continued, "Thing is, the place had a security system. No entry alarms, but two hidden cameras and a video recorder."

That was a surprise. I sure as hell hadn't seen any cameras!

"It looked like they were brand new," Fox said. "Nicely concealed wireless jobs. The receiver was in the office. It was motion activated and wrote everything onto a computer hard drive."

I could see where this was going, and I didn't like it.

"Every twenty-four hours, it'd burn a DVD and then record over what was on the hard drive. We didn't figure it out until it'd already overwritten everything that'd been on the hard drive."

I almost let myself breathe a sigh of relief, but then Fox pulled an envelope out of his pocket.

He said, "We pulled the discs out of the DVD drives and took them in for analysis, and guess what the techs found?"

I held my breath, waiting for the hammer to drop.

"They found diddly-squat," he said, tossing the envelope to me. "I guess the system wasn't working right—that or else the discs got mixed up somehow."

I did my best not to let my relief show. "That's too bad," I managed to say.

"Yeah," he agreed. "It would have been interesting to see if anyone ever went in there and tampered with Elgin's car—you know, like installing tracking equipment, shit like that."

I had told him that, so I just nodded.

"You know how we nailed Elgin?" he asked, changing the subject.

"No, actually I don't," I said, pretending that Kim hadn't told me.

"Elgin got careless," he said. "We managed to pull up a partial print, and because Mrs. Devonshire had mentioned Richard Elgin, we checked it against the prints on file with Portland Police Bureau. Bam, a definite match. What do you think of that?"

"Sounds like good police work."

"Damn right. It was good police work."

Fox was going somewhere with this, but I didn't have a clue.

"See, he left that 'partial' on the barrel of that little Beretta," he said, eyeing me carefully. "Never would have figured it. Pretty careless, huh?"

"On the Beretta?" I blurted.

Fox leaned across the table and said, "That's right, Corrigan. On the Beretta. You see, we didn't *need* your help. Got that? We didn't *need* it."

"Jesus Christ," I mumbled.

"Are we clear on this?"

"Yeah, we're clear."

"When I want your help, I'll ask for it."

Appropriately chastened, all I could say was, "Right."

"I want everything you have on Elgin," he continued. "And I want to know all about his connection with that crispy critter on Highway 99."

"Trey Bourne," I said.

"Yeah, Bourne. We have a file on him. He's been in some shit down here, and I'd like to know if I can pin that on Elgin, along with the Devonshire thing."

"I'll give you what I have. I did some trash collecting last month, and Elgin's phone bills show a solid link to Bourne—and some other people, including Devonshire."

"We've subpoenaed his phone records, but that might take awhile. The bills will help. What else?"

"Witnesses. Elgin's ex-wives will connect him with Bourne."

"How did you get onto him?" Fox asked.

"I first heard of Bourne in connection with the deaths of two deputies who were investigating the Mendelson-Devonshire case back in 1980. I believe that Bourne killed them because they were pressing the investigation too hard," I told him, knowing perfectly well that he'd heard all this from Kim two days earlier. I guess he was just double-checking.

"So what was Elgin's connection to that?"

"When Alan Blalock was Portland mayor, Elgin was his driver. Devonshire was Blalock's top aide."

"So?" he pressed.

"The ex-wives told me that part of Elgin's job was to procure women for important public officials," I said, "and little girls for the mayor."

"They told you that?"

"I'll send you the audiotapes of my interviews."

"I can see what you're driving at. How much of it can you prove?"

"Well, that's a problem," I admitted. "So far, I can't prove anything on that part of the case."

"If you get something, I want to know about it," Fox said.

We finished lunch, and I paid the bill.

"One more thing, Corrigan," Fox said as we were leaving the restaurant.

"What's that?"

"Best thing to do with those"—indicating the DVDs—"is burn 'em. Make sure of that."

"Thanks, Fox. I owe you," I said sincerely.

"Damn right you do," he said.

CHAPTER 71

he drive back to the Devonshire mansion gave me time to contemplate what I'd learned from Kevin Fox. I had looked around pretty carefully the first time I went into the RTE Consulting building, and I'm sure that if there had been any security cameras, I'd have spotted them.

But I recalled that Elgin had his GPS tracker installed on my Yukon that day, so when he checked where I'd been, he'd have realized that I'd followed him to the garage.

That's probably when he decided to install the security cameras. On my subsequent visits to the garage, I hadn't bothered looking for a camera since the place had been clean the first time I was there. I was just lucky that Elgin hadn't checked his DVDs after I'd installed the tracker on his Subaru. If he had, I have no doubt that my tracker would have taken a journey similar to the one I'd started for his—and more importantly, I'd have never known about his trips to Salem.

When we resumed our search, I found it difficult to concentrate on the task—and why not? Sumner had already taken the brass ring. We went upstairs and went to work searching the bedrooms. Believing that there was nothing left to find, I had to force myself to be thorough in my search.

We were just finishing our search of the guest room when Barbara's phone rang. Barbara hurried into the master bedroom, where there was an old fashioned hard wired telephone. The handset volume was set so loud I could hear both ends of the conversation even from the next room.

"This is Barbara Devonshire."

"Hello, Barbara. This is Robert Sumner."

"Oh yes, Mr. Sumner, how are you today?"

"Have you seen Mr. Corrigan today?"

"Yes, we spent all day searching, but we drew a blank."

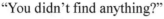

"You didn't find anything?"

"No, not a thing."

"Hmm. Well, the reason I'm calling is that among your husband's papers on file here in my office, I've found a paper referring to a safe deposit box at Salem State Bank."

"Salem State Bank? No, I'm sure he didn't—well, if he ever had a safe deposit box there, I never heard about it. The only safe deposit box I know about is at US Bank downtown. We did all of our banking there."

"There's no question he did have a box at Salem State Bank."

"Why do you think that, Mr. Sumner?"

"There was a key attached to the note card."

"Oh. I see. Well then…"

"Mrs. Devonshire…Barbara, I really should open that box. It could contain something very important to you—possibly something of value, jewelry or something like that."

"Do you think it might contain—"

"Corrigan's incriminating documents? Doubtful—very doubtful. I'm afraid those documents exist only in Mr. Corrigan's colorful imagination. No, this is most likely some long-forgotten stock certificates or—whatever."

"Yes, of course."

"I will need your permission to open the box and retrieve the contents, though."

"When were you thinking of doing this?"

"Well, the sooner the better. I'd like to get it done this afternoon if possible."

"I see. Did you want me to meet you at the bank?"

"Oh, that won't be necessary. I don't want to put you to any trouble. I'll just send a messenger over with a form for you to sign, and I'll take care of it for you."

"No, actually I think I'd like to be there in person."

"That seems like a lot of—I mean, I know you don't have a car now. Why don't you just let me handle it?"

"It's no trouble. I can get a ride. Or take a cab."

"Of course, but it really isn't necessary for you to be there. I'll just pick up whatever's there and put it with the rest of the things we have to go over together next week."

"Mr. Sumner, if my husband was keeping something secret from me, I want to be the first to know what it is. And unless it pertains to a legal matter, I will be the only one who knows what it is. Is that clear?"

"Uh…uh…well…uh…yes. Sure. I didn't mean to—but you know that whatever I find there is privileged information. I couldn't reveal it, even if I wanted to."

"That's very comforting, Mr. Sumner, but if you never see it, that isn't an issue, is it?"

It wasn't a question. It was a statement. Barbara Devonshire was no fool. She could see the same thing that I did. The contents of that box might well be the very thing we'd just spend all day looking for. Sumner made one last attempt to talk Barbara out of opening the box herself before finally agreeing to meet her at the bank at ten thirty the next morning. She hung up the phone and came back into the guest room, where I was packing-up my flashlight, stud finder, and other tools.

"You heard?" she asked me.

"I didn't mean to eavesdrop," I apologized.

"Wilson was damn near deaf. He had the phones turned up so loud, they might as well be speaker phones," she explained. "Anyway, I'd like you to take me to Salem State Bank. I don't want to be stuck there with Robert Sumner—he can be awfully pushy when he wants something."

"Then I'll pick you up at ten tomorrow morning," I told her.

By the time I got back home, Martha had already closed up the office. I spotted her sitting on the deck of Daryl's boat with—Bud? The sight was almost too much to bear. Bud was one of the crustiest individuals I've ever known, and that's saying something.

Kim was still on duty, so I had a little time to myself. I took the first of the three DVDs that Kevin Fox had given me and dropped it into the DVD drive on my computer. This disc showed what appeared to be the technician installing and testing the cameras. The last thing on the video was a glimpse of Elgin's gray Taurus backing out toward Caruthers Street.

The second disc was more troubling. It showed me—very identifiable despite my ODOT disguise—from two angles walking into the garage with my new Spark Nano. There was no question what I was doing when I lay on the floor and squirmed under the Subaru. If Elgin had seen this recording, he'd have not only known that I'd broken into his garage, but also that I'd installed the tracker. I thanked my lucky stars.

The third disc was the one that could have cost me time in the state penitentiary. It showed every detail of how I had captured Elgin's fingerprint from the door handle of the WRX. Taken together with the chicken-oil print on Devonshire's Cadillac, I'd have been dead meat for an evidence-tampering charge.

As Fox had advised, I burned the discs.

Thinking of Kevin Fox led me back to the computer, where I pulled up the transcripts of my interviews with Alicia Jefferson, Kathy Saginaw, and John Whitney. I attached those and the audio files to an email to Fox. I was browsing absently through the investigation files when Kim drove up.

"Tough day at the office?" I asked, seeing her tired expression.

"Any day that I have to spend in the office is tough—especially now. Kerby may have backed down from my suspension, but he's still keeping the heat on," she said.

"Would a glass of wine help?"

"How about a beer?"

I put a six-pack into a little cooler and dumped a layer of ice cubes over the top. I grabbed a bag of pretzels, and then we walked down to the dock. Bud and Martha were still chatting on the afterdeck of the boat, and they paid no attention to us as we went down the steps to the beach.

"Did you find what you were looking for at Devonshire's place?" Kim asked, after we'd settled in and opened our beers.

I hesitated, deciding that it was best not to mention the DVDs.

"We didn't find anything in the house," I said, "but Sumner may have found what we're after—a safe deposit box in Salem. What's funny about it is that he thought he'd be able to get access to the box simply by representing himself as Devonshire's attorney. But the bank wouldn't let him. He had to call Barbara Devonshire, and she has asked me to accompany her to the bank. So just when Sumner thought he had us, it looks like he's out of luck."

"Well, that's great. I love it when someone beats an attorney at his own game."

Evenings were different on the river after school started. There were almost no "family" boats out—mostly just twenty-something guys with way too much testosterone and stereo systems loud enough to rattle windows from a mile away in wakeboard boats that they couldn't possibly afford. And there were a few girls out attempting to slalom ski amid the mayhem kicked up by the wakeboard boats. It seems that only girls have any interest in learning to slalom ski.

Looking upstream, we watched the western sky gradually turn from blue to a deep pink punctuated by soft clouds. These were the evenings that make the river life golden. We stayed on the dock until hunger drew us back up to the house in search of something to eat.

"There's a take-and-bake pizza in the refrigerator," I suggested.

Kim made a face. I guess three pizzas in a week were over her limit.

"I have some ham and a fresh loaf of hazelnut bread," I told her.

"That's more like it," Kim said.

I helped her slice tomatoes, onions, ham and cheese, from which we built our deli sandwiches. We carried them out to the porch with the last two of our cold beers. It was dark by the time we went back inside. I glanced at my computer screen as I walked past. The last thing I'd been looking at was Dick Hammond's photo of the entry hall in Wilson Devonshire's house on the morning of July 26, 1980.

For perhaps the hundredth time, I sat down and gazed at the photo, hoping to see something new. The familiar reddish-brown stain on the carpet, the long, narrow side table where the eagle sat, and, of course, the eagle—the probable murder weapon. I gazed at it, wishing it could speak. Finally, I closed the file and turned off the computer.

CHAPTER 72

FRIDAY, SEPTEMBER 16

At twenty-five minutes after ten the next morning, Barbara and I walked into the lobby of Salem State Bank. The look of surprise on Sumner's face when he saw me was worth all of the previous two days of frustration. He thought he'd gotten me out of the picture. Until I walked in, he believed that he was still in charge.

I offered a welcoming handshake and cheerfully said, "Hello, Sumner, nice to see you again!"

He ignored my hand and spoke to Barbara, "I don't think you should have brought him along."

"I didn't. He brought me," she corrected. "Now let's have that key."

At the counter, Barbara explained to the teller, whose badge said Harriet Mosier, that she was the widow of the safe-deposit-box holder and that she'd come to remove the contents. The teller had her sign an affidavit confirming the death of her husband and made copies of the Devonshires' marriage certificate and Wilson Devonshire's death certificate.

"Very well," Ms. Mosier said, "shall we go to the vault?"

"I'm Mr. Devonshire's attorney, representing his estate—Robert Sumner. I'd like to be present," Sumner said.

Ms. Mosier gave Sumner a long look and then said with a frown, "Mr. Sumner, unless you know of some recent change in Oregon law, Mrs. Devonshire is the natural heir to Mr. Devonshire's estate. I'm sure that if she wants you to be present, she'll invite you."

She turned to look at Barbara, who simply shook her head.

"We'll just wait out here," I said to Ms. Mosier.

When I attempted to nudge Sumner toward a row of vinyl upholstered chairs in the lobby, he brusquely turned away and marched toward the waiting area alone. It was obvious that it had been a long time since a mere bank teller had beaten him in a legal argument.

After about fifteen minutes, which seemed like a couple of hours, Barbara came out of the privacy room carrying a small stack of papers, which she laid on the low table in front of Sumner and me.

"Looks like an old insurance policy—on me," Barbara said. "Little did I know that I was worth one hundred thousand dollars to Wilson if I'd died. It goes way back. I had no idea he'd kept paying premiums on it."

"Is that all?" Sumner demanded. "There was nothing else?"

"Oh yes, there was more," she told him as she laid out the documents one by one. "There are certified copies of his birth certificate, his college and law-school transcripts, his diplomas, and certificates for a hundred shares of Enron stock. And one more thing."

Sumner and I looked at her expectantly. With a flourish, she laid down the last piece of paper. "The AKC registration certificate for our Pomeranian. He died about ten years ago."

It was quite a disappointment. More so for Sumner, I think, since he'd gone to such great pains to intercept the contents of the safe deposit box.

"That's all there was?" he persisted.

"That's it. I may want some advice on that Enron stock, but it can wait."

"Of course," Sumner mumbled.

"Mr. Corrigan, would you mind giving me a ride back home?" she asked. "You are still on the clock, aren't you?"

"That's up to you," I said.

"Then let's go," she concluded.

During the drive back to her place, she extracted two folded papers from her purse.

I almost drove off the road when she said, "This is the letter that Mr. Sumner said existed—how did he put it—only in your colorful imagination."

Back at the Devonshire mansion, Barbara led me into her husband's study and waved me to the leather chair at his desk. Then she handed me the two-page typewritten letter.

Dear Barbara,

The fact that you are reading this means that I am dead. So here I will tell you the *true* facts of what happened to Jessie on July 25, 1980. I know that a part of you has always believed that I killed her, but I want you to know that I did not, although the things that I did do are perhaps even more contemptible than the murder itself.

Alan Blalock killed Jessie, along with that young gardener. But I will take the full blame for setting up the circumstances that led to the killing, and I will, to my everlasting shame, confess that I helped Blalock cover up the crime and literally get away with murder. My dear Barbara, I can only hope that you will find a way to forgive me, though I know I do not deserve it.

I think you have always suspected the things that went on when Jessie was in the mayor's so-called internship program, though we've never spoken of it. I didn't know until after I was brought in as Blalock's aide that the internship program was just a way for the mayor to get close to young girls. Believe me, had I known in advance, I'd have never let Jessie be a part of it.

By the time I found out, it was too late. Jessie was the mayor's mistress. And it is true that the only reason I was given the big promotion was to guarantee that I'd never turn against Blalock. I simply sold out, and the price was Jessie. I sold out again when I helped Blalock conceal the murders he'd committed. My reward for that was my seat on the Supreme Court. So, you see, everything that I am is built on betrayal.

On July 25, 1980, Blalock knew that you were out of town. He took advantage of that occasion to meet with Jessie at our home for a "special afternoon," as he called it. Most of his "special afternoons" took place in motels in Portland, though several took place right in his office in City Hall.

Blalock bought Jessie a gift for that last meeting—a lingerie set that I saw her wearing after she was dead. If her body is ever found, it is what she will be wearing. I don't know what went wrong that afternoon. I removed two empty Champagne bottles from Jessie's room, so I know they'd had a lot to drink--Blalock was still drunk when I arrived home. I assume that Jessie was more than likely drunk as well.

I've often wondered if perhaps Jessie had gotten pregnant, although Blalock had provided her with birth control pills. Or maybe Jessie had simply had enough. In any case, there was an argument that became heated. Jessie left the room, and when she returned, she had the revolver that I kept in the nightstand.

Blalock described the event to me in detail. Jessie threatened him with the gun and threatened to expose his affair with her. She went downstairs, cursing him-- Blalock said she was completely out of control--and headed for the front door. Blalock felt that he had to stop her. He grabbed the only thing handy--which turned out to be the eagle bank that Jessie got when she opened her first bank account--and struck her in the head.

I don't know if that killed Jessie, but she went to the floor. Blalock took the gun from her hand, and at that moment, the gardener knocked on the door. Apparently, he had heard Jessie's shouting, and he wanted to see what was wrong. Blalock let him in, and when he knelt over Jessie, he shot him in the side of his head. He then added a gunshot to Jessie's injuries, to make sure that she was dead as well.

When he collected his composure, he started figuring out how to hide the crime. If he could clean up the blood and put the bodies someplace where they wouldn't be found, Jessie and the gardener would simply have disappeared. He phoned me and insisted that I get home as quickly as possible.

The scene at home was horrible beyond belief. Jessie and the gardener still lay in the entry hall. Blalock had gone out and moved the gardener's car into the garage. He talked me into helping him carry the bodies out and put them in the car, and then we started cleaning up.

We worked for at least an hour trying to get the bloodstain out of the carpet. We ran gallons of water through the Shop-Vac, and we tried everything. In desperation, I came up with the idea of spilling paint over the bloodstain, though I still can't believe the police actually believed the story. Blalock called the paging service, and Richard Elgin showed up from whatever bar he'd been hanging out in, and Blalock had him park the car at Mark's Tavern and take a cab home. I went out and bought a can of paint. I painted the door and then poured paint on the carpet.

Blalock and I worked for the rest of the evening, into the night, cleaning up and making sure that there wasn't a trace of blood to be found. He took the gun apart and wiped off fingerprints. Then he put the gun in the car with the bodies. He told me that if the bodies were found, it would look like a murder-suicide. I wasn't so

sure, but I was in too deep to argue. He
told me that he was planning to run the car
down the boat ramp into the river. He said
that if it drifted out far enough before
sinking, it might never be found.

In some ways, I wished it would be found,
so this whole nightmare could end. When you
search my study, you will find the proof of
what I have said here—proof of Blalock's
murder of Jessie and the gardener, and
proof of my own cowardice. Do with it as
you wish.

Wilson Landis Devonshire

March 31, 1986

"The letter was written about two months after we moved into this house," Barbara explained. "I guess that's when he rented the safe deposit box."

I took a slow look around the study that we'd already spent close to seven hours searching. I thought we'd done a pretty thorough job. Perhaps whatever Devonshire had hidden in 1986 was no longer here.

"What do you think?" I asked.

"Could we have missed it? Wilson was not one to change his mind about something like this," Barbara told me. "It was important enough for him to write the letter in the first place and then to keep paying rent on the safe deposit box. Whatever he hid, it's still here."

"I can't argue with the logic," I agreed.

So Barbara and I commenced a new search, starting with the bookshelves. Shelf by shelf, we pulled down the law books, fanning the pages in search of documents or hidden compartments. Before putting the books back on the shelves, I tapped and pushed on every panel. We worked through the noon hour into the afternoon and still found nothing.

Barbara brought in glasses of iced tea and a plate of snacks, which we finished off quickly before resuming our search. Once more, I pushed and prodded on every panel in the wainscoting, and I inspected the mortar around every brick in the fireplace and hearth. I went over every square inch of wall, ceiling, and floor with my electronic stud finder but again found nothing that would indicate the presence of a hidden compartment.

Late in the afternoon, we were running out of energy and ideas. I virtually took apart the desk and credenza, looking for something as subtle as a hollowed-out leg or a false back. We took down the drapes and looked for things hidden in the hems. I attempted to lift the window sills to find the hidden compartment. I took down the ceiling light fixture and inspected it, and I removed the faceplates from all of the wall sockets.

By dinner time, I was out of ideas. I was starting to think along the lines of microfilm dots hidden on an ordinary page of words, as was done by spies in the Cold War days. Barbara ordered some Thai food, and while we waited for delivery, I worked at putting the room back in order.

The doorbell told us that it was dinner time. I went to the door and accepted the sack of food in little cartons with wire handles, while Barbara set out plates on the breakfast bar in her kitchen. She opened a bottle of red wine to go with the Thai food, and for most of the next hour, we attempted to put our futile search out of our minds.

When I went back into the study to gather up my tools, it was already dark outside. I plopped into Devonshire's leather chair and reread his confession letter. Barbara came in, carrying her glass of wine, and sat on the footstool in front of me.

"When you search my study, you will find the proof of what I have said here," the letter said.

I could see the disappointment on Barbara's face. I shook my head in frustration. We seemed so close but had found nothing. Was this Wilson Devonshire's last joke, or had someone else—maybe Richard Elgin—gotten in here and removed the evidence?

My eyes landed on the bronze eagle on the credenza. Devonshire's letter said that it was a gift to Jessie from the bank when she'd opened her first savings account as a child. How sad and ironic it was that it had been used to take her life. And here, more than thirty years later, it still decorated the Devonshire house.

As I gazed at the eagle, my mind drifted to the photo I'd been looking at on my computer the evening before: the entry hall with the stained carpet, the narrow table, and the same bronze eagle. But it wasn't the same. I looked again at the rectangular brass plate with the inscription attached to the base of the eagle, and it struck me. There had been no rectangular plate there in the 1980 photo.

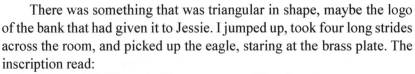

There was something that was triangular in shape, maybe the logo of the bank that had given it to Jessie. I jumped up, took four long strides across the room, and picked up the eagle, staring at the brass plate. The inscription read:

SI VERUM, TESTIMONIUM EST INTUS

How many years had gone by since my teachers in high school had tortured me in their futile attempt to teach me Latin?

"Barbara, can you read Latin?" I asked.

She laughed. "No chance. That bad memory has been blotted out for many years."

I continued to stare at the inscription. I had shaken the eagle before and found nothing rattling inside. I shook it again, and still nothing rattled. Long-buried memories gradually reemerged: *verum*—"truth," *testimonium*—"proof," *intus*—"inside."

"If you wish truth, proof is inside," I translated.

"Huh?" Barbara asked.

Turning the eagle over and looking at the bottom, I found the coin slot and nothing else except the four tamper-proof screws that held the bottom plate in place. The screws were recessed deep in little round plastic feet at the corners of the eagle's base.

Carrying the eagle to Devonshire's desk, I held it beneath his desk lamp, trying to see down inside through the coin slot. At that moment I got a momentary whiff of gasoline—not enough to get my attention, but enough to register. I adjusted the lamp and got a glimpse of what looked like yellowish plastic inside of the eagle—not what you expect in a bank.

But there was that gasoline smell again, this time stronger. I looked up from the eagle and saw that Barbara had a look of concern on her face. She too had smelled the gasoline. Even as we looked at each other, the smell became stronger. I dropped the eagle on the desk and bolted toward the door to the central hall. Just as I reached for the handle, I felt a huge hot pressure wave as the door blew open, knocking off my feet.

A ball of flames rolled across the ceiling, igniting the drapes behind Devonshire's desk. Barbara still sat on the foot stool, glass of wine in one hand and Devonshire's letter in the other. I scrambled across the room, knocked the wine glass from her hand, and pulled her down to the floor.

"We have to get out of here!" I shouted.

I glanced at the windows, but pieces of flaming curtain were falling and igniting the carpet. Through the open doorway, I could see flames rippling along the ceiling paneling in the hallway as the eighty-year-old varnish bubbled and ignited. But it was still clear at floor level.

"That way!" I shouted, pointing toward the hall.

We were almost to the door when I remembered the eagle. I couldn't leave it behind. I pushed Barbara toward the door and scrambled back to the desk. It was like being under the broiler in the oven. Heat radiated down, and bits of burning varnish fell onto the carpet around me. I grabbed the eagle off the desk and caught up with Barbara in the hallway.

It was stunning how fast the fire was spreading. There was no hope of getting to the front door. Our only option was to turn right and head toward the back of the house. A layer of thick smoke was forming above us as we crawled past the stairway toward the kitchen.

There was another soft explosion, and a fresh ball of flames rolled out of the kitchen. We were blocked. The dining room was fully involved. The heat was causing the wallpaper to curl and pull away from the plaster, igniting and dropping to the floor in flaming strips. I quickly pulled Barbara back to the stairway.

It makes no sense to climb stairs to get away from a fire. Heat and fire rise. But it was the only place we could go. Keeping low, we crawled up the stairs. Already, the stairwell was working like a chimney, though the flames hadn't yet ignited the second floor. It was just a matter of time.

We rushed to one of the bedrooms on the front of the mansion, where I hurried to one of the windows. It was a casement window hinged at each side with a pair of latch handles that engaged the center mullion. I handed the eagle to Barbara and tried to open the window. I found the first latch immovable, probably corroded from decades of disuse. The other proved to be the same.

I picked up a wooden chair and swung it at the window. The glass shattered, and the chair disintegrated, but the window frames remained intact. A closer look at the window revealed that the frames were not made of wood, as one might expect, but rather were solid steel. The openings left by the broken-out panes were far too small to crawl through.

Desperately, I looked for something that I could use as a lever or even a hammer to work the seized-up latches. Smoke was seeping out through cracks in the walls, and the floor was getting warm. There was a sharp cracking noise as the main floor window directly below us disintegrated under the heat and pressure. Flames bloomed up from below and licked into the window I had just broken, igniting the curtains.

Barbara and I retreated to the hall. We could no longer get to the rear part of the house because flames were now roaring up the stairwell. To our right, the guest bedroom was already illuminated by flames that had broken through the floor or walls. To our left was the pull-down ladder that led to the attic. Once again, the only way we could go was up.

I dragged a chair into the hall and stood on it to reach the cord on the attic ladder. The smoke was thick and fiercely hot up near the ceiling, but I was able to pull the ladder down. Pushing Barbara ahead of me, I scrambled up into the attic. With some effort, I was able to fold the steps and pull the spring-loaded hatch closed, buying us a few precious minutes of relief from the scorching heat.

I ran to the far end of the attic, where I had seen a large louvered vent during our search. I kicked at it and managed to break one of the boards. I kicked again and then again. Another board cracked. Smoke swirled past me out into the fresh air outside.

I rushed back to the pile of things we'd searched and picked up one of the boxes containing the encyclopedia. I heaved it like a battering ram at the vent and felt the frame move. On my second swing, the box disintegrated and books tumbled out. I went back for another and heard a satisfying crack as the frame split. I could hear fire crackling beneath my feet, and I knew that flames might burst through the dry flooring at any moment.

The third box broke through, leaving a ragged hole big enough for us to squeeze through. But then what? We were thirty-five feet above the ground. While Barbara hammered at the remaining slats with the eagle, I went back and looked at the two large boxes of Christmas decorations. I dumped them out and found several strings of old-fashioned outdoor lights—the kind with big colored light bulbs and heavy-duty wire.

Hoping that the wire would hold her weight, I wrapped one end of a string of lights around Barbara's chest and tied it in a crude knot. Then I knotted that string to another and that to a third. The attic was suddenly illuminated by flames as the wooden hatch on the access ladder burned through. We were out of time.

I helped Barbara squeeze through the vent opening, holding tightly to the string of Christmas lights as she transferred her weight to it. Hand over hand, I let out the strings of lights, lowering Barbara toward the ground. Behind me, the flames had reached the dry wood of the rafters and were spreading quickly toward me. As soon as Barbara reached the ground, I took my end of the Christmas lights and wrapped it around a two-by-six rafter brace and tied it off.

Looking below, I saw Barbara struggling to get loose from the wire. The heat of the fire was at my back. I shouted a warning and then tossed the bronze eagle out past where Barbara stood. Then I got my feet out through the vent, pulled up the slack in the wires, and eased myself outside. Rappelling down the side of a brick-faced wall on a string of Christmas lights is not something that can be done with any finesse.

Working my way down the wire, trying not to cut my hands on the broken bulbs, I lowered myself down the wall. With a sudden roar, flames burst out through the attic vent, and I knew that the copper wire was going to burn through in a matter of moments. Moving as quickly as I could, I worked my way down past the second story windows.

Sirens and air horns sounded as fire engines and ladder trucks approached. From somewhere inside the house came a rumble as something gave way. The whole building shuddered. I was about eight feet above the ground when my lifeline let go. I dropped like a bag of sand. Foolishly, Barbara attempted to catch me. Had she not done that, I'd surely have incurred some broken bones.

We crashed together in a heap, tangled in knotted wire studded with jagged remains of broken Christmas lights. Embers rained down, and we heard more crashing from inside the house. Clawing at the ground, we dragged ourselves away from the house, looking no doubt like a pair of crabs trapped in a fish net.

Windows began cracking above us, and shards of glass rained down to the ground where Barbara and I had been just moments before. We worked at disentangling ourselves from the Christmas lights as the flames broke through the roof, soaring sixty or seventy feet into the air, illuminating the entire block in a shimmering orange light.

To my left, I caught a glimpse of movement in my peripheral vision. Instinct rather than thought caused me to roll abruptly to my right on top of Barbara just as a two-by-four smashed into the ground. Not yet completely free of the Christmas lights, I jumped to my feet and immediately fell backward. The man with the club was dressed in dark clothing, and his face was mostly covered by a bandana, like a bank robber in an old-time Western movie.

I rolled again and avoided another swing of the club, but in the process, I was winding the wires around my ankles. The attacker's third swing connected with the thick part of my thigh when I was unable to get completely out of the way. He raised the two-by-four to deliver the killing blow, which I was now helpless to avoid.

Just as he started to bring it down, he jerked suddenly and pivoted to his right. The board fell harmlessly to the ground as the man's hands went to his head. Clutching his skull, he staggered blindly a couple of yards before collapsing to the ground next to the foundation of the burning house.

Barbara stood next to me, holding the eagle that had, for the second time, been used as a weapon. I pulled at the wires and finally got myself loose from the Christmas lights. There was a loud popping noise as more windows shattered. Our attacker screamed in panic and pain as dozens of glass knives rained down upon him, followed in an instant by a shower of embers and burning bits of debris. He attempted to get up, giving me a clear view of his grievous injuries. Blood spurting from a severed carotid artery, he crumpled lifeless back to the ground.

Firefighters, having heard the screams, appeared around the corner of the house. They rushed to Barbara and me, and I gestured toward the dead man. Two firefighters hurried over and dragged him away from the house, where they quickly determined that he was beyond their help. They escorted Barbara and me out to the curb, where the rescue vehicle was parked, and got busy treating our injuries.

While the paramedics cleaned and bandaged my cuts and scratches, I watched the house burn. My Yukon, which was parked on the circle drive about thirty feet from the front door, caught fire, and with a loud *whump*, the nearly empty fuel tank exploded, causing firefighters to retreat.

A dozen fire hoses shot streams of water at the burning mansion, but the fire was burning too hot to be extinguished. There was a loud cracking sound followed by a muffled roar. A huge ball of flames and sparks rose toward the sky as the roof collapsed into the shell of the once-elegant mansion.

"Maybe you should take these," Barbara whispered.

She handed me Devonshire's letter and Jessie's bronze eagle piggy bank. I discretely wiped off the blood and hair that stuck to the base.

In answer to the paramedic's curious expression, I said, "This belonged to the lady's daughter, who died a long time ago."

We accepted an ambulance ride to Salem Memorial Hospital, mostly just to get away from the horror of the fire scene. In the emergency room, our cuts were inspected and rebandaged and our bruises and burns treated with ice packs. I pulled my phone from my pocket to call Kim but found the LED screen shattered and the phone dead. Eventually, I was able to use a hospital phone to make the call.

It took nearly an hour for Kim to get to Salem to pick us up. We both still had ice packs held in place by elastic bands, in addition to our many small bandages, singed hair, and soot-stained faces.

"Another day in the glamorous life of a private investigator," I said as she looked me over.

She didn't even smile at my quick humor. "What the hell happened?" she asked.

I looked around to make sure that nobody was listening before saying, "Pretty sure someone torched Mrs. Devonshire's house, and we had the misfortune to be inside at the time."

"Where are the police?"

"It'll be a day or two before they determine that the fire was arson. Then they'll want to talk to us."

"Who set the fire?"

"I don't know, but when we got out of the house, someone tried to club me with a two-by-four. I'd bet that he was the one who started the fire."

"So who was he? Where is he?"

"He's dead. He got caught in a shower of glass when the windows blew out—a lucky break for me because he had me dead to rights."

I saw no need to mention to a law-enforcement officer that Barbara had brained him with the eagle before the glass came down on him.

Looking at Barbara, I asked, "Do you have a place to stay tonight?"

Her expression was blank. "My whole life was in that house," she said.

"Is there someone you can call?"

Barbara slowly shook her head. "Everything I owned—"

"You're welcome to stay at my place. I have a spare room," Kim offered.

"I don't even have a toothbrush," Barbara said.

"We'll stop at Fred Meyer and buy whatever you need," Kim said.

Staring at the floor, Barbara shrugged. "I don't have any cash."

"Don't worry about that," I said. "Let's get out of here."

CHAPTER 73

SATURDAY, SEPTEMBER 17

woke up feeling pain in every part of my body. For a few disoriented moments I tried to figure out what had happened. Then I remembered the fire, the climb down the side of the house on a string of Christmas lights, and the man with the two-by-four. Panic hit when I remembered the eagle.

Throwing off the covers, I sat up too quickly and experienced a wave of dizziness. After a brief pause to let my circulation catch up with my movements, I dropped my feet over the side of the bed and stood up. I pulled on my jeans, limped to the kitchen, and started a pot of coffee. In my desk drawer, I found my old prepaid cell phone and called Kim.

"Do you have the eagle?" I asked as soon as she picked up.

"Good morning to you," she said. "The eagle is safe. I have it right here."

"The last thing I remember was leaving Fred Meyer."

"I'm not surprised. You were pretty well out of it—the miracle of modern drugs."

"How's Barbara?"

"Still asleep. I'm going to have to go to work pretty soon, though."

"I'll get up there. Half an hour okay?"

"That'll work," Kim said. "By the way, how are you feeling this morning?"

"Not so great, but I think I'll live," I answered.

I took a shower, the hot water causing my little burns to sting relentlessly. I washed about half a pound of soot out of my hair, blew an equal amount of black slime from my nose, and coughed up even more. By then, I was wondering if the hospital had sent any of those pain tablets

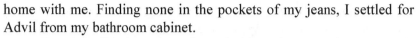

home with me. Finding none in the pockets of my jeans, I settled for Advil from my bathroom cabinet.

After struggling into some clean clothes and gulping down a couple of cups of coffee, I dug up the phone number for my insurance agent.

"Good morning, Corrigan," the agent said brightly. "What can I do for you this morning?"

"I'm going to have to file a claim on my auto insurance," I said.

"No problem. What happened?" he asked.

"The Yukon got caught in that big fire in Salem last night." I assumed that he'd have heard the news.

"Is that right? The big mansion that burned down?"

"I was in the mansion. I got away, but the Yukon went up in smoke."

"Need a rental?"

He told me that Enterprise would deliver a nice Hyundai sedan within the next couple of hours. I gave him Kim's address and then called a cab to take me up there. Kim was on her way out the door when I arrived.

"She's still sleeping. I'll see you tonight," she said as she got into her Explorer.

"The eagle?" I asked.

"It's on the counter. And I'm running late."

The eagle stood next to the morning *Chronicle* and a plate of hot eggs, bacon, and toast. The front page article featured a photo of the fire when it was at its peak, with flames pouring from every window and soaring a hundred feet toward the night sky.

Devonshire Mansion Destroyed by Fire

Two weeks after the death of Oregon Supreme Court Justice Wilson Landis Devonshire, his 1925 mansion was destroyed by a three-alarm fire Friday night. One person was killed, and several others were injured in the blaze, whose cause remains unknown. The identity of the victim has not been released.

At least two people are known to have escaped from the burning mansion by climbing down a makeshift ladder from the attic. One of the survivors is believed to be Wilson Devonshire's widow, Barbara Devonshire. The other survivor has not been identified. Both were taken to Salem Memorial Hospital with what were described as non-life-threatening injuries.

First responders found the structure fully involved and immediately placed a second alarm. A third alarm followed a few minutes later. In all, 72 firefighters and eleven units were involved in fighting the fire. Two firefighters received minor injuries when struck by falling debris.

The story went on to describe the history of the mansion but said surprisingly little about Wilson Devonshire or the revelations that preceded his death. The arrest of Richard Elgin for Devonshire's murder was mentioned, but without detail.

I heard Barbara stirring in the back room, so I put on some more eggs and bacon. She was surprised to find me in the kitchen, so I explained that Kim had gone to work.

"How are you feeling this morning?" I asked.

"Numb," she said. "I still can't believe it."

"Are there any phone calls you need to make?" I asked, offering my phone.

"I guess I'll make some calls after this," she said, accepting the plate I offered. "I don't even know where to begin."

While Barbara ate breakfast, I said, "I'm having a rental car delivered. When we have that, I think the first thing we should do is get these locked up." I pointed at the eagle and the folded letter, which was wrinkled and smoke stained but still intact. "It makes me nervous to have them sitting out where anyone could grab them."

"Where can you lock them up?" Barbara asked.

"I have a secure safe at home. We'll stop there and then go shopping. I'm sure you'll need more than what we bought last night."

The rental car arrived, and after a quick trip home to lock up the eagle, Barbara and I headed to Clackamas Town Center. Our first stop was at the Verizon kiosk. I showed them my broken phone, and despite its appearance, they were able to transfer all of my data to a new phone.

It was more difficult for Barbara, with no old phone to work from and no ID. But when we explained that we were the people who escaped from the burning mansion in Salem, they became more helpful. We had to tell the story of our narrow escape and show a few of our injuries, but that was enough to get a new phone.

We both took a few minutes to check our voice mail. I had a couple of messages from Kim, left during the time before I phoned her from the hospital. There was also a brief message from Kevin Fox, asking me to call him right away.

"Corrigan, where the hell are you?" Fox yelled when I called him.

"At the moment, I'm in the middle of Clackamas Town Center," I answered.

"You took your damned time returning my call!"

"Just got your message. My phone was trashed in the fire. I just got a new one, and called you as soon as I listened to my voice mail."

"Okay, okay. I'll buy that," he conceded. "What do you know about the dead guy?"

"I know that he tried to kill me."

"What the hell are you talking about?"

I described how Barbara and I escaped from the attic only to be attacked by the bandana man. "He was about to deliver the finishing touches when debris started raining down from the upstairs windows."

"He was shredded by shards of glass," Fox said.

"I know. I saw him die. Do you know who he was?" I asked.

"Name's Earl Jasper. That name mean anything to you?"

"Never heard of him."

"He's a small-time local hood. His sheet includes some B & E and assault. No arson."

"Are you saying that the fire last night was not arson?" I asked.

"You tell me. You were in the house," Fox replied.

"We smelled gasoline just before the first explosion."

"The *first* explosion?"

"Yeah. The first explosion was at the front of the house. The second one was at the rear, when we were trying to get to the back door."

"That doesn't sound like an accident to me," he said. "You know, we found an old van registered to Jasper parked around the corner from the Devonshire place. There were two gas cans in the back—along with half a dozen empty wine bottles. Looked like he'd been making Molotov cocktails in there."

"Known associates?" I pressed.

"We'll know more when we get his phone records. For now, he's just a stiff on a slab."

"It wouldn't surprise me if his phone records have some common ground with Richard Elgin's."

"That thought had crossed my mind."

"Fox, some major shit is going to hit the fan up here in the next few days. It's going to have huge political implications."

"Let me guess, you found something to back up Barbara Devonshire's claims."

"I think so. We haven't gone through it yet, but that's what it looks like."

"Do you know where Mrs. Devonshire is? No one has seen her since she was at the hospital."

"She's right here. We're going to get her something to wear."

"Stop down here when you have a chance—both of you," Fox concluded. "We need your statements."

For the next two hours, Barbara and I went from store to store buying several sets of clothes, shoes, accessories, luggage, and toiletries, all on my credit cards. When the little rental sedan was filled with bags and boxes, we went back to Kim's place and unloaded.

We ended up at my place where Barbara, with help from Martha, used my computers to look up phone numbers for her contacts in Salem—including her insurance agent, who said he'd been trying all day to call her on her home phone. *Duh.* Meanwhile, I called dealers around the area, trying to locate a replacement for my Yukon. I found one in Beaverton that sounded enough like my old one to be familiar, but sufficiently different to avoid being repetitive.

The dealer agreed to hold onto it for a few days while my insurance company processed my claim. While Barbara continued talking to her insurance agent about temporary lodging, I waved Martha over to take a look at the Devonshire letter.

"I'll need high-resolution scans of this, and I think it ought to be cross-referenced in Merlin so we can double check timelines and facts," I explained.

Martha started reading the letter and exclaimed, "This can't be true! It has to be some kind of a hoax."

"It's possible. That's why we need to cross-check the facts."

When she got to the part about the evidence hidden in Devonshire's study, Martha commented, "I guess if there really was any proof, it's gone now."

She looked up quickly when I said, "No, I think we found it just before the fire. It's here in the safe."

"What do you mean, you 'think' you found it?" she asked.

"I haven't yet opened it up yet. I'm going to do that when Kim gets here. I want an official witness."

"This is just…so unbelievable."

"Are you sure about that? Remember what Elgin's ex-wives had to say about Blalock. Their statements certainly support what the letter says about Blalock and little girls."

"I still think it's all political slander, and I'll bet none of it can be proved," she concluded.

Barbara had finished her phone call and overheard the last part of my conversation with Martha. She said, "I know that Blalock's political supporters—and you obviously are one of them—won't believe it without hard proof, but you can believe me because I was there. Everything my husband wrote in that letter is consistent with what I know."

"But…still…" Martha groped for something to counter the statement but finally just left it hanging.

CHAPTER 74

"**W**hat's the occasion?" Kim asked when she got home.

"You remember my attorney, William Gates," I said, motioning to Gates, who was seated in my office, along with Barbara and Martha.

"Of course," Kim said, shaking his hand.

"How do you feel about witnessing the possible recovery of evidence in the Mendelson-Devonshire case?"

Gates asked her. "We're going to see what's inside the eagle that Corrigan and Mrs. Devonshire found yesterday."

"Officially?" she asked.

"Officially and on the record," I said.

"I can't be a party to evidence tampering," Kim said.

"We don't know that evidence is present. We can't know that until we see it. At this point, all we're looking at is a private communication between husband and wife," Gates explained.

Kim slowly shook her head. "How do I get myself into things like this?"

"Just to make this official, I've typed up a formal affidavit for all of us to sign, attesting to the origins of the eagle and its contents," Gates explained. "Mrs. Devonshire and Corrigan have already signed a similar document relating to the discovery of the Devonshire letter in the Salem State Bank safe deposit box."

I went to my safe and extracted the eagle. I placed it on my dining table and then handed my video camera to Martha and asked her to record what we did next. For the record, I had everyone present state their names on the recording. I described the inscription on the eagle and my translation of the Latin phrase, and I shot a series of still photos of the eagle from every angle.

The irony of Devonshire hiding his evidence inside the murder weapon was not lost on me. It was the perfect place to put it—in plain sight—but never to be found by accident. I commented on Devonshire's cleverness in having the Latin words engraved on the eagle and also at the relatively long odds against anyone ever translating them. How many people had looked at those words without realizing that they actually said something?

I already had my Dremel tool ready, and after explaining what I was doing, I cut new slots in the tamper-proof screws. Then I carefully removed the four screws and the plastic feet from the bottom of the eagle's base. When I pried the bottom loose and got a clear view up inside the eagle, I could see that it was filled with a yellowish plastic foam of some kind.

The foam crumbled when I scraped at it with the screwdriver blade. I carefully dug out the foam, revealing a small Ziploc bag. As more and more of it became visible, I could see that it contained some folded pieces of paper and a couple of micro-cassettes.

When I finally had dug enough of the foam out, I was able to extract the Ziploc bag. I shook out the two micro-cassettes and three sheets of tightly folded paper.

"Don't touch anything," Kim warned. "I have gloves in the car."

She went outside and returned with a pair of latex gloves, which she handed to me. I put them on before picking up the first of the folded papers. I found it to be a credit-card slip from the downtown Portland Meier & Frank department store for the purchase of a pink lingerie set. I would bet that the product number would match what Jessie was wearing when she was killed. The name on the credit-card slip was Alan Blalock.

The second paper was another credit-card slip, this one from a pharmacy for a prescription in Jessie Devonshire's name for Ovral-28. Again, the name on the credit card used to pay for the birth-control pills was Alan Blalock.

The third piece of paper was a handwritten note:

The full explanation for what you have found here is in my safe deposit box at Salem State Bank. This is the proof of the things I said there. The tape recordings are self-explanatory.

I found the Meier and Frank receipt in Jessie's bedroom while Blalock and I were cleaning up after he killed the kids. The pharmacy receipt was something I found in the wastebasket in Jessie's bathroom months before her death. I pray that I may be forgiven for what I've done.

Wilson Devonshire

For the benefit of my video recording, I said, "We are now going to play the two audio cassettes that we recovered from inside the eagle, along with the note and receipts previously described."

I got my old Sony micro-cassette recorder out of my desk and plugged it into the computer—to amplify the sound but also to make a digital copy. I inserted the cassette marked One and looked from Kim to Gates to Barbara to Martha. They all nodded. I pressed the play button.

> **Devonshire:** I am making this recording because something has happened. Uh, I...uh...don't know for sure, but I think Alan did something to Jessie. He called me in my office half an hour ago, and uh...he said...he said that he needs my help. He told me not to, you know, talk to anyone about it, just to get home as soon as possible. Blalock said...something about Jessie. Uh, like "Jessie's hurt." So, uh, I'm making this recording to, uh, protect myself, you know, in case he did something that could get me...could get me in trouble. Legal trouble or something. So I'm going to start recording...when I get home. I'm carrying the recorder in my inside jacket pocket. I hope that works.

> *Click. Click.*

> **Devonshire:** Okay, I'm pulling into the driveway. Uh, Alan's car isn't here. But I don't think he left. Wait. There's a car—a black car in the garage...what the hell...uh, it looks like the gardener's car. I don't...Okay. I'm parking on the driveway and closing the garage...Something wrong here.

> [*Car engine shuts off. Car door opens. Footsteps of Devonshire walking to the door. Sound of key, then door opening.*]

> **Devonshire:** What's all this about?

> **Blalock:** Big trouble.

> **Devonshire:** What trouble? What's going on?

Blalock: She had a gun! I didn't know what she was going to do!

Devonshire: A gun? Who, Jessie? How did Jessie get a gun?

Blalock: How the hell should I know? One minute she was there, and then she was back, waving the gun.

Devonshire: Oh, Jesus! Oh, Jesus Christ! What the hell have you done?

Blalock: She was heading... She was going outside. She had the gun.

Devonshire: What have you done?

Blalock: She was crazy. She just went nuts and started shouting, and then she went and got the gun.

Devonshire: Oh, Jesus! Are they dead? Oh my god.

Blalock: I didn't mean to do it. I just hit her... I had to stop her from going outside. She was going to tell... the whole neighborhood. She was screaming.

Devonshire: What the hell! You killed them both?

Blalock: I had to... The kid heard... probably heard the screaming. He started banging on the door. I didn't have time to think. Jessie was on the floor and she wasn't moving.

Devonshire: What did you do to her? Good god! Look at her! All that blood!

Blalock: I hit her... I had to stop her, you know. She was going outside and she was screaming. She just went nuts. I hit her... with that.

Devonshire: The eagle? You hit—Dear god! Alan, you crushed her skull!

Blalock: I know, I know. I just panicked, and then that kid was banging on the door. I didn't know what to do, so I took the gun out of Jessie's hand... and then I opened the door. I said, "Jessie's hurt," or something like that, and the kid came in. When he got down to look at Jessie, I shot him.

Devonshire: Dear god!

Blalock: Then I didn't know what to do. I waited. I waited to see if anyone heard the shot. But then Jessie started making…sounds, and maybe she wasn't dead, so I shot her. Oh, Jesus Christ! And then I just sat down on the floor.

Devonshire: I have to call the cops. I'm not going to go to prison with you!

Blalock: No, wait! I've had time to think about it. There's a way out of this.

Devonshire: There's no way out of this! They're dead! You can't bring them back to life.

Blalock: Nobody needs to know. Listen to me. We can get rid of the bodies. We can clean up.

Devonshire: Good God! Do you know what you're saying?

Blalock: Listen to me! We can make this work. We'll put the bodies in the kid's car. But I need your help. I can't carry them by myself.

Devonshire: Then what? Alan, you can't just make this go away!

Blalock: Yes, we can! We wait until after dark…until the middle of the night, when nobody's out. We can make it look like a suicide—make it look like he killed her and then killed himself.

Devonshire: I think that's harder to do than you think. How the hell—

Blalock: No, listen. I have it all worked out. We'll run the car into the river…with the bodies inside. It'll sink, and probably nobody will ever find it. But even if they do, the gun will be there, and they'll just think that he did a murder-suicide. It'll work!

Devonshire: No goddamned way! I don't want to be involved—

Blalock: You *are* involved, damn it! Don't you think there'll be a ton of questions? You aren't innocent, you know. If I go down, so do you!

Devonshire: Oh, no no no! This is just—we're screwed!

Blalock: Get control of yourself! I have it all figured out. I'm going to have Richard park my car down at that tavern—the one down in the old...where the road goes down the hill to the boat ramp. All I'll have to do is walk back up, get in my car, and drive home.

Devonshire: You're completely out of your mind!

Blalock: Listen to me! I'm going to be the next governor—but right now I need your help to make it happen. And I won't forget it! I'll get you a seat on the Oregon Supreme Court.

[*Five seconds passed in silence.*]

Blalock: Look! Think about everything that'll come out if we call the cops. You'll be destroyed too, you know. We at least have to *try* to get out of this!

Devonshire: I don't see how we can possibly get away with it.

Blalock: I'm telling you, it'll work! Just help me carry them out to the garage.

Devonshire: Oh my god! Oh my god!

It went on, and on, and on. For an hour and a half we sat in silence listening as Blalock coerced Devonshire into helping with the cover-up. It was all there: the placing of the bodies in the El Camino, the cleaning of the murder weapon, the scrubbing of the walls and ceiling, the futile attempts to clean the carpet, and finally Devonshire's suggestion that they conceal the stain with spilled paint.

When the recording finally ended, we all sat still, just staring at the cassette recorder. Barbara's face was pale, and her hands were shaking.

"It's worse than I could have imagined," she whispered.

I handed Martha the gloves and asked her to scan the three paper documents and store copies in our database.

"I'm going to have to turn all of this in," Kim said.

"I know," I agreed. "How do you think Kerby will react?"

"If the past is any clue, he's going to be none too happy," she said.

"You probably should take our affidavits along—and the video we made while opening the eagle to get this stuff out," Gates suggested.

"Bag up everything," Kim said. "I have to do this now."

On the drive up to the sheriff's office, Kim put in a phone call to Sheriff Kerby. He didn't answer, so she left a voice message telling him what she was bringing in. Then she called Larry Jamieson.

"Jamieson here," he answered.

"This is Stayton," Kim said. "Hold onto your hat, Larry. I'm bringing in some pretty solid evidence that says the Mendelson-Devonshire murders were done by Alan Blalock."

"What?" Jamieson exclaimed. "Blalock? What the hell do you have? Where did you get it? Have you called Kerby?"

"I called him first, but just got his voice mail. The evidence was found in Wilson Devonshire's private study."

"When? Who found it?"

"His wife—widow—found it last night. It was hidden inside a bronze statue."

Jamieson sounded puzzled. "How the hell did you end up with it?"

"Mrs. Devonshire hired Corrigan to help her find it after she found a letter from Devonshire in a safe deposit box," she told him.

Jamieson groaned. "Oh, please don't tell me that Corrigan contaminated the evidence!"

"Corrigan *found* the evidence. He handled it by the book and documented every step. The chain of custody is completely clean."

"It goddamned well better be," Jamieson grumbled. "Kerby's going to have a coronary."

"Don't I know it! How can we cover our asses on this?"

"I'm trying to figure that out. Let me call in David Elkton. I want the preliminary processing done before Kerby gets involved—and you know why."

"He can't possibly blow this off," Kim objected.

Jamieson said, "Not if we handle it right."

"Okay, I'll be at the office in five minutes."

"I'll be right behind you. See you there."

While Kim took care of that, I phoned Kevin Fox and brought him up to date, promising to email him copies of everything we'd found. I figured if anyone deserved it, Fox did.

CHAPTER 75

SUNDAY, SEPTEMBER 18

When I opened my eyes, I still felt like I'd been run over by a truck. The Cascade train going by told me that it was seven, so I reached over to shake Kim awake, only to find that she wasn't there. Gradually things came into focus. Oh yeah, Kim was at her condo with Barbara.

That should have meant that I could sleep in, but once awake, I couldn't get back to sleep. Instead, I dragged my aching body into the kitchen and made coffee. While that perked, I washed down two ibuprofen tablets with a glass of grapefruit juice.

I flipped through the Sunday *Chronicle*, unable to generate any interest in their milquetoast substitute for news, their predictable editorials, or even the comic strips. The only thing I found remotely interesting was that the Oregon Ducks were dealing with yet another scandal involving members of their football team.

Kim phoned to say that she was on her way to work and that Barbara was still asleep when she left her condo. A few minutes later, I heard the familiar rumble of the sheriff's Jetcraft as Kim sped upriver.

❧❦

On Monday, I took Barbara to Salem and helped her get new checks and a debit card from her bank. From there we went to the DMV office, where after a forty minute wait in line, she got them to issue a duplicate drivers license. I then helped her move into a temporary apartment pending an insurance settlement.

I put the heat on her insurance agent to get her a rental car—at least until the police released the Cadillac.

Of course, I knew that Barbara would never get into that car again and suggested that the insurance company take care of its disposition after it was released. The agent tried to argue that there was no insured loss involved, but I challenged him on that. At the very minimum, a biohazard cleanup would be required, and it was likely that the headliner and other interior parts would have to be replaced. Would his insurance company *really* try to dodge the claim? He finally conceded that *maybe* Barbara had a case.

My insurance company was a lot more cooperative. By Monday afternoon, we had reached a settlement, so I called the Beaverton dealer and told them I'd pick up my new Yukon on Tuesday. It wasn't that there was anything wrong with the little rented Hyundai. It just didn't fit my self-image.

Not surprisingly, the sheriff's office kept silent about the things we'd given them. Nor did they contact me or anyone else in an effort to validate the chain of custody.

That was disappointing because it hinted that Kerby was going to try to bury the whole thing. I'd really hoped to see him do the right thing. But I guess he never had that option. Kerby belonged to Blalock. When my phone rang on Wednesday morning, the display told me that it was Kevin Fox calling.

"I just wanted to thank you for sending me that stuff," Fox said.

"You listened to the recordings?" I asked.

"Yeah, that's a hand grenade with the pin pulled."

"Anything in there you can use?"

"Too soon to tell. At the very least, it shows how everyone fits into the big picture. I sent the recording to an audio lab. They're going to try to match voice prints with known recordings of Devonshire and Blalock."

"How long will that take?"

"Who knows? They said that they might have a preliminary report by the end of the week. A full analysis might take a month or more."

"Have you found out anything about the fire?"

"Yeah, the fire marshal confirmed multiple points of origin, and they found evidence—an accelerant on the concrete back porch. Those two things taken together prove that the fire was deliberately set. In the absence of any contradictory evidence, our conclusion is that Earl Jasper was the arsonist."

"And what've you found out about him?"

"You'll love it. Like I said before, Jasper was a small time thug. He's a welder but doesn't always have a job. Seems like every time he finds himself unemployed, he gets in trouble with the law. He hasn't had much work lately—the bad economy and all—so guess who he calls? Our old friend, Richard Elgin—Jasper talked to him about a dozen times in the last month."

"So Elgin was talking to Jasper even before the Devonshire murder."

"Yeah—makes you wonder if maybe Elgin wanted Jasper to do the job."

"Or maybe Jasper's job was to clean up after Devonshire was dead," I speculated, "and make sure that Devonshire didn't leave anything behind."

"Could be," he said, "but after we locked up Elgin, why follow through? I mean, he had to know that Elgin wouldn't be paying him for the job."

"Did Jasper talk to someone else after Elgin was locked up?"

"We're looking into that. There were several calls to and from one cell-phone number last week—the last one just an hour before the fire started. We traced the cell phone to a guy who turns out to be an attorney. Now we're wondering why Jasper would run out and set fire to Devonshire's place right after getting a phone call from his attorney. It makes no sense."

"Was Jasper being prosecuted for something? I mean, why did he need an attorney?"

"That's the thing. This isn't even a criminal attorney. He does contracts, estate planning, wills, things like that. Jasper doesn't strike me as the kind of guy who would be setting up a living trust, ya know what I mean? Anyway, we're checking out the attorney—some shyster named Sumner."

"Oh, crap!" I exclaimed. "Robert Sumner?"

"What, you know him?" Fox quickly asked.

"You bet I do! He was *there* when Barbara Devonshire got the letter out of the safe deposit box!"

"Hold on! What the hell was he doing there?"

"He was Wilson Devonshire's attorney. The day we first started looking for the letter, Sumner stole the key to the box out of Devonshire's study. He tried to get into the box without telling Mrs. Devonshire, but the bank wouldn't let him. Then he tried to get her to sign a document authorizing him to open it without her—but she refused to sign it."

"So he knew about the letter?"

"Well, no. Barbara went into the vault by herself. I think by then she was suspicious of Sumner's motives, and she didn't tell him about the letter. She didn't tell me about it until after we were back at her place."

"But if Sumner didn't know about the letter..." Fox began.

"Damn!" I said, finally putting two and two together. "He had Devonshire's study bugged. That's why he met with Elgin!"

"What the hell are you talking about?"

"When I had the tracker on Elgin's Subaru, he drove to Salem—a sports bar right next to Sumner's office—just a few days before Devonshire was killed. Elgin was big on listening devices. I'll bet he gave one to Sumner to plant in Devonshire's study."

"Before Devonshire was killed?"

"Sure. He'd have wanted to know how Devonshire was reacting to all the publicity about the new evidence," I said. "I'll bet Sumner planted a bug and then heard Devonshire say something to someone about what he'd do if he faced charges."

"And that's why he was killed," Fox concluded.

"Exactly. But the bug was still there when Barbara and I were talking about what was in the letter from the safe deposit box—and he was still listening while we searched the office the next day."

"Sumner heard what you were doing and called Jasper," Fox speculated.

"He was desperate. If we found the evidence, it would be all over," I added. "He had one chance. Burn the house, destroy the evidence, and get rid of us all at once."

"They must have talked about it earlier. Jasper had already gathered up what he needed to make the fire bombs—there wouldn't have been time between the phone call and the fire."

"You know, when I first found out that Sumner's office was right next to the pub that Elgin visited, I intended to take another look at the phone bills I got out of Elgin's trash."

While I spoke, I motioned to Martha to pull up the phone bill on the computer. In a few seconds, the columns of numbers came up on the screen. Once Elgin had been arrested, we'd stopped tracking down his calls, so a lot of the numbers hadn't been identified.

"Do you have Sumner's cell-phone number?" I asked Fox.

I wrote down the number and held it up next to the computer screen. And there they were: calls to and from Sumner in mid-June, during the week following the recovery of Randy's El Camino. The calls were interspersed with Elgin's calls to and from Washington, DC.

"They were connected," I confirmed. "Elgin was talking to Sumner in between calls to Blalock. You have Elgin's phone records?"

"Yeah," Fox said, "but we were looking at the calls he made to Devonshire. At the time, the other calls didn't matter."

"I was looking at the calls to Washington. Those calls correlate directly with events in the Mendelson-Devonshire investigation."

"This is shaping up into a neat little package. I'll talk to you later, Corrigan. I need to get a court order for Sumner's phone records," Fox said just before the line went dead.

I dialed Larry Jamieson's direct line.

"This is Corrigan," I said when Jamieson answered.

"I can't talk to you, Corrigan. You should know that," he said.

"You don't need to talk. Just listen. Salem PD is closing in on this case. They already have Richard Elgin, and they've connected him with the stiff who torched the Devonshire place. Now they've connected both of them to an attorney named Sumner and all of them to Alan Blalock."

"That's all very interesting, but—" Jamieson started.

"Just listen," I interrupted. "They've sent the Devonshire recordings in for voice analysis. They'll have preliminary results in a few days."

"Son of a bitch!" Jamieson muttered.

"I'm just giving you a heads-up. No need for you to go down with the sinking ship."

"Why didn't you tell me that you gave the recordings to Salem PD?"

"I'm telling you now."

"So now it's a horse race," Jamieson said cynically.

"Not if you work with them," I hinted. "Detective in charge is named Fox. Kevin Fox."

CHAPTER 76

WEDNESDAY SEPTEMBER 21

gainst Kim's advice, I called Amy Powers and Gerald Banks at the
Oregon City Journal. I explained what I had and offered them the
opportunity to see the documents and listen to the recordings. No
reporter can pass up an "exclusive."

We met at my place in the early afternoon. I explained why Barbara
Devonshire and I had started searching and how we'd first found the
letter and then the eagle. I told the story of how we'd been trapped inside
the burning mansion and how we'd barely gotten out alive only to be
attacked by Earl Jasper.

"Kevin Fox on the Salem PD is investigating Jasper," I told
them. "All I know right now is that Jasper has a record—mostly
small-time stuff."

I showed them Dick Hammond's 1980 photo of the eagle, together
with a photo we shot just before taking the bottom off the statue. There
was an air of breathless anticipation when I showed my copies of the
Devonshire letter.

They read in silence. Then I showed them the note and receipts
recovered from the eagle. Finally, I played Devonshire's audio recordings.

"Unbelievable," Banks whispered when the recording ended.

A full minute passed in silence. "All of this was turned over to Larry
Jamieson at the sheriff's office last Saturday,"

I finally said. "Because it is material evidence in a capital murder
investigation, I'm going to have to ask you not to reveal any specifics.
You'll need the sheriff's permission on that."

"If we can't use it, why did you show it to us?" Amy asked.

"I showed it all to you so that you'd know that I'm not just blowing smoke. You need to know that there's real evidence, not just a good story," I explained.

"This is dynamite," Amy commented. "How much trouble are you going to be in for showing it to us?"

I shook my head. "The more people I show it to, the safer I am. Blalock's people would've killed me to prevent me from revealing any of this—God knows, they tried—but once it's all public, they have nothing to gain by coming after me."

"Can't the sheriff's office charge you for interfering with the investigation by making this public?" Amy asked.

"Sure they can, but they didn't even *have* an investigation until I gave this to them."

"What's next then?" Banks asked.

"Ideally, Sheriff Kerby will quickly complete his preliminary validation of the evidence, and then he'll hold a press conference to announce that new evidence has been found pointing to a new suspect in the Mendelson-Devonshire murders. Meanwhile, his people should be interrogating the new suspect—Alan Blalock—to see if he'll trap himself relative to the new evidence."

"Do you think Kerby will do that?" Amy asked.

"Given the way he treated the evidence recovered from Randy Mendelson's car, it's hard to have any confidence in him. I think he'll try to sit on it—but I know that you folks won't let him. You have the knowledge to force the issue. Just call him up, tell him what you know, and ask him for comments."

"What does he have to do to validate the evidence?" Amy asked.

"First he'll validate the chain of custody. He already has sworn affidavits regarding the recovery of the evidence from inside the eagle, backed up by a video recording of the process. I expect him to interview everyone involved in that, just to make sure that everyone saw the same things, but I haven't heard from him yet.

"Meanwhile, lab technicians will look for fingerprints on the papers and cassettes. Devonshire's prints could be on everything, and Blalock's prints could be on the receipts. Fingerprints would be a big step toward validation, although absence of prints doesn't necessarily invalidate the evidence. They can also try to determine the age of the materials—the papers and cassettes. And the stores might be able to validate their receipts.

"The main thing will be having an analysis done on the audiotapes—see if the voices match Blalock and Devonshire. I'm sure there are plenty of voice samples available in media archives for comparison. Technicians will also be able to tell if the recordings have been doctored."

"How long is all that going to take?" Banks asked.

"A full technical analysis of the audio recordings could take weeks," I admitted. "But preliminary results ought to be in by the end of the week. Checking for fingerprints should be done already. Validating the receipts, who knows? Same for determining the age of the paper used for Devonshire's notes."

"So it could be awhile," Banks said.

"If Kerby sees no reason to expedite the investigation, it could take forever. On the other hand, given the proper incentive, he could have preliminary validation done within a couple of days. I'm hoping that you folks can give him that incentive."

Banks shook his head. "It's a fine line between incentive and extortion."

"Look, I'm not trying to tell you how to do your jobs. I'm just giving you information. If you ask Kerby to comment on what you know, you'll have put him on notice. What happens then is up to him."

Looking at Banks, I said, "It's your call, of course, but I'd say if the sheriff's office hasn't held a press conference by your press time next Tuesday, you should break the story. Blow it out on Wednesday, and then we'll all just duck our heads and ride it out."

"Does that give him time to interrogate Blalock?" Amy asked.

"It should, but I don't think it matters. Don't get me wrong—I'd love to see Blalock caught in a lie. But I'd be willing to bet that Kerby has already told him all about the new evidence."

"Probably true," Banks said, "but should we gamble on it?"

"You'll be able to judge that by how Kerby reacts to your request for comments. If he clams up, you can safely assume that Blalock's running the show—which I think he's been doing all along."

CHAPTER 77

Silence. Wednesday, Thursday, and Friday went by without an announcement from the sheriff 's office about major new developments in the Mendelson-Devonshire case. Surely by then, Kerby must have known that this was going to blow up in his face.

Martha and I concentrated on catching up on the work we were doing for William Gates and Xycon. I heard cars approaching and was surprised to see two Oregon City Police cruisers stop in front of my cottage.

Two uniformed officers got out of each car, and all approached my front porch.

"What can I do for you today?" I asked through the screen door.

"Are you March Corrigan?" one officer demanded.

"Just Corrigan," I corrected. "Come on in."

"If you're March Corrigan, we have a warrant for your arrest," he said without a smile, as he came inside.

"My arrest?" I repeated stupidly. "Arrest for what?"

"For interfering with an official investigation, obstruction of justice, and destruction of evidence."

"Are you serious?" I sputtered.

"You're going to have to come with us." He extracted a pair of handcuffs from his duty belt.

"That isn't necessary."

"It's department policy," he said. He spun me around and snapped the handcuffs onto my wrists.

"You have the right to remain silent—" the officer began reciting.

I turned to Martha and said, "Will you please call William Gates?"

They marched me out and stuffed me into the backseat of one of the cruisers and drove to the city lockup, where my pockets were emptied, my watch and belt removed, and I was placed in a cell. When I asked about my phone call, they told me that I'd have my chance to make a call—but not yet.

I waited impatiently for the opportunity to call my attorney. Finally, late in the afternoon, a pimple-faced kid straight out of the police academy unlocked the cell and escorted me to an interview room. There I found Gates and the arresting officer, together with my old friend District Attorney Roger Millican.

"Have all of your rights been explained to you?" the officer asked rhetorically.

"Yes, and for the record, I want my attorney present during any and all questioning," I said.

"We have no need to question you," Millican said. "We already have all the evidence we need."

"Then maybe you should tell me what this is all about," I suggested.

"We have a sworn statement that you illegally obtained a piece of material evidence in a capital crime, described as a bronze metal coin bank in the shape of an eagle, and that in the presence of witnesses, you proceeded to dismantle the bank, in the process destroying possible evidence, and that you subsequently handled the contents of the bank, tainting whatever evidence may have been present, and that you then proceeded to listen to and make copies of audio cassette tapes that were taken from the bank, and that you then, without authorization, distributed copies of the evidence to an unknown number of other parties, including newspaper reporters. Do you deny that this is true?"

I gave him a cold stare and said nothing.

Millican continued, "You will be held here until arraignment, at which time your attorney may request a bail hearing."

Of course, Millican had sprung this on a Friday afternoon. Arraignment couldn't happen until Monday, so I was stuck in jail for the weekend. His arrogant little smile made me want to throttle him.

"I would like to speak with my client," Gates said. "In private."

After the officer and Millican left the room, Gates told me that the charges were completely baseless and that the case wouldn't make it past the arraignment. He'd been trying all afternoon to get a judge to ditch the case, but Clackamas County employees don't work on Fridays and nobody could locate a judge.

"So I'm stuck here," I said.

"We'll make this right," Gates assured me. "Not only will you get out of here, you'll win a fat lawsuit against the district attorney's office."

I gestured toward Millican, who was standing outside the door. "I'd settle for seeing that arrogant ass sitting in a cell with a few of the people he's convicted."

"I'm working on that," Gates said.

So I spent the last weekend of September in the Oregon City jail. Monday afternoon, I was finally taken downtown to the Clackamas County Courthouse for arraignment. Contrary to Gates's assurances, the charges were not dropped, and I was remanded to county custody.

The judge set bail at fifty thousand dollars, and Gates immediately posted it, but not before commenting that fifty grand seemed extremely high for a nonviolent crime.

Of course, whatever they set for bail, you actually have to post only ten percent, so I got out for five grand. I went home and took my first shower since Friday morning.

CHAPTER 78

TUESDAY SEPTEMBER 27

It was Tuesday morning before I got around to checking the nineteen messages on my voicemail. One by one, I took notes and deleted the messages until I got to number fourteen.

"Corrigan, this is Mickey Odell. You came around here a couple of months ago, pretending to be a reporter or some shit—remember that? Word is that Sheriff Kerby is pissing in your mess kit. It's time to take him down a notch. Call me."

Mickey Odell was one of the retired deputies who'd refused to talk to me way back in June. I wondered what had changed his mind.

When I returned his call, Odell said, "I never believed you were a reporter. That was just plain amateur. You shouldn't try to pull that crap. Not on a cop."

"What is it that you want to talk about?" I asked, ignoring the rebuke.

"I heard they came down on you for finding evidence connecting *Senator* Blalock to the Devonshire and Mendelson murders."

His emphasis on the word *senator* dripped with contempt.

"How do you know about that?"

"I still have friends on the job. Thing is, most of us knew way back in 1980 that Blalock was up to his ass in that case. Nobody dared say anything though, 'cause Sheriff Barrington was Blalock's good buddy and supporter."

"Tell me what that means."

"Back in the fifties and sixties, the Democrats couldn't *buy* an election in Oregon, though God knows they tried. Then along came Alan Blalock—a good-looking guy with a silver tongue. He could talk the hide off a buffalo. Glib as hell. Nobody could ever catch him without a quick answer.

"He went up against old man Farmington for Portland mayor in '76 and just tore the crooked old bastard apart. He was such a smooth talker. People gravitated toward him. Blalock was a winner, and everyone knew it. He had a way of controlling everyone who approached him.

"The Democrat power brokers thought Blalock was courting them, but it was actually the other way around. Blalock had them kissing his feet, and they didn't seem to notice. Meanwhile, the news reporters, they all *loved* the new mayor. He had glamour and charm, he entertained them, and they made him the Golden Boy.

"Well, Ralph Barrington was one of those old-guard Democrats. He'd been elected sheriff in the late fifties and reelected time after time ever since, and that made him one of the few successful Democrats at the ballot box until Blalock came along. Naturally, Barrington was happy to welcome this bright new star into the party and even offered to show him the ropes.

"Didn't take long before Barrington and all the rest were eating out of Blalock's hand. It was Blalock who told the others how to run a campaign and win elections. He just had this—I don't know what to call it—it was like everyone wanted to do what he said because he was a *winner*."

"Yeah, I know all that. But what was his hold on Barrington?" I said.

"Don't ya see it? Blalock showed 'em all how to win. They *depended* on him, so they all did what he said," Odell explained. "Pretty soon, no Democrat could win an election unless Blalock wanted him to.

"It was in '78, I think. Barrington had been on the job too long. He had a couple of challengers going into the primaries. There was a deputy who was half Barrington's age, better looking, and a hell of a lot more competent—a shoo-in.

"Barrington went to some kind of party and got together with Blalock. The next thing you knew, that good-looking deputy dropped out of the race, just like that. Barrington got reelected, and that deputy resigned to take an appointed position in the attorney general's office, making twice what the sheriff got paid."

"So you figure Blalock rigged the appointment for the challenger so that Barrington could get reelected," I commented.

"Hell no! He rigged the appointment so that from then on he'd *own* them both. And he did too. When that Devonshire girl went missing, word got around real fast that Blalock was involved. That's when Blalock called in his chips. Barrington *owed* him, and Blalock reminded him of that fact. Piece by piece, Barrington took that case apart. He made sure that nobody ever so much as spoke Blalock's name.

"Just when everyone thought the investigation was dead, along came those two, Turner and Hammond. They just wouldn't leave it alone—kept insisting that there was more evidence. And then one day, Hammond turned up dead of a heroin overdose. Barrington claimed he'd stolen a load of smack out of the evidence vault and drummed him out of the office—after he was dead!

"You know, they still don't even acknowledge that Hammond ever existed. Well, the rest of us just looked at each other and said, 'Whoa there.' We didn't know what to think. Two weeks later, Hammond's partner winds up dead in a ravine off a country road where he had no reason to be. Now him, they buried him with honors, but you can be damned sure that nobody around the office ever asked any questions. Turner was dead. Hammond was dead and dishonored. That's all we needed to know. Nobody ever mentioned the Devonshire case again. Not for the next thirty years."

"What about Kerby?"

"When Barrington announced that he was going to retire, Bill Kerby was handpicked by Blalock's cronies to run for sheriff. His nose was so far up Blalock's ass, he could blow snot out his belly button. Blalock pulled the strings, and Kerby's been sheriff ever since."

"Thanks for the history lesson," I said.

"Not so fast, Corrigan, there's more," Odell said. "See, I was Bill Kerby's partner. We were close, ya know, like partners are—even after he became sheriff. We been drinking buddies for, like, twenty-five years, and sometimes he'd come to me with, you know, *special* assignments."

"What does that mean—'special assignments'?"

"You know, things that nobody ever found out about," Odell said evasively.

"*Illegal*, you mean."

"Things that needed to be done," he said dismissively.

"The point is, Kerby *trusted* me—still does. And sometimes he comes to me when he has a special kind of problem, ya see."

"Explain that," I pushed.

"Couple a months ago, I got a call from Kerby. He says, 'There's an asshole trying to mess things up for everyone, and he needs to be taken care of.' I say, 'What do ya mean taken care of?' He says, 'We're gonna take him down, but we'd like to find some serious stuff.' I figure he means drugs, ya know."

"Kerby wanted you to plant drugs?"

"Yeah, he says the DA is going to search his place, and he wants to find a good-sized stash of drugs—you know, a dealer-sized stash. Kerby gave me a couple of bricks—uncut, straight from Asia."

"For you to plant in the guy's house," I said right away.

"*Your* house," Odell corrected. "*You* were the mark. I took it to your house, but then I found your badass security system, and I couldn't get in. But your car was there, so I put it in the spare tire well—figured they'd find it there for sure."

I stared at him incredulously. "You planted Asian heroin in my car?"

"Yeah," he said, "that beige-colored Suburban."

"Yukon," I corrected.

"Whatever. Thing is, you weren't there when they showed up with the warrant, and your car ain't there either. The drug dog makes a beeline for the neighbor's garage, where they find a big pot-growing operation. The dog's going nuts, so they lock him in the car. They never found the drugs, and the DA's pissed at Kerby, and Kerby's pissed at me."

Damn. I remembered seeing the dog in one of the cars when I got home that day. I thanked my lucky stars for Red Harper's pot growing operation.

"I told him that I'd done my job, and it wasn't my fault they screwed-up the search," he said, "but Kerby said they'd deal with it a different way.

"Next thing I knew, there was your picture in the paper talking all about how you saved some lady from going over the falls in a boat. That's when I recognized you as the phony-ass reporter. And the same article talks about a guy who got creamed on the highway with a load of explosives in his car. I put two and two together and figured that bomb was meant for you."

"Did Kerby ever say why he wanted me taken care of?"

"Hell, he didn't have to! I knew what it was about—same thing as always. Got to protect Blalock. That's Kerby's main job. Always has been."

"Why are you telling me all of this now?"

"This shit's gotten out of control. It's not enough that old Blalock killed those two kids. They gotta go kill the two detectives to protect him. Thirty years later, they kill Devonshire, and then I read about the shooter, that Elgin guy, and find out that he probably murdered a couple of his wives. They torch Devonshire's house in a last-ditch attempt to destroy the evidence and damn near kill you again, along with the Devonshire broad. All this shit just to keep Blalock's ass out of prison. I'm done with that. I never liked him to begin with."

"So what's next?"

"You tell me. Is this new evidence you've found going to go anywhere?"

"Damn right it is. Kerby and Millican cooked up these charges against me just to discredit the evidence, but they don't know that Salem PD has been working on authentication for over a week, and when that's done, Blalock is finished. Add your testimony, and Kerby goes down with him, maybe Millican too."

With a sly tone in his voice, Odell said, "It isn't just my testimony. I recorded all of my phone conversations with Kerby. He talked about Millican by name several times—in connection with the planted heroin and the stuff they found in the search. Kerby told me that Millican found your hidden safe. He knew I couldn't have hidden the smack there, but he figured that's where you kept the evidence."

"You have that on tape?" I asked.

"Every word," he said.

"Are the recordings in a safe place?"

"Yeah, I got a lockbox in the bank. I don't know who I can trust with 'em."

"There's a Salem cop, Kevin Fox. I trust him. And I trust Larry Jamieson. He's given me some help along the way."

"Sorry, I don't trust *anyone* at the sheriff's office. Kerby's got a hold on everyone there."

"You want my advice then, get a message to Fox."

"I might just do that," he replied.

"One more thing," I said. "Watch your back."

❧❦

First thing the next morning, I drove my new Yukon up to the *Oregon City Journal* office and picked up an early copy of the newspaper. The front page article was accompanied by file photos of Jessie and Randy, the Devonshire mansion fire, and the recovery of Randy's El Camino.

Under the headline, "New Suspect in Mendelson-Devonshire Murders," the story started by saying that the sheriff's office was keeping quiet about the latest evidence. From there, it gave a detailed review of the case, including Richard Elgin's involvement in Devonshire's murder and the subsequent discovery of new evidence hidden inside Jessie's bronze eagle.

The *Journal* stopped short of revealing the nature of that evidence but reported that it had been turned over to the sheriff's office. This would put pressure on Kerby to do something—at least to give some hint of what we'd found.

CHAPTER 79

THURSDAY SEPTEMBER 29

R eports of the pending press conference first hit the news at ten thirty that morning. The preliminary report said that a press conference on the steps of the Clackamas County Courthouse at noon would reveal a major break in the Mendelson-Devonshire murder case.

In reporting the pending announcement, the newscasters made reference to the *Journal* story of the day before and speculated that the new suspect would be named.

Rather than watch on television, I went downtown and staked out a good viewing spot on the sidewalk opposite the courthouse. The first thing I noticed was that half a dozen Oregon State Police officers were stationed on the courthouse steps. All four Portland television stations were busy setting up their remote transmitters on the side streets around the courthouse, and reporters crowded the sidewalk at the foot of the steps.

Oregon City Police closed Main Street and were busy detouring traffic around the courthouse block. As noon approached, a lectern and portable PA system were set up in front of the courthouse doors. The state police officers formed a cordon as uniformed deputies from the Clackamas County Sheriff's Office started filing out of the courthouse and lining up behind the lectern.

Kim was there, along with Sammy Cushman, who'd helped pull Randy Mendelson's car out of the river. I also recognized Carrie Silverton and David Elkton, the CSI criminalists who had processed the evidence from the El Camino. Larry Jamieson stepped to the microphone.

Conspicuously absent was Sheriff Kerby. "I am Deputy Larry Jamieson, lead detective for the Clackamas County Sheriff's Office Homicide and Violent Crimes Unit. I am pleased to be able to tell you that we have reached what we believe to be the final resolution of a thirty-one-year-old investigation.

"One hour ago, our office issued a warrant for the arrest of United States Senator Alan Blalock for the murders of Jessie Devonshire and Randall Mendelson on July 25, 1980. I have been informed that he is currently being held by Washington DC Police, pending extradition.

"Also arrested this morning were Clackamas County District Attorney Roger Millican and Sheriff William Kerby, both charged with obstructing justice and attempting to hinder prosecution in a capital-murder investigation. They are currently being held in the Clackamas County Jail.

"As you know, the first break in the mystery surrounding the disappearance of Jessie Devonshire and Randy Mendelson in 1980 was the discovery last June of Mendelson's car in the Willamette River, at the site of the old boat ramp in West Linn. Evidence found in the car proved conclusively that the pair had been murdered by an unknown third party.

"Other evidence subsequently proved that the late Supreme Court Justice Wilson Landis Devonshire had deliberately concealed blood evidence in his home. The blood was proved through DNA analysis to be from Devonshire's stepdaughter, Jessie.

"A former Portland police officer, Richard Elgin, has been charged with Wilson Devonshire's murder in Salem. Both Elgin and Devonshire worked for Alan Blalock when he was Portland mayor.

"Elgin is also under investigation in the 1980 deaths of Clackamas County Sheriff's Office deputies Richard Hammond and Gary Turner and the deaths of two of his wives, Carrie Whitney Elgin in 1994 and Christie Brogan Elgin in 2004.

"In a related investigation, Salem Police have arrested Attorney Robert Sumner for his role in attempting to prevent the recovery of the evidence that conclusively ties Alan Blalock to the 1980 murders. Sumner is accused of hiring Earl Jasper to set fire to the Devonshire mansion in Salem thirteen days ago. Barbara Devonshire escaped the fire with an Oregon City private investigator named Corrigan. Jasper was killed by falling debris from the burning mansion.

"Finally, on behalf of the Clackamas County Sheriff's Office, I want to extend a public thank you to investigator Corrigan, whose work on behalf of Lila Mendelson was instrumental in solving this case.

"For all of you in the media, thank you for coming here on short notice. Our public information officer, Cal Westfall, is working on a detailed press release, which you will receive electronically within the hour. I will now take your questions."

What followed was forty minutes of chaos as the swarm of TV, radio, and newspaper reporters peppered Jamieson with questions, most of which could have been answered by reading Wednesday's *Oregon City Journal*. I stayed around until the event wound down, and I caught up with Kim as she headed toward her Explorer parked alongside the courthouse.

"Hey, Deputy," I said. "Are you still on duty?"

"No, Thursdays are my day off," she said.

"Then, can I buy you a glass of wine?" I asked, pointing to the Verdict Bar & Grill across the street.

"That's the best offer I've had all day."

"And we can talk about that trip to Vegas."

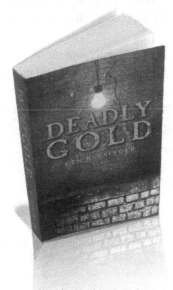

Deadly Gold

Thirty-four gold miners lay dead on a gravel bar where Deadline Creek flowed into the Snake River in the depths of Hells Canyon. From the surrounding bluffs, a small gang of cattle rustlers had poured gunfire down on the defenseless mines, who had committed two cardinal sins: they were Chinese, and they had found gold.

A hundred twenty-five years later, a woman's body is found in the Willamette River, wrapped in a piece of carpet and weighted down by a cast iron anchor. Corrigan, having just completed his investigation of the notorious Mendelson-Devonshire murders, once again finds himself trying to solve the murder of a victim whose body was pulled from the river many years after her death. In the course of his year-long investigation into the death of Tara Foster, Corrigan learns that there is no limit to the mayhem that is triggered by lust for the *Deadly Gold*.

ISBN: 978-1-947491-99-1 ©2017

Yorkshire Publishing   402 pages $19.99

www.kenbaysinger.com

Missing and Exploited

A car collector looking for a place to store his vintage Studebakers stumbles across a name carved in a wooden beam from a century-old building. Just a quarter-mile away, the skeletal remains of a young woman are found outside a homeless camp.

The investigation that Corrigan starts as a favor for his old friend quickly becomes a nightmare beyond anything he could have imagined. As the body count rises, the mystery becomes ever deeper, until it takes on a life of its own.

For three decades, children have been vanishing without a trace, until Corrigan uncovers the terrible truth. And nothing comes without a cost.

Relationships are torn apart, and at times even nature works against Corrigan and his small team of investigators as they chase down obscure clues from the cold case files. Chasing leads across five states over six months, Corrigan faces the greatest challenges of his investigative career.

ISBN: 978-1-5245-5269-5 ©2016
Xlibris 390 pages $19.99

25% of the author's first year royalties for *Missing and Exploited* will be donated to the National Center for Missing and Exploited Children

www.kenbaysinger.com

CPSIA information can be obtained
at www.ICGtesting.com
Printed in the USA
LVOW07s1921240817

546255LV00012B/73/P

CPSIA information can be obtained
at www.ICGtesting.com
Printed in the USA
JSHW010044010623
42520JS00003B/6